...e. Right now. Right or wrong.

...ouldn't think of a better place for something
— ...d waited a lifetime to do. Moving closer to him,
...r focus dropped to his mouth.

"Holly." He shook his head.

"What?"

"This is not a good idea." His voice was rough.

"I don't know what you're talking about." But her
focus remained on his lips, which had haunted her
for over a decade, now a mere breath away.

"Yeah. You do." But despite his hesitation, he
reached up and smoothed some strands of her hair
back from her face. He caught her hair in his fist and
gently pulled her toward him. His mouth touched
hers, gently, tentatively... But then he drew back,
making her heart cry out. He watched her, carefully,
intently.

"It's just a kiss," she whispered. She could hear the
pleading in her own voice.

"We both know it's a hell of a lot more than that."

* * *

Redeeming the Billionaire SEAL

s part of Mills & Boon Desire's No 1 bestselling
series, Billionaires and Babies: Powerful men...
wrapped around their babies' little fingers

REDEEMING THE BILLIONAIRE SEAL

BY
LAUREN CANAN

MILLS & BOON

First Published in Great Britain 2016
By Mills & Boon, an imprint of HarperCollins*Publishers*
1 London Bridge Street, London, SE1 9GF

© 2016 Sarah Cannon

ISBN: 978-0-263-91863-2

51-0616

Our policy is to use papers that are natural, renewable and recyclable products and made from wood grown in sustainable forests. The logging and manufacturing processes conform to the legal environmental regulations of the country of origin.

Printed and bound in Spain
by CPI, Barcelona

Lauren Canan has always been in love with love. When she began writing, stories of romance and unbridled passion flowed through her fingers onto the page. Today she is a multi-award-winning author, including the prestigious Romance Writers of America Golden Heart® Award. She lives in Texas with her own real-life hero, four dogs and a mouthy parrot named Bird.

She loves to hear from readers. Find her on Facebook or go to her website, www.laurencanan.com.

This book is dedicated to Laurel Hamrick
for the endless support and the many hours
she gave so willingly. And to Kathleen for
her patience and determination to make this
story the best it can be. And to my closest friends
(you know who you are!) who provided so much
support when it was needed the most.

One

Watching a newborn foal rise to its feet for the first time was a sight Holly Anderson would never tire of seeing. With a few staggered steps and some encouragement from its mother, the foal located its dinner bucket and didn't have to be shown how to latch on to her first meal. The fluffy little tail flipped and turned as the warm nourishment filled her tummy.

"I thought we were going to lose this one," said Don Jefferies, owner of the mare that had just given birth with considerable help from Holly. "I've been raising quarter horses most of my life and I guess I've been lucky. I've never had to deal with a breech birth."

"They don't happen that often," Holly agreed. "Thank goodness."

"I can't say how much I appreciate you, Doc."

"Glad I could help." Holly took one last glimpse at the foal before stepping out into the hallway as Don closed the stall door behind her. She began gathering her implements, then walked to the truck and dumped them into a white bucket filled with a special cleaning solution. "I should come back out and check them both in two or three days. I'll need someone here to contain Mother. She's probably not going to like having her baby kidnapped for a few minutes."

"No worries. I'll call your office tomorrow, schedule a time and make sure someone is around to help if I can't be here myself."

With a final handshake, Holly tossed the last of her gear in the holding compartment in the back of her truck, climbed in behind the wheel and headed back to the clinic. The sun had set and twilight was quickly folding into night.

She'd finished scouring the equipment and was rinsing her hands when the little bell over the front door chimed. Someone had entered the building. She must have forgotten to put up the closed sign again. It had been a twelve-hour day with an emergency wake-up call at seven thirty this morning, and her body was screaming for a long hot soak in the old claw-foot tub.

Drying her hands on a paper towel, she made her way through the back of the clinic, rounded the corner and stopped at the edge of the front counter. She had already turned off the overhead lights but the glow from the lab area provided some illumination. Two men stood just inside the door of the small waiting room. She immediately recognized Cole Masters, one of the three owners of the ninety-two-thousand-acre beef operation across the road. She'd grown up with the three Masters sons; her aunt's small house, where she lived now, was just across the road from their mansion on the hill. Although they were several years older, that hadn't stopped any of them from forming a lifelong bond of friendship that was more like extended family.

As to the identity of the man who stood next to Cole, she had no clue. He must be a business associate out for the weekend. Cole and his brother Wade randomly brought people to the Circle M for a leisurely weekend in the country with horseback rides and cookouts over a campfire—by an accredited chef. Why anyone would need a professional chef to cook a hot dog over a grill was beyond her realm of understanding. To each his own, she supposed.

She didn't sense any type of tension indicating an emergency. Cole just stood there with a stupid grin on his face. It was late. She was tired. And she needed to get home to the baby so Amanda, her friend and temporary babysitter, could go home. Whatever he was up to, she needed him to pull the prank and be done with it.

"Hey, Cole," she said. He nodded. "Did you forget your way home again?"

"Ha. Ha."

"How can I help you?"

"I wanted to pick up the antibiotics for the sorrel mare that cut her foot. Caleb intended to get them but something else came up. I told him I would stop by if you were still open."

"Right. I'd forgotten. They're in the fridge. Be right back."

She slipped into the main room of the clinic, grabbed the drugs out of the refrigerator along with a few syringes, dropped them all in a plastic ziplock and returned to the front. "Here you go. Caleb knows what to do but if he has any questions, tell him to call."

"Sure thing."

Cole stood in the same place, making no effort to move.

"Was there something else?"

Cole glanced over to the other man next to him, then back to Holly.

Holly bent slightly forward and held out her hands, palms up, a silent way of asking, *What do you want?* "It's a little late for charades. I'm sorry, but I've had a really long day. How about you skip the theatrics and just tell me what you need?" She glanced at the other man. "I apologize. He gets this way sometimes."

The man shrugged, pursing his lips as though finding the situation funny. Cole's grin grew wider. "Ah, man... this is too good," Cole muttered to his friend. "We should have brought Wade."

Holly didn't know what to make of that statement. What was *too good*?

"Okay." She patted the counter. "You both have a good evening. If you don't mind, lock the door on your way out." She turned to leave, headed for the rear entrance and made it all of three steps.

"Why do you have to leave so soon, Muppet?"

Holly froze. Her heart did a tiny dance in her chest. That voice, deep and raspy. That name. Only one person called her Muppet. But it couldn't be. Could it? Holly turned as the big man with wide shoulders walked toward her, removing the Western hat that had been pulled low over his eyes. In one blinding flash the past twelve years vanished and she was looking into the eyes of her best friend.

She should have known him even if she hadn't seen his face. It was the way he moved, silently, with the grace of a cougar. It was how he held himself, feet apart, broad shoulders back, big hands at his side, ready to handle any potential threat that came his way by any means necessary.

He had a ruggedly handsome face, with high cheek-bones and a sharp jaw that stood out despite a five-o'clock shadow. His hair was the same dark saddle-brown color as his brothers' but instead of a suave businessman's cut, it was shaggy, disheveled—which capped off his devil-ish, sexy looks. His appearance had once driven most of the county's female population crazy. The Roman nose would have given him the distinction of royalty had it not been broken due to his preference of football in his youth and no doubt some hard-fought battles on enemy lines. The cleft in his chin completed the image.

Holly knew those full lips were punctuated by dimples on either side and hid strong white teeth. It was the kind of smile you waited for. Hoped for. And when it finally came it was more than worth the wait. But it was the crys-tal blue of his eyes that conveyed the true power of his persona. It was as though they were lit from inside. His gaze could be as daunting as a thief at your window on a moonless night, as hypnotizing as a cobra, as erotic as two lovers in the throes of passion or, like now, it could sparkle with humor. She'd once wondered if he even no-ticed the second glances from people he passed on the street. Or was he so accustomed to people taking another look that he no longer paid any attention?

He was dressed in desert fatigues and a light brown T-shirt, which showed the chiseled muscles of his arms and chest to full effect. There was a black-banded watch that had more dials than an Apollo spacecraft on his tanned wrist.

In front of her stood a warrior. A US Navy SEAL.

Chance Masters had come home.

"Chance," she whispered. She reached her hand out to him, needing to prove to herself he was really here. He caught her smaller hand in his, placed it firmly against his chest and held it there. She felt his heartbeat, steady and sure, beneath the thin material of his shirt.

Tears stung her eyes and she blinked rapidly, trying to prevent them from falling while she scrambled to gain control of her emotions. He'd been her best friend, her first crush and her first heartbreak when he'd left for the navy. The entire community had felt his absence. Some, mostly the women, had been saddened by the void his leaving created, while others, primarily the parents, had breathed a sigh of relief that he was gone. But his leaving had affected everyone in one way or another for three counties around. Her older brother had once told her he wished he had a nickel for every woman Chance turned down.

She stepped into his arms, her hands encircling his lean body while he held her close and let her cry. Hot, raw vitality surrounded her, causing her senses to ignite in a fire that swept through her. After a few moments, she stepped back and wiped the tears from her cheeks. She sniffed and with a quick movement tossed the strands of hair that had come loose from her braid away from her face, determined to regain some measure of control. She pulled in one shaky cleansing breath, placed her hands on her hips and jutted out her chin with purpose. "Commander? It's about damn time you came home."

That earned her a smile. He looked down, shaking his head.

"I was about to say you've changed, Muppet. But maybe not," he said teasingly, his voice deeper than she remembered. "But no braces. No pigtails. And you seem a bit taller."

Holly smiled. "You think?"

She'd been barely twelve when he'd joined the military immediately after graduating high school, so yeah, in twelve years there had been changes. But all the change wasn't on her side. She was intensely aware of the pure animal magnetism oozing from every pore in his body; he was an alpha male in every sense of the phrase. A jolt of awareness shot through her veins, pooling in her belly, making the temperature of the room rise fifteen degrees. At least.

Gone was the swaggering teenager with an easy smile and a reputation for knowing where to find trouble, the cocky guy who was too smart for his own good. He'd been replaced by a man who had seen the world through different eyes, used his above-average intelligence for things that mattered and trained to hold his emotions carefully in check. It was all there in his face. He oozed self-confidence; his nearness and the underlying power of his physique made her intensely aware of his utter masculinity.

Easily six foot four of hard muscle, he was more dangerous than she would ever have guessed a dozen years ago. She could see small glimpses of the old Chance beneath the hard exterior but it was as though the Chance of yesterday had faded away, leaving only minute traces behind. He'd finally made peace with whatever demons had been haunting him all those years ago, making him everyone's number one nightmare. But she could tell the impatience and restless energy were gone, held tightly in check by the powerful man he had become.

"I'm so sorry about your dad." Her glance swung to Cole, including him in that statement.

"Thanks," Cole replied.

Her eyes returned to Chance. "He was so proud of you. We all are."

Chance nodded, for the most part letting the comment slide. Holly remembered there had been rumors of discord between Chance and his dad. She hadn't known

Mr. Masters very well. He was rarely at the ranch. She remembered her brother once confiding that according to Chance, the man wasn't proud of anything money couldn't buy, except more money, adding he hoped when his old man died he could manage to take some of it with him because he'd never cared about anything else.

Holly stood next to Cole as Chance walked around the clinic noting the instruments, X-ray machines and microscopes. Two additional rooms were fully set up to conduct a surgical operation, and there was a separate smaller space for patients recovering from surgery. The kennel area for boarding was at the end of the hall, clearly marked by a sign on the closed door. "This is nice, Holly," he said, glancing around. "Calico Springs has needed a vet for a long time. You always said you were going to get your license and build a clinic. You're the one who should be proud."

"I had a lot of help. Kevin Grady is co-owner. I couldn't have pulled this off without him. He is a licensed vet who has wanted his own clinic for years. It worked out that I had the building, and in exchange for the use of, I could work under his supervision for my last two years of clinical instruction—the hands-on experience diagnosing and treating. And your brothers helped a lot with a loan for the equipment. But yeah, I'm glad it worked out. The hours are long, the work is hard at times, but it's fulfilling."

His eyes found hers. "I couldn't have said it better." A silent understanding passed between them. Chance felt the same way about the life he'd chosen.

His expression turned serious. "I'm sorry about Jason," he said, referring to Holly's older brother, who'd been killed in Iraq. "He was a great guy."

She nodded and glanced down, suddenly uncomfortable. "There are some days I forget he's gone. I'll pick up the phone to call him then realize…he isn't there."

Chance and Jason had been best friends since fourth grade when Chance's mother had finally won the battle for her sons to grow up in a normal environment, pulled them out of boarding school and enrolled them in the local public school. The two had hit it off immediately and remained best friends until the day Jason died. Holly imagined when Chance received the news that Jason had been killed it had been hard for him to take. Chance was closer to Jason than his own brothers.

"Listen, you're tired. I'll be here a while. We're gonna head out but I'll catch you tomorrow."

"I'll hold you to that."

Chance nodded. "Absolutely."

"And *you*…" Holly pointed at Cole. "You are so mean for not telling me Chance was home." She scooted over to give him a sisterly hug. "But I guess we love you anyway."

He just chuckled. With one last look at Holly, Chance followed Cole out the door.

Rather than drive, Holly took the footpath that extended from the clinic through the trees, over an old wooden footbridge that spanned Otter Creek and on a few yards farther to her small house. *Chance is really home.* He'd made it through how many deployments? She could only imagine. And he looked good. Better than good. It had been so many years. What had he done all that time? Fight wars? Dodge bullets? Probably accomplished feats that even if he could talk about them, she wouldn't fully comprehend. Things she was no doubt better off not knowing.

She picked up her pace. Amanda Stiller, her good friend for many years and her temporary babysitter, might be anxious to go to her own home unless she'd become engrossed in something on television. At fourteen months, baby Emma could be a handful, and Holly was anxious to relieve Amanda.

But Amanda was a TV junkie and Holly had a satellite dish with some three hundred channels to keep Amanda occupied, so it was a good arrangement. Amanda often preferred to crash on her sofa instead of making the drive into town, especially now that she was in between jobs. She was an RN specializing in surgical care, and the local hospital had been forced to lay off half of its medical staff, but assurances had been given they would be recalled as soon as budget demands were met. Amanda saw it as an opportunity to catch up on her second job: being a couch potato.

Holly stepped through the back door and heard the sound of one of Amanda's favorite shows. The background music foretold something bad was about to happen. Seconds later there was a gunshot. A woman screamed and another began to sob. This was Friday night. So that meant Amanda was watching *You Can't Hide. Good grief.*

"Who died?" Holly asked as she dropped her bag into a chair.

"That old witch, Ms. Latham. She got shot."

"Again? Are you sure it isn't a rerun?"

"It's not."

"I wonder who did it this time." Holly tried to contain the sarcasm. The fictional character had been shot, stabbed, choked and drowned more times than Holly could count and she didn't regularly watch the show. Amanda and half the town were more than willing to bring her up to speed on who had done what, then ask if she had a guess who was behind it.

"I'm betting John because he wants to marry her daughter and the old biddy had it out for him. I mean, whoever pulled the trigger, she had it coming. She was up to something. I could tell. If somebody didn't shoot her, she'd have really hurt John sooner or later."

Holly clamped her mouth shut and headed for the kitchen. Amanda got so caught up in her soaps that she talked about the characters as though she'd just watched the evening news. Dear old Ms. Latham would be back in one form or another. Just today, the owner of one of Holly's patients had remarked that the actress who played the crotchety old biddy had signed a contract for another year. But Holly wouldn't spoil it for Amanda.

"Are you staying over?"

"Yeah. This sofa is way softer than my bed at home. And I still don't have cable or satellite. All I can get is the local news and weather, and nothing exciting ever happens around here."

"You do know there are stores that are only too happy to sign you up for three hundred plus channels?"

Amanda shrugged. "I'd rather be out here with you guys than sitting in that apartment alone. David won't be back for another month. Oh. Almost forgot. I promised Emma we would go see the kites tomorrow."

"Out at the lake?"

"Yeah."

"I'd forgotten it was this weekend. That should be fun. She'll enjoy it. It's my Saturday to work but it's only half a day." Holly looked over the counter into the den. "Amanda, you don't have to go to the park. You do so much for us anyway."

"Please. I want to or I wouldn't do it."

"Thank you. I'll close the clinic and get out there as soon as I can."

The commercial ended and Amanda turned back to her program. Holly made herself a pimento-and-cheese sandwich before heading for the baby's room, eating as she went. Emma was asleep on her back, her little arms splayed out on either side of her head. The silver-blond curls surrounded her face like a halo. She bent over the bed and placed a kiss on the small forehead.

Regret again filled her heart that Emma would never know her mother or father. Jason would have made a terrific dad. She hoped the pictures she had of her brother and the few she'd obtained of his wife would help Emma relate to them when she was older.

Every minute she was forced to leave the baby in someone's care, guilt hit hard and heavy. Often on the days she worked in the clinic, Emma stayed with her, either behind the counter or in the small office just off the lab, in her playpen. But on those days of ranch calls, like today, even knowing Amanda was taking care of her didn't help reduce Holly's self-reproach.

Jason, her brother, had been killed two years ago in Iraq when an underground IED exploded, taking out his patrol vehicle and everyone on board. His death had brought on their father's fatal heart attack. Four months later Jason's wife died giving birth to Emma, making the baby an orphan before she ever opened her eyes. Now all they had was each other. Emma was safe and protected, and until the baby was grown and could make her own life choices, Holly would do everything in her power to ensure it stayed that way.

She switched on the little night-light in the corner of the room and set her sights on the bathroom and a long hot soak in the tub. After undressing and filling the tub, she turned off the tap, settled back into the hot water and let her mind drift. It immediately went to Chance. He'd

changed, but then didn't everybody in twelve years? Cole
had told her a couple of months ago that Chance had been
wounded during a mission. She'd felt her blood turn cold
as the shocking news had set in. No further information had been forthcoming, and all Holly could do was
cling to the old belief that no news was good news. When
Chance hadn't appeared at his dad's funeral, she'd just
known something horrible had happened. She'd carried
that fear for days, refusing to bother Cole or Wade during their time of grieving. If they got any news—good
or bad—surely they would tell her. Then tonight when
Chance walked into the clinic, the relief had been so overwhelming all she had been able to do was hold on to him
and sob like a baby. He must've thought she'd turned into
a total and complete dork.

Bath over, she pulled on an old blue T-shirt, checked
on Emma once more and fell into bed. She smiled in the
darkness. Chance had finally come home. That thought
ran through her mind over and over again as though daring
her to believe it. She'd almost reconciled herself to the idea
he might never return. In a way, he hadn't. At least not the
old Chance she'd known all her life. When she'd hugged
him, it was like hugging a warm pillar of marble. The small
scar on his jaw added to his intensity. There was a fierce-
ness in his eyes. His face denoted wisdom far beyond his
years. Cole had once mentioned Chance was thriving in
the navy, moving up in rank much more quickly than others. Once he set his mind to do it, she wasn't surprised.

The rabble-rouser he'd been in his youth, the solitary
bad boy, had been reshaped into a soldier: the best this
country had to offer. He was big and dangerous and no
doubt very capable. But while they may have redirected
his spirit, no one would ever control it. It was that streak
of wildness that made him who he was. His brothers

didn't have it. Just as their brown eyes would never be a hot icy-blue like Chance's, their spirit would also never rival his. Chance had always been different, always found his own road. He'd found his place in life, a place he was meant to be. Unfortunately, it required him to put his life on the line each and every day, and that was something Holly wouldn't let herself think about.

For the first time, she knew why the older girls had gone a little crazy those dozen or so years ago. It was not something Chance did purposely. It was just part of who he was. It was in his stride, his voice, his touch—in the way he presented himself. It was the way he looked at a woman, making her very much aware of her own femininity and what he could do with it.

Just being in his presence for a few amazing moments, she'd felt that silent challenge to come to him. If she did, instinct told her she would never be the same again. Before, she'd been a child and sexual attraction wasn't even in the picture. Chance had seen her as a little sister. Now, as an adult, the look of male want in his eyes reinforced the fact that she was a woman in every sense of the word and he knew it. And her body had responded accordingly.

With a moan she rolled over onto her side. Despite the years of dreaming he would someday come back and she would be *the* one in his life, she couldn't imagine this was her wish coming true. Reality had long since become her guide. Chance was home because he'd been wounded and needed a place to recuperate. Then he would once again be gone. Twelve years and her life had gone on. She needed to let go of the little-girl fantasies. The world had changed and so had they. It was sad in a way, but the happy memories from her childhood, made even better with the passage of time, would always remain close to her heart.

She couldn't help but wonder if Chance would still enjoy working with new colts and riding out to check the fences or rounding up the calves for annual inoculations and electronic branding. Horses used to be his passion. More than likely he hadn't had that opportunity in a long while.

He had also loved the river that ran for miles through the ranch land. Before Emma, she would often ride out to the place he loved the most, sit on the boulder that jutted out over the rushing water and try to imagine where he was and what he was doing. As the years rolled past, like fallen leaves carried out of sight by the waters in the stream, she'd had to accept she might never see Chance Masters again.

But he was here. She would see him. *Tomorrow.* She wouldn't think any further into the future than that. She absolutely would not, on the day of his arrival, consider how hard it would be when he left yet again. *He is here.* She could touch him, talk to him face-to-face and have an opportunity to make some new memories.

She had to wonder how he was doing up in the big house. Suddenly being thrust into the lap of luxury probably wasn't comfortable to him. While some dreamed of having even a tenth of the wealth of the Masters family, Chance had always shrugged it off, never wanting to talk about it. Holly imagined that the living accommodations he'd had for the past few years were vastly different from the mansion. Was he sleeping? Was the fact he was at the ranch making him restless? Or maybe he normally kept different hours, awake at night and asleep during the day.

If she didn't get to sleep pretty soon, she might go down to the barn. Anything beat tossing and turning in this bed. And if Chance Masters couldn't sleep, the barn was where he would be.

Two

"I'm not saying you *have* to leave the SEALs and transition into the corporation," Wade defended himself. "I'm just saying I think that's what Dad would have wanted."

How in hell could Chance argue about something neither he nor his older brother could prove or deny? His father had said nothing about time frames the day he'd told Chance he was washing his hands of his youngest son and his outrageous behavior. He'd strongly suggested Chance join a branch of the military before he ended up in prison. So he'd enlisted in the SEAL program. He very much doubted his dad cared if he ever laid eyes on his youngest son again—and he never did—let alone expected him to slide into an executive position in the billion-dollar conglomerate upon his death. Apparently Wade hadn't been told everything that had gone down that day in their father's office. And tonight at least, Chance wasn't about to enlighten him.

Wade had taken to the role of CEO in the corporation as easily as downing the first cold beer after working the cattle chutes on a hundred-and-ten-degree day. As chief financial officer, Cole had pretty much had the same experience. But corporate America had never appealed to Chance. Not when he was younger. And damn sure not now.

"It's always been a family business," Wade continued. "When his brother died, Dad carried on by himself. And he did pretty damn good. I think it was always his intention that his sons would join him."

The kitchen staff entered to remove the empty dinner plates, inquire about dessert and offer more coffee. Chance nodded and pushed the twenty-two-carat gold-rimmed cup toward the man standing to his left. He knew the family saga. He didn't have to hear it again. It was painfully ironic to him that their dad had devoted his entire life to building a dynasty for a family he'd all but ignored for the sake of building it. Wade could call it what he wanted, but that was screwed up. And from what Chance could see, Wade was going to be just like their father. He just hadn't as yet met a woman who would put up with it. It was a bit disconcerting to think of the type of woman who would.

"Why don't you take a day and fly into Dallas with us while you're here." It didn't sound like a request to Chance, but he let it go. "Take a look at some facts and figures and get an idea of what Masters Corporation, Ltd., is about. What we do. What we are trying to achieve."

Wade seemed impervious to the fact that Chance already had a company. It was the US Navy. And for the life of him, Chance didn't know how to get that across without an out-and-out clash that might leave one, or both, wounded inside. Now was definitely not the time to go there.

"No problem," Chance agreed and stood up from his chair, ready to get out of this room and check out something that did interest him: the ranch. "Name the day and let's do it."

It wasn't that he had no concern or curiosity for the business. He would be glad to have an inside look at what had provided income for all the Masterses exceedingly well for three generations. He just doubted he was ready to put down his weapon and pick up a pen and a calculator. Still, he owed Wade enough to let him have bragging rights. Wade had always been there for him so a trip into Dallas was the least Chance could do.

Wade reached out, offering Chance his hand, which he readily accepted. "It's good to have you back, little brother. Don't think too badly of me for wanting to keep you around a little longer."

"Oh, I absolutely understand. You're still ticked off that you never could beat me in a game of chess."

Wade's smile was immediate. "Something I intend to change."

"Yeah? Good luck with that."

Wade laughed and Chance took the opportunity to leave on a high note. He'd known this visit would be hard. He just hadn't realized he'd be drawn into such a nettle-filled quagmire. His emotions about his father dying were screwing with his head; he wasn't sure if he should feel saddened or relieved. Wade was determined to make him part of the corporation, pushing him to leave the military. And heaven help him when he was near Holly. His body had hardened just saying hello to her earlier in the clinic. He was mentally at war between wanting to know this very sexy, beautiful young woman a lot better and staying well clear of his best friend's little sister. It hadn't been a full twenty-four hours since he'd arrived at the ranch and already she had him in knots.

It was dark when Chance ventured outside. The fresh night air felt good. He inhaled the scents of pine and freshly cut alfalfa. He was determined to not give in to the stiffness in his knee where the surgeons had removed a bullet and tried their best to repair bone fragments and torn ligaments. He'd never made it through a full thirty-day leave without being called in early for immediate deployment. But this time, he knew that was not going to happen. He rubbed his left arm, hoping it might relieve the dull pain that lingered from the injury to his shoulder. The last mission had taken out two of his men and left him with a couple of brass .45-caliber souvenirs. The first bullet had missed his heart by millimeters, so it could have been a hell of a lot worse. But the rounds from the AK-47 had still managed to do enough damage to kick his butt and put him in the hospital for a few weeks. The round that blew out his knee had been the real zinger. That was the injury that could change his life.

The attending doctor hadn't been convinced Chance could get back to 100 percent. For the missions Chance was trained to do, it was crucial. The doc had been upfront with him. Further medical evaluation was warranted and he was sending the case to the medical evaluation board for review. A soldier might be physically able to return to a full life as a civilian, but the injuries could prevent him from performing his duties, especially the duties of a SEAL.

Chance had been told straight up this might result in a medical discharge, something he was not willing to even think about. What in the hell would he do if that should happen? The issue was not about money, but the way he lived his life. He'd found his place. Hell, he'd *made* his place, worked harder than most men to attain it. He wasn't ready to step down to a trainer position or become a desk jockey, but at least he would have those options. Hopefully.

He was grateful for the time he had here with his family. He loved his brothers and he didn't want to cause any hard feelings. If that should happen he would carry the regret with him a long time. But their roads had gone in different directions. He respected what they had accomplished. He hoped they would do the same.

He spotted a dull light on the next rise that seemed to flicker behind the branches of the trees as they caught the evening breeze. The main barn. As schoolkids, he and Jason had spent hours in there, grooming and cleaning tack—not because they had to but because they'd both enjoyed it. Holly was usually tagging along or hanging out with them. Busy hands provided a good environment to talk. When they weren't in the barn they were in the saddle, riding the hills, checking fences, enjoying each day without considering that eventually it would all come to an end. It was strange. Only after seeing Holly tonight did he feel like he was truly home. But still, it was not the same without Jason.

His brothers had told him Holly had only one year left before she received her veterinary license and that she had a clinic across from the ranch entrance. But they omitted how much she'd changed, and for a guy who'd seen pretty much everything life could throw at him, he'd been unprepared for the vision standing before him. He's been blown away.

He'd always thought her older sister was beautiful and had been surprised when she'd agreed to go out with him back when they were high school seniors. That one date was all he'd needed. Karley wasn't the kind of girl he usually dated. She was a breath of fresh air in the purest form, and he was anything but. He'd never asked her out again. When she'd called, he'd shut her down. He knew she'd been hurt, but he'd needed to make sure there was no further contact between them. Through the booze-and drug-filled haze, he'd done the right thing. Now he was again facing temptation with her younger sister, but this time it was far worse.

Holly was utterly feminine, almost fragile in the way she moved, like a ballet dancer on stage, and conveyed an innocence wrapped up in a tough persona. He was intrigued from the second he'd stepped inside her clinic. She was nothing remotely close to the scrawny little kid who'd followed him around the ranch, asking one question after another, ranging from why frogs hopped to where the clouds went on a clear day. He had often wondered when she found time to breathe.

She was still slim, but maturity had added some appealing assets. Her hair fell in a long, flaxen braid down her back. Her fine features were timeless; the delicate arch of her brows enhanced soft, honey-brown, almost golden eyes. The small button nose was now refined, adding to the delicate balance of her face. And heaven help him, her lips were made to be kissed. He let out a long breath and tried to gain control of his body, which suddenly had a will of its own.

In the years he'd been away, Holly Anderson had matured into a remarkably beautiful woman. Chance abruptly realized where his mind was headed and brought it to a halt. That type of awareness was completely inappropriate. Holly had always been like a kid sister to him. Theirs was a special friendship, a unique bond, and he would not do anything to change that. At least that was his steadfast intention.

Without conscious thought he walked across the natural stone courtyard around the pool, bypassing the twelve-foot-high waterfall, to the wrought iron gate between open pasture and the estate grounds.

Like the main house, the huge barn structure utilized a lot of natural stone beneath log beams reaching up some fourteen feet high to support an A-frame dark green roof. Accents of the same mossy color were added to the cross boards in the doors and the shutters outside each stall. Inside the massive structure, there was a lobby with trophy cases and a sitting area. To the left, a hallway with mahogany wainscoting led to the office on one side and two wash and grooming stalls on the right. Straight down the main aisle of thirty-six stalls, there was a grain room, blanket closets, tack room and two separate oversize stalls for foaling. To the right, there was a three-bay equipment garage. The indoor arena, with its elevated viewing area, was only slightly smaller than the outside arena.

Soft nickers welcomed him. The vibrant scents of cedar and pine shavings, alfalfa and leather soothed him. The barn, for all its amenities, seemed smaller than he remembered. He strolled down the center aisle, glancing at the horses in their stalls, some still munching their evening grain or pulling a bite of hay from their overhead rack. They were all bred to be the best and they appeared to fulfill that expectation. Their silky coats shone, even under the dim nighttime lighting. Alert and curious, some were excited at the prospect of leaving their stall for exercise in one form or another, regardless of the time, day or night.

He reached the open door to the tack room, and the scent of all the leather and the oils used to clean and condition the various pieces of tack lured him in. Western saddles sat five deep on the twenty-foot-long racks. Bridles covered one wall, halters another, with various other tools and grooming equipment in the floor-to-ceiling cabinet in the corner. He noticed an English saddle at the end of one of the saddle racks. That was new. You sure couldn't work cattle with it. But then a lot of the wrangling was done on four-wheelers today. He reached over and picked it up. It was light, less than half the weight of a Western saddle. It was probably there to appease some guest who came out for a weekend and didn't care for the Western riggings.

Back out in the central hall, he walked to the far end of the barn to an open area where hay for the stalled horses was kept. He sat down on a bale, leaned back against the wall and gazed at the sky. He missed this. He'd done plenty of night maneuvers, but the last thing he thought about then was gazing at the stars.

He drew in a deep breath and blew it out. Until a decision was made regarding his ability to perform his job, all he could do was walk the tightrope and keep his fingers crossed. He'd been assigned to see a civilian doctor while he was here. Hopefully he could add some positive input. But Chance had a sickening feeling in his gut that his life as a SEAL was over. It was how he'd deal with the news that caused the turmoil in his head. He was thirty years old. A lot of guys dropped out of the program by now. No doubt all of them wished they had the opportunity Chance was being given by his brothers. But he didn't want to go there. If his brothers were content with the corporate side of things, good enough. But he wanted no part of it.

Holly again flounced onto her back, staring at the ceiling fan's blades whirling silently in the darkened room.

This was so not working. She was tired. She'd had a long day. But even after a soak in the tub she couldn't go to sleep. Her mind refused to shut down. Glancing at the clock, she calculated she'd been lying in bed tossing and turning for almost two hours. Sleep was not even in the neighborhood, let alone knocking at her door. And she knew the reason was because Chance was home.

He was probably up in the big house with Wade and Cole. It was well after midnight. They were probably asleep. Even if they weren't, she wasn't about to disturb them on Chance's first day home. *But.* What if he wasn't with them? What if he was restless and couldn't sleep either? What if he'd wanted some air? There was only one place he would go at one o'clock in the morning.

Swinging her legs off the bed, she grabbed a pair of jeans and a T-shirt. A quick peek into Emma's room assured her that the baby was sleeping soundly. Finger-combing her hair, Holly grabbed her phone and slipped into the tennis shoes by the back door.

"Are you leaving?" Amanda mumbled, half-asleep but still glued to the television.

"Couldn't sleep. Just going to take a walk. Have my cell if you need me."

"'Kay."

Holly stepped outside and began jogging toward the main barn. If he wasn't there, at least she could run off some restless energy. But if he was there, she didn't want to waste a second that she could be spending with him.

The night air was cool to her skin with a hint of moisture. The creatures of the night continued to chirp as she jogged down the path, across the bridge and onto the main ranch road. She passed the driveway to the big house and finally reached the barn on the far rise.

The large outside double doors were open. The center hall had been swept as usual and there was no sign of anyone inside other than the current four-legged residents. She took a quick peek into the office. Finding it empty, she ventured down the hall, glancing inside the grain and tack rooms. No sign of Chance. Her shoulders dropped in disappointment. She turned around and started walking back the way she'd come when she heard a sound. It sounded like a snore. She stopped. After a few seconds, there it was again. It was coming from the far end of the building. Curious, she headed that direction. Sure enough, in the open area on the left, intended for keeping a monthly supply of hay for the horses that were stalled, two long muscled legs were propped up on a bale of hay. As she stepped closer, she knew it was Chance. He was sound asleep, his hat pulled down over his eyes. She should just go and let him sleep.

She really should.

She chewed her bottom lip and glanced at the stacks of baled silage. He could always go back to sleep. This was too good to pass up. Pulling a foot-long strand of hay from a nearby bale, she checked to make sure it had the dried seedpod on one end before slowly creeping toward him. Crouching on her knees, she reached out and touched the wispy end of the straw against his nose. He stirred and batted at his face. Holly had to work hard to stifle a giggle as she reached out again.

In less time than it took to blink he grabbed her arm, propelled her over his body and down onto the hay with him on top, one hand around her throat, the other holding her hands above her head.

Time stopped. His face was mere inches from hers, his look fierce, his eyes hard and deadly. She didn't know if she should try to speak or just remain absolutely still. She'd heard of soldiers with PTSD having bad nightmares. But Chance's eyes were open, glaring and focused on her.

"Chance?" She said his name, barely over a whisper. "Chance, it's me, Holly."

"I know it's you," he assured her, his voice low and angry. "I know what you were doing. And I know you came damned close to getting yourself killed."

"Sorry. Lesson learned," she squeaked. But he wasn't letting her up. His granite body was pressing her down into the hay, making her intensely aware of the absolute power and total control he commanded. He released her neck, but still held her hands above her head. His eyes were mesmerizing, entrancing, and changed her need to escape into an almost desperate desire to stay. Her fright faded, turning into something else entirely. She could feel part of his body becoming more rigid, more unyielding, and she fought the overwhelming temptation to press her hips against him. She threw her head back, closing her eyes as she battled the need for him. She could smell the sweat from his body. All sounds around them stopped. Then it was too much. She was burning and she knew Chance was the only one who could make it stop.

She felt his warm breath on her face and her eyes opened, her gaze falling on his lips, full and enticing, only inches away. Absently she pulled her bottom lip inside her mouth, moistening it with her tongue. In the dim light she saw his face harden, the muscles of his jaw working overtime. In spite of his anger, she craved to know what his kiss would feel like. Twelve long years ago when she'd jumped into his arms and kissed him goodbye, she'd just been a kid. Her action had taken him by surprise and he had immediately set her away from him as shock and aggravation covered his face. But she'd held on to the memory even though it hadn't been enough. Not nearly enough. It only provided a child-ish dream she'd carried in her pocket all this time. Now he lowered his head, his mouth coming closer while at the same time she felt the solid ridge of pure adult male begin to throb.

"*Goddammit*, Holly."

With an abrupt move, he rolled off her and onto his feet. Disgust at himself for almost kissing her waged war with the frustration that he hadn't. It wouldn't have stopped after a few kisses. She was too damn enticing and it had been too long since he'd felt the pleasures of a woman. *Damn*. Gritting his teeth, Chance strove for control. Holly was more than just another available fe-male. He would not take her like this, even if she asked. Not in a barn. Not in a bed. Not anywhere for any rea-son. He sucked in a deep breath and held out a hand to help her up.

She scrambled to her feet without acknowledging him then sent a glare in his direction. He probably should apologize, but he had a tough time saying he was sorry for something he didn't regret. She appeared decidedly uncomfortable, looking in any direction but at him. She'd offered herself and he'd rejected her. But dam-mit, didn't she understand? She wasn't a one-nighter, a onetime roll between the sheets. She was so much more than that.

"Use a small bit of common sense."

"You sure do wake up grumpy."

Grumpy? He'd call what had almost happened a lot of things. Grumpy wasn't one of them. He dropped his head and let out a sigh. Rubbing the back of his neck, he contemplated how to explain why he appeared *grumpy*.

"Holly, I spend most of my time, night and day, in

areas of the world—in situations—where the only way you stay alive is by use of a sixth sense. It's awareness. And you can never turn it off. If someone sneaks up on you, you have to assume it's the enemy, and we are trained, if he's that close, to take him out and ask questions later. If you don't assume it's the enemy, in all likelihood you'll be dead before you figure it out. It's an automatic reaction."

"I didn't know."

Chance nodded. "Now you do." He rested his hands on his waist. She hadn't commented on the fact he'd come perilously close to permanently changing their friendship, and as long as she was feeling insulted, he might as well get it all out. "And there is one other thing I feel the need to mention. I will not have sex with you. We will *never* have sex. You are a friend. A very special friend. You are also Jason's little sister." He drew in a deep breath and blew it out. "I will not touch you in that way. Ever. It would end what we have now and I don't want to lose that." If she had so much as raised her head a quarter of an inch, touching those amazing lips to his, they might be having a completely different conversation about now. Or no conversation at all.

"Fine by me," she huffed right back at him. "What makes you think I would ever want to have sex with you anyway? Of all the unmitigated gall. Your arrogance defies description."

"Is that right?"

"Yes," she hissed. "I don't even find you interesting… in that way."

"Sweetheart, make no mistake. Our feelings greatly differ in that regard. I want *you* until it hurts. You are without doubt the most beautiful and the sexiest woman

I've ever seen in my life. But I will not touch you, even if it kills me. And it very well may. Now, why are you here? What did you need?" He couldn't keep the frustration out of his voice and no doubt sounded a lot more surly than intended.

She adjusted her stance and the look on her face was somewhere between insulted and incredulous. "What did I *need*?"

"You woke me up, so you must have a reason." He barked out his explanation then waited for an answer.

Her arms hugged her body in a protective stance as she glared at him. Silence ensued.

"What?" He enunciated the question. "Has it become a secret all of a sudden?"

She narrowed her eyes in anger. "I was just trying to place who you are. Because you're sure not my friend Chance."

He shook his head and huffed a sigh. "Holly…look. I'm sorry, okay?" How long had it been since he'd apologized to anyone?

"I didn't *want* anything, *Commander* Masters. I didn't expect to be attacked. I didn't come looking for a good time. And I sure didn't anticipate a lecture on how not to wake up an ill-tempered, arrogant grump. When did you get so bossy? You used to be nice. Sorry I bothered you." She spun around and marched toward the exit at the front of barn.

"Holly."

"Good night," she snapped without turning around.

Just let it go. You're asking for trouble if you don't let her go.

"Holly." *Shit.* He ran a hand over his face. "Wait."

She slowed her steps, finally stopping, but she still

didn't turn around. Her hair fell in gentle silver-gold swirls past her waist. Small bits of hay clung to the silken strands. He watched as she slowly turned around, saw her chin jut out, displaying the stubborn streak she'd had since she could talk, and silently cursed himself for getting into this situation. With that angelic face and a body *Playboy* would kill to add to its centerfold collection, he knew he'd just made a big mistake. Another one. His body was still erect and throbbing, ready for action of a different kind that had nothing to do with the battlefield. Spending too much time around her he could easily lose his mind. Or find himself in a whole lot of trouble. Maybe both.

"I...I couldn't sleep," she said finally, her voice soft. "I guess it's because you're home." She huffed out an embarrassed laugh as though she now thought the idea was completely lame. "I considered maybe you might be out here and could use some company. I thought we could talk. Like we used to. Sorry I woke you up."

Chance muttered a string of silent curses, all aimed at himself. He could feel all the little spears of warning jabbing his body and mind, each one screaming *No!* as he nodded, sat back down on the old blanket he'd found in the office and patted a corner, silently inviting her to join him.

"I would like your company. I'll try to be nice."

With a shift in body language, Holly approached him, moving the loose strands of hay around and fussing over the makeshift bed like a hen building a nest. When she finally had her spot the way she wanted, she sat down and grinned up at him. She was radiant. She smelled of some kind of berries, probably her shampoo. It was nice. Not all flowery like what some women used. He could feel the slight heat of her smaller body next to him as she relaxed against the wall.

This was a very bad idea.

"So have your brothers hit you up about quitting the SEALs and coming home permanently?"

He wondered which of them told her about their little plan. "Wade?"

"Cole." She smiled. "I take it that's a yes. And let me guess. Might your answer have something to do with you being out here in the barn?"

"You know, Naval Intelligence could use your talent."

"It isn't that I'm snoopy," she countered. "All that much," she qualified. "People just like to blab. Especially men."

"I'm going to let that pass."

"That might be wise." A frown covered her face, an indication of sincerity.

"So tell me about your clinic."

"It's there. You saw it. We've had this conversation. I'd rather talk about you."

"I'm sure I'll regret this...but what about me?"

"Exactly."

She sounded pleased that he understood. He didn't understand a damn thing except the need to adjust his pants. He turned his head and looked down into her eyes. Their faces were separated only by the width of their shoulders. He watched as her eyes dipped to his mouth. And stayed there. Her teeth were so white against her slightly open lips. His ability to remain indifferent dropped to below 2 percent. Give or take. With jaw-clenching determination, he looked away. "What can I tell you?"

When she didn't immediately answer, he turned back to her, noting how she'd again lowered her gaze to his mouth.

"I'm not exactly sure how to put it." She chewed her lower lip. Then let it slide from between her teeth until her mouth was again slightly open. Moistened. Full. Ready for kissing. Her soft honey-brown eyes looked directly into his.

"Is it hard?"

Three

Chance froze as a flare of heat once again surged to his groin. He cleared his throat and tried to weigh the question. He'd been around the men in his platoon too long. They all tended to break the tension and stress by intentionally putting the wrong connotation on something another said. This was Holly. Especially after what just happened, it was better to be safe.

"Is what hard?"

"What you do. For a living. Being a SEAL." She looked down at her hands, fiddling with a piece of straw. "I know you guys are the best, but even then, sometimes… Sometimes bad things happen. Like…what happened to Jason. I know you were hurt. Wade told me. I hear about an accident in Iraq or Afghanistan, like a chopper going down or our men being killed by some hidden bomb, and it's all I can do to take another breath. I know what it's like to get that phone call from a near hysterical wife who is calling to tell you your brother—her husband and the father of their baby—is dead. I can't imagine what it must be like on the other side. To actually see someone killed or badly injured."

He felt her struggle to not break down.

"After Jason… It became so real. It was no longer just a news report that happened to someone else. They could be talking about you. I pretty much held my breath every time they announced another casualty or bombing involving our guys, only relaxing when Wade didn't call to tell me anything after a few days."

That surprised him. He'd never considered that Holly would follow the news reports from that part of the world out of concern for *him*. He sensed she needed to know more than she'd probably been told. "It's a job, Holly. One that needs doing. I try not to think any further than that. I trust my team. I know they've got my back and in return they have confidence in me and we get it done. Sometimes bad things happen. But that's true wherever you are, whatever you're doing." They all prepared for that moment; they all knew the next breath could be their last, especially in SEALs. But he refrained from saying that out loud.

She was quiet for a long time.

"I wanted to write to you." She shrugged. "Especially after Jason was killed. Wade offered an address." She shook her head. "I was afraid I would say something that might cause you to lose your focus."

"Nah. You should write. I'd enjoy hearing from you."

She looked up at him. "Really?"

"Well, yeah."

She settled back against the board wall and he felt her relax. One of the horses nickered; another answered.

"The horses are always ready to go. Night or day. I

love their spirit. So eager to be saddled and taken on an adventure. I think they enjoy it as much as the riders do."

"I would have to say you're right. The biggest problem I used to encounter was holding them back when they wanted to tear ass and run."

"Do you think you can still do it?"

Chance had to get a grip on this. There were so many ways this question could go.

"Do what?"

"Ride a horse." This time she looked over at him, frowning. "What did you think I meant?"

He shrugged and hoped she would let it go. Distraction was the key. "Hell, yeah, I can still ride. It's like a bicycle. Once you learn…"

"Isn't that what they say about sex?" she asked. "I suppose it fits both scenarios."

Sex? Did she bring that up on purpose? He glanced over and saw the look of pure innocence on her face. *Nah.* "What do *you* know about sex anyway?" It was out before he could stop it.

The cool look she gave him didn't require words. But she answered anyway.

"Really. Are you honestly going there?" A look of disbelief covered her fine features. Her mouth was open in awe. Again. "Chance, I'm twenty-four years old and a year shy of being a doctor. I probably know more about sex than you do."

He absolutely refused to take up that challenge. "I didn't mean it that way."

"What *way* did you mean it? That I'm just a dumb little girl who never left the farm?"

"Your intelligence has never been questioned. I know you're smart," he murmured, adjusting his jeans in the most unnoticeable way he could. "You always have been."

"Okay. Well, that kinda narrows the options."

Chance didn't like where this conversation was going. He didn't want to think about Holly in another man's arms let alone his bed. *Hell.* It was none of his business. Holly was an adult and she could date whom she wanted. But he still didn't like it. Those bullets had done more than knock out his knee and shoulder. Apparently they had severely screwed with his head.

"Who is your boyfriend? Maybe I know him." *Safe subject.*

"Don't have one. Once the clinic caught on, I barely had time to breathe. That's when we hired Jolie to run the office, take the calls, set up the appointments."

"You said Kevin Grady is the co-owner?"

She nodded.

"I remember him. Red hair? Thick glasses?"

"Yeah." She nodded and smiled. "You should see his kids! Anyway, he has the experience but couldn't handle the workload by himself. I had the land and the old house that was left to me when Aunt Ida died. And that old masonry building sitting empty. So we formed a partnership. So far it's working. There are two high school boys who work weekends and evenings, cleaning and caring for the boarded animals. Even then it's still hectic at times. Right now we are all struggling to learn the new computer system."

"You'll get there. Look at how much you've accomplished already."

"I guess. I owe a lot to your brothers. They fronted the money for the equipment. We're making payments but I'll be so glad when I've paid them back.

"Hell, I doubt if they're worried about it."

"So when are we going to saddle a couple of horses?"

Chance hesitated. In actuality, he wasn't so sure he

could still swing up into a saddle. His right knee was still healing. It was mended enough that he could hide the tendency to limp. And the left knee took the brunt of the weight when he put his foot in a stirrup. Maybe he could manage without doing any more damage. "I don't know. I think Wade is expecting me to spend some time in Dallas but that probably won't be until next week."

She let her head fall back against the wooden wall and grinned like a cat that had just found the key to the milk vault.

"What?"

"I have something I want to show you while you're here. Something I've recently gotten into. I'll bet if you give it a try it will have you flat on your back and begging for mercy in about eight seconds."

Mother of God. He wasn't going to ask. He. Would. Not. Ask.

"Aren't you going to ask what it is?"

"No."

"You sound grumpy again." Her eyes narrowed as she gave him the once-over. "You must be really tired. I know you've experienced a lot of emotions today. I'll wait until you get your strength back and show you. Give you a live demonstration. It's easier than trying to describe it anyway. I guarantee you're going to think I've gone absolutely wild-child crazy. But I love it. You get into this rhythm and feel all that power beneath you, pushing you up and slamming you down, and know you control it... ah man, there's nothing like it."

He pinched his eyes closed and took a deep breath. He could feel her looking at him. For the life of him, he didn't know how to tactfully respond.

"Can we change the subject?" He cleared his throat. Why had he ever decided to come to the barn?

"Sure. Are you in pain?"

"No." *Yes.* But not in a way he could do anything about at the moment.

She nudged his arm playfully. "What do you want to talk about?"

He hadn't found one safe topic of conversation so far and he was quickly running out of ideas. When he'd thought about coming back to the ranch to recuperate, he hadn't envisioned this. He hadn't considered how Holly would have grown and matured into someone he would love to know better. A lot better. And thoughts like that wouldn't cut it. He needed to clamp down on his wayward thinking and he needed to start right now.

"How about on Sunday we grab a couple of horses and disappear for a while? I'll tell Wade we will go into Dallas later in the week. I'd like to see how things have changed on the ranch."

"That sounds great." She yawned. "Maybe then I can show you my new passion."

He let his head bounce against the back wall. *God-damn.* This was so messed up. He needed a smoke. Or a beer. Or both. The last time he'd seen Holly she'd been a child. For some reason she'd taken to him and he'd not been able to stop her from following him around the ranch, first with her brother there, then the few times when he wasn't. She'd been too young to take a hint and he wasn't about to hurt the feelings of a little ten-year-old by telling her to get lost and leave him alone. She had persisted and not only had he begun to enjoy her presence, he'd missed her when she wasn't around.

She'd been a cute kid, smart, never hesitating to speak her mind and not caring if she insulted someone in the process. He'd respected that. Especially in one so young. It was just over fifteen miles between her home and the school, so hanging out with her friends and classmates had rarely been an option for her, even after she'd joined 4-H. He'd definitely been like a second big brother. That status forever changed the second he'd stepped inside her clinic earlier tonight.

He felt Holly snuggle into his shoulder, her hand falling across his waist. It wasn't long before the sounds of the night were the only things he heard. He leaned farther back against the board wall, scooting down in the hay, absently smoothing his hand over her long silky hair.

How many times over the past ten years had he sat for hours against a stone wall, his senses alert to any sound out of the ordinary? The desert air had been dry, dusty, with a smell like something was rotting, the nights cold, the landscape harsh. In his mind he'd always walked through the plan of attack they would carry out just before sunrise, going over it in detail time after time. Recently, though, images of this ranch had pushed strategic preparations out of his head. The lush green pastures, the smiling faces. And sometimes he'd begun to wish he could come home to exactly this, although he hadn't really envisioned Holly snuggled in his arms. But that made it even better.

He had to question what was changing inside to make him start thinking of home after twelve years. Twelve years next month. At that time he would sign up for another three-year stretch if the medical evaluation board didn't determine he was out of the military forever.

Chance heard footsteps and looked up to find Wade walking in his direction. The smile on his face and a slight shake of his head said he wasn't surprised to find Holly asleep in his brother's arms.

"Just checking," he said in a lowered voice. "You both okay?"

"Yeah. I was just about to walk her home."

Chance stood up, then gathered Holly into his arms. She weighed next to nothing. A couple of tentative steps told him his knee could do it.

"Her house is behind the clinic a few yards. There's a path and light. You'll see it. It was her aunt's old house, if you remember."

"Thanks."

Walking to the front of the barn, Chance stepped out into the semidarkness. Holly had tucked herself into his arm, her head resting on his shoulder. He could feel her soft breath against his neck. When the smell of berries infused the night air, it was intoxicating. She was intoxicating.

A sudden sense of being home wrapped around him like a heavy fog. He could see only the road beneath his boots and the gentle face of the woman who slept in his arms. Drawing a deep breath, he inhaled the familiar smells of the ranch and heard the sounds of nature that stirred in his mind memories he'd carried since forever. He felt uplifted, although exactly what caused it, he didn't know. For the first time since he was wounded—maybe further back than that—he didn't feel the restlessness that speared him on each and every day. He felt at peace.

Stepping off the gravel road onto a well-worn path, he heard the water running in the stream seconds before he felt the cooler temperature inside the tree line. He smelled the rich, raw earth. Then he heard the hollow sound of his footsteps as he crossed the wooden footbridge that had existed long before he'd discovered it. He skirted the clinic, and with one last glance down at Holly, he stepped up onto the small patio of her home and opened the door.

If the woman watching TV in Holly's house thought it

strange to see a man step inside with Holly in his arms, she hid it well.

"And you are?"

"Chance Masters. And Holly is fine. Just asleep."

"That way." The woman pointed to her left. "Down the hall on the right."

"Thanks."

He laid Holly on her bed, pulled off her shoes and covered her with the blanket. He had to get a grip on this. Fast. Less than twenty-four hours back on the ranch and he was putting her to bed and fighting the desire to climb in with her.

Holly was a beautiful temptation. But Chance knew it would be unethical to come on to her, especially when his future was not set in stone. Some women were in it for the sex and were okay with no promises of forever. When he disappeared on a mission, the women he dated just found someone else. He couldn't see Holly in that light. She was as special now as she'd ever been and she would expect more from him. Maybe a lot more than he could give.

He needed to find something that would guarantee that distance was maintained between them. With every breath Holly reminded him he was a man. Every muscle in his body tightened, making him throb with painful need. The vision of Holly beneath him, the delicate features of her face glowing in mindless captivation of their sexual joining, her eyes locked to his as he moved inside her.

He had to stop it. Now.

But even so, the innocence of their friendship was forever gone. Whether a good thing or bad, there would be no going back to the way they were.

Four

Holly awoke to Amanda shaking her shoulder. "It's almost eight. Are you opening the clinic today?"

Holly moaned, nodded her understanding and sat up.

"You slept in your clothes?"

Looking down, Holly realized she was fully dressed except for her shoes. "I guess I did."

"And you fell asleep in Chance Masters's arms? Are you like kidding me?"

Holly nodded. "We were talking and I guess I did fall asleep." And Chance had brought her home. More than likely she'd been in his arms. It was typical of her rotten luck that she couldn't remember it. "We've known each other as far back as I can remember. He and my older brother were really tight."

"If I was with that man, the last thing I would do is fall asleep." Amanda sipped her coffee. "Go. Have your shower. I'm preparing Emma's cinnamon oatmeal. How long is the hunk staying, and is he married, engaged or involved?"

"I don't know. I don't think so."

"Mmm, mmm, mmm," Amanda muttered as she returned to the kitchen. "That is one fine man."

When Holly emerged from the shower, Amanda had already dressed Emma and was helping her eat breakfast. Holly paused to kiss the baby good-morning and gave Amanda a grateful hug before she left the house.

A quick peek around the corner of the clinic to the front parking area showed no cars in the lot. After entering the building, she put on some coffee, turned on the computer and scrolled through the appointments for the day. There were eleven scheduled and none was serious: annual vaccinations, a horse for pregnancy confirmation and a pig that limped. Probably stepped on a nail or cut its hoof in some way and it had become infected. Not a biggie. But hogs took everything to the extreme. One touch in an area they didn't want you to touch and they would scream. And scream. And scream. And they were loud. The town should find a way to use them for storm warnings. Everyone in the county would hear it.

She poured a cup of coffee and headed back outside to the far end of the building where there were four pipe-and-cable pens. Inside two of the pens were two mares that were due to be picked up today. They were recovering from founder brought on by too much spring grass. Some horses could handle it. Some couldn't. But both mares were looking good, back on their feed and ready to go home. And with no boarders scheduled, the clinic would be closed.

It was shaping up to be a perfect weekend. She could make it to the Kite Festival and enjoy the afternoon with Emma. And then Sunday maybe she and Chance could go riding. Just as she stepped back inside the building, the little bell over the front door chimed and she welcomed the first appointment of the day.

Following the curving road through the trees, Holly slowed the truck as she neared the parking area for the Calico Springs County Lake. It wasn't a huge lake, but covering several hundred acres, it was big enough for skiing and fishing tournaments. Its ever-growing popularity attracted families from Dallas on summer holiday. They had recently added more camping grounds and additional shower facilities. She found a parking spot and hopped down from the truck. Kites in every shape, size and color filled the sky. Amanda said they would be near the B section of the campgrounds and Holly headed in that direction.

A lot of the people brought their own food. Ice chests and containers of various sizes filled every available space on the picnic tables and lined the brightly colored quilts that had been spread out over the green grass. The aroma of hickory and mesquite wood filled the air as people grilled hot dogs and hamburgers. There was face painting, and vendors sold an array of food and sweet temptations along with lemonade, souvenirs and, of course, hundreds of kites and plenty of cords of string to fly them.

Holly caught sight of Emma as Amanda knelt before her holding a pink kite. Jogging over to them, Holly swung Emma into her arms, giving her a big kiss that made her giggle. Emma pointed to the colorful paper *birdies* in the sky and couldn't contain a squeal of excitement before Holly put her down. Taking her hand, they made their way through the crowd toward a grassy knoll that bordered the lake. Amanda held a pink kite and a spool of string while Holly attempted to tell Emma what they were going to do with it. The baby's eyes were wide as she sucked on her first finger and looked at the sky.

"Kite," Emma said, pointing to the object in Amanda's hands.

"Yeah. That's right." Holly grinned. "It's a pink kite, isn't it?"

"Pekite."

"Are we going to fly it up in the sky?" She pointed up at all the other kites, bobbing and twirling on the breeze.

"Fye!" And Emma pointed up, mimicking Holly's actions.

"Okay, you guys ready for the launch?" Amanda asked as she held the kite over her head and let out some string. "Here we go."

With near perfection, the kite caught the wind and took off, rising as fast as Amanda could let out the string. Emma laughed and pointed to the kite. "Pekite."

"Are you ready?" Amanda asked.

"Ready for what?"

"Blake Lufkin just spotted you." She nodded her head in a direction just behind Holly. "Yep. Here he comes."

Holly closed her eyes. Why wouldn't the man take no and just find someone else? "Wonder what he wants now."

"If I had a guess it would be that he's going to ask you to go to the rodeo. Isn't that coming up in a few weeks?"

Holly shook her head. "I've got to work. They're setting up a tent for me next to Doc Hardy."

"I wouldn't tell Blake or you'll have company all night."

"Pekite." Emma pointed to the water. Holly looked in that direction and saw the kite floating precariously close to the lake's surface.

"Uh-oh," Amanda said to Emma before running hard in the opposite direction. The kite hesitated, dipping even lower before a gust of wind sent it soaring again. Amanda returned to where Holly stood, still laughing.

"I want to go back to the couch, the air-conditioning and the TV," Amanda said. "Too much exercise for this girl. Oh. Here he comes. Think I'm gonna go and find something cool to drink." She shoved the cord of string toward Holly's hands.

"No. Amanda, pull the kite in. We're all leaving." *Crap.*

"Hey, Holly," Blake said in his annoying nasal tone as he stepped up next to her.

"Hi, Blake." Holly forced a smile at the cowboy. "How are you today?"

"Good, thanks. I just got off work. Thought I might find you here."

Holly nodded. He might be a nice guy, but there was nothing appealing about him. Over the past few months, it had started to become a problem. He would show up at the clinic, materialize in the aisle of the grocery store, even come walking into the dry cleaners, offering to carry her clothes. Every time he'd asked her out, she'd turned her down. There was nothing about him that she wanted to know better. She thought by now he would have taken the hint.

"Pekite," Emma told the strange man and pointed up.

"Yeah. That's a fine kite." He grinned at Emma. "Here, let me take that string for you, Amanda."

"No. Really. That's okay." She gripped the cardboard a little harder. "We were just leaving."

"Then, let me reel it in for you."

Holly switched the baby to her other arm and watched as Blake took over the honor of official kite reeler and waited for the inevitable question to come. Amanda made her escape.

Where was Chance when she needed him?

If someone had told him to go fly a kite with even a small degree of seriousness, Chance would have thought they were crazy. He'd honestly never seen a sight like this. Kites everywhere. The vividly colored paper contraptions with long tails flying against the stark blue sky, all reflected in the serene surface of the water, were such a contrast to what he'd become used to for over a decade, he couldn't quite get his head around it. There was color everywhere. It was like waking in the Land of Oz.

He'd been told in town that Derek Brown, a longtime friend, would be out at the lake. Chance decided to track him down, wondering at the same time if he would know him if he saw him. They'd told him to look for a silver Ford truck with spurs hanging from the rearview mirror. It would most likely have a boat trailer attached. Or a red fishing boat, if the crappie weren't biting. The guy who'd given these directions had failed to mention the Kite Festival.

As Chance made his way through the maze of erratically parked cars and trucks, he kept his eyes out for anyone who looked somewhat like Derek.

"Well, I'll be damned." A voice behind him sounded very familiar.

Turning, Chance looked into Derek's familiar face as he stepped from behind a tree. He hadn't changed. Not one damned bit.

"How're you doing, my man?" He pulled Chance to him in a manly hug of friendship. After a couple of slaps on the back, Derek stepped back and just looked at his old friend.

"When did you get in?"

"Yesterday."

"I'm sure sorry about your father."

"Thanks."

"So how long are you here?"

"I'm not really sure. Maybe a month."

As they continued to talk and catch up on what had transpired since the last time they had been together, a flashing motion a few yards behind Derek caught Chance's eye. A woman's long blond hair had come lose from its stretch band and she was struggling to hold it back with one hand while holding her baby in the other. It was a small family: a man trying to reel in a kite, a baby laughing in the arms of its mother.

Nothing unusual. Except the mother looked a lot like Holly.

Chance refocused on Derek, nodded at what he was saying—something about his eldest son—then gazed again at the couple. The woman had turned and was pointing up to the kite, her face now clearly in Chance's field of vision. It *was* Holly. Who was the guy? More important, whose baby was she holding? They looked like the typical happy family. Holly hadn't said anything about being married. In fact she said she didn't have a boyfriend. So who was flying her kite? About then she looked in his direction and made eye contact.

He once again focused on Derek. It was none of his business whom Holly saw or what she did in her life. He had no right to even speculate. He refused to acknowledge the feeling of his stomach plummeting to his knees.

"If you have time," Derek was saying, "I'd like you to meet my family."

"I'd like that," Chance told him honestly. He needed to be someplace else. *Any*place else. "Are they here?"

"Yep. My wife—you may remember Mary Beth Carter? She's grilling some burgers as we speak. Have you had lunch? There's one with your name on it."

Chance nodded. "That sounds good. If you're sure she won't mind."

"She'll be tickled to see you. It's just over this way."

Chance would enjoy spending some time with the friend he'd come to see. And he would not give Holly a second thought. He could keep his eyes on the ball during a reconnaissance mission where he led his team deep into the heart of enemy territory time and time again. He should have no problem focusing on lunch with one of his good friends.

But by the third time Derek asked him if he'd heard what he'd said, Chance knew it was time to give it up. He shook Derek's hand, nodded to his wife and thanked her for the great meal, promising Derek they would get together again before he left. He apologized for his inability to focus, blaming it on jet lag. As he walked back to the parking area, he couldn't prevent his eyes from roaming once more to the spot where Holly stood.

"Are you Chance Masters?" A pretty brunette with her hair pulled into pigtails grabbed his arm.

Frowning, Chance nodded. "How can I help you?"

"Not me, Holly. I'm Amanda, her best friend and part-time babysitter. I was there last night watching TV when you brought her home? Anyway, I'll explain all that later, or she can. Right now I need you to walk over to her and tell her it's time to go." She spoke fast, but he understood everything she said.

Chance frowned at the odd request. "Why would I do that?"

"Because that creepy guy won't leave her alone."

She grabbed his shirtsleeve and forcibly turned him

around. There was Holly, a baby still in her arms. She was reaching out to take a kite from the man, who didn't appear to want to relinquish it.

"Got it?" the brunette asked from just behind him.

"Got it."

"Tell Holly I'll see her back at the house." She beat a path toward the main parking area.

As Chance stepped forward, Holly had apparently given up on retrieving the kite and was walking toward the parking lot at a swift pace, frustration and a hint of anger covering her face. The man she'd been talking to was trailing behind. Chance changed course, which put him directly in her path. She appeared shocked to see him there but immediately smiled in relief.

"You two look like you've had a good time."

"Gootine."

This one would be talking Holly's ear off in a matter of weeks.

"Pekite." The baby pointed to the kite in the man's hand.

"Yep." Chance nodded. "That's definitely one pink kite."

"Fye!" Emma pointed to the clouds.

"What brings you out to Kite Day?" Holly smiled up at him. He clearly read the silent message of "don't leave us" in her eyes.

Chance glanced at his watch. "Did you forget you asked me to pick you up at three?"

That brought a full grin. "Oh! I did! I totally forgot."

The man who'd been standing behind them stepped up next to Holly. He didn't look happy. He wore a Western hat, had a short beard, thin nose and narrow, glaring eyes. He was shorter than Chance but a good fifty pounds heavier, most of it around the waist.

"Oh, sorry," Holly said. "Blake, this is US Naval Commander Chance Masters. Chance, Blake, ah...Lufkin."

Chance offered his hand to the man. He seemed to consider his options before he accepted it, apparently deciding that to refuse in front of Holly would not be wise. As first impressions went, Chance didn't like the guy. Holly's friend had been right. Something about him felt off. Holly seemed determined to leave his company. Hell, Chance would help her with that in a heartbeat.

"Are you guys ready to go home?"

"Yes," she responded immediately. "It's been a long day."

"Why don't you let me take you home?" Blake asked, his hand rubbing her back with a familiarity that suggested it was something he did all the time. "We could run into town and grab an early dinner?"

"Uh, thanks," Holly said and moved away from his touch to stand next to Chance. "But actually I'm not hungry."

Holly was being way too polite. Chance slid his arm around her shoulders, giving her a kiss on the temple. "I'm parked right over here, sweetheart." Chance pointed in the opposite direction. "I'll take their kite off your hands."

When Chance grabbed the kite, the man didn't immediately release it. Chance didn't really care how he retrieved the baby's kite. The man could hand it to him from flat on his back, or save himself a whole lot of trouble. But after staring at Chance a few more seconds, he did the wise thing and let go, dropping his hand.

Holly wished Blake a good evening. He returned a stiff smile, clearly not happy Chance had interfered with whatever he had planned. Chance understood all too well. The man was a parasite, thinking Holly was alone and vulnerable, which only proved that the guy didn't know Holly at all. She might be alone, but *vulnerable* wasn't in her vocabulary.

He opened the back door of his truck and set the kite on the seat. He didn't have a baby seat. It wasn't something he'd ever needed. Holly hopped up into the passenger side and set Emma on her lap, drawing the seat belt around both of them.

Chance got in behind the wheel and started the engine, still watching as the man walked off, finally disappearing amid the trees and parked cars.

"So spill," Chance said. "What's the deal with that guy?"

"I don't really know." She shrugged. "He moved here sometime last year. He came into the clinic for some flea and tick meds. The next thing I know he's showing up almost everywhere I go."

"He's asked you out?"

"Yeah. Like today. I've never accepted. The last time, I was pretty blunt. And I lied. I told him there was someone else in my life and I would not accept any invitations from him or anyone else." Holly took a deep breath. "I was afraid for a while I'd hurt his feelings and felt really bad about it, but two weeks later, here we go again. Small town. Guess it wasn't that hard to find out the truth. There is just something about him that makes me very uncomfortable."

"Has he ever threatened you?"

"No. Nothing like that. He's always polite. But…he's pushy. And he gets in my personal space." She shuddered. "I just wish he would go away. Go hit on somebody else."

Chance put the transmission in Drive. He would ensure Holly's wishes were met. No woman should have to deal with a stalker. He glanced at the baby in Holly's arms. "You haven't introduced me." He looked back at Holly. "Is she yours?"

That brought an immediate smile. "I thought you knew. This is Emma."

Obviously some things had definitely changed around here. Holly was a mother. And no one had thought it important enough to share that little tidbit of information?

Chance turned the truck toward the exit and the road that would take them back to the ranch.

"I'll send a ranch hand back for your truck, if that's okay. I'd prefer to make sure you both get home safely."

"Thank you, Chance."

He couldn't help but speculate about the father of the baby. Holly didn't wear a wedding ring, and although they hadn't had a chance to talk very much, surely she would not have come out to the barn and snuggled up next to him if she had a husband waiting at home.

A baby. Yet Holly still had that air of innocence. Obviously he was reading her wrong. Way wrong. Between her natural beauty and the fact she had a child, she couldn't be all that naive. Obviously there was a man in her life or had been at some point. These days, women didn't need a wedding ring on their finger to have a child. Some preferred it that way. He knew plenty of women, both in the military and not, who had one or more kids. Most said they neither wanted nor needed a man to complicate their life. He respected them even though he tended to be from the old school. Of the three Masters sons, he'd been the one closest to his mother and consequently had been raised with her principles. Old family values he'd never had reason to question. But in today's world, those ideas were outdated.

Chance's life didn't make it easy to have a permanent girlfriend or a wife, although some in his platoon were married and, at least on the outside, appeared to make it work. He liked his life the way it was. He was responsible only to himself and during a mission, the safety of his team. Kids were not something he wanted to be around, let alone be responsible for. Generally a baby was not something that put a smile on his face. They were a constant reminder of just how narrow the line between life and death was. They made him see the hopelessness of ever having peace in this world. He needed to stay away from Holly anyway, out of respect. A baby might just be the ticket to ensure he kept his distance.

Five

Sunday morning Holly finished feeding Emma her breakfast of oatmeal and juice, then set her down on a pallet to play with her five-note legless piano, her favorite toy.

"Aren't you late for your date?" Amanda asked as she refilled her coffee cup. "It's after eight o'clock."

"I told you, Amanda, it isn't a date. And we really didn't set a time." Holly stepped into the bathroom and began braiding her hair. "Are you sure you're willing to watch Emma on a Sunday?"

"Absolutely. As hard as you work, you deserve to enjoy a day off now and then. Anyway *Slanders Ridge* is coming on at two. That's about when Emma takes her nap. I'll just let her doze on the couch with me. We'll be fine. Go. Enjoy your day. With that hunk, how could you not?"

Holly took in a deep breath and sighed. She was separated from Emma too much during a normal workweek.

She hated missing a day with her on a weekend. The guilt weighed heavily. But this was only one day. Not even an entire day. And how often did she get an opportunity to go riding with Chance? She would make it up to Emma. Definitely.

She hadn't made it out the door when her cell went off. Chance.

"Good morning."

"Good morning to you. Are you ready for that ride?"

"Definitely."

"I'll see you at the barn."

"On my way."

With a hug for Amanda and a kiss for Emma, Holly slipped on her boots, pulled the jean pant legs down over the boot tops and she was ready. "I'll see you later."

"Be careful. Have fun."

The increased volume of the television drowned out anything else that might have been said.

Stepping into the barn, she saw no sign of Chance. She walked down the main aisle to the big gray gelding that nickered when he saw her. She grabbed the halter that hung on the stall door, slipped it on and led him to the grooming area next to the tack room.

"Good morning," Chance said as he walked inside the barn a few minutes later. His deep voice sounded husky, as though he'd just awakened. His short dark hair was in disarray. He was wearing jeans and a blue sleeveless shirt, unbuttoned and hanging from his broad shoulders. The sculptured muscles of his chest and abs were amazing.

"Good morning to you."

Holding his coffee cup in one hand, Chance sidled toward her, approaching the gray horse cautiously as if he was afraid his presence would startle it.

"I didn't know we had any thoroughbreds."

"I don't think you do. This is Sinbad and he's mine. He's actually a thoroughbred-Arabian mix. Cole lets me keep him here in exchange for being on call for the ranch but I pay for his food."

Chance ran his hand over the velvety neck. "He's nice."

Holly smiled. "Thanks."

Chance nodded his head in approval. "Well, I guess I need to catch up."

Stretching his arms, he walked to the center aisle, scanning the horses. He selected a big bay quarter horse that nickered to him as he passed, a good indication he was ready to leave his stall for a while. With the efficiency gained over a lifetime, Chance quickly brushed down then saddled the gelding.

"Do you need any help?" he asked, returning to Holly, leading the bay behind him.

"No, thanks. I've got it." She threw a red plaid saddle blanket onto Sinbad's back, then followed with a Western saddle. She tightened the girth, switched from a halter to a bridle and was ready to go.

Holly couldn't help but notice that Chance seemed to hesitate before climbing into the saddle. She'd forgotten he'd been wounded.

"Chance, if you're still recovering, we don't have to do this. Don't do anything that might set your recovery back."

Absently he rubbed his left arm. He obviously didn't want to talk about it and he was right. Talking wouldn't make it heal any faster and the last thing he needed was pity. Still…

"You might tear cartilage or undo the healing. It isn't worth the risk."

He looked out over the vast pastureland. "Yeah, it is."

The gelding was spirited and anxious to get started, but had been well trained, as had his rider. The horse stood in place while Chance jumped up, slid his left boot in the stirrup and threw his right leg over the saddle. He looked back at Holly. "We're good. Let's go."

Gathering the reins, he directed the bay toward the main gate that led to the bulk of the ranch land. Holly was happy to follow. They headed west, toward the river. Neither seemed inclined to talk. It was a day to relax and enjoy and Chance seemed intent on fully taking advantage of being here. Holly sensed he needed the quiet so she rode along next to him without attempting conversation.

They rode for miles. Spring rain had made the rolling pastures a deep, rich green. Chance appeared to visibly relax as they rode farther into the trees that dotted the land. Eventually they topped a rise and saw the river below. She could hear the sound of rushing water over the rock bed.

"Want to stop for a while?" She hoped he wouldn't think she was mothering him, even if she was.

"Yeah," he replied. "We can do that. I remember... there. On that gray boulder. You and Jason and I would sit and talk. Remember?"

"Yes. About girls." She rolled her eyes but was pleased he remembered. A lot of life had been discussed on that boulder. Past worries laid to rest; future dreams shared. Sometimes she'd been allowed to go along.

"How old were you back then?"

She thought for a moment. "I think around nine, maybe ten. You and Jason were still in high school. Aunt Ida used to make Jason take me with him. He would get so mad." Holly had to smile at the memory. Gosh, how she missed Jason. Aunt Ida, too.

Dismounting, they tethered the horses and climbed onto the large rock that jutted out over the water. The shade of the oak and cottonwood trees was cool on her back. The sound of the rushing water was always melodic and relaxing. Soon Chance sat down next to her.

"Remember when we all used to come here thinking we could catch fish for supper?"

He chuckled. "Yes. And if memory serves, we did catch some once. They weren't as big as your hand but you insisted on taking them home anyway."

"Your chef looked at that stringer as though he was being asked to panfry a snake."

"I know. But the guy tried. Then after one bite you determined they were uneatable." Chance laughed. "Double whammy. Poor man."

"Didn't he quit not long after that?"

"Yeah, he did."

Holly lay back on the rock. The radiant warmth felt good.

Chance chuckled. "Do you still have the old shoe?" he asked, referring to a centuries-old high-top shoe they'd found inside the remnants of an old cabin.

"Yep. It's wrapped in tissue and inside a ziplock bag. It seems a shame to keep it tucked away. I mean, it would be nice to display it somewhere, but I'm so afraid something might happen to it. I wish we could have found the other one."

"So do I. That was definitely one of our better finds."

"Yes. That and the compass." Holly glanced over at Chance. "Do you still have it?"

"Yeah. And Jason brought the razor and the musket balls over to the house before he left for college. It's hard to believe part of the Civil War took place in our own pasture. I wonder if the old cabin on the rise is still standing."

"I doubt it. But maybe we can check it out before you… while you're here."

There was a lull in the conversation. Then…

"How old is your baby?"

She rolled toward him, a smile pulling at the corners of her mouth. "Fourteen months," she answered without any hesitation.

Chance lay on the boulder, one boot crossed over his raised knee, his hands threaded under his head, his eyes closed as he doubtlessly listened to the peacefulness around him.

"She's Jason's daughter. You do know that, right?"

He looked over at her. "No. I didn't have any idea."

"His wife died giving birth a few months after Jason was killed. Carolyn didn't have any family so I brought Emma home. When I look at her I see a little bit of Jason. But Emma is a person in her own right. She's so smart she's a handful. You work to keep up with that one."

Chance rolled toward her, his head propped on his hand. She looked into those smoky-blue eyes and wanted to drown in them. She saw his pupils widen as he gazed at her with serious intent.

She wanted to kiss him. She wanted to know how he tasted, how his hot breath would feel on her skin, how his big hands would feel when they touched her. He was so sexy, so handsome. Most of all, he was Chance. He'd saved her from school bullies, taught her to ride a bicycle, then bandaged her knee when she took a tumble. She'd loved him when he'd signed up and joined the navy and had never stopped thinking of him in the twelve long years he'd been gone. He wasn't the same man she'd known then. Wherever he'd been, whatever he'd been doing had changed him from the happy-go-lucky cow-boy, defying his billionaire status, into a hardened war-rior. Clearly he was used to being in command.

"I'm surprised you're not married." she said, feeling a bit awkward for some reason.

"What I do doesn't leave a lot of room for serious re-lationships. Here one day, gone the next, and no way of knowing when I'll be back. Sometimes it's a week. Some-times nine months or longer."

"I can see how that would be tough," she agreed. "A woman would have to be strong and completely head over heels in love to deal with that."

"Yeah. And have the trust and patience of a saint. And they are rare. Some of the guys in my platoon are married. But it's hard on the relationship. Eventually he begins to question if she's faithful, and if that concern takes root and stays on his mind it can get him killed. It's equally hard on the woman for obvious reasons. One guy in my unit, Ray Shields, has three kids. He never got to be there for the birth of any of them."

"But some do make it work."

"Yeah. Some do."

"Why did you never come back here before now? You loved the ranch so much."

He was quiet for so long she wasn't sure he would answer.

"Too many memories. And most of them were not so great. I guess you knew my father and I didn't get along. I think the entire county knew. Or maybe you were too young to pick up on it. But there was a lot of resentment. On both sides. I blamed him for the death of my mother. Still do. He blamed me for a hell of a lot, as well." He paused, as though transported deep into his past. "It seemed like the wisest move to take my leaves somewhere else."

After a long silence, Chance sat up and scanned the horizon. "It looks like rain is coming our way. Are you ready to head back?"

"I guess. If you are."

She wanted to ask him so much more about his mother. Holly had very little recollection of her. But now wasn't the time. She sat up next to him and their gazes met and held. How she wanted to kiss him. Right here. Right now. Right or wrong. She couldn't think of a better place for something she'd waited for for a lifetime. Moving closer to his muscled body, her focus dropped to his mouth. Absently, she moistened her lips.

"Holly." He shook his head.

"What?"

"This is not a good idea." His voice was rough, as though he was holding himself back.

"I don't know what you're talking about." But her focus remained on his lips that had haunted her for over a decade, now a mere breath away.

"Yeah. You do." But despite his hesitation, he reached up and smoothed some strands of her hair back from her face. He caught the back of her hair in his fist, gently pulling her toward him. In what seemed like slow motion, she watched as his face came closer. His lips parted, showing a glimpse of strong white teeth. Then his mouth touched hers, gently at first, his lips moving over hers tentatively, as though he was giving her every opportunity to change her mind. He drew back, making her heart cry out. He watched her, carefully, intently, as though he had to be sure this was what she wanted.

"It's just a kiss," she whispered. She could hear the pleading in her own voice.

"Don't bullshit me," Chance said. "We both know it's a hell of a lot more than that."

She raised her hand and touched his face, letting her fingers trail over his deep jaw, feeling the stubble, while her eyes remained fixed on his handsome face. With a last glance, the lure of his lips could no longer be denied. She tilted her head and swayed toward him. Chance pulled her the rest of the way. Strong yet supple, with his tongue he moistened her as though preparing her for something more to come. Then the gentleness was gone as he took her mouth fully and completely. His tongue pushed inside and she was lost. A shiver ran through her at the speed of his immediate possession.

Holly savored the feel and taste of him. Her arms came around his neck, holding him to her. She heard him inhale a deep breath, felt the grip on the back of her hair tighten in his fist. He tasted of raw, hungry male, his mouth and tongue so hot, so demanding, it threatened to overwhelm her senses. Heat surged through her veins like liquid lava, pooling at the apex of her legs.

She felt the warm sensation of the rock against her back and absently realized she was lying prone with Chance's hard body covering hers. He was ravenous. His mouth moved rapidly over hers, taking her over and over, pushing his tongue in deep time after time. She heard him emit a growl, long and low, and her body responded. She wanted more. She needed more as his mouth continued to ravish hers, over and over, entering the deep recesses of her mouth, seeking the hidden depths, encouraging her to do the same.

His big hand cupped her breast, kneading her almost to the point of pain but never crossing the line, making her sensitive flesh swell under his touch. She arched her back, wanting to cry out at the sheer pleasure. She couldn't get close enough, couldn't open to him wide enough, take him deep enough.

As if he could read her mind, he made a simple adjustment and Holly felt his erection pressed hard against her. She couldn't hold back the moan, the last sound she heard before reality disappeared and left her floating in Chance's arms. Something seized her deep inside. It was a feeling that burned her like an invisible ray of the sun, heating her skin, surging through her body like a forest fire out of control. It made her forget to breathe, caused her heart to speed up and her mouth to go dry. The sheer intensity of it was indescribable. Her body ached as though she was experiencing withdrawals. She had never felt such a strong physical attraction to anyone before in her life.

Suddenly Chance raised his head, separating their hungry lips, breathing hard. Their gazes locked for endless seconds before Chance rolled away, mumbling some not-so-nice words under his breath. Still, his nearness made her intensely aware of his rock-hard masculinity, the sheer density and power of his body. The sudden stillness poured over her like the cold waters of the stream. Holly wanted to scream at him, beg him to release the building frustration and make it stop. She wanted him to free the overwhelming desire rising inside her, ease the terrible throbbing need to be loved by him.

The world came sliding back and try as she might, she couldn't stop it. The sound of the running water slowly returned. Birds called in the trees. The branches above them swayed in the gentle breeze, the shadows moving over the two people below like soft caresses.

Holly realized she was lying on her back on the huge rock, her blouse unbuttoned, her body seizing up and needing more. She squeezed her legs together, trying to ease the need, and rolled onto one shoulder to watch as Chance wrestled with what had happened.

"Don't you dare even think about apologizing." He turned his head to look into her face. Remorse showed clearly in every feature, confirming that was exactly what he was thinking.

"Holly—"

"No. Not one word. Not one syllable. Please don't ruin it. I'm just sorry you stopped."

"Don't say that." His voice was incredibly deep and gravelly with a hint of desperation.

"Why not? It's the truth."

Chance shook his head, then rubbed the back of his neck and mumbled something she couldn't understand.

"Don't grumble," she said as she began buttoning her blouse.

Chance looked over at her as though there was something he needed to say. A whole bunch of things. Instead, he straightened his spine, ran one weary hand over his face and groaned.

The ride back was quiet, but not strained. Holly let Sin go at his own pace. She kept her head turned away so Chance didn't see the smile that refused to leave her face as she relived their embrace. That had definitely been worth waiting for. But it wasn't just the kiss or the passion that flared between them. Chance had been right when he'd said there was a lot more to it. Their embrace had been life changing. It had affirmed that childhood was over. Thinking of him as merely a friend was history.

Part of her was thrilled that Chance was attracted to her. The other part reminded her that whatever they shared while he was here would soon be just another memory. And she'd be well advised to remember that.

Six

The sprawling city of Dallas spread out beneath them as the chopper headed toward a landing pad located somewhere in the muddle below. It was a far different sight from flying over the cities in Afghanistan and Iraq. Sitting next to Cole, Chance was content to gaze out the window and let the pilot do his thing. No reason to try to talk over the roar of the engine. They both knew where they were headed and why. It wasn't enough for Wade to tell him about the corporation and the plans for future development—he wanted to show him. Chance had refrained from telling him he didn't succumb to arm-twisting and wasn't about to start now.

Cole pointed to a skyscraper on Chance's right. Constructed of steel and smoked glass, it gave the impression of wealth, power and sophistication. Soon the helipad came into view and the pilot set down in a near-perfect maneuver on top of the building. A short trip to the elevator and then they were walking down a richly carpeted hallway to Wade's office.

Chance expected to greet only Wade, but the sprawling office and reception area was filled with people. Applause broke out as soon as he walked through the door. Chance understood they were heralding one of their soldiers' return home from the battlefield, but he could have done without the attention. He shook hands and received gentle pats on the back as he made his way to where his eldest brother stood as the employees who'd welcomed him filed out the door.

When they all had departed, Wade lost no time getting down to business. Literally. For the next five hours Chance was given a thorough glimpse into Masters Corporation, Ltd. It was impressive. Wade had done an excellent job and Chance lost no time telling him so. The plans for future expansion in key areas were brilliant. Wade was made for this and he handled it beautifully. Cole proudly gave Chance a bird's-eye view of the books: where they had been, where they were now and where they expected to be in the next two years.

"Where are the figures on the ranch?"

He caught a quick glance pass from Cole to Wade. Suddenly the feeling of camaraderie in the room shifted to one of nervous tension. It was the same sensation Chance felt on missions when they had been given wrong intel and rather than a simple reconnaissance his team found themselves in the middle of an all-out skirmish. There was always a moment of realization that they'd been set up just before shit hit the fan and bullets started to fly, not unlike what he was feeling right now. The hair on the back of his neck stood at attention. Chance stepped back from the conference table and waited.

"The fact is," Cole said, meeting Chance's eyes, "the

ranch is not profitable. It hasn't been for the past five or six years. Beef prices fluctuate but the cost to maintain it steadily goes up."

"There is a lot more to it than that. Have you taken an in-depth look at the figures?"

"Yes. And no."

"What the hell does that mean?"

"It means we've decided to get out of the cattle business. There is a lot more money to be made in other areas of the corporation. Frankly, we are not ranchers. We've tried several times to bring in someone to manage a turnaround. Nothing they tried worked. It's just not worth the money and time to try to fix whatever might be wrong— if there is a fix—when that time could be better spent working on financially sound investment opportunities."

"The ranch was Mom's dream."

Wade nodded. "Yes, it was. But she's gone. And times have changed. The land itself is worth more divided into parcels and sold for development than it is as a feeding trough for cattle. Plus, the entire west end of the property runs parallel to the rail system, which triples its worth."

Chance clenched his jaw, determined to keep that sickening twist in his gut from spilling out in a completely different form, all directed at his brothers. He clenched his fists as fury battled desperation. In all the covert missions, he'd never felt such a strong sense of pending disaster. There was always a plan B. There was always hope. But this was a dagger right to the heart. And he had only himself to blame. He was the one who'd chosen to walk away, leaving Wade and Cole to handle it all. As it stood, he had no right to say anything. He'd long ago made choices, and those choices took him out of the game. But that didn't stop the bile from rising in his throat.

From the home office, they were driven to the original Masters mansion in North Dallas, where dinner would be served and they would spend the night. Their grandfather had built the original structure back in the 1940s. Their father had doubled its size, and the entire building had been updated just before he died. Complete with turrets, it had always reminded Chance of something out of the Middle Ages. This was where Wade and Cole had lived the first few years of their life and, when business brought them to Dallas, this was home. Their mother had not been raised in a city and longed for the wide-open spaces, so to appease her, the gigantic log-and-stone house at the ranch had been built. That was the only home Chance could remember.

While Wade and Cole kept up a lively conversation between courses, Chance's mind wavered between the loss of the ranch and Holly. Somehow he saw both in the same light. In a matter of weeks, he would lose them both. He would head back to his world, and life would continue as it had for the past twelve years. He couldn't help but surmise what would happen to her business if Wade sold the land. Could a veterinarian clinic survive amidst the housing developments and commercial ventures? He supposed it could happen. Maybe she would be better off. Maybe Cole would help her relocate. Whatever happened, Holly would survive. She was a fighter. Always had been.

Chance shouldn't have kissed her. He'd promised himself he wouldn't touch her. But damn. He was glad he had even if it was wrong. She'd felt amazing in his arms. Her skin was velvety soft and smooth. She'd melted against him until it felt as if the two had merged into one. He'd never felt that close to any woman, even during sex. The silky sweetness of her mouth had been almost more than he could handle without taking her fully. And he'd wanted to. The way she'd opened to him, offering more… Her soft moans telling him of her need. Holding himself back had taken more strength and determination than a lot of the missions he faced as a SEAL.

She had a baby. A baby not a lot older than the one he'd let die. He'd been in plenty of situations he would label uncomfortable. Being around her baby was another one. He couldn't tell Holly he no longer wanted to be around her because she had a kid. And he wanted to see her again. Whether it was right or wrong, whatever this thing was between them had changed from childhood friendship to adult desire, and it gripped him hard and heavy. He'd felt the very real, very hot flames of it when he'd kissed her. When she'd responded.

His brothers' laughter brought him back to the present.

"That sound okay with you, Chance?"

"I'm sorry?"

Wade had that stupid knowing smile on his face again. "I was saying a welcome-home celebration was needed. It'll give you the opportunity to meet some of the executive staff here in Dallas. We have some really good people and they've all been waiting to meet you. I think once you have a chance to talk with them, get to know them and feel comfortable, this whole corporation thing won't seem so alien to you."

Chance sat up in his chair. The last thing he wanted to do was become a G.I. Joe puppet on Wade's center stage. Clearly this was another attempt by his brothers to bring him on board at the company, and after their earlier revelation about the ranch, he wanted nothing more than to tell them both to stick it. "And who else will be there?"

"Excuse me?"

"Other than your employees?"

Wade dropped the linen napkin on the table. "There might be some representatives from companies we do business with."

"You see me as a salable, item and you're not going to let the opportunity pass to draw interest to your latest project by introducing them to a SEAL. And the fact that it's your own brother makes it more palatable. You never were one to give up an opportunity to grab for the brass ring. Just like Dad."

Wade shrugged. "I'm not saying you're right, but even if you are? So what?"

Chance looked at Cole, who had silently observed the exchange. "You want explain it to him?"

"Cole doesn't have to explain anything to me," Wade barked, his voice edged with aggravation and long-practiced intimidation.

Yeah. Good luck with that.

"I get that you want no part of this company, Chance. I think I can change your mind but you've got to give me an opportunity. What can it possibly hurt for you to put a little effort forward and meet some people? People who care a lot about you."

"I don't even know them. You said that yourself."

This conversation had no end. He and his brother could keep arguing until the next full moon. No, it couldn't hurt for Chance to agree to attend this fiasco, but at the same time, it wouldn't hurt for Wade to let it go.

Chance blew out a breath. "It seems ridiculous to me when I have no plans to stay. I'll do it. But one evening is it. After that, no more."

"Done," Wade confirmed.

"If you gentlemen will excuse me, I think I'll say good-night. I've had about all the happy news I can stomach for one evening." Chance stood and looked around at where he'd been sitting. They'd used three chairs out of the forty that surrounded the elaborate table, the rich mahogany gleaming under the glow of three chandeliers. "Why don't you put some effort toward getting a smaller table? Eventually somebody's going to think there are a lot of guests who didn't show up for dinner. Not good for the image." He pursed his lips at the humor apparently only he could see. "Good night."

As Chance's long strides carried him down the hall to the elevator, he heard his brothers discussing what they had asked him to do. Cole wanted the party held here, in the center of Dallas, which would be easier on everybody. Except for the star attraction, aka the bait. In two days he had an appointment with the civilian doctor. Depending on his findings, Chance would be one step closer to getting back to his team.

The next morning, not willing to subject himself to the possibility of any belated plans Wade may have thought of overnight, he asked the chauffeur to take him to the heliport. Wade and Cole had meetings scheduled in Dallas over the next two days, so there was really no reason to stick around just to say goodbye. They knew where to reach him if need be, plus there was an abundance of choppers if anyone needed to make a fast trip back to the ranch or anywhere else.

Soon Chance was behind the controls, the rotors gaining speed as he lifted off, heading the chopper north. This was a toy compared with what he'd been trained to fly, but it handled well enough. When the sprawling ranch came into view, only then did he begin to relax.

He had just shut down the engine of the Bell 407GX and stepped away from the chopper when his cell began to ring. It was Holly.

"Hey, Holly."

"How was your visit to Dallas?"

"Oh, wonderful." He could hear the heavy sarcasm in his own voice. There were dogs barking in the background on her end so he didn't hear her reply.

"Come to dinner. Tonight at seven. It's meat loaf night."

"Meat loaf, huh? How can I pass that up?"

She giggled. "Gotta go. See ya then."

He couldn't help but notice his steps were lighter than they'd been before she called. But as he reached the flagstone area around the pool, he remembered the baby who would no doubt be there tonight. How was he going to spend time in the presence of…what was her name? *Emma?* How could he carry on as though it was nothing? Every time he looked at Holly's baby he saw the baby girl in Iraq. She'd been sitting on the ground innocently playing with a doll. Chance had heard the missile seconds before he saw the exhaust as it lined up trajectory to the target: a building directly behind where the child sat.

He'd hauled ass toward the baby, muscles straining as he pushed himself past his physical limits, determined to get there in time. The explosion had blown him back some thirty feet. He'd lost hearing in one ear for almost a month, and they'd pulled shrapnel from his head and shoulders, requiring several days in the infirmary. And when the dust settled, there was nothing of the baby that remained. Just one foot of the little doll. All he could do was lie in that hospital bed and relive the incident over and over. Three seconds. If he'd had three seconds more, he might have saved her.

It was a child Emma's age who brought on the nightmares. Of all the things he'd witnessed during his time in the service, that had been the worst. It had brought the reality of just how innocent and fragile a little life was screaming to the surface. After that experience, he'd stayed well away from members of his platoon who incessantly talked about their families. He didn't blame them. Not at all. But it was nothing he would ever be a part of, and he found reasons to leave the room before new baby pictures made the rounds. He was happy for Holly. She seemed to really love Emma and no doubt was a great mom. But it was none of his business and it needed to stay that way.

Chance ran a hand over his face. He should listen to his own common sense. This wasn't Iraq. There were no guided missiles. Holly's baby was fine. He would be there an hour tops. He could do an hour. He wanted to see Holly again. If that's the only way he could do it, he would get through it somehow.

"Come in!" Holly called upon hearing the knock on the door. Seeing Chance step into the room, she left the potatoes frying in the pan and hurried over to give him a welcome hug.

"Smells good," he said and hugged her back.

"I hope you like it. It's my granny's recipe." She hurried back to the stove. "There's cold beer in the fridge and dinner is almost ready."

This was the first time she'd ever cooked for Chance. She'd debated for two days what to fix. She wanted it to be something he couldn't get anywhere else. That ruled out steak and baked potatoes. With her limited culinary skills, she'd settled on her Granny's secret meat loaf recipe, homemade French fries, green beans from Miss Annie's garden and cold beer or mint tea. Holly would have never been able to pick out or afford a good wine anyway.

Placing the food on the table, she told him to take a seat before hurrying from the room to get Emma. Chance's body language changed when she carried the baby into the dining room. He appeared to withdraw. She had to wonder what that was about. Setting the high chair at the table between them, she seated Emma, then fixed her plate: noodles, some of the fries, green beans and applesauce. Finally, Holly sat down in the vacant chair across from Chance.

"Please, help yourself."

Without uttering a word, Chance cut a sizable portion of the meat loaf and helped himself to the fries, green beans and a hot roll. He periodically glanced at Emma almost as though she made him nervous. Odd. He'd seemed fine with her at the Kite Festival at the park. Maybe he'd just had a bad day.

With Emma, it was sink or swim. She would either like you or she wouldn't. It was her decision. If she took to Chance, he'd made a friend for life. Holly sat back, content to see what Emma would do.

It didn't take long.

The baby was fascinated with the big man. She chewed a noodle and watched him fork a bite of meat into his mouth.

"This is great, Holly." He glanced at Emma, who still sat staring at the new person in their house.

"Bea." She pointed to the green beans on his plate. When Chance didn't move she apparently thought he didn't understand her command. She leaned over toward Chance, her hand almost touching his plate. "Bea."

"Right. Bean."

But he didn't put any beans on his fork. He didn't pick one up. He didn't put any in his mouth. And Emma became more determined, staring as if trying to figure out why this person sitting at the table wasn't eating his food.

Chance speared some fries. That seemed to appease her somewhat. She looked at her own plate and picked up a fry. As she chewed, she continued to stare at Chance. Holly had to wonder if Chance felt like a specimen under a microscope. It was then she noticed the beads of perspiration on his forehead. She stood from the table and walked to the thermostat on the wall, cranking it down a few degrees. When she returned to the table, Chance was wiping his face.

"Are you okay?"

"Yeah. Fine. This is really good."

"So seriously, how'd it go in Dallas with your brothers?"

He shrugged. "Pretty much the way I expected."

She saw the muscles in his jaw working overtime. He took a deep breath as though trying to gain control. Something unexpected had happened. Something he clearly didn't want to talk about. She wouldn't push him to tell her. If he wanted her to know, he would when he was ready.

"Fy." Emma held out a French fry to Chance.

"Emma, here." Holly put some applesauce in a spoon and held it to Emma's mouth. "Take some applesauce. Mmm. Good."

The baby took the bite, never taking her eyes off Chance. Holly sat mesmerized as Emma grabbed a noodle in her chubby hand and held it out to Chance. The baby leaned far out of her high chair in an attempt to feed Chance the noodle. Holly would swear the color drained from his face.

"She won't give up until she sees you eating a green bean or a noodle. Those are her favorites." Holly smiled in apology. "She's like that. She tends to want to take care of people she likes."

Chance nodded his head and speared a bean. "She doesn't know me."

"She knows enough." Once Chance ate some of the green beans, Emma sat back in her chair, content. "Remember you telling me about that sixth sense you rely on? I'd have to say knowing which people she likes and doesn't is something like that. I've seen her scream bloody murder if a person she doesn't like tries to pick her up, even if it's a grandmotherly type and innocent as can be. You've just witnessed what happens when the vibes are right."

Chance cut a glance back at the baby. She sat quietly, watching him while she chewed on her bean. He picked up a French fry, broke it in two and gave her half. They both chewed their potato.

As the meal went on, Chance seemed to relax. A little. They shared green beans and more potatoes until finally Emma was full and wanted down to play.

"So where is your roommate this evening?"

"Roommate? Oh, you mean Amanda. She went home. Said she had errands to do. I think she had a date. She'll be back eventually. She gets lonely sitting in her apartment by herself. She's in between jobs right now."

"What does she do?"

"RN. Surgical nurse."

"You've known her a while?"

"Yeah. We've been friends since grade school. Her dad is the pharmacist at City Drug. You might know him. Doug Stiller?"

"Yeah. Yeah I remember him." Chance wiped his hands on the napkin. "He was always very understanding when a guy's hormones began to kick it. But you didn't walk away with a foil packet in your back pocket without a speech about being responsible." He glanced at Holly and smiled. The glimmer was back in his eyes. "I tended to listen."

Emma banged her spoon on her tray and kicked her feet. "Out," she demanded loudly. Holly reached for Emma and knocked over a glass of lemonade. The liquid spilled onto Chance's half-eaten dinner.

"Oh! I'm sorry. Here, let me get another plate and some—"

"Don't worry about it, Holly. It was all delicious but I'm full."

"Boo-boo," Emma proclaimed.

"Yes. Boo-boo," Holly agreed, still mopping at the spill with whatever napkin she could find.

"It was really good, Holly. I'm sorry to eat and run, but there are some things I need to do before tomorrow."

He stood from the table, careful of the baby, and headed to the back door.

Why did she suddenly feel like a waitress in a really bad restaurant?

"Sure. Maybe we can do it again sometime." She followed him to the door.

"Yeah. That'd be nice."

He pulled open the outside door and hesitated. She heard him mutter to himself before turning around and catching her face in his hands. He absorbed her lips, kissing her deeply, then took one last glance at Emma. "Good night."

And just like that he was gone. Holly turned to look at Emma, who sat contentedly on the floor, playing with a toy. Something had totally unnerved Chance. She had no clue what. Surely not Emma? Yet that was what appeared to be the problem. She began gathering the dirty dishes.

She knew some men didn't like to be around children. Apparently Chance was one of them. One more reason for Holly to keep her distance.

For more than half of her life she'd daydreamed about Chance. Of the home they would have, the family... The reality was very different and it was a hard pill to swallow. Knowing he would soon leave again, plus seeing his reaction to Emma pretty much said it all. There would never be a future for them. And the sooner she accepted it the better off she would be.

"Commander Masters?" Chance stood as the doctor held out a hand. "I'm Dr. Lopez. Good to meet you, sir. Please come in."

Chance followed the doctor into the small examination room.

"Your doctor at the VA forwarded a summary of your injuries. Tell me about them. How do *you* think you're doing?"

It was an intensive hour. This doctor, while not military, knew his stuff. After Chance explained how he felt physically and emotionally, the doctor examined him head to foot.

"Do you have full range of motion in your left shoulder?"

"Pretty much." He rubbed the site of the bullet's entry on his chest. "I still have minor pain around the site itself, but everything else feels normal. It's my knee I'm worried about."

The doctor nodded. "Hop on the table and let's have a look."

When the exam was finished, Chance went through a battery of tests including X-rays and an MRI on both his chest wound and his knee. Finally back in his office, the good doctor explained that the preliminary results looked good.

"It will take forty-eight hours to get all of the results back but I don't anticipate seeing any problems. Are you taking any physical therapy?"

"No."

"You might want to consider it. I would suggest you start out slow. Don't push your knee too hard at first. If you have access to a pool, that would be an excellent way to work the knee without an extraordinary amount of pressure."

The doctor leaned against the counter, looking at his file. "Are you going to return to active duty?"

"That's the plan."

The doctor tore a slip of paper from his prescription pad and handed it to Chance. It had a name, address and phone number. "Physical therapist. He's good. Call and set up a few sessions. I'll call you if there is anything that concerns me when the last of your tests come in."

While it was good to hear some positives, this doctor didn't know the specifics of Chance's job. Therefore he would have no way of knowing if Chance could return to doing it. It was damn hard to stay positive when it was your life on the line and your future was ultimately in the hands of the Naval Medical Evaluation Board.

Seven

"Let's start him out slow today," Mark Johansen called to Holly, who was seated atop her gray gelding, Sinbad. "Ease him into a slow canter, keeping to the outside of the cross rails."

Holly did as she was instructed. She loved riding Sin and he seemed equally happy to give her the ride. He was an amazing animal. He carried her smoothly twice around the large arena, never once slowing or breaking stride.

"Now," Mark called from the center of the ring, "when you get to the opposite end, gather him, take a half halt into a figure eight and ask him to change his gait. Then reverse when you reach the other end. We need him to feel like that's a normal motion."

Holly took Sin around again then gathered the reins, gave the cue, and within a few strides Sin switched from leading with his right front foot to his left.

"Try that again. He needs to respond more quickly. Take him around a few more times. Keep in a figure eight. He should start to feel it as part of his natural stride, changing without you asking him to do it depending on the direction."

Holly gave a nod and followed Mark's instructions. The fourth time, Sin switched his lead perfectly. Holly finished the round, patting Sin on the neck, then directed him toward the inside of the arena for the jumps.

The first cavalletti was a cross rail: two poles that crossed one another with a straight beam over the top. At four feet in height, it was a piece of cake for Sinbad. Holly lined him up for the jump, gathered the reins and gave the cue. With graceful ease, the powerful gelding sailed over the jump as though he was floating on air. Her body automatically swung forward as Sin left the ground. The horse's natural motion lifted her rear out of the saddle, then her weight sank back into the stirrups as they landed. She continued around the small course, Sin taking each jump as perfectly as the first.

Twice more through the maze and Mark waved her over. "Okay. He did great on the jumps but he still needs some work on dressage."

She glanced over toward the indoor bleachers. Near the front entrance Emma contentedly played with her own little plastic horses and cows inside the playpen. The indoor arena was actually a little larger than the one outside. It allowed for storage of the jumps and ensured Emma a near-perfect temperature year-round. Out of the corner of her eye she caught movement. Chance was leaning against the railing. How long had he been there?

"Chance. Come over and meet Mark."

"Mark, this is Chance Masters. He is one of the owners of this ranch."

"Mark Johansen. Nice to meet you." The men shook hands. "You have an incredible spread here."

"Thanks."

Holly turned to Chance. "Mark was once a contender for the US Olympic team. He and his wife moved here last year and he's been kind enough to give me some dressage and show-jumping lessons," Holly said. "What's it been? Six months?"

"About that," Mark replied. "She's doing great."

Chance nodded. "Yeah. I saw. Lots of *passion* in that ring. It would undoubtedly have me on my back begging for mercy in about eight seconds." His deep blue eyes sparkled with dark humor.

Holly knew he was referring to their night in the barn when she told him about her new fervor. "Yep. It tends to make a girl wild-child crazy. Controlling all that power." She couldn't help but grin as Chance put two and two together.

"I should have known you were talking about a horse." He shook his head.

"Why, Commander, what else could it have been?" she asked, a grin edging her lips, a look of pure innocence on her face.

Chance didn't reply to her challenge but his eyes told her in no uncertain terms that payback would be hell.

"I'm out of here," Mark said. "Mary Ann, my wife, has a list of to-dos. It was nice to meet you, Chance," he said and headed for his truck.

"I need to talk to you. Would you mind stopping by the house when you're finished?" Chance asked Holly when they were alone.

She shrugged. "Sure. Let me put Sin back in his stall and I'll be there."

"Take your time," he said before turning and disappearing around the corner of the barn.

After Sinbad was showered down, brushed out and returned to his stall with some apple slices in his feeding trough, she picked up Emma and headed for the big house.

Holly rarely came here. She'd been inside once or twice as a child, gotten lost and, after a kindly housekeeper showed the way back outside, she'd never tried again. Chance was rarely in the house. Their time together was always spent in or around the barn.

She let herself through the back gate that opened into the courtyard. From here she had a view of miles and miles of rolling hills blanketed by well-fertilized grass, so green it almost didn't look real. She passed the waterfall at one end of the large lagoon-style swimming pool, and Emma laughed when a few drops of cold water hit her in the face. She squealed and worked her feet in an attempt to get down. Holly held firm. Emma would be in that pool in a heartbeat and all the beautiful tropical plants she could reach along the way would meet their demise. Emma had a deep love for all things nature, especially the flowers. But she wanted to pick them all. Holly hadn't as yet convinced her they could be enjoyed just as much on the bush outside. She passed through the outdoor kitchen and under the large pergola to the back entrance.

She rang the bell, letting Chance know she was there. She thought she heard a voice, so she opened the door. "Hello?"

Chance appeared on the catwalk above with a towel wrapped around his waist. "Come on in. I had to take a quick shower. Be down in a minute."

"Okay." She stepped inside and looked around. Someone had gone to great lengths to downplay the family's wealth in the decor, but while she liked the Western theme, it failed to conceal the pure luxury around her. With a stone fireplace on the wall to the left large enough to roast an entire cow, this single room was larger than her entire house. The furnishings were leather, the kind that a person could just sink down into. Curious, she peeked around the corner just beyond the fireplace. The kitchen. She saw dark glistening wood and more counter space than she could have ever imagined topped with brown-and-buff-swirled marble. The hardwood floors gleamed while the copper canopy over the huge stove gave a rustic feel and brought out the veins of dark gold in the countertops. A pan holder above the long work space in the center of the room was filled with copper pots. The designers had utilized brick in the spaces between the cabinets, all blending perfectly and framing the glass-enclosed eating nook that offered the same view of the rolling hills outside. Which went on as far as the eye could see. And it all belonged to the Masters family. It was mind-blowing. And it drove home the enormous difference between the Masterses and everyone else.

As odd as it seemed, she'd never consciously made that realization before. As a child, things had just been the way they were. She had never placed any significance on anyone's wealth or standing within the community. People were people and you either liked them or you didn't. Against the majestic background of the ranch and this great house on the hill, suddenly her small home and equally small clinic that she had worked hard to attain became as insignificant as one blade of grass on the ninety-two-thousand-acre ranch.

She heard footsteps coming down the stairs. Chance walked into the kitchen wearing only jeans, his broad shoulders and sculptured chest and abs standing out in stark relief. "Are you thirsty?" He didn't stop until he stood in front of the fridge. "Want a beer? Coke? Lemonade?"

"Lemonade sounds great. Thanks."

Chance popped the tab and handed her the ice-cold can, then grabbed a beer for himself.

"Let's sit." He nodded toward the round oak and black wrought iron table in the breakfast area.

Holly selected a chair and settled Emma on her lap. Chance pulled out a chair, scooting it some distance from where they sat before sitting down.

"You looked good on your gelding." He took a sip of his beer. "How did you ever get started on the dressage thing?"

"I've always been curious about it. Last year I went with Amanda and one of her friends to a competition in Dallas. I was fascinated. Then I met Mark's wife when she brought their dogs into the clinic and we talked. Found out he has been a major contender for years. He helped me get Sinbad."

"And when you're in that English saddle, you control all that power." A sparkle of humor danced in Chance's eyes. "And I would imagine taking him over the jumps flings you up then slams you down when he lands."

"How did you ever know?" Obviously Chance had figured out what she was speaking of that night in the barn.

"And now you throw sin into the mix. A guy had better watch out for you."

"You'll never see me coming."

Chance barked out a laugh and shook his head.

Emma began to whimper, wanting to get down. Holly placed her on the Spanish-tiled floor and away she went—directly to Chance.

"So what's up?"

Chance's eyes were glued to the baby, who held on to a fold in his jeans with one hand and patted his knee with the other. She was doing a little hop dance, wanting to be picked up. Either Chance didn't understand or he was ignoring her. Emma was grinning, those two bottom teeth clearly in sight, so she wasn't distressed either way.

"Cole and Wade are throwing some kind of party in Dallas. Saturday night. I can't get out of it." He looked from the baby to Holly. "I need a date. Would you consider?"

Chance was asking her on a date? She didn't know whether to be elated or frightened. It was something, as a child, she'd thought about. But in a few weeks he would be gone. He was a soldier. His SEAL team was his family. And this was, after all, just one date.

This party would, presumably, have a lot of attendees. They would want to talk to Chance and find out what he could tell them of his success on the battlefield. Or if most were friends and associates of Wade and Cole, the talk would eventually turn to business. Either way, she would be a shadow in a corner somewhere, there only if Chance needed her.

But it was one date. One evening. She could do it. She would do it. How could she not?

"Sure. I would love to. How dressy will it be?"

"Haven't a clue. And I don't much care. We will probably stay overnight, so bring a change of clothes. Any way you want to dress will be fine."

"Will I get a hot dog grilled by your chef?"

The light danced in his eyes. "I never figured that one out, either. But if that's what you want, consider it done."

By the end of the week, Holly was a nervous wreck. She'd be lying if she tried to convince herself otherwise.

Amanda had joyfully agreed to keep Emma, saying she was proud of Holly for finally agreeing to go out on a date, comparing it in importance to buying a new house. Granted, she hadn't accepted many invitations, because she hadn't wanted to leave Emma. Not that she felt she'd given up all that much when she'd politely refused other offers. This time was different. This time it was Chance.

"Okay, have you got everything?" Amanda stood in the hall just outside Holly's bedroom door.

"There really isn't that much to take." Shrugging her shoulders, she once again looked at her reflection in the mirror. The strapless black dress clung to every curve of her body, from her breasts to her hips. Just past her waist, varying tones of gray were layered to midthigh. Black heels capped it off.

"You look hot." Amanda grinned. "A bit different from your customary jeans and boots. Chance's eyes are probably going to bug out of his head when he sees you."

"Yeah, right." She swung Emma up in her arms and walked to the living room. "I appreciate the loan of the dress and the shoes, Mandy."

"Not a problem. Has Chance ever seen you in a dress?"

Holly took a second to think about the question. "No. I don't think he ever has."

She put Emma in the playpen, making sure she had plenty of toys and her juice.

Amanda hurried over to her purse and withdrew a small bottle of perfume. "We almost forgot this." Before Holly could say no, the fragrance floated in the air around her.

"I don't wear perfume."

"Tonight you do." Amanda smiled in smug triumph. There was a knock on the back door. Chance was here to pick her up. Grabbing the black clutch and a small overnight bag, she walked to the door.

"Hi." She welcomed him in.

"Wow." His eyes traveled over her from her head to her feet. "Actually, I'm here to pick up Holly… Is she here?"

"Very funny."

He took her bag. "You look amazing. Thanks for doing this."

"My pleasure. And you look amazing yourself." He was wearing his full dress whites, with a number of medals pinned on his chest. Not surprising.

"Since this debacle is the work of my brothers, primarily Wade, in an attempt to lure future business associates into his web, he wants to trot out a SEAL. So I'll give him the whole show. But this is it. Never again."

Holly had anticipated that a drive into Dallas would take a couple of hours. When Chance turned left toward the barn, in the opposite direction from the main road, she sat up and took notice. Where was he going? Over one hill and up another and they were parking in front of the hangar at the ranch airport. Chance was out of the car in a heartbeat and had her door opened, offering his hand before she could come to grips with what this meant. They most likely were not driving to Dallas. The thought of flying there had never crossed her mind.

He held her hand as they crossed to the other side of the asphalt runway where two white-and-blue helicopters sat on their round concrete helipad.

"Are you kidding me?"

"Nope."

She stopped but he didn't let go of her hand. "I'm not getting into that."

Chance tilted his head and pursed his lips. "Why not?"

"I'm not a bird. Do I look like I have feathers? If I die,

I don't want to be twenty thousand feet above the ground when it happens."

"You won't be that high, but if you're dead, what difference will it make?"

Holly glared at him. "You know what I mean."

"Come on. It'll be all right." She still wasn't moving. He looked down into her eyes, then brought his hands to cup her face. Before she could grasp his intentions, his lips briefly touched hers. "I would never put you in a dangerous situation. Do you believe that?"

"Yes. I guess I do." She looked up at him, frowning. "Although you are the one who said it would be safe to cross that new bull's pasture to get to the river quicker. That sucker almost ate our lunch."

Chance pulled a hand down over his mouth. She knew she had him there.

"But no one was hurt."

"Only because old man Reichter saw what was happening and released those two heifers into the pasture to distract him."

"Come on. This is not a bull."

"And you've driven one of these before?"

He nodded, taking her hand. "A couple of times. Yeah. What *is* that perfume?" he asked as he settled her into her seat. "It's amazing."

"I don't know. Amanda just grabbed the bottle and dabbed—"

"Find out the name." His eyes sparkled dangerously. "It makes me hungry. Come on. You can do this."

Chance made sure she was buckled in. Once inside, he handed her a headset with a mic before putting on his own.

"Ready?"

"No."

He grinned. That charming, seductive, devil-may-care, bad-boy smile complete with dimples made it no contest. He would win this battle. The engine began turning the rotor blades, faster and faster until she felt the helicopter lift and move forward.

"Wait! Stop!"

Chance looked at her and lowered the chopper back onto the ground. "What's the matter?"

"I wasn't ready. You didn't say we would take off so soon."

He spared her a look clearly saying, *Are you kidding me?* "Holly, get ready. We are going to the moon. Is there anything else?"

"Where are the parachutes?"

"There are no parachutes."

Her eyes got big. "Then, what do we use if we crash?"

"Ah… That would be the ground. Hold on."

With a shake of his head, they were off yet again. The chopper climbed high as Chance circled the ranch then headed south.

"Holly, loosen up. You have a death grip on the seat."

"I think I'm going to be sick."

"No, you aren't. Relax and enjoy the flight."

She nodded, scooted as far away from the outside door as her seat would allow, and in a show of bravery, managed to pry her fingers off the leather seat. Her hands found each other in her lap and she held on tight. The warmth of Chance's hand covered hers, and only then did she begin to relax.

She had to admit, it was an amazing sight. The closer they got to Dallas, the more roads there were and the busier it was. It was twilight, so the sun had set, but darkness hadn't fully taken over. The lights of the city began to come on and it was amazing.

She glanced at Chance. He was so capable, so incredible. He caught her look and winked. "We're ahead of schedule. Do you want to circle Dallas?"

Holly knew this was the chance of a lifetime. When would she ever again be in a helicopter? *Put your fear in your back pocket and trust Chance.* She looked at him and nodded. "I would love it."

He grinned. "That's my girl."

It was just a turn of phrase, but his words hit her hard just the same. Was she his girl? Would she ever be?

The giant skyscrapers of Dallas unfolded below them. As they circled, Holly spotted Pegasus, the flying red horse. Formerly a symbol of Mobil Oil, it now served as both a symbol of Dallas and a representation of its history.

After circling the downtown area, they headed northeast. The city gave way to beautiful estates. They finally touched down at a small suburban airport.

"We're here."

Chance killed the motor and helped her from the chopper, grabbing her overnight bag and handing her the small purse. Just ahead was a stretch limo, the driver patiently waiting next to the car. Placing his hand on the back of her waist, Chance guided her to the vehicle.

This was a day of firsts. While she'd seen limos in and around the big house at the ranch most of her life, she'd never been close to one let alone *in* one. Even when Jason died, a military-issue sedan had picked her up at the airport and taken her to Arlington Cemetery, where her brother had been buried with full honors.

"Since this is our first official date…" Chance said, looking straight ahead as the chauffeur started the limo and drove out onto the highway. Then he turned toward her. "I would like to kiss you."

"I would like that very much."

Chance leaned toward her, put his arm around her shoulders and lowered his head. She felt his hand press against her face, turning her to him. Then his mouth covered hers, his tongue seeking permission to enter, which she happily gave. Typical of Chance, his kiss, like the rest of him, was strong and decisive. He tasted of brandy, a hint of peppermint and his own unique masculine flavor. She again felt the heat in her lower regions. A single thought crossed her mind that if they didn't stop, they were definitely going to be late for his party.

Chance raised his head, separating their lips, but seemed to hesitate as though he'd been forced to stop. His thumb lightly moved over her bottom lip, swollen and moist from his kiss.

"We're here," he said, his voice coarse and deep.

"Oh."

The limo turned into a driveway, coming to a stop in front of tall black wrought iron gates. They opened immediately, and the limo proceeded up the hill and to the right, where a circle drive dipped under a high portico. It was the largest house she'd ever seen. She was certain of that. A mansion complete with turrets made of stone and brick with blooming vines clinging to the mortar, which made it appear more castle than house.

"Is this where Wade lives?" The sheer colossal size of it required confirmation.

Chance nodded as the driver opened his door. "And Cole also stays here when he is in town."

She leaned toward the window and glanced up at the top of the turreted roof then back to Chance. "Promise me the dragons are securely locked in the basement."

He looked at her with surprise. One eyebrow lifted higher than the other, then he pursed his lips as he fought not to laugh. "You know, I'm not entirely sure anyone remembered to do that. We might have a problem."

She drew back and saw the teasing glitter in his steel-blue eyes. She also saw the need.

"Damn, Holly." And his mouth returned to hers, hard, almost frantic as if he wanted to taste all he could before circumstances forced them apart. He was so masculine. He reeked of sex appeal. His lips were unexpectedly tender yet firm. His mouth widened over hers as his tongue deepened its penetration. She felt the sizzle of heat shoot down her spine, pooling in her belly as she melted into him.

A light tap on the glass brought reality creeping back. When Chance hesitantly pulled away, Holly saw Wade standing outside the car window, his brown eyes glittering in amusement. Apparently deciding now was appropriate, he opened the door, bent down and looked past Holly at his brother. "We have rooms upstairs. Shall I tell the guests you'll be a little late?"

"No," Holly answered before Chance. She could feel the deep blush cover her face and neck.

Then Chance's lips were near her ear, his hot breath causing shivers over her already heated skin. "He's messing with you. But if you change your mind, there are, in fact, rooms available."

"Stop. Both of you!" She laughed. Grabbing Wade's offered hand, she stepped out of the car.

"Wow." Wade held her hands and stepped back for a better overall look. "Holly, you are stunning."

"Thank you. I just hope I don't fall flat on my face in these crazy shoes."

Wade's deep laughter followed her and Chance into the entrance hall.

Holly looked back at him and mouthed the word *What?* which only served to renew his laughter.

The only words to describe the inside of the home were *palatial elegance*. This place made even the big house at the ranch small in comparison. Three-story ceilings, crystal chandeliers, glass walls, steps leading to still more luxury. A huge indoor terrarium dominated one vast corner. Holly had never seen anything like it. They continued through the marble-and-glass foyer and into a huge living room to the right and a dining room that could easily seat forty people on her left. A man in a white jacket offered to take her overnight bag. Chance whispered something in his ear, received an "Of course, sir," and the man hurried away with her bag.

By now some of the guests had begun to notice their arrival. At least they'd realized Chance was there. In his full navy dress whites that served as a backdrop for the medals that almost covered the left side of his broad chest, he was the target of every wannabe macho male and lusty female in the entire house. The music from discreetly hidden speakers blended with the sounds of laughter and excited voices.

"Let's get this over with," Chance whispered to Wade, who stood next to them.

"Ladies and gentlemen." Wade's baritone voice carried through the den of people. Everyone turned and a hush fell over the crowd. The eyes quickly deflected from Holly to Chance. The smiles grew bigger, the eyes brighter, and it seemed as though everyone in the room advanced toward them at the same time. Toward Chance, more specifically.

"Thank you all for coming. I'm delighted to introduce my brother, Lieutenant Commander Chance Masters, US Navy, Special Forces Division, and his close friend Dr. Holly Anderson. Please join me in making them welcome."

There was united applause. Holly knew it was for Chance. She took a few steps back and brought her hands together for Chance. A receiving line formed, everyone anxious to meet Chance and thank him for his service. She felt out of place big-time. This was his night to shine. And he deserved all the accolades these people were willing to bestow.

A waiter in a white coat walked through the crowd carrying a tray filled with champagne flutes. Holly grabbed two and handed one to Chance. There were several hundred people clustered around him. He hadn't mentioned there would be this many people. Maybe he hadn't known. The music filtered into the room, mixing with excited banter. Twice Holly tried to make her escape but found her arm seized and held securely in Chance's hand before she could take one step. *Did the man have eyes in the back of his head?* Eventually most of the people had come forward and introduced themselves, all adding questions about the SEALs, Iraq, BUDS training or the Masters Corporation. Chance said a lot of words that told them nothing. She was amazed at how he could do that.

"I'm starved," he said after the last group had finally dissipated. Taking her hand in his, Chance led her toward the buffet. While he filled his plate with various meat and cheese selections, Holly went for the fruit: bite-size slices of melons, strawberries, cherries and grapes. Then it was finding a place to sit down and eat. With well over three hundred people in attendance, no chairs were available in the living or dining areas.

"We can just stand up," Holly offered.

"I have an idea. Follow me."

Back out in the great hall, Chance walked toward the

back of the house. Before they got to the kitchen, he turned into a small alcove on their left. Probably intended as a smaller, more intimate dining room, there was no table or chairs, just one lone sofa and a small flat-screen TV on the opposite wall. The far end of the room was glass panels, giving a view of a large fountain in a garden outside.

Holly walked to the couch and was unable to hold back a sigh of relief when she sank down into the plush leather. By the time Chance joined her, she'd already kicked off the four-inch heels. They ate in unison, enjoying the quiet.

"So do you know all those people?"

"Nope."

"Who was that brunette who was so determined to get close to you? She actually tried to step on my foot in an attempt to make me back away."

"You're kidding." Chance looked from his plate to Holly. There was a frown of concern on his handsome face.

"No. Not kidding." She took a bite of a strawberry. "But no worries. Every time she tried it, I just poked her in the ribs. Oh, these strawberries are so good."

Chance laughed out loud. "You're priceless."

"I'm ornery."

"That, too."

She adjusted her body into a more comfortable position. Doing so caused her plate to tilt. Before she could catch it, a cherry slid off, rolled over Chance's leg and onto the leather of the couch, stopping at his crotch. She looked at him with dismay. He bit down hard, his eyes dancing. Which told her he was going to have fun with this one.

"You uh…lost your cherry, Ms. Anderson," he said, trying to keep a straight face.

"So it would seem," she replied, stiffening her spine, unable to keep from staring at the small red piece of fruit. "Would you be a gentleman and hand it to me?"

"Nope. You'll have to get it yourself."

Holly looked around, making sure no one else was within hearing distance. "Chance Masters," she said through gritted teeth. "Do not do this. This isn't the place or the time. Give me my cherry."

"You want the cherry? Reach down and get it."

The bad-boy light was dancing in his eyes. He was enjoying this way too much.

"Fine. I'll just leave it there and you'll have a stain on your pants."

"Dry cleaners can get it out," he said, sounding totally unconcerned.

Chance reached out to her plate and picked up one of the two remaining pieces of fruit. With his fingers he removed the stem and brought a green grape to her mouth. She opened to accept it, biting down, enjoying the sweet, juicy flavor. He watched as she chewed. Then he scooped up the last piece of fruit, a small strawberry. This time, he put it to his mouth, his teeth holding it in place.

His eyes glittered in challenge. He wanted her to take it. From his mouth. She could do it. Leaning toward him, Holly touched her lips to his as she bit down on the fruit. She felt his hand come around to the back of her head, holding her to him. With his tongue he made sure the fruit was well into her mouth. It turned into a deep, smoldering kiss until she neither knew nor cared where the strawberry went. Against her lips, Chance murmured, "Get the cherry, Holly. Do it. Do it now."

Eight
___

"Just remember, Commander. Paybacks are hell," she said against his mouth and felt him smile. As she reached out to retrieve the crimson fruit at his crotch, his lips again found hers. He pressed her hand against his swollen erection. The fruit was forgotten. His hard body pushed up against her hand, his own hand pressing hers down on his thickness.

Someone cleared their throat. It wasn't her. It wasn't Chance. All movement came to a screeching halt. Reality flooded into the little room. Chance drew back and she looked up to find Wade standing in the opening next to a chef, who for all intents and purposes appeared as though he wished he was anywhere else. So did Holly. The heat of a deep red blush crept up her face.

"We couldn't find you two." Wade was trying so hard not to grin it would, without doubt, do damage to his facial muscles. "Chef Andre has something for you."

Holly looked at the silver tray in the chef's hand. He lowered it and removed the silver dome cover. It held a hot dog in a bun with an assortment of relishes and condiments on the side.

"As requested, madam. Grilled over an open fire. For you."

He held the tray toward them. Thankfully Chance reached out and took it. Her hands were shaking so badly she would have probably dumped the whole plate in his lap. A new rush of heat ran up her neck and face as an image flashed in her mind of how Chance would ask her to clean that up. This had to stop.

"Thank you."

"You are quite welcome. I hope you enjoy," Chef said before turning away.

"Something is begging me to ask what you both were up to when I walked in here," Wade said. "But, nah. I don't think I really need to ask, do I? And if I did, you probably wouldn't tell me, would you?"

"Honestly, Wade. It's all just a big misunderstanding." Holly would not leave him thinking she'd come to his elaborate party just to make out with his brother. Even though she had been doing just that. There was a distinct difference between making out and *making out*. "What you saw was not really representative of what we were doing."

Chance snorted and she sent a glare in his direction.

"Oh?" Wade's dark eyes glimmered with barely contained amusement.

She shook her head. "I was simply helping Chance find my cherry."

No one moved.

It took about five seconds to realize what she'd said.

Her admission didn't faze Chance as he dangled the small red fruit from its stem.

"And I got it," he said, before popping it in his mouth, grinning like the Cheshire cat.

The hot dog was delicious, and in spite of having already eaten all that fruit, she downed every bite. Chance disappeared for a couple of minutes and was soon back with a lemonade and a cold beer.

"Wade is offering his guests beer? That seems a little odd."

"He keeps them in the fridge. I never really formed a liking for champagne."

Holly took a sip of her lemonade. Neither had she, but probably not for the same reasons. People on her side of the road generally didn't attune their taste buds to the full-flavored bouquet of the world's finest champagne.

"What now?" she asked, setting her empty plate aside.

"Put your shoes on and I'll show you."

Stifling a groan, she stood up and slipped her feet into the shoes. Chance took her hand and led her to a large room adjacent to the atrium. Above them there was a dome ceiling decorated with twinkle lights. At the back of the room a six-piece orchestra was tuning up. As the music filled the space, Chance took Holly into his arms.

"This is so nice," she said, smiling up at him. "I didn't know you danced."

"You're about to find out I don't. Watch your toes."

He danced beautifully. It felt so good to be held in his strong arms, pulled tight against his powerful body as they swayed to the strings of the slow, soul-touching melody.

As they danced it felt as though the temperature in the room got warmer. The songs being played now were slower, the melodies strumming the strings of her heart. Holly felt as though she'd stepped up to an entirely new level, feeling a closeness to Chance she'd never felt before. There were plenty of women at the edge of the dance floor who were ready to pounce and take her place at the first opportunity, but selfishly she held on tight. And it seemed Chance was equally unwilling to release Holly.

"When you're ready to call it a night and head upstairs, just let me know. We've been here over four hours. I'm more than ready to get the hell out of here."

Holly stepped back. "Let's go."

He took her hand and led her through the throngs of people still making the most of the party. Just outside the double doors that opened into the great hall, they found Cole.

Chance leaned forward and quietly spoke a few words to his brother, who nodded and gave Chance a couple of pats on the back. Cole looked at Holly and winked.

Then Chance guided her farther down the hall to a small elevator. A couple of seconds later they stepped out onto a higher floor. It was peacefully quiet and every bit as elegant as the first floor had been. These people knew how to live. Antique mirrors randomly adorned the walls along the hallway. In between were very old, beautifully framed pictures, presumably of Chance's ancestors. Men standing with a crowd of smiling people in front of the entrance to a mine, next to an oil rig or next to a gorgeous thoroughbred held by a groomsman with a jockey on its back and a blanket of roses over its neck.

"That's my uncle on the day he won the Triple Crown."

"He's magnificent."

"I assume you mean the horse?"

"There's a horse?"

Chance laughed and it was a nice sound to hear.

"I think you'll be comfortable in here." He pushed open the door to an amazing bedroom suite. It was decorated in varying shades of blue in a French motif with a fireplace on one wall. A large canopy bed dominated the room. "I'll be just next door."

"Okay. I'll see you in the morning."

"I'm an early riser."

"So am I."

Chance leaned down, his face close to hers. The dim lighting in the hall shadowed just enough of his features to make him devilishly handsome.

"I had a good time," she whispered.

"I can almost say the same. You made it bearable. Thank you, Holly."

Then his lips, gentle, sweeping, were joining hers. He ventured inside just enough to taste and let her do the same. Then he was pulling back.

"Good night."

"So did you have fun?" Amanda asked the next day as Holly sat holding Emma, bouncing her on her lap. She couldn't kiss the baby enough, hold her tight enough. The fragrance of baby powder, shampoo and Emma was a much-needed relaxant after her overnight stay in Dallas. She now knew how Cinderella had felt going to the ball. Thankfully Holly had returned home intact—with both shoes. And the great blue-and-white flying coach had made a perfect landing with the prince behind the controls.

"Holly?"

"Oh. Yes!" Holly came back to reality. "Sorry. Just a bit jet-lagged."

"Jet-lagged? You only went to Dallas. This just keeps

getting better. I'm going to want to hear all about it. Every delicious savory detail. Promise me."

"Sure." *Not.*

"Okay, then. I've gotta head out. I'll talk with you soon."

"Thanks so much, Amanda." Holly stood and hugged her friend's neck. "Really. You are so great to keep the baby for me."

"Anytime." Amanda touched the tip of Emma's nose. "See ya, kiddo."

"Keyo."

Holly saw Amanda to the door, then called Kevin. She and Emma checked the clinic and made sure all was in order for tomorrow. Monday. Always a busy day.

Something woke Holly out of a sound sleep. The dogs in the kennel were barking in that way dogs do when there is someone or something in their immediate vicinity. Two shepherds, a terrier and a mixed breed named Henry were definitely acknowledging something.

She slipped out of bed, tiptoed across the hall and into Emma's room. The baby was sleeping peacefully. About the time she returned to the hallway, the sound of breaking glass reached her ears and the dogs were now going crazy. It sounded as though it was coming from the clinic.

Pulling on a pair of jeans, she slipped into her shoes and stepped out into the cool night air. She hadn't gone but a few steps when the back door to the building swung open. The security lights, one on each end of the clinic, had been turned off. From the small amount of moonlight, she saw the darkly clad figure throwing something out. It crashed when it hit the ground. Her computer?

Holly turned and ran back inside the house, making sure the door was locked behind her. She didn't want to turn on any light to draw attention. Grabbing the cell phone from the kitchen counter where it was charging, she quickly called 911. The dispatcher answered immediately. Holly quickly gave her name, address and the reason for her call and was assured the police would be sent right away.

Ending the call, she slipped her cell into the pocket of her jeans and hurried to Emma's room. More sounds of glass shattering and continued barking tore open the night. It was over fifteen miles to town. Chance was across the road. Without giving it a second thought, Holly dialed his cell. He picked up on the second ring.

"Holly?" His voice sounded amazingly awake for two o'clock in the morning.

"Chance, I think someone is in the clinic. I've called the police but Emma and I are here alone and—"

The connection went dead.

Returning to the front room, Holly peeked through the blinds behind the sofa. From here she could see the back of the clinic. Suddenly light from a vehicle flashed across the window. She heard a door slam, and seconds later the driver ran in front of the lights toward the clinic's front door. It must have been Chance.

Immediately she regretted calling him. If someone was in there, the person might have a gun. She couldn't bear to think she might be the cause of Chance getting seriously injured. She couldn't leave Emma alone so all she could do was watch and wait. Someone in dark clothing ran out the side door they used for deliveries but it was too dark to make out more than a shadow. Seconds later the back door to the clinic opened and Chance lumbered out through it, making a straight line for her house. Holly quickly ran to her back door and opened it.

"Are you okay?"

"Yes. Was someone in there?"

"Definitely. But they got out before I could get in there. My truck lights probably warned them I was coming."

"Them?"

"Them. Him. I don't know, but there is a lot of damage for just one person to do."

"Damage?" Holly reached for the door. "How much damage?"

"No, Holly." Chance kept her from going outside. "We don't know how many there were. We don't know why. And we don't know if it's safe. I cleared all the rooms but whoever did this might be lurking in the wooded area between the clinic and your house."

"The dogs. I've got to at least make sure the dogs are okay."

"How many?"

"Four."

"I saw them and they all appeared okay. I'll go back and check them again when the police get here."

Before she could voice an objection she heard the sound of a siren. Officers from the Calico County sheriff's office were on the way. Once they arrived and checked inside and out, Holly was allowed to go into the clinic. It looked as if somebody had set out to destroy everything possible. Expensive microscopes had been thrown through walls. X-ray screens were on the floor in pieces. There was no sign of her computer, which probably meant she was correct to think it was lying in pieces outside.

It definitely wasn't someone trying to steal and resell. It was vandalism with a vengeance. She hurried down the hall to the kennel, switching on the lights. One by one she checked the animals for any cuts or indications they were hurt. They were all fine. Still excited, but fine.

"Holly." John Green, a deputy for the county, called her back to the main part of the clinic, where Chance stood. "Do you have any idea who might have done this?"

Holly shook her head. "No. Not at all. Most of our patients are healthy and happy. I've only lost two. A seventeen-year-old beagle belonging to J.D. Cordiff. But Mr. Cordiff is in his eighties. He understood his dog had health issues no vet could cure. And Sammy Bartlett lost his Bubbles to cancer a week ago. Sammy is seven. I know his parents. No way they would ever do anything like this. I can't think of anyone who would have done this or why. Excuse me, I've got to go and check on Emma."

As Holly hurried back to the house, she couldn't stop the tears from welling in her eyes. Who would do such a thing? And why? Thankfully insurance would cover most of the loss, but even then it would take weeks to get back up and running. She needed to call Kevin.

Emma was still sleeping soundly in her bed, snuggling her stuffed goat. Holly took the cell from her pocket and speed-dialed Kevin's number. She probably should wait until the morning, but this was serious. It would impact his family's earnings. After three rings, she heard Kevin's sleepy voice on the other end of the line.

After explaining what had happened and hanging up, Holly ventured back outside. She wasn't sure what to think or where to begin. Walking back to the clinic, she began picking up pieces of her equipment. Broken monitor frames, a smashed keyboard, the frame of a very expensive microscope Wade had given as a grand opening gift.

"Holly." Chance reached out to her, taking the shattered pieces of various instruments from her hand, tossing it all to the ground then drawing her into his arms. "Leave it until the morning. You don't need to be out here trying to clean up in the dark. The sheriff is going to keep one unit out here overnight. I've already called and arranged for a couple of ranch hands to keep them company just in case."

She nodded. "I called Kevin. He's going to contact the insurance company. Maybe they will send someone out fairly quickly. Oh, Chance, I have patients who need medical attention. How am I ever…"

"Shh." Chance's hand gently pressed her head against his chest, keeping her close. "We will get through this. One step at a time. I want you to go inside your house and get Emma. Pack a few things for both of you. You're coming to my house until the authorities can get a handle on what's doing."

"No, that isn't necessary. We'll be fine…"

"I intend to make sure. Go. Pack a bag and let's get you out of here."

"But, Chance—"

"Now, Muppet. Stop arguing and go. There is no way you're staying in that isolated house tonight." He stepped back and with his finger, raised her face to his. "You can save that stubborn set of the jaw and battle stance for when they catch the perp. This is one argument you will not win."

She turned and walked toward her house. Chance wouldn't leave her out here in a wooded area with no alarm system and no way to defend herself. Even though a couple of sheriff's deputies and a few of the cowboys were stationed in the area, he would not let her stay here tonight. She supposed there was some logic to it. She had to think of Emma. But what she really wanted to do was hide somewhere and wait for the vandal or vandals to come back. Her shock was rapidly changing into anger.

"Pick any bedroom you want. Wade and Cole are in Dallas so it's just us." He stepped over to the outside wall and flipped open a small, discreetly hidden panel. Punching a few numbers, he then shut the lid. "Security. Tonight I don't trust anything. Come on, you're exhausted. Lets get you and the baby upstairs."

"I'm not exhausted," Holly retorted. "I'm mad as hell."

To that, Chance could only smile. When Holly had initially called, it had frightened him. Something that didn't happen very often. He had heard the fear mixed with fury in her tone. He had a feeling were it not for the baby, Holly would have jumped right in the middle of the situation, confronting whoever it was destroying her clinic, and God only knew what would have happened then. She'd never been afraid of very much of anything; whether that was an admirable trait or a fool's mission he wouldn't say. But before tonight, he'd respected it. Now he was just glad the baby had instilled a degree of protective caution in her.

He followed Holly up the stairs. She stopped at the top as though lost and unsure of what to do next. Chance stepped forward and opened a door to one of the bedrooms next to his. She walked past him, still holding the baby, checking it out. During the day, the view from here framed the barn and various outbuildings. Step out on the balcony and it had a good view of the courtyard below and the pool with the waterfall.

Seeing Holly inside this house affected him in ways he didn't want to think about. In all the years they'd known each other, she'd never ventured farther into the home than the kitchen and den downstairs. Now, seeing her in a bedroom, a king-size bed three feet away from where she stood, did something to his equilibrium. For just an instant he let himself envision Holly lying in the center of that bed wrapped in his arms, the sheets tangled around their legs while he took her again and again.

Chance was doing it again. He was envisioning something that could never happen. He needed to stop.

"I asked a couple of men to bring the baby's bed over." He was prepared for her objections and raised his hands, palms out. "It's just for a couple of nights. I thought you both might sleep better. You won't have to spend the night worrying that she might fall off the bed, and I think she'll be more at ease in her own bed, with her toys. It might help to comfort her." Holly was not going back to her little house until a good security system had been installed. But he didn't want to add that argument to the problems she already faced. At least not tonight. If there was luck to be had, it would be a done deal before she knew anything about it.

By now Emma was awake, her eyes as big as saucers as she took in her new surroundings, her first finger getting quite a chewing. Holly let her down to wander around and she made a beeline for Chance. She was so tiny. So innocent. He was afraid to pick her up for fear he would hurt her, but apparently the child had different ideas. She looked up into his face, her blue eyes asking a silent question while she gripped the pant leg of his jeans in her tiny hand.

"Up," she said with absolute clarity.

Chance glanced at Holly. She just smiled. If he didn't know better he would swear she had set him up. Feeling uneasy, Chance reached down and picked up the baby. She immediately laid her head against his shoulder, her hand gripping his shirt, settling in as though she had always slept there. He gently patted her back with his free hand. He couldn't believe how right she felt in his arms. He wouldn't admit, even to himself, how much he liked holding her.

"I imagine the sheriff will try to lift some fingerprints from your clinic tomorrow. I know over half the town has been inside the building, but maybe he'll get lucky in the lab area. I assume not everyone goes back there."

"No, they don't." She shrugged.

A rap outside the door drew their attention. "Got the little one's bed, boss. Where you want it?" Two of the ranch hands looked inside the bedroom, finally turning to Chance for directions.

"Just put it… You know, I guess you'd better put it close to the bed so if she wakes up she can see her mother."

The two stout cowboys soon had the bed sitting next to the large bed where Holly would sleep. With a tip of their hat, they said good-night and left the room.

"You really didn't have to do this. It's a lot of trouble for one night."

"No big deal." Chance walked to the baby's bed and deposited Emma in it. She immediately sat up and looked around, her pointer finger securely in her mouth. "See you tomorrow."

"Thank you." Holly sat on the edge of her bed and stared at the baby. If he had a guess, he'd bet she wouldn't sleep tonight.

Chance nodded, closed the bedroom door behind him and headed for the stairs. He wanted to take another look at the clinic and see if he could pick up on anything he may have overlooked the first time when he was hurrying to try to catch the perp. The clinic might be a target for whatever drugs she kept on hand, but the damage done was far and above just someone looking for drugs. Somebody wanted to do damage. A lot of damage.

Nodding to the deputy standing guard at the front entrance of the clinic, Chance again looked at the damage covering the counters and floor.

"Have you checked the fridge?" he asked the deputy. "I was thinking this might be about narcotics."

"Yes, sir," the officer respectfully replied. "We haven't checked each item off a list but it appears that area of the lab was about the only part untouched. I had the same thought that it was somebody looking for drugs, but apparently not. This whole thing is really strange." He looked at Chance. "I've known Kevin most of my life. Both he and Holly were very organized. In the drawer containing sedatives and pain relievers not one vial was out of place, no bottles turned over. So more than likely this wasn't about pharmaceuticals or theft. That narrows the suspects considerably."

Yes, Chance thought as he bid the officer good-night. It certainly did.

When he returned to the ranch house, he reset the alarm and went upstairs to check on Holly. When a knock on the bedroom door didn't get an answer, he opened it. The room was dark. The ambient light let him see that the baby was again sound asleep. Holly had removed her jeans and boots, but she still sat on the side of the bed, clad in a T-shirt, her hands folded in her lap. He couldn't see her face, but he would bet she was crying. For someone who had worked so long and hard to accomplish her dream, to find it trashed must have been devastating.

"Holly?" He walked toward the bed.

"Who would do that, Chance?" Her voice was so soft he had to strain to hear. "They weren't hurting me. They were taking away medical care for dozens of innocent animals. Who would do that?"

"I don't know, but eventually the sheriff will figure it out."

She couldn't sit like this all night. She'd had a shock and needed to get some sleep. He walked to the far side of the bed and pulled down the covers.

"Come on. Climb in and try to go to sleep."

As though hypnotized, she stood and walked around to that side of the bed. He covered her with the comforter and turned to leave.

"Will you stay?"

Chance hesitated. "I'm not sure that would be a good idea."

Holly nodded and looked down at her hands. Shit. Under the circumstances, how could he say no?

"Scoot over next to Emma's bed."

When she complied, he removed his boots and lay down on top of the bedding. He understood her need for his presence. The break-in made her feel as though she herself had been attacked. She felt unsafe and vulnerable.

For maybe the first time in his adult life, he stretched out on a bed next to a beautiful woman and sex never entered his mind.

Nine

Mondays were always busy. This one was insanity. The pet owners she couldn't reach showed up with their dogs and cats and iguanas and pigs to be told the clinic was closed. The more severe cases were referred to the clinic in the next county.

By nine o'clock the police were doing their follow-up inspection, inside and out. Holly sat outside under a tree answering the phone while Kevin spoke with the officers and tried to wrap his mind around the destruction. Amanda, bless her, was at Chance's house with Emma after Chance assured her there was cable and a couple of flat-screens and she could help herself to anything in the kitchen.

A little after two that afternoon the claims adjuster arrived and began the process of assessing the damage so a dollar figure could be determined.

By the end of the day, Holly was exhausted. But Chance

had once again stepped into the role of protector and became her rock, just as he had when she was ten and a bully had tried to take her lunch. She noticed even Kevin asked for his opinion several times.

Dinner that evening was prepared by the Masterses' chef on the outdoor grill. It smelled heavenly, making her realize she hadn't eaten all day. But at least the worst was over. New equipment had been ordered and would start arriving tomorrow, again thanks to Chance. Holly had argued vehemently against taking money from him but finally agreed on behalf of the animals and Kevin, whose family depended on the business's income. She did, too, but she also had a small inheritance from Aunt Ida and only Emma to care for, versus three kids and a mortgage. She and Kevin would just sign the insurance check over to Chance when it came. The clinic, while strangely bare, was clean and ready for the new equipment to be installed.

Emma was fretful for the first time Holly could remember.

"What's wrong with her?" Chance asked. "Is she sick?"

"I don't think so," Holly said. "I think it's because she's in strange surroundings. Maybe she's picking up on my emotions."

"You look dead on your feet."

"Yeah. That's pretty close." She tried bouncing Emma on her knees, but to no avail. "I want to thank you for all you've done, Chance. I don't know how any of us would have gotten through it were it not for you." Especially last night, but she wasn't going to bring that up. She wished the circumstances could have been different.

"You would have been fine."

She shook her head but was too tired to argue. "I'm

going to take Emma upstairs and see if I can get her to sleep."

"All right. Get some sleep yourself. See you in the morning."

Because of Emma's fussiness, Holly let her play longer than usual in the big bathtub of the en suite where Holly was staying. Story time followed, and finally with a warm bottle of comfort milk, Emma fell asleep.

Holly ditched her dirty clothes and headed back into the bathroom. That jet tub had her name written all over it. Lying back, she let the jets massage away the weariness. An hour later, dressed in clean clothes and feeling a lot better, she jumped in the big bed, hoping tonight she could sleep. But sleep didn't come easy. Chance wasn't here tonight and there was no reason to ask him to be.

Still, the silk sheets felt amazing, especially compared with her sturdy cotton bedding at home. The thick silk comforter made a soft rustling sound when she moved; the fragrance in the room was a beautiful blend of cedar and honeysuckle. All of it served as a heady reminder that she was in the ranch mansion with Chance sleeping steps away.

She must have slept a while but before long, she was again wide-awake. The large house was quiet. Feeling thirsty, Holly slipped out of bed, checked on Emma, who was sleeping peacefully, and headed to the stairs. She should have thought to bring a glass into the bedroom before retiring, but then she rarely became thirsty during the night. It was nerves. Had to be.

The large timber joists crossing the top of the den and on the staircase were amazing from this elevated angle. At the bottom of the stairs she padded into the kitchen, found a glass and filled it with cool tap water.

Sipping the water, she meandered toward the huge den

and the French doors that opened out onto the flagstone patio with the giant columns bordering the outside dining area, the lagoon-style pool and the large waterfall in the background. A splash drew her attention. Minutes later Chance's head broke the surface of the water. He began to swim the length of the pool, back and forth, his powerful arms and his muscled legs propelling him at a fast pace. Curiosity got the better of her and she walked up next to the glass panes of the French doors.

He was magnificent, so powerful. Put all the sexier-than-hell ingredients into a bowl and stir. The final product was right in front of her. And his apparent unawareness of how he affected the female species just made it worse. Or better, as it were.

She set her glass on a nearby table, careful to make sure it wouldn't leave a ring. When she looked again, Chance was coming out of the water.

Without one stitch of clothes on that hard, muscular body.

He grabbed a towel and began to dry himself off. Holly realized he was headed for the door, directly in front of where she stood. He was coming inside and she was standing there gawking. He hadn't seen her yet. She turned, intending to make a break for it. But where? She'd waited too late to run up the stairs. There was no place to hide in the kitchen. She spun around and folded herself into the linen draperies framing the French doors.

Holly listened as Chance pulled open the door and closed it behind him. The lights came on in the kitchen. She heard movement. Then the lights went out and all was quiet. Peeking through a slit between two drapery panels, she saw him walking toward the stairs, one thick white towel fisted in his hand. His body was incredible.

The muscles in his back moved beneath the tanned skin; his legs were equally well defined.

When he made it three steps up the stairs, he stopped. Holly held her breath. She didn't want to be caught lurking, ogling a naked man, even if it was Chance. Especially if it was Chance. She snapped her head back, closing the tiny gap in the blinds, and made like a statue, barely allowing herself to breathe. After what seemed like hours, she again cautiously moved the panel aside. No sign of him on the stairs. No indication he was in the kitchen. She strained to listen and heard nothing. Feeling assured he must have gone on to another part of the large house, she stepped out from behind the drapery.

"Well, well," he said, standing right next to her, one bulging arm braced on the wall. His gaze held her motionless. His lips pursed as he hid a smile. "It would appear we have a Peeping Tom."

She could feel the deep blush run up her face and back down her neck. "No…no, you don't. Me? You mean *me*? I was just going to the kitchen to get some water." She knew her eyes were as big as saucers. "See?" She pointed to the small occasional table and the glass of water sitting on top.

A few droplets from his hair dripped onto his broad shoulders. She watched them trickle down over his chest.

"The kitchen is over there."

"I know where the kitchen is," she snapped back at him. "You scared me, that's all."

"I scared you? How exactly did I do that?"

"You were in the pool."

"Oh. People swimming frightens you."

"Nobody goes swimming at two o'clock in the morning. Especially without any… Especially outside."

"Especially buck naked?" Yet again, those sexy dimples cracked the surface and that devilish bad-boy look danced in his eyes.

"I didn't say that."

He frowned and sidestepped until he was in front of her, placing his other hand against the wall on the other side of her and leaning in. He tilted his head, as if trying to figure something out. "You're twenty-four. And you're a doctor."

"Almost."

"And you know more about sex than I do. Isn't that what you said? That first night in the barn?"

"I really don't remember."

"Uh-huh. So seeing a naked man cooling off in his own pool is no big deal. Right?"

She shrugged her shoulders, acting nonchalant. "Right." Her chin jutted out as though daring him to contradict it. "So why are you making this such a big deal?"

"Me?" He adjusted his stance. "Sweetheart, I'm not the one hiding in the draperies."

With an unhurried motion, he shook out the towel and draped it around his hips, tucking in the corner. "Better?"

"It doesn't make any difference to me."

"I wouldn't have thought a grown woman—a *doctor*, no less—would be embarrassed by a little nudity."

"It wasn't a *little* nudity."

He raised his eyebrows and tilted his head once again, suggesting she might want to explain that remark. The devilish light danced in his eyes.

"That's not what I…I mean…" The blush returned, this time twice as strong, covering her face and neck. She even felt her ears burn. "You're twisting what I say."

"How am I doing that?"

Chance ventured closer to her and she couldn't breathe. The awareness overwhelmed her once again, making little prickles dance over her skin, her senses excruciatingly acute.

Placing her hands against his broad chest, she attempted to push him back. Granite boulders the size of her house would be easier to move. His bare skin was cool at first touch but heated to a sweltering glow beneath her hands. "You're in my space," she snapped. "Please move back."

"Why? I like being in your space." A wicked smile turned up the corners of his mouth. "I'll share mine if you'll share yours. Tit for tat. How about that?"

"This is ridiculous. I'm not having this conversation. It's pointless and stupid."

She heard his masculine chuckle as she spun on her toes, ducked under his arm and headed for the stairs.

"Maybe ridiculous is not what you're feeling. Maybe *frustration* is a better description?"

"What's that supposed to mean?" Then she caught herself. She was walking into his web. She raised her hand in a signal of stop. "You know what? I don't want to know. Forget I asked. I'm not having this conversation."

She paused at the bottom of the stairs, feeling a little bit safe now that she was a few feet away from him. "But if it was frustration—and I'm not saying that is true *at all*—you caused it. You probably did it on purpose."

"So hiding in the drapes gawking at a naked man is my fault?" He barked out a laugh.

"You're the SEAL, not me."

Chance frowned and raised his hands to his hips. "You're going to have to explain that one."

"If you weren't a SEAL you would never have known I was in the drapes and none of this would be happening."

With a flip of her hair she again turned toward the stairs. She almost made it to the fourth step before she was scooped into his arms. And as soon as he turned around and crossed the threshold of the French doors, she knew where he was going.

"Don't you dare. Don't you dare even think about it."

He stopped at the edge of the pool. It appeared he was still struggling to contain a smug grin. "Don't you know a SEAL can't resist a dare?"

His face was so close, his handsome features so charismatic. Chance was the epitome of an adult alpha male in every sense of the phrase, by anyone's definition. To be held in his arms, so close she could smell the essence of his body, was a heady sensation.

"Chance. Put me down," she said, choosing her words carefully. "Please."

"Just put you down? That's all you want?"

"Yes."

The grooves on either side of his mouth deepened and the dimples made another appearance. "Bribe me."

The breath caught in her throat.

"What do you want?" she asked, afraid he would say what she wanted to hear.

"You."

A shiver that felt very much like anticipation crawled over her skin. His voice was deep and coarse, sounding as though he was as affected by their closeness as she was.

Her gaze drifted down to his lips. She couldn't stop it.

"But for now, I'll settle for a kiss. It would be a shame to get you wet before you're ready for bed. But—" he frowned in contemplation "—maybe I could help with that, too."

"Put me down."

"Do it, Holly."

"I've already kissed you."

"No. I've kissed *you*. There's a difference. My arms are getting so tired. Hope my strength doesn't give out."

His strength wouldn't give out if he stood here like this for a week. But with her arms already around his thick neck, she leaned toward him and pressed her lips to his.

"There. Happy? Now please put me down."

The light in his eyes danced wickedly.

"I've had handshakes that were more enticing than that kiss. That wasn't a kiss. It was… You know, I'm not sure what it was." Then in a softer, absolutely mesmerizing whisper, "Let's try it again."

Holly's lips found his like a magnet pulled to a giant piece of steel. It was a hot, intense sensation and she wanted more, especially when the master took over and provided another lesson on how it was done. A small moan escaped and Chance responded, taking her mouth, taking what he wanted.

She knew an instant of breathless elation before he lifted his mouth.

"I think it needs some work."

She was stupefied. "What do you mean it—"

Before she could finish her sentence, she was flying through the air, her mind trying desperately to catch up before she hit the chilling water with a splash. She went down like a floundering goose with a bowling ball tied to its feet. Kicking off from the bottom, she broke the surface sputtering and spewing, still not able to believe what he'd just done. If looks could kill, he would be a dead man.

A large hand reached down to her. With a glare she brushed it aside.

"I would offer you my towel but…"

"Shut. Up."

"Tomorrow night? About the same time?"

Holly made no further remark. She didn't open her mouth. She marched past him, not stopping until she was up the stairs and headed to her room.

"Do you still want something to drink?" Chance called from below.

She stomped down the hall, slinging water as she went. She slammed the door, belatedly remembering the baby. She hoped it didn't wake Emma.

She could still hear his laughter echoing through the house.

Ornery man.

Ten

Chance threw a saddle on the bay he'd ridden a couple of weeks before. He'd tried to call his CO to see if there had been any news on his pending medical decision. He'd had to leave a message and he didn't like doing that. There was no telling when he would get the call. It could be days. He hated the idea of missing it. But he disliked sitting by a phone and waiting for it to ring even more. *Dammit.* He felt fine. He was ready to get back to the SEALs. He was ready to pick up his AK-47 and complete a mission. He needed the focus. He wanted a way to expel some of this pent-up energy that had him bouncing off the walls. He needed his team. They understood. Hell, they might be the only ones who could.

Wade and Cole were making him absolutely crazy. They wanted him working in the company and, Wade at least, wouldn't drop it. The man had looked him right in the face and declared his intent to sell the ranch, knowing what it meant to Chance. And knowing there was probably little to nothing Chance could do to stop it without returning as a partner in the Masters Corporation.

He would like to get his hands on the books. Every question he'd asked about the ranch met a dead end. Wade talked in circles, something he was very good at doing. Were they hiding something? He was used to getting inside intel immediately, and this cat-and-mouse thing Wade had going was making him nuts. Obviously it was a ploy to try to make Chance conform. *Good luck with that.*

Regardless of how long he'd been away, he wasn't some stranger facing Wade over a bargaining table. This wasn't about a corporate takeover or the buying and selling of stocks or companies. It was about his life. And Wade was in line for an eye-opener if he thought he could coerce Chance into leaving the SEALs.

Securing the cinch, he exchanged the halter for a bridle, led the gelding out of the barn and climbed in the saddle. When Chance was younger, this was the way he'd dealt with all the crap he faced on a daily basis. People had their own idea of what the son of a billionaire should act like, talk like, be like. The toughest lesson had been the realization that because somebody said you were a friend, it didn't necessarily mean shit. People always wanted something. Whether it was a claim of friendship, a favor or money, Chance Masters had quickly become the go-to guy.

Living up to the expectations of others was the worst. No one had been willing to accept him for who he was inside. Over the years it soured him until finally, he'd had enough and began to strike back. He would talk and act exactly as people around him expected. If someone wanted a car, hell, he'd help the person steal it. Who cared if they got caught? Certainly not his old man. If somebody dared him, he'd no longer brushed it off and walked away. Fights? Bring it on. Girls? There were two kinds. He'd learned the difference. The innocents, the girls like Holly's sister, he'd given a wide berth. With the others he'd gained a reputation. Love 'em and leave 'em. He didn't care. They used him, so he'd returned the favor. He'd been on a downhill spiral and only two things had saved his ass. The friendship of Jason Anderson and the lynching committee that had finally approached his father and demanded he do something about his son's illicit behavior. He guessed the good citizens of Calico County had finally determined they cherished something more than money, so his father's little payoffs—some called them bribes—had no longer worked.

Passing through the gate leading into the north range, Chance urged the bay into a slow canter. He knew this ranch like the back of his hand. And he knew how to disappear. Let his CO leave a message. Let his brothers find something better to do.

Holly was the one thing he hadn't envisioned when he'd decided to return to the ranch for his mandatory medical leave. He'd known what his brothers would try to do. He'd come up with a plan of what he'd do if any of the old gang wanted a rematch. But he'd never seen Holly coming.

Keeping his hands to himself was a lesson in futility. No matter what he planned or what safeguards he put in place, when she came near he had to touch her. He had to hold her. He had to kiss her. And he wanted to do a hell of a lot more than that. Knowing she would let him because she thought she was in love with him only made it worse. He would soon be leaving, one way or the other, and had no plans to come back. If the MEB granted him active status, he would be on the first flight back to his team. If they didn't, he had a couple of options, but returning to Texas wasn't one of them. He'd had enough. Wade's intentions to sell the ranch had pretty well, pretty effectively driven the stake into his back. And turned it.

Holly was raising a baby. Jason's baby. That small family had already lost enough. Chance damn sure wouldn't put himself in the situation of being responsible for any tiny life. Babies were too fragile. He'd already proved he could not protect a child. The thought had crossed his mind that maybe he could ask Holly to come with him. In how many languages could he say *stupid idea*? She had Jason's daughter and had achieved a lifelong dream of opening a vet clinic. She was less than one year away from obtaining her doctor of veterinary medicine license. She was safe and happy, and no way would he screw that up.

Reaching the top of a small rise, Chance paused to get his bearings and just appreciate the view. The green of the land against the dark blue sky. How often had he wished he could be exactly here when instead he was stretched out on a roof in Pakistan with his sniper rifle, waiting for someone to come out of a house carrying a bomb? And praying it wouldn't be a child.

Chance encouraged his horse to continue forward. A lone cow bellowed in the distance, somewhere a hawk found its meal and an American bald eagle circled overhead. In spite of the vague rumble of thunder in the distance, it couldn't be a more perfect day.

The sound of rushing water and the smell of the river found his senses. Reining the bay to the right, he followed the riverbank. The one place he hadn't visited in too long was his mom's cottage. Heaven help Wade or Cole if anything had happened to it. It was a small house in the trees, sitting back from the river enough to ensure it never flooded. It was where she'd finally found some peace and maybe a small bit of happiness. It was where, when she'd given up on her husband ever coming home and simply loving her, she had spent the last six or seven years of her life. It was where Chance had found her, her thin body still in the rocking chair, a picture of his father clutched against her breast.

Chance had to wonder if Wade—or Cole—had ever seen their mother break down and openly weep because the man she loved never seemed to have time for her. Never gave her the same consideration he gave to a business associate. Chance damn sure had seen it. He'd sat with her while she'd wiped her tears on more than one occasion. Wade and Cole had been away at school. One time he'd sneaked a phone out of the house and called Wade, telling him their mother was not doing well. He didn't know what else to say. When Wade finally did return home, his mother had hid her grief well and his eldest brother had looked at him as if he was crazy.

Did Wade never wonder why the little house had been built out here? Had he asked their mother why she'd moved out of the mansion to spend her remaining days on the earth in that cabin? A blanket of panic and misery had fallen over Chance when he'd realized his mother had finally given up. She'd given up on their father. She'd given up on life. She'd never confided in him, but he'd known. Somehow, he'd known. He actually couldn't remember if their father had come to her funeral. Surely he had. But Chance didn't recall seeing him there. Or in the house before or after the services. But then, Chance hadn't looked very hard.

Holly sat by the pool, keeping an eye on Emma as she alternately played and begged to get out of her playpen.

She wanted to shred the plants and Holly was having no part of it. She was glad to see Amanda's car come up the long drive.

"Well, don't you two ladies look like the privileged elite," Amanda said as she climbed out of her vehicle. She entered the gate and joined Holly, pulling up a padded lawn chair. "So what happened with the clinic?"

"We don't know anything yet. The replacement equipment has been ordered and should be delivered today or tomorrow. Kevin is overseeing that. I know how to read a slide under a microscope, but how to connect a microscope to the computer is beyond me."

"Well, look at it this way. You weren't going to get any time off for a couple of years. You should make the best of it."

Holly nodded. "You're right."

"And this—" Amanda held out her arms to indicate where they sat "—is not a bad way to start."

Amanda was right. There was only one main ingredient missing.

"Hi, Emma." Amanda stood and walked to the playpen, picking up the baby when she raised her arms.

"Don't let her near the plants. She likes to pick them, which means she will shred every one of them."

"You wouldn't do that, would you, sweetie?"

"Do at."

"Where's the hunk this morning?" Amanda settled back with the baby perched on her lap. "I've been dying to ask how it's been going."

Before Holly could formulate an answer, one of the Masterses' housekeeping staff called to her. "Ms. Anderson?" A tall, elderly man accompanied by a postal employee walked toward where they sat.

"Hey, Holly," Joe Green said. "Chance has a certified

letter from the US Department of Defense. Can you sign for it? Do you know when he'll be back?"

"I don't even know where he went." Chance had already been gone when she'd woken up around eight o'clock. She hadn't knocked on his door, but she felt relatively certain he would have made an appearance by now if he was still around the house. She'd assumed he was down at the barn.

"Commander Masters rode his horse out to see his mother's house," the butler said. "I will find someone to take the letter to him. It might be important."

Holly sent a quick glance to Amanda and received a nod. She held her hand out for the electronic confirmation of receipt. "I'll take it to him. I know about where his mother's house is."

"Sections of the road have flooded in the past. As I understand, even a Jeep can't travel the old road that Mrs. Masters used to use."

She nodded and looked at the white envelope in her hands. This was it. This had to be what Chance had been waiting for. A decision had been made as to whether he could return to active duty. She just knew it. Holly was suddenly bombarded with emotions that hit her from every direction. She'd known this was coming. She thought she'd steeled herself from feeling anything other than happy for Chance, but that tiny hole in her heart began to emerge.

She rose from the chair, the letter clutched tightly in her hand. Emma was still contentedly sitting on Amanda's lap. She gave Emma a big hug and kiss.

"Thanks, Mandy."

"This is it? He's leaving?"

Holly glanced at the letter in her hand. "I have no way of knowing for sure, but that would be my guess."

She ran into the house and changed into jeans and a clean shirt. Her heart was beating as though she'd run a marathon. She grabbed the letter and forced herself to smile as she passed through the flagstone courtyard and waved goodbye to Amanda and Emma. In the barn she went straight for Sin. She wanted a mount she could absolutely trust. Positioning the blanket on his strong back, she threw a Western saddle on top, quickly adjusting it before tightening the cinch. Rather than his eggbutt snaffle bit, she chose a Western headstall from the tack room. The sky was becoming dark and thunder rolled across the sky in the distance. She had no way of knowing what she would face. It was a long ride.

Swinging into the saddle, she headed to the gate that opened to the northern acres. Leaning forward, Sin took the cue and immediately set off in a canter, his dark gray mane and tail flying out behind him.

Chance sat on the front porch of the small cabin as the memories continued to wash over him. It had been so many years ago that he'd stood next to his mother watching as the house was built. He'd sensed something was wrong, but being just a kid he probably wouldn't have understood it if she'd taken the time to explain it to him. His mother hadn't lived for riches and social status. She'd lived for the love of her husband. And after waiting for years for him to return that love, she'd finally given up. Who was she to compete with the elation in his face when he had again succeeded in buying out yet another company, increasing both his reputation as a highly successful businessman and his wealth? In Chance's father's eyes, nothing could compare with that.

She'd brought to her new house only the things she'd brought into the marriage and not a lot else, other than pictures of her children and a few souvenirs of happier times. She'd loved art. Drawing and painting had been her passion and she was good. Sadly no one had ever seen her talent. Except Chance. He'd asked her once why she didn't sell her paintings or display them in a gallery. He remembered her sad smile when she'd shrugged and said they were worth something only to those who appreciated art. "I paint them because I enjoy it, not to sell for money," she'd said. It was years later he'd realized what she meant. They were not Rembrandts or painted by Michelangelo or da Vinci. So in his father's eyes they had been worthless. The hours she'd spent painting was time forever lost.

The thunder rumbled overhead and Chance noticed the darkening sky. He'd better get back to the ranch. Maybe his commanding officer had returned his phone call. Hell, maybe he'd even called to give Chance some good news. And maybe pigs would start flying tomorrow.

He rose from the small chair and headed around to the back of the house where a small barn and corral had been built. The big bay nickered at him, a clear indication it was ready to go home.

Quickly saddling the horse, he mounted and headed south. He hadn't gone far when the first drops of rain made a light tapping sound on the brim of his hat. Before he'd gone a mile the rain increased to a steady downpour. He took the gelding into a canter. Rain had never bothered him but the ground was beginning to move—a sure sign of flooding. Just ahead was the river. The water was running fast and rising. He considered the best place to cross and in that moment he saw something at the river's edge some distance ahead. A gray horse was standing with its front feet in the river, pawing at something in front of him on the ground. As Chance got closer he saw it was a person.

He urged the bay into a flat-out run. The closer he got the more he felt fear. It was a feeling he'd not previously experienced, but there was no shaking it. And the closer he got the worse it grew. It was Holly. He was certain of it. She lay on her stomach, her head toward the rising water. What had happened? Was she alive?

He jumped from the saddle before the horse had a chance to come to a complete stop.

"Holly? Baby, can you hear me?" He knelt next to her on the soaked earth. When she didn't answer, something close to panic gripped his throat. "Holly."

He heard a small moan. Then remarkably, she moved her arm under her and attempted to push up.

"Take it easy, sweetheart," he said. "Try not to move. Can you tell me where you're hurt?"

His SEAL medical training kicked in, and thank goodness for that. Once he was sure she was relatively unharmed, he helped her sit up. She was groggy after apparently having the breath knocked out of her. Sin nickered and tried to push Chance out of the way. The rain was still coming down.

"Holly, we've got to get you to a dry place. I'm going to pick you up. Tell me if it hurts anywhere." He saw her nod her head. As Chance drew her into his arms, she made no sound. But he wouldn't know with any certainty if she was okay until he got her to his mother's house, where he could check her more attentively. With Holly in his arms, he walked toward the gelding.

"Wait. The letter. Must find the letter." She spoke in a whisper. It was hard to understand what she was saying. He felt her take a deep breath. "The letter. Chance, I won't leave until I find the letter."

What letter?

"Holly, this storm is building and about to kick our butts."

She tried to push out of his arms. "Let me down. Chance, put me down. I've got to find the letter."

He didn't understand what could possibly so be so important that she would risk her life. But he set her on the ground.

"Just stay there, I'll go look." He walked back to the spot where he'd found her, and sure enough there was a white envelope half covered in mud. He picked it up, slung off most of the mud, folded it so that he could shove it into his back pants pocket, then he ran back to Holly.

"I found it. I've got the letter. Now let's get you out of here."

She nodded. "I can ride. I just got the breath knocked out of me when Sin fell coming up the side of the embankment. Is he all right?"

"He seems fine."

When Chance didn't move, she added, "I'm all right. Go. Get your horse." She was now yelling to be heard over the wind and thunder. Chance lifted Holly onto the saddle. As he approached the bay, the lightning crackled overhead and the horse flinched and began to back up. Chance swung out his arms and managed to catch the reins. With a few calming words, he leaped into the saddle and maneuvered the horse toward Holly and Sin.

"You're okay?"

She nodded.

"I don't think we have time to make it back to the ranch," Chance said. "I think we should head for Mom's cabin. It's not far from here."

Holly nodded her agreement. "Lead the way."

As soon as Chance cleared the tall, rocky uphill grade

and reached level ground, he pulled his mount to a stop and waited for Holly and Sin to make it up the rocky hill from the river below.

"Ready?" she asked when she caught up to him.

"It's this way. Let's go." Gathering the reins, he headed back to his mother's small cabin.

The thunder continued to roll across the sky. It was so dark, it looked like midnight. The wind picked up. They were in for a whale of a storm. Only a couple of hours earlier, it had been a bright sunny day with not a cloud in the sky. Typical Texas weather. If you don't like it, stick around a couple of minutes. It will usually change.

Holly urged Sin into a gallop. The thunder became louder, streaks of lightning hitting the ground all around them. The faster they went, the harder the rain stung Holly's face. They had to traverse about a mile of open range before once again entering a tree line. His mother's small house sat some distance deeper into the forested area. Entering the thickening trees, Holly slowed, allowing Sin to pick his way over fallen branches and around thornbushes.

"There." Chance pointed ahead.

Holly could just catch glimpses of the blue roof almost hidden behind the trees. Chance guided them into the clearing around the house and into a small barn slightly to the left and behind the cabin. Jumping down, he pushed open the tall double doors and motioned for Holly to go inside. Compared with the main barn at the Masterses' ranch, this was tiny. At some time in the past one of the six stalls had been converted to a feed-and-tack room. It appeared fresh bedding had been spread in the stall floors, the individual water troughs filled with fresh water.

"Somebody knew we were coming." Holly laughed and slid down from Sin's back.

"I think the foreman keeps this area fairly clean for just what happened to us today. The storms come on fast. This is about the halfway mark between the house and the butte with the views, where most guests eventually wind up."

After riding up under the protective covering, Chance began to unsaddle his gelding and Holly followed suit with Sin. Everything needed a chance to dry out. Holly led him into the closest stall and removed his saddle, blanket and the headstall. With a good shake of his massive body, Sin dried himself off.

"I think there is some hay at the far end. You might check and make sure it's fresh."

Holly headed in that direction and sure enough, five bales of hay had been set in the corner. Breaking apart one of the bales, she checked for any sign of mold. All was good. She grabbed a couple blocks of the bale and tossed them into Sin's stall before going back for more for Chance's gelding.

While Chance took care of the tack, Holly stood in the structure's opening. The rain was still coming down in heavy torrents. A glance up at the charcoal sky made her wonder if they were going to be bedding down in the other stalls. As a kid, she'd slept in worse. The image came to mind of her huddled next to Chance in the hollow of a giant hickory tree, listening for signs that the black bear had come back. But she'd never felt true fear. Not when Chance was there with her. But being stuffed in that tree hollow had made it a very long night.

"Let's go," Chance said, coming up from behind her.

"Where?"

"In the house."

This was where his mother had lived the last years of her life. It was a special place. Holly hesitated, thinking it might be better if she just remained on the porch.

"If there is a blanket, I'll be fine out here."

His dark brows drew together in a frown. "Holly, it's fine. Come inside. You need to get out of those clothes. We're both soaked."

She looked at Chance long and hard before finally nodding her head in agreement. She'd been very young when his mother died but she remembered the deep grief that had plagued him for weeks—no, months. She'd once overheard Wade ask Chance where he'd been for three days. He'd said, "Mom's house." It was a two-word answer that had been tossed to his brother as he'd walked past him headed to the barn.

"You can't find her there, Chance. You need to accept she's gone and get over it." For the first time Holly had witnessed Chance lose it. He'd had his eldest brother on the ground, his fist slamming his face in less than a heartbeat. Some ranch hands had pulled him off. With one last glare at his brother, Chance had disappeared into the barn. Instinct had warned Holly that it wasn't the time to approach him. She remembered the haunted look that covered his features, the straight line of his mouth, the dead look in his eyes. He'd disappeared shortly after. He'd reported to the Naval Special Warfare Center in Coronado, California, and she'd never seen him again. Until two weeks ago.

He broke into her reflections. "Holly?"

"Yeah. I'm coming."

Holly knew that even after all these years the memories would be as fresh as if the events had occurred yesterday. Though he tried to hide it, she could feel his pain and regret at losing his mother at such a young age. And the anger at his father for contributing to her sadness and consequently, her early demise, stirred the anguish in Chance's heart.

Inhaling a deep breath and blowing it out, Holly walked to the front door and stepped inside.

Eleven

The house was small, especially when compared with the mansion on the hill, but she could see how Chance's mother could be comfortable here. Raised ceilings made it feel a lot bigger than it probably was. The kitchen with granite countertops and oak cabinets opened into the den. Frilly curtains hung over the windows. The four canisters on the counter intended for flour, sugar and such were shaped mushrooms, with small bright orange spotted mushrooms painted on the sides and lids. It was colorful, bright and cheerful.

Holly walked through the house at a leisurely pace. The bedrooms each had an accent wall painted in a cheery color of blue, yellow or green, the decor just as delightful as the kitchen's. *Whimsical*. That was the word. The entire house was whimsical. And she loved it.

"Okay if I take a shower?" The force of the storm was increasing. It would be a while before they were able to return to the ranch. She could feel the dried mud on her face.

"Of course. Help yourself."

The robe she found in a bedroom closet must have belonged to his mother. After taking a quick shower, she reentered the den. The robe fit perfectly. She set her dirty clothes on the kitchen floor, spreading them so they would dry a little bit. Chance had a small fire going in the fireplace. She couldn't help but notice he still wore his wet jeans but his shirt had been removed and lay on the floor of the kitchen.

"There's a washer and dryer in a utility room behind the kitchen. You can dry your things there."

"Okay. What about your jeans?"

"I'm fine."

"No, you're not." Holly held out her hand, palm up, her fingers waving in a gesture of "give them here." "Give."

"I don't think that's a good idea."

"You need dry clothes." She tilted her head, defying him to argue with logic. When Chance didn't respond, she said, "Now who's suddenly playing Mr. Modest? Sounds like a dare is needed. Let's see…"

"You are just about the most ornery woman I've ever met in my entire existence."

"Funny. That's exactly what I say about you. Give me your pants."

Shaking his head, he headed for the bathroom. A few minutes later he poked one hand outside the door and dumped his muddy clothes onto the floor.

"I'm covered in mud. Gonna take a shower."

Holly grabbed his jeans, picked up his shirt and her clothes and headed for the laundry room. Every article of clothing was caked with mud. If she didn't wash them, they would be ruined. Tossing everything into the washer, she added the detergent and hit the button. She returned to the den just as Chance was adding a couple of logs to the fire. He'd found an old pair of jeans from somewhere. The warmth spread out into the room, giving it a cozy, inviting feeling.

Holly idled around the room. In one corner a painting of the three Masters brothers sat on an easel.

"Did your mother paint this?"

"Yeah."

She had captured each of their characters beautifully. Wade, the eldest, with that stern, in-charge face even when he was about fifteen. Something about the brown eyes softened his features, making him appear a little less arrogant. The picture showed his strength and determination. Confidence. He was very much in charge. Next to Wade was Cole, the middle son. At fourteen, he had a straightforward grin and his honey-brown eyes sparkled. He'd always had the tendency to see the humor in the world. He never appeared to take anything all that seriously, a trait that duped a lot of people. He was as sharp and cunning as a fox, something business adversaries discovered after it was too late. Holly had heard Cole was one hell of a negotiator. She had no reason to doubt it.

Then there was Chance, the playboy of the three: the impossibly handsome bad boy, adorable even at the tender age of ten. All of the brothers had had their fair share of women ogling them since they'd reached adolescence, but from what her brother told her, Chance had latched on with both hands. Once again, Elaine had captured him perfectly. There was a distinct difference between Chance and his brothers. His vivid blue eyes glowed in contrast to their brown. His hair was a bit lighter in color. Even so long ago, Chance had been unique.

"There is coffee in the kitchen," he said. "On the

counter to the right of the sink. The cups are in the cabinet above it.

"Thanks."

When she came back with her steaming brew, Chance reached out to his own coffee cup he'd set on the edge of the stone hearth. He took a sip and put it back down, never taking his focus off the letter in his hand. Suddenly, with the small fire blazing behind him and his face drawn in concentration, she was looking at Lieutenant Commander Chance Masters, US Navy SEAL. Serious. Strong in both mind and body. Of above-average intelligence with a physique to back up any immediate, life-threatening decisions he made. It must have been how he'd looked planning his team's next mission down to the last detail. They counted on him and he was there for them.

He always would be.

He was being summoned to California for the final decision by the medical evaluation board. Chance didn't know if that was a good thing or not. He had assumed they would just send a letter notifying him he was either in or out. Apparently they wanted to do it in person.

"So is that your clearance? The news you've been waiting for?"

Holly stood next to him. Seeing her in his mom's robe did odd things to his gut. She was so beautiful with her long hair unbraided so it could dry, the golden waves falling over her shoulders. He couldn't imagine any other woman doing justice to that robe. From the sexiest of negligees to nothing at all, he'd seen everything. No other woman could compare with the vision of Holly he was seeing right now.

"The letter?" she prompted.

"Ah, kinda. I've been asked to appear at a final hearing in front of the medical evaluation board in three days. I guess I'll find out then."

"So after all of this waiting, you get to wait more. That is so unfair."

"Sounds like you're trying to get rid of me," he joked. Holly apparently didn't take it that way. He saw her blink her beautiful eyes in rapid succession before she turned away.

"Don't be silly," she said as she walked to the kitchen. "What do we have in here to eat?"

Holly rarely showed signs of an appetite. Grabbing a piece of cheese or a carrot and eating while on the go had always been her MO. She was upset. She was upset about the letter and what it meant.

"Holly," he said, getting to his feet. He could see how she was fighting to maintain the thin sliver of control as a battle raged within her.

"Got any peanut butter?" She opened a cabinet, closed it and moved to another one. She grabbed the small jar of Peter Pan and lowered it from the shelf, turning it round and round in her hands. He knew her mind was a thousand miles away. In Coronado.

"Holly," he said, leaning over her, his arms on either side, balancing his weight on the counter. "I'll come back. Even if I'm cleared for duty, I swear I will come back." Coming back to the ranch was not a promise he wanted to make, but it was a promise he would keep. For Holly. If Wade gave them time.

He saw her nod and brush her hand against her cheeks.

"Come on, Holly. Turn around and tell me you believe me."

"I believe you," she said but didn't turn to face him.

Damn. He couldn't do this anymore. He could not

deny them what they both wanted. The muscles in his body tightened as the idea took hold, and before he could talk himself out of it, he grabbed her shoulders, turned her around and cupped her face in his hands. "I will come back." He leaned toward her and their breaths fused into one as his lips covered hers, their tongues mating until she sighed and her exquisite feminine body melted into his.

Holly opened her mouth wider, giving him as much as she got, and his body surged to readiness as the kisses deepened and grew more impassioned with every breath. His hands encircled her waist and he set her up on the kitchen counter.

With the ease of experience, he parted her legs, opening them wide enough to accept his girth. Then he stepped up to fill the space. One hand cupped her face, caressing the velvet softness of her cheek. His other hand reached behind her and pulled her forward to the edge of the countertop, nestling his erection at the apex of her thighs. She made a sound somewhere between a sigh and a moan and moved against him. He felt the heat between them scorch like fire and her body went limp. She grabbed the belt loops on his jeans, holding him to her as she pressed harder against his throbbing shaft.

Hell. He wanted to say no. He wanted to stop this before it changed everything, before it could never be taken back. He wanted to ask her if she was sure. But he did none of those things. Instead, he scooped her up into his arms and walked into the bedroom, kicking the door closed behind them.

Settling her gently on the bed, he felt almost disconnected with what was happening. They had denied the passion growing between them for so long, to know what was about to happen felt surreal. The thought of it increased the fire in his loins, his erection throbbing.

"Be sure this is what you want." Was that his voice? So deep and demanding with more than a hint of frantic worry that she would say no. "Because in about three seconds there will be no turning back."

She looked up at him, her eyes soft and clouded, her lips swollen and moist from his kisses. A fierce possession gripped him.

"One. Two. Three," she said. "Take off your jeans."

Chance unsnapped the button on his waistband and lowered the zipper. Then, bending over her, he parted the robe. Drawing back, he let his eyes roam over her. Holly was so perfect; her skin was so fair, like a porcelain doll. Her breasts were full and heavy, the light pink tips fully erect. Chance lowered himself to suckle one pale rose tip while his hand kneaded the other, his thumb rubbing and teasing. She inhaled deeply, then moaned and arched her back. Her response told him she needed more, and he was ready to give her what she needed.

But she wasn't ready to take him yet. He kissed her silken skin as he worked his way down her body from her lips to her belly. The dark blond curls at the joining of her legs enticed him to explore what other secrets she was keeping. Pushing her knees apart, he cupped her hips, raising her to him. He had to taste her essence. He wanted to acquaint himself with all of her.

She drew in a deep, long breath when his tongue tasted her for the first time. As he completely enjoyed the silken skin and scent of her, her legs dropped open fully and his erection surged past hard to painful. He was about to lose it, but this had to be for Holly. Suddenly her hands gripped his hair and she stiffened, then cried out. Chance continued to draw out her climax as long as possible, loving the idea he had brought her pleasure. After several minutes she collapsed back on the bed.

Like a wild animal ready to mate, he ditched the jeans and crawled up her body until his swollen shaft was pressing against her. Returning to the succulent nectar of her mouth, he fed, his tongue probing deep before withdrawing, again and again. A slow, increasing beat of pleasure gripped them both.

"Are you ready for me, Holly?"

Her breathing was fast and shallow and she only managed to nod. Her hips pushed against him. "It's so hot... there."

"It's about to get a lot hotter." He smiled at her through the darkness. Removing a silver patch from inside his wallet, he tore it open and slipped the condom on. With his hand, he positioned his heavy erection at her core. She was so wet. And she was right about the heat. He couldn't remember ever being so turned on by a woman. He wanted to take her hard, give in to the lust that gripped him, sink into her womanhood, feel her grip him with her silky wet core and send them both to the moon. Some sixth sense axed that idea. She was small of stature and he didn't want to hurt her. Slowly, inch by excruciating inch, he entered her, his hands fisted to maintain control. Suddenly, she grew very tight inside and cried out, pushing at his shoulders. All movement stopped. He drew back and their eyes locked. He saw her look of discomfort and was shocked. This was not happening.

"Holly, tell me you've had sex before."

She shook her head. "I never wanted anyone but you. There was no one else I felt drawn to. No one I wanted to be with. Please don't be mad."

His nostrils flared; his jaw clamped down so hard it was sheer luck his teeth didn't shatter from the force.

For a second he considered pulling out before it was too late. Even through the shock, he was still highly aroused. She'd saved herself for him. She had never been with another man. Holly moved her hips, pushing up and against him and hurting herself in the effort. It would take more than that. It would require him to do his part. Another look into her beautiful face and Chance knew he would see this through.

He cupped her face in his hands, drawing the sweetness from her lips. "There will be a sharp, deep pain, sweetheart. But it won't last long. I'll do everything I can to make it pleasurable for you."

"Its okay, Chance. I want this. I want you."

Lowering his face to hers once again, he kissed her gently, gradually building back up to the passion of moments ago. When he felt she was ready, he pushed in all the way. Her single cry was swallowed by his mouth.

It was done.

There was a feeling of euphoria, and his passion could no longer be held in check. She was frantic and sexier than ever as he poured every bit of his experience and expertise into making this moment a good memory for her. Then she embraced him, sobbing, panting and crying out his name. Her climax ignited the spark that sent him over the top and beyond. It went on and on until finally, fighting for breath, he pulled her head to his shoulder, his arms holding her against him.

"Holly?" he said, kissing her neck and jaw where it was still moist from their passion. "I need to know that you're all right."

Through the ambient light of the passing storm, he saw her smile. "Wow." She raised her head and kissed him. "Thank you, Chance," she whispered against his lips.

Silence filled the room. The only sound was Holly's

soft, steady breathing and the guilt that screamed in his head. Who would have thought Holly would still be a virgin? Chance wasn't sure what to do. This was a first for him. But his protective instincts were on full alert. He would do what was needed to protect her, to keep her safe even from her own heart. She was his. Totally and completely. A fierce pride rumbled through him. But it didn't stop him from remembering there were issues preventing them from being together. Issues he had no clue how to solve.

She ran a veterinarian clinic and was raising a baby. He was a SEAL and never had any intentions of doing anything else. He didn't want a wife to go through three-quarters of the year alone, waiting for her husband to come back, hoping he would. When he came home, he couldn't tell her where he'd been or what he'd been doing. With any luck, he would have a few months before he'd be gone again. Sometimes not that long.

It was an impossible situation. Wade was selling the ranch. If Chance wasn't cleared to active duty, what would he do? He'd never been the type to sit around on his ass.

Lightning flashed and Holly snuggled closer. He'd never held a woman after sex. Once he and a date got what they'd come together for, one of them always left with an "I'll call you" thrown over a shoulder on the way out the door. He had to admit, holding Holly, the way she was curled up in his arms, felt good. He could get used to this.

This was all too crazy. Something had to give. He just didn't know what.

When Chance awoke the next morning, Holly was already up. There were mouthwatering smells coming from the kitchen. He headed for the bathroom. When he came out from taking his shower, his clean clothes were laid out on the mattress. The bedding had already been stripped and was no doubt in the wash.

Shuffling into the kitchen, he saw Holly was frying bacon and eggs. Her back was to him. He went to her and put his arms around her. She turned in his arms and pulled him down to her. No words were needed as she stood on her tiptoes and kissed him.

Then drawing back, she said, "There's fresh coffee. I didn't know if you took cream or sugar. The sugar is next to the coffeepot. If you need cream, you'll have to find a cow." By the time he poured a steaming cup of black coffee, she was setting the bacon, eggs and toast on the table.

"Holly," he began as he pulled out a chair. "About last night—"

"No. We are not going to do the guilt-trip thing. It happened. It was beyond wonderful. I don't expect anything from you and I'm not asking for anything. Now eat your eggs before they get cold."

"I don't want to let this drop. Last night was special, but you should have told me you were a virgin."

"Why?" she asked, pouring a cup of coffee with a steady hand. "Would you have done something different?"

"Maybe."

She rose from her seat, leaned over and gave him a kiss full of passion edged with temptation. "I don't think a first time can get any better. Thank you, Chance."

Chance still didn't feel right about taking her virginity. Hell, he hadn't intended to make love to her, but as usual with Holly, things had gotten out of hand. All he knew to do now was keep a close watch on her, be alert for any signs of regret and be there for her if any remorse made its presence known.

"Now eat your eggs before they get cold."

He closed his mouth and realized it had been gaping open. "Yes, ma'am." And he attacked the best breakfast he'd ever had. Somehow, from Holly, he expected nothing less.

Twelve

The clinic was back in business and playing catch-up. With the new equipment installed, they had never been busier, which was a good thing for lots of reasons. The number one reason was because it kept her busy. Holly didn't have time to dwell on what had happened with Chance. He'd made it clear he wanted her then and forever but on the heels of that, he'd left for his hearing and wasn't sure when he would be back.

Holly didn't know what to expect after they made love. Obviously they had taken their relationship to an entirely new level, but they hadn't worked out how to overcome the barrier between them. Probably because there was no answer.

Holly never thought it was possible to love anyone as deeply as she loved Chance. She knew he wasn't the type to settle down, marry and raise a family. If that had changed, he could find somebody a lot better than her.

Someone who could give options of whether or not he wanted kids, where they lived and how they wanted to enjoy their life together. She couldn't offer him any of those things. She had a clinic and couldn't walk out and leave Kevin holding the bag. She had pledged her help just as he'd promised her the same. And she had a baby girl to raise. A very special, very beautiful baby girl. And even if Chance actually asked her to come with him, she would have to say no. It was his life, the one he'd chosen. It was not hers. That was something she couldn't let herself forget, regardless of how much she wanted to be with him. Regardless of how much she loved him.

She knew that his hearing had been scheduled for yesterday at 1:00 p.m. No phone call yet. What could that mean?

She finished the last farm call around four that afternoon and she still didn't want to go home. She knew when she did she would feel Chance's absence as she had every day since he left. Emotionally it had been a very difficult week and she was still on pins and needles. Would they reinstate him or set him free?

Amanda had taken Emma to visit her parents, promising to have the baby home by six. Holly didn't know how, but she'd swear that Amanda knew something had happened between her and Chance. Was Holly that transparent? She supposed it didn't matter that Amanda was suspicious. She appreciated her friend's help and understanding.

She'd overheard Cole tell the general manager of the ranch he didn't think Chance was coming back. But Chance had promised he would. She believed him because not believing Chance was unthinkable.

It was the scream from a wild mustang that shattered the evening calm. Eight of them had been brought to the ranch to be trained and cared for with the hope of finding each a good home when the rehabilitation was done. But there was so much public outcry that their population was increasing too fast, doubling every four years and wreaking havoc. Ranchers in the area claimed the damage done to the open government grasslands prevented others from using it for feeding their livestock. There was talk of thinning out the herd by any means available. That meant rifles. That meant innocent horses would die.

The Circle M was one of many ranches to become involved with saving the mustang. It had joined with other ranches in an effort to bring the wild horses back for rehabilitation. For four years crews from the ranch had journeyed to New Mexico and Arizona a couple of times a year. The results so far had been good.

The office door burst open. Amanda's eyes were wild as though in shock. "Is Emma with you? Do you have her?"

"No," Holly answered as a bolt of pure fear shot down her spine.

"She was standing just inside the office door. I stopped to talk to Kenneth and apparently Emma ventured back outside. I can't find her. Anywhere."

Holly burst into a dead run, heading for the holding pens and calling over her shoulder for Amanda to go to the barn.

Chance stepped out of the chopper, thanking the pilot for the ride. As soon as it was airborne again, he walked to the nearest holding corral, watching while the cowboys separated the mares from the stallions. In this bunch that had just come in, there was only one male. And it appeared he wasn't going to go quietly. Finally, in a combined effort, he was separated from the rest and placed into another pen by himself. He was not happy. A few days to settle down and he would start the long training process. Chance wished he could be here to help. But he had other battles to fight, namely the war against the terrorists in Afghanistan.

He'd been reinstated. He should be doing backflips. But he was grim. He'd done a lot of thinking over the past few days. For all his SEAL training, he hadn't come up with a solution to keep Holly in his life. Being back on the ranch, he felt the situation was as hopeless as when he'd left. He hadn't wanted to tell her over a phone. And he hoped she might have some idea, regardless of how crazy, that would let them stay together. For the first time in his life, Chance was ready to say "I do" and afraid she would say "I don't." Slapping his gloves against his leg, he walked toward the house.

He hadn't gotten very far when he heard a woman calling Emma's name. As the tension in her voice grew more and more frantic, it immediately made Chance go on full alert. Out of the corner of his eye he saw Holly running toward Amanda like the devil himself was on her tail. Why would Holly's friend, Amanda, be calling Emma as though she didn't know where she was? Chance stopped. That sixth sense he'd always relied on had the hairs on the back of his neck standing straight up. Something was wrong. He turned around and started jogging back to the barn. Then Holly took off, running toward the other side of the barn where the mustangs were being kept. She was running frantically in circles, now screaming Emma's name.

He caught up with her, his hands holding her shoulders as he tried to understand what was wrong. She was almost hysterical.

"Holly, talk to me. Where is Emma?"

"Chance? You're here?" She fell into his arms before pushing back. "We can't find Emma. I got a call from Jim Dugan, your ranch manager, asking me if I could please come up and take a look at the new batch of mustangs and see if I can spot anything that needed immediate attention. I was in his office and Emma was standing next to me. Amanda had just brought her inside. The door was closed. The next thing we knew she was gone."

"Okay. Try to calm down. We'll find her."

"How could she have gotten out of that room without me seeing her?" Then, as though she realized talking about what happened was wasting time, she once again started screaming for the baby. Her face was red, her eyes swollen and it appeared shock was settling in.

In between the screams Chance heard something. It sounded like an infant's laughter. Where was she? She couldn't be far. Apparently Holly had heard it, too. Her frantic calls stopped and she, too, was trying to home in on where the laugh had come from. Chance watched as Holly walked toward the holding pens on the west side of the barn. She paused. Seconds later she was screaming again. This time it was his name.

Chance ran toward her faster than humanly possible. From the direction Holly was looking he knew the only thing she saw were the pens that contained the wild mustangs. As he reached Holly, one glance told him the little kid was in big trouble. Emma was holding up her hand, clinching what looked like some grass. And she was offering it to the mustang stallion.

Like a crazed person, Chance took off for the baby, fear tearing down his spine, closing his throat and shutting down his mind to all but one thought: get to Emma before the mustang did. In his mind he was back in Iraq commanding his body to make up those three seconds.

Another tiny life rested in his hands, and that thought turned to pure adrenaline. He would not let another child die needlessly. He would not let Emma be hurt.

He cleared the six-foot-high fence as though it didn't exist. About the time he landed on the other side, the stallion had seen the baby. She was still walking toward it holding up the grass in her hand. The mustang's ears were flat against its head as it pawed the ground and bared its teeth, all signs of imminent attack. There was a distance of about ten feet between the mustang and Emma. The horse could lurch that far in one stride. Chance had to run faster, harder. He needed those three seconds.

The situation played out in slow motion with every sinew in his body straining to go faster. Chance caught the baby in his arms, never breaking stride. He jumped up onto the fence on the east side just as the stallion pounced. Knowing it missed its target, it first reared up, then wheeled around and kicked the fence, the strike landing less than a foot away from where Chance held the baby.

By now the cowboys had heard the commotion and were coming out to help. When he jumped down on the outside of the fence, Emma's head was against his shoulder, her little arms around his neck, and nothing he'd ever experienced in his life had ever felt so great.

He walked toward Holly, who was running to him.

"Hoshee!" Emma exclaimed, giggling.

"Yeah," Chance answered. "Bad hoshee. Emma stay away from that hoshee. Okay?"

"Bah hoshee."

He handed her to Holly, who hugged her as though she never wanted to let her go. Tears were flowing down her cheeks.

"Thank you, Chance. Oh, my gosh. *Thank you.*"

As she hugged him to her, the baby turned in her arms and was patting his chest. "Ta you." And Chance hugged them both.

Holly paced the floor. The incident with Emma had shaken her up so badly her heart hadn't slowed down even two hours after it happened. Amanda had offered to take Emma back to her parents, but Holly refused to let Emma out of her sight. She would have nightmares for a very long time after what had happened. She and Amanda had talked and neither could understand how the baby had gotten out the office door, walked all the way across the private road and into the pen with that mustang. Thank God for Chance. Emma could have been dead right now. Holly couldn't even get her mind around that. She owed Chance more than she could ever repay.

But what was he doing here? She knew his hearing had been scheduled for yesterday afternoon. She'd been waiting for the phone call that never came. Then suddenly he'd shown up in time to save her baby. She didn't know what to make of it. She thought about going to the big house and asking him. But in addition to the fact she was still trembling over Emma's close call, she believed if Chance wanted her to know the outcome of his hearing he would tell her. It wouldn't make the answer different if she went over and beat on his door, although that was exactly what she wanted to do.

Lightning flashed in the distance. Standing at the window, Holly wished this nightmare could be over. Chance would be leaving. She felt it. The doctor here had given him a clean bill of health, saying the wounds were healing nicely. That was a good thing. The medical evaluation board had probably decided in his favor and allowed Chance to go back to his team. She and Emma would continue their lives and maybe, someday, Chance would come back. He still loved the ranch. Maybe if he retired from the military he would come here to live out his life.

As the thunder rolled in, she continued to pace. She hated waiting for something to happen once it was a done deal. She had learned the hard way she was lousy at saying goodbye. Ironically Chance was always the one she was saying goodbye to. While she didn't want Chance to leave—ever—if he was going to she wanted it over with. Counting down the hours and minutes until he boarded the plane and left her was tying her insides into knots. A tear broke loose and fell down her cheek. Absently she brushed it away. Only to have it replaced by another.

She really needed to stop this. She'd accepted that Chance would never stay. It was so stupid of her to have her own little pity party like this. She walked into the bathroom and grabbed a section of tissue to blow her nose and wipe her eyes.

Someone knocked on her back door. *Please don't let somebody have an emergency tonight.* She was almost to the door when the knocking came again. She realized she was wearing only an oversize T-shirt and her panties. "Give me just a minute," she called out, and scurried to put on a pair of jeans. Then she came back and cracked open the door just enough to see who was there.

"Holly?" It was Chance.

Had he come to say goodbye? He must have really wanted her to know he was leaving to show up in person at midnight.

"I know you're leaving," she whispered through the crack in the door. "You didn't have to stop by and tell me in person, but thank you. And I can never thank you enough for saving Emma. Please take care of yourself. Okay?"

A strong gust of wind brought the rain slamming against her house. The tears returned about the same time.

"Holly, let me in."

"No. Chance, you need to go." Yes, she wanted to be in his arms again. But she didn't want to prolong the goodbye.

"I'm not leaving until I make sure you're all right. Until we've had a chance to talk." She heard the determination in his voice and knew he would stand outside in the rain with lightning crackling overhead all night if that was what it took.

With both hands she wiped the moisture from her cheeks and stepped back into the room, letting the door fall open.

Chance stepped inside and closed the door behind him. His eyes were on her face. On the tears that refused to stop falling. "Holly, don't do this."

She turned away from him. "If you don't have an animal emergency…"

He put his hands on her shoulders and spun her around to face him. He should never have come back to the ranch. He'd told her he would call and that was what he should have done. He should never have made love to her knowing full well he would be leaving. He knew her heart. She lived life, she didn't just walk on the edge of it. Small things that most people didn't notice made Holly laugh for joy. But it worked the other way, too. Things that made others feel a little sad could rip a hole through her heart. She'd lost so much. He had a feeling that in her mind she was losing him, as well.

He loved her. He probably always had. But he couldn't stay. What would he do if he left the military? He just couldn't see himself wearing a suit to work every day and becoming a pencil pusher like his brothers. He was not cut out for that. If he tried to force it, Holly would pay the price by putting up with what she called a grouch.

"Are congratulations in order? Are you going to be reinstated?"

He hesitated, knowing the answer was not what she wanted to hear. "Yes. I leave in the morning to report to the naval base in Coronado."

"Then definitely, congratulations. I'm very happy for you."

She did her best to smile, but he could see the truth in her eyes.

"This, what we have, is not over, Holly. That's why I came back. To tell you, in person, I want you in my life."

She walked to a chair and leaned against the back of it as though she needed the support.

"And what, exactly, do we have, Chance? A childhood full of memories and making love in the rain?" She looked down to where her hands gripped the chair back. "We both know you don't have to come all the way here for that sort of thing. In fact, I'm sure there are plenty of women who have vastly more experience than me who would love to take my place."

He walked toward her. "Make no mistake, Holly. It's you I want." His voice was rough and low even to his own ears. "I want you in my arms, I want to kiss you like there's no tomorrow. I want to bury myself inside you, as deep as I can go. Deeper. I want to tease you about riding English. I want to teach you how to swim. I want it all." He stepped closer. "I want you to come with me. I want to marry you, Holly. Please say yes. I don't know when I'll be back."

The tears swam in her eyes. "I can't, Chance."

"Why?"

"Let's just say I know how to swim and leave it at that, okay?"

"No. We're not leaving it there. I thought…I thought you loved me."

"I do. With all my heart and soul. It would be my dream come true, but eventually reality comes knocking," she said. "You have a team who counts on you, who cares about you. I have patients who need me. And of course, my number one priority is Emma. I'm all she has, Chance."

"I'm not asking you to leave Emma." He frowned, upset that she would ever think such a thing. "I would never do that."

"Chance, please understand what I'm saying. She will never know her mother or father. But at least here, in Calico Springs, she will grow up in a community where they lived. She will meet people who knew them and loved them and she'll hear good things. She'll grow up proud she is Jason's daughter. And they will love her as one of them. I won't take that away from her. It's all I have to give her."

Chance looked into Holly's eyes, and saw her determination to protect and do what was right for Emma clearly reflected there. He took her into his arms. He needed to hold her, to feel her next to him. He was a bit surprised when she made no effort to push away because clearly she was upset. He bent down and kissed the side of her face. She turned toward him, her lips seeking his. He could taste the salty remnants of her tears.

As always, her lips were so soft. Like the softest velvet he could imagine. As he kissed her he felt the stiffness leave her body, and her arms came around his neck.

And she kissed him back as if this was the last time she would ever see him.

Eventually, they pulled apart.

"So I guess this is really it."

"I guess so. We had a good time, didn't we?" She crossed her arms around her as though giving herself some needed support. He could see the tears still falling down her face even as she tried to blink them away. It was so Holly. She'd always been so tough, so determined. Especially when it meant keeping up with her big brother and his friend Chance. Thank heavens that hadn't changed.

"Holly, I keep thinking there is some sort of solution here. The money is there, but I've never been one who could sit on my hands. A few months with me underfoot, you really would be calling me a grouch. And…there's something else you should know. Wade is selling the ranch, so prepare for some new neighbors."

The shock on her face was immediate. "*What?* How can he do that?"

"He is the head of Masters Corporation. The corporation owns the land. He can do anything he wants."

"But the ranch… It was the beginning of all of us. Jason, you, Wade, Cole. It's where your mother is laid to rest. It should be yours. This is so wrong. I'm going over there and light into Wade Masters like…"

"No, Holly," he said. "Wade is doing what he thinks is best. The ranch isn't profitable, and it's too big to try to support it. He will do right by you, Holly. Don't hold it against him." Chance looked around the room as though unsure what his next move should be. "Okay. Well, I'd better get going. I'll be in touch, okay?"

"Sure. You take care and don't get shot again, for gosh sakes." Again she tried her best to smile.

There was nothing else to say. There was no use in prolonging her sadness. Or his.

With a nod to her, Chance turned and walked out the door.

He didn't see Holly double over in pain. He didn't hear the hopeless cries of anguish or her soft but broken voice saying, "I love you, Chance Masters. I always will."

Thirteen

The combined sounds of announcements over the loud-speaker and the disgruntled mooing of cows told Holly the rodeo was well underway. A loud buzzer signaled the end of time for a wild bronc rider. Holly had grown up at these events and she never could quite understand why any man would put his life on the line if he didn't have to. Who in their right mind would try to go eight seconds on a bull with three-foot-long horns and a really bad attitude? Her brother and Chance used to ride those bulls. She'd thought they were crazy then. She still thought it was insane. But she always admired the roping competitions and had won her share of ribbons for the barrel-racing event.

She walked toward the area that had been set up for her use. Next door, another tent, quite a bit larger, had been erected for the area doctor. She loved old Doc Hardy. It was easy to understand why this community refused to let him even think about retiring. He welcomed her with a hug.

"Let's hope neither man nor horse gets injured tonight," he said. "Are you here for both nights, Holly?"

"No, sir," she said. "I've got it tonight. Kevin will be here tomorrow."

"I like that young man. Seems like a hard worker. And his boys were in to see me for preschool inoculations and they are just as nice and respectful as their father. The mother, too."

"I couldn't agree more."

Holly inventoried the medical equipment brought over by members of the Calico County Rodeo Association. As far as she could tell, everything was here. She shared the hope that neither she nor Doc Hardy had to use any of it. Her for the animals. Dr. Hardy for the people.

"Say, Holly. Did you know Chance Masters?"

Her heart plunged to her feet. "Yes. Yes, I did."

"He and your brother were always at the rodeo. I heard he was back in town after a dozen years or more. Can't rightly recall how long. I always wondered what happened to him. The only time he wasn't getting himself in trouble was when he was with Jason. I think your brother put his foot down and wouldn't stand for any of that rabble-rousing. But you know, it might have been a lot different if his father had given two hoots about his sons. I think he was cruel to Chance and Chance finally had enough. A lot of that trouble he caused was because of his father."

"Really?"

"Yeah. Like I said, I always wondered what happened to him. I know there was some good in that boy."

"I heard he is a navy SEAL." Holly volunteered the info, still trying to digest what Dr. Hardy had said.

"Is that right? Good for him. It's like I thought, after his father threw him out of his house there were all kinds of directions he could have gone. He made the right choice. I'm happy to know that."

It had been three weeks and five days since Chance had walked out of her house and out of her life forever. Thankfully Amanda didn't mention him. Her friend knew Holly's heart was still healing. But it was unexpected inquiries, like Dr. Hardy's, that slipped through her defenses. Those were hard. But she was making progress. She no longer cried herself to sleep every night. And she'd begun eating regular meals, required if she was to do her job. But even she could look in the mirror and see the dark circles under her eyes and a general pallor to her skin. It couldn't be helped. She was doing the best she could.

"I'm going to go and get one of Judy's corn dogs. Would you care for anything, Dr. Hardy?"

"Thank you, Holly, but Martha sent me with a thermos of coffee and a bunch of lettuce and told me I'd better not set my sights on a dessert."

Holly couldn't help but smile. "I'll be right back."

With a couple of cowboys standing watch to ensure her supplies and equipment didn't grow legs and walk off, she strolled through the crowd, looking at the various vendor booths selling everything from tack to Western-related jewelry. But her focus was on Judy Cooper's hot dog stand.

"Hi, Doc." Judy spotted her in the crowd. "I've got that corn dog and homemade lemonade almost ready for you."

"Great." Holly smiled. "It wouldn't be the annual rodeo were it not for your corn dogs."

Leaving a five-dollar bill on the counter, Holly waited for the lemonade to be freshly made.

"Well, hello, stranger. Long time no see."

Holly cringed and turned to face Blake Lufkin.

"How have you been doing?"

"Fine. I've been good. How about yourself?"

How long did it take Judy to mix up one glass of lemonade?

"Is that guy you were hanging around with still around?"

"No. He had to go back to his SEAL team. But he will be back." She didn't know if he would or not, but the least Chance could do was be her excuse to keep this irritating man away.

"Here ya go, Holly," Judy said, handing her one dog and a large lemonade.

"Thanks."

"You are entirely welcome." She then turned to Blake. "Can I help you, sir?"

Holly didn't stick around to hear his answer. She was done being nice to the creep. Sipping her lemonade, she made her way back to her medic tent and thanked the cowboys who'd watched it for her.

"Some guy was by here looking for you," Larry offered. "About ten minutes ago. I told him you'd gone to get something to eat and would be back."

"Thanks, Larry."

Great. Now she had people helping the creepy guy track her down.

Holly pulled up a chair toward the front of the tent so she could catch the evening breeze. She had just finished her corn dog and was sipping the last of her lemonade when Blake walked into her tent and pulled up the other chair next to hers as though he had every right to be there.

"Enjoy your food?" he asked. "Frankly, I don't see

how you can eat that stuff. How about let's go into town after the rodeo and grab something decent?"

"No, thanks. After the events are over I'll have to get home."

"How about if I come over there? Once you get the kid to bed we could watch a movie. I love the *Mission Impossible* films, so we've got that in common."

Holly was determined to look unimpressed. "I really don't like those kinds of movies."

"I thought I remembered seeing a box full of them next to the TV."

Must belong to Amanda, she mused. Then the deeper meaning of what he'd just said hit her like a blow to the solar plexus. Blake had never been inside her house.

"So how about that dinner? Anywhere you want. Or we could go to my place and see what we can find there." Blake stood up, facing her. He leaned forward, his hands resting on the arms of her chair. Too close. But what she saw made her eyes pop out of her head. He was wearing a pendant. When he leaned toward her it swung forward. And Holly grabbed it. It was a pendant made and given to her by a ten-year-old. It had hung in the clinic.

She saw a moment of surprise in his creepy face. If he left he would destroy the pendant and no one could ever prove he had it. It would be her word against his.

"I love this pendant," she said, making her voice a breathless whisper. "It's beautiful." She looked up into his eyes as though the bastard had walked out of a dream. Heaven help her.

The cut-glass charm depicted a mare and foal in a green pasture. It was one of a kind.

"Oh, Blake." She let her fingers touch the glass. Flipping it over, she found Toby's initials. "I don't suppose the store has any more?" She rose from the chair, purposely standing well within his personal space. Blake had forgotten about the token in her hand, distracted by being this close to Holly. Their faces were inches apart; his breath reeked of alcohol and tobacco, and he generally smelled of someone who hadn't taken a bath in a very long time. She hoped she didn't throw up.

"I'll tell you what. You have dinner with me and I just might be persuaded to give this little medallion to you. Free."

"Really?" she squeaked, keeping up the dumb blonde persona.

"Well, sure." He went to hug her and she dropped her napkin accidently on purpose.

"Oh, Blake, I have to go find the ladies' room. Oh, I'm so excited. Will you wait for me? Right here? Don't go anywhere. I might not be able to find you." She would probably go to hell for the look of love she plastered on her face.

A disgusting gleam filled his eyes. "Why, sure, Holly. You just take your time. I'll be right here."

She turned after giving him one last smile and stumbled out of the tent. Once out of sight, she ran as if a rabid dog was on her trail. She had to find a deputy, and fast. That necklace had been hanging inside her clinic when it was ransacked. Blake was the culprit.

The crowd parted and just ahead she saw John Green, the deputy who had come out the night the clinic was almost destroyed.

At a dead run she fought to catch up with him. "John. Wait!"

It took two times to make him understand what she was saying. She was panicked that the creep would get away and if that necklace disappeared, they would have no reason to hold him. There might not be any other way to prove he did it.

She made her way back to the tent with John following close behind her. See spotted Blake sitting back in her chair. Unfortunately, he spotted her at the same time. And John Green. Blake was out of the tent, running toward the parking area like the coward he was. Holly refused to let him go and she took after him. After everything he'd put her through, he was going to pay. She heard John calling her name but she wasn't about to stop or slow down.

Blake had disappeared in the parking lot but she had predicted his course. Jumping over parking chains and around bumpers, she managed to get ahead of him, duck down behind a car and wait. Sure enough Blake jogged by, slowing down, obviously thinking he'd lost the cops. He hadn't lost Holly. She put one foot on the bumper to give her leverage and threw herself on top of the man. He was bigger, older, meaner, but she held on. She dug her fingernails into his face and wrapped her legs around his chunky, stinky body. He was cussing, trying to get free. Holly was like an octopus and held on to him with everything she had. They went down in the loose dirt and still she refused to let go. He managed to get on top. She saw the snarl on his face and his fist lift high in the air, and she braced herself for the pain.

But it never came.

She saw strong hands grip Blake's neck and haul the man off the ground.

It was Chance!

Blake took a swing at his captor and Chance flattened him. With one blow. The man was out cold on the ground as John arrived, two deputies in tow.

Offering his hand, Chance helped Holly to stand.

"Well, you damn sure know how to enjoy a rodeo,"

Chance teased. "The bull riding is on the other side of the fence."

She was covered in dirt from her tussle. She would probably have a couple of bruises, but she didn't care. Chance was here and that creep would soon be behind bars.

"I can't let you out of my sight for an instant," Chance said, trying for a gruff tone but failing miserably. He pulled Holly to him. His lips were on hers, hard, heavy and glorious. In spite of the dirt. In spite of the crowd of curiosity seekers standing around them.

It took her a few minutes to regain her senses. "What... what are you doing here?"

"I missed you, Muppet. I had to come back." His eyes moved over her, top to bottom. "Although I didn't expect to find you rolling around in the dirt with some scumbag."

"That man is the one who ransacked the clinic."

"I hoped he'd done something other than say hello. Let's get you cleaned up."

"The medic tent... I can't leave—"

"Kevin has it all under control. Anyway, another half hour and this rodeo will be one for the history books. In more ways than one. Come on."

The big shower of the en suite room she'd used before when she stayed in the mansion was just what she needed. But she didn't stay under the soothing spray very long. Chance was downstairs. Waiting for her.

She stepped out and grabbed a large towel, wrapping it around her. A quick brush of her hair and she was out the door heading to the den. Chance was in the kitchen, looking into the refrigerator. "Are you hungry?" How had he known she was there?

"Lemonade?"

"Coming up."

She looked at him and it was the most beautiful sight she'd ever seen. And this time she couldn't wait patiently to be told what was happening. "Okay. Tell me why you're here."

He leaned against the kitchen bar, sipping his beer. "I'm here to get married if the beautiful lady I'm in love with still wants me." He set the can down and grew serious. "I quit the SEALs, Holly. It came time to sign up for another three years and I couldn't do it. I looked at the guys I'd served with and I saw your face. And I knew any one of them would call me everything but smart if I didn't get my ass back here and ask you to marry me."

"You're really not going back?"

"Nope. And I'm okay with that. I've done my part."

"What about Emma? You don't like kids."

"I love kids." He was quiet for a moment. "Before we get married, if you agree to marry me, you need to know what kind of man you'll be pledging your life to."

Holly looked at his face. Did he feel as uncomfortable as he looked?

"There is more to it than what it seems. I was in a recon mission. We were provided intel that one of the leading terrorists was in the area hiding out in a small town nearby. We were set to go in, secure the town and capture the guy."

Chance drew in a breath, obviously not wanting to go on. But she had a feeling it was something he needed to say. "At the height of the fighting, a child about Emma's age walked around the corner of a building. She sat down and proceeded to play with this old doll. That's when I saw the bomb coming in fast."

He looked up at Holly, who was frozen in shock. "I hit

the ground at a dead run, determined to save her." He ran a hand over his lower face. "I couldn't do it. I couldn't get to her fast enough to save her. The brass wrote it off as collateral damage. But it was the life of a little girl who will never see her second birthday."

"Chance. You can't blame yourself."

"I can and I do. It's reality. It is what it is. I'm afraid of being near your baby because I know someday I might make another mistake. Wait too long. Run too slow. The next time, it might be Emma."

"Chance Masters, you *saved* Emma. Had it not been for you…"

"I got lucky."

"No. What I saw wasn't luck. It was the superhuman effort of a man who cared, determined to save a baby's life. There was no luck involved. And I have no doubt it was the same scene played out when you tried to save the other child."

"You'll have to excuse me if my opinion differs."

Holly didn't know what to say. How could Chance possibly think he was responsible for that baby? But Chance wasn't the kind of man who accepted pity. Anything she said would sound like that to him. At least now she understood why he didn't want to be around babies. She wasn't worried. Emma would fix that.

Holly crossed the space between them, looked up into his face. His eyes said it all. She leaned toward him and placed her arms around his solid waist and her lips against his. He didn't turn her away. Muscles as hard as iron lay beneath her arms. He cupped her face, his rough thumbs rubbing her cheeks. These were the same hands and strong arms that held a rifle with the intent of killing if necessary, if he was ordered to pull a trigger. Now they were so gentle, holding her as he would a baby kitten. He'd put his life on the line every day for his country and dealt with the horror he'd described, carrying it around in his mind. In his soul. It took a very special individual to do that and still go forward.

"I swear, Holly, I'll be the best dad to Emma that I can be."

"I have no doubt of that, Chance," she said, holding him tight. "None."

She felt him inhale as though a weight had been lifted from his shoulders.

"There's one other thing I feel you should know."

Holly waited, not certain what was coming next.

"Wade sold the ranch," he said. "Thought I'd better mention that, too."

She was shocked, but it didn't matter and she wasted no time telling him so. They would find a place of their own.

"I'm so sorry, because I know your love for the Circle M."

Before Holly could wrap her head around that, Chance added, "He sold it to me. We made a deal. It represents my share of the family company. I'll tell you about the particulars some time. But if you will marry me, this will be your home. And Emma's."

"She's gonna love your plants."

"Make love to me." His heavy arms came around her and pulled her tightly against him. With a flick of his wrist, the towel that covered her fell to the floor.

A soft moan, the sexiest Chance had ever heard in his life, gave him her answer.

She pulled his head down to her, her lips on his, her tongue entering his mouth with a desperate need, giving him all she had to give. And he took it. His hands reached to cover her hips, kneading the firm flesh before he lifted her up and against his throbbing erection. Chance was on fire. The heat that tore through him was burning him alive, and every time she moved the slightest bit his internal thermometer inched up a notch. His hands went to his belt. He had it unbuckled, his jeans unsnapped and his zipper down in seconds. The fact that Holly watched his every movement had the fire once again running through his veins. His jeans fell to his feet. He stepped out of them, tore open the foil packet and put his hands around her waist. He lifted her, positioned his member against her and pushed inside. He was like a wild thing, taking the female he'd chosen as his mate.

Her silver-blond hair splayed out around her head and shoulders. Her eyes were closed, her lips open as she immersed herself in what he was doing. That look of fulfillment brought on the mindless insanity. He didn't want to think. He only wanted to feel, and that feeling was incredible.

Holly's face had always been pretty much an open book and now was no exception. As she opened her eyes, her honey-brown gaze focused on his mouth. It drove him crazy. If she wanted his kiss, he would gladly give her what she wanted. On every square inch of her luscious body.

She brought her silky-smooth legs around him and he began to move. The tension began to build and build until seconds later Holly cried out his name. But he wasn't finished. Not by a mile. Her hands gripped his hair, and she kissed his lips, hungry for anything he could give. And he had plenty he wanted to give. Everything he had was hers.

She was so sensitive, reacting to every touch, every word spoken. How long had he wondered if such a woman existed? Something she said made him break out into a sweat. He felt the familiar tingling in his lower back as his own release overcame him. It seemed to go on and on, every time he heard her saying, "Yes."

Finally, he withdrew from her. Sweeping her into his arms, he carried her to an upstairs bedroom, placed her on the bed and climbed in after her.

Wrapped in each other's arms, they slept. Before morning broke, Holly kissed him awake. She didn't have to tell him why. He grabbed another of the foil packets from the bedside table and took her to the heavens yet again.

Epilogue

Six months later

The small chapel was filled with friends and neighbors who smiled and whispered with hushed excitement about the wedding between two of their own. Who would have ever thought little Holly Anderson would be the one to tame the wild, charismatic, bad-boy billionaire, Chance Masters? Some were here to see it for themselves. Others had already decided they wouldn't believe it regardless of whether they saw it with their own eyes. Some could not contain the pure jealousy evident in their faces. But most were here to see the joining of two people who had loved each other since forever.

The soft strains of a harp combined with the beautiful rhythms of a piano as the front doors opened to allow the bride and her detail to enter. First came two-year-old Emma with her basket of rose petals. Holding Amanda's hand, she walked down the center aisle carefully holding the woven wood basket in front of her. Setting it on the floor, she reached inside and grabbed a handful of petals and dropped them to the floor. After saying hello to the people sitting on both sides, she dutifully picked up the basket, walked another three or four feet, set the basket on the floor and grabbed more petals.

Next to her, the maid of honor, Amanda Stiller, looked behind her to the bride.

"If she doesn't pick up the pace, we are all gonna be here the entire night," Amanda whispered.

Holly grinned at the thought and nodded. She knew Emma would do it her way, so yes, they all might be here for a while. She looked at Emma in time to see her throw down the little basket and run to the front of the chapel, squealing a happy laugh and calling, "Cha, Cha," her little arms held high above her head.

Holly watched as Chance leaned over and picked her up. A lump formed in her throat. They were a family. Chance had overcome his fear he might hurt her and Emma had taken his training over from there. She loved her Cha. Holly caught the radiant blue eyes of her husband-to-be and saw his dimples were showing once again.

I love you, he mouthed.

I love you right back, she mutely answered.

It didn't matter how long the ceremony lasted. She had the rest of her life to love this incredible man. Her hero, her protector, her only love. And she'd make sure he felt that love each and every day for the rest of their lives.

"Emma! Come and get your basket," Amanda said in a loud whisper. "Emma!"

"I'ne get now." Emma wiggled to get down from Chance's arms. She ran halfway down the aisle back to the basket, picked it up and continued to throw the flower petals.

"Good. That's very good," Amanda told her as they made their way to the altar.

And wasn't that the way things were meant to be?

* * * * *

What was Alex doing in Washington?

It was almost as if she'd known he couldn't stop thinking about their night together.

He stood as the door opened and Alex spilled into the room. Her face glowed and something seized his lungs as he stared at her. She'd stolen his ability to think simply by walking into the room. That was not supposed to happen.

Her eyes shone with unexpected moisture and he lost his place again. This wasn't a social visit, obviously. "Is something wrong?"

"Maybe." She hesitated, biting her lip in that way that said she didn't know what to say next.

If only he could take her in his arms and kiss her hello, like he wanted to. He sighed. "I like you a lot, Alex, but I'm not sure we're meant to continue our affair. It's complicated. And not your fault. I wish things could be different. And not so complicated."

She choked out a laugh that sounded a bit like a sob. "Yeah, I wish that, too. Unfortunately, things are far more complicated than you could ever dream."

"What—"

"I'm pregnant."

* * *

A Pregnancy Scandal
is part of the Love and Lipstick series:
For four female executives, mixing
business with pleasure leads to love!

A PREGNANCY SCANDAL

BY
KAT CANTRELL

First Published in Great Britain 2016
By Mills & Boon, an imprint of HarperCollins*Publishers*
1 London Bridge Street, London, SE1 9GF

© 2016 Kat Cantrell

ISBN: 978-0-263-91863-2

51-0616

Our policy is to use papers that are natural, renewable and recyclable products and made from wood grown in sustainable forests. The logging and manufacturing processes conform to the legal environmental regulations of the country of origin.

Printed and bound in Spain
by CPI, Barcelona

Kat Cantrell read her first Mills & Boon novel in primary school and has been scribbling in notebooks since then. She writes smart, sexy books with a side of sass. She's a former Mills & Boon *So You Think You Can Write* winner and an RWA Golden Heart® Award finalist. Kat, her husband and their two boys live in north Texas.

To Anne Marsh for about a million reasons
but mostly because you're always there on
the other side of my chat window.

One

The third time Alex ducked behind the Greek statue, Senator Phillip Edgewood's curiosity got the best of him. Yeah, he'd been watching her from across the crowded room as she chatted with her friends and coworkers. How could he not?

Alexandra Meer was the most beautiful woman in the room.

Surprisingly so. Phillip had half expected her to show up to his fundraiser-slash-party in jeans, which he would not have minded in the slightest because he liked her no matter what she wore. But this dressed-up, made-up, transformed version of the woman he'd first met a couple of weeks ago at the Fyra Cosmetics corporate office—*wow*.

Senator Galindo cleared her throat, drawing Phillip's attention back to their conversation. Ramona Galindo, the other United States senator from Texas, and Phillip had a lot in common and they often socialized when they were both home in Dallas. But it was hard to focus on the senator with Alex's secretive actions going on. He pretended to listen, because the whole point of this evening was to network with his colleagues outside of Washington, while he also strained to catch a glimpse of Alex.

Was she covertly dumping canapés before anyone figured out she wasn't eating them? Or was she hoping to meet someone interesting in the shadowy recesses?

If it was the former, Phillip felt it was his civic duty to inform her that, while this was his party, he hated the canapés, too. If it was the latter, well, it might also be his civic duty to grant her wish.

Honestly, Phillip needed the distraction. Today was Gina's birthday. Or rather, it would have been. If his wife had lived, she would have been thirty-two. You'd think nearly two years of practice being a widower would afford a guy a better handle on the designation. But here he was, still stumbling through it.

And that decided it. He could spend the rest of the evening morose and moody. Or he could fan the sparks that always kicked up whenever he was around Alex. When Phillip had agreed to help Fyra Cosmetics navigate the FDA approval process for a new product, he'd never expected to meet someone so intriguing, especially not when that someone was the company's chief financial officer.

He and Alex had been developing a "thing" over late lunches and one-on-one meetings. She laughed at his jokes and made him feel like a man instead of a politician. And she'd come to this party stag when he'd been almost positive she'd decline. How much more of a hint did he need that their relationship might become more than two people working together?

"Excuse me," he murmured to Senator Galindo as he skirted her expertly, tugging on the white shirtsleeves under his tuxedo as he beelined across his cavernous living room to catch the most interesting woman at his party in the act of…whatever she was doing.

He crossed his arms and stepped behind the statue, boxing her in. The scent of Alex overwhelmed him first… light, fruity…and then the woman did. He let both wake up his blood. Which didn't take long.

"Fancy meeting you here," he said blithely. "I hope I'm not the bore at this party that you're avoiding."

Alex's eyes widened and then warmed dangerously fast. Her eyes were the most fascinating shade of green with a little brown dot in the left iris that he couldn't help but notice. She was easily the most distinctive woman he'd ever met, and that was saying something when he regularly mixed with the elite of both Dallas and Washington.

"No, of course not. You couldn't pry that title away from the mayor with a crowbar." And then she groaned, which made him grin. "I mean, I'm not avoiding the mayor. And he's not a bore. Neither are you! I'm not avoiding anyone."

Was it wrong that he enjoyed flustering her so much? It was so easy to do and she always said something outrageous that never failed to make him smile. He needed to smile, especially tonight. And she was the only person in attendance who had managed that feat. The only person he'd met in a long time who seemed unimpressed by his position or wealth. He liked that.

"But if you *were* hoping to avoid someone, this would be the opportune spot." He leaned against the wall and crossed one ankle over the other. "No one would know you were back here unless they were already watching you."

The shadows weren't deep enough to cover her blush. "You were watching me?"

"Oh, come now." He tsked. "When a woman wears a dress like that, surely it's not a shock that a man would spend a great deal of time looking at her."

She glanced down and scowled.

"It's just a dress," she mumbled.

No, it was anything but. The off-white dress had a hint of gold sparkle that caught the light when she moved, and the fabric draped over her curves in a way that announced she had some. That was news to Phillip and he'd call that a front-page story, because she was an amazingly beautiful woman already, even before this evening's transformation.

But *with* the transformation…well, she'd captured his interest thoroughly, because he hoped it meant she wasn't averse to the occasional dress-up event. Politicians attended a lot of those and Phillip had a huge void in the plus-one category.

Maybe he'd found a potential candidate.

"Yet I've never seen you in a dress." He raised one eyebrow in emphasis, which she did not miss. "I've come by Fyra for FDA meetings, what, like three or four times? And you, my dear, have reinvented the concept of casual wear. Cass, Trinity and Harper always wear suits, but you're most often in jeans."

The other three cofounders of Fyra dressed well and without regard to price tags. Phillip appreciated a woman who knew her way around a stylist, and normally he would have said he preferred a sophisticated woman. Gina had never met a rack at Nordstrom she could leave untouched, and the small handful of women he'd preoccupied himself with after Gina died could only be described as high maintenance. He'd lost interest in them pretty quickly.

But Alex…well, Alex intrigued him. She'd instantly stood out from her three counterparts when his cousin Gage had introduced Phillip to the founders of Fyra Cosmetics.

He couldn't ignore the demure, brown-haired woman clad in a T-shirt, hair scraped back into a ponytail. It was baffling to walk into a meeting with Fyra's executives and see the chief financial officer's face bereft of makeup. It would be like introducing himself to someone as Senator Phillip Edgewood and then claiming he had no interest in the laws of the United States.

He was intrigued. He wanted to know her better. Understand why he couldn't stop thinking about her. Why she was so different from any woman of his acquaintance. But he had to tread carefully with the opposite sex for so many reasons, not the least of which was his aversion to scandal. And then there was the other thing: he was on the lookout for a permanent plus one. Only the right woman would do for that role and his criteria were stringent.

No point in getting a woman's hopes up unless she filled them. He didn't know if Alex fell in that category or not, but he planned to find out.

"Don't you have guests?" she asked and glanced over his shoulder. "I'm keeping you from them."

"Seventy-eight, if I recall." Yes, he should be doing host-type things, definitely. He didn't move. "And you're one of my guests, as well. I'd be remiss if I didn't see to your welfare as you skulk about behind this very large statue."

"My dress is…uncomfortable." She waved at her torso. "None of this stays in place like it's supposed to."

Naturally, his eye was drawn to the area in question. "Looks like everything is in order to me."

"Because I just adjusted it all," she hissed fiercely.

The image of Alex ducking behind his statue to dip her hands under her dress to *adjust things* flooded through his senses, unchecked. He couldn't unsee it. Couldn't unexperience it. And now this small space in the corner wasn't nearly big enough to hold a senator, a CFO and the enormous attraction sizzling between them.

He stopped himself from asking if she needed help adjusting anything else. It was right there on the tip of his tongue. But United States senators didn't run around saying whatever they felt like, no matter how badly he wanted to flirt with her. Among other things.

Phillip's life was not his own, never had been, nor would he have it any other way. He was an Edgewood, born into a long line of statesmen, and an even longer line of Texas oilmen, and his family was counting on him to be the first one to make it to the White House.

To accomplish that, he needed a wife, plain and simple. A single president hadn't been elected in the United States since the eighteen hundreds. The problem was that his heart still belonged to Gina, and he'd met few women willing to play second fiddle to another woman, even one who'd passed away.

The catch-22 was brutal. Either he'd marry someone in name only and make his peace with loneliness for the next fifty years or hope that he magically stumbled over a woman who was okay with his ground rules for marriage—friends and lovers, sure. But love wasn't on offer. It would feel like a betrayal of the highest order.

It wasn't fair; he knew that. But Phillip didn't believe in second chances. No one got lucky enough to find their soul mate twice. But if Alex was the right woman for him, she'd understand.

Instead of the dozens of other offers he'd have rather issued, he asked, "Would you like a glass of champagne?"

"Do I look that much like I need a drink?" she asked wryly. "Or are you a mind reader?"

He grinned. "Neither. I thought it was a shame you were stuck back here in the corner with your dress problems and couldn't enjoy the party."

Tucking an errant lock of hair behind her ear, an escapee from her upswept hairdo, she rolled her eyes. "It'll take a lot more than champagne to get me to enjoy a black-tie party."

There she went again with her outrageous statements. He smiled. "Should I be insulted that my party isn't up to par?"

A horrified light dawned in her expression. "No! Your party is perfect because, well…you're *you* and your house is amazing and the guests are great. I'm just clumsy with small talk. Obviously."

She blinked up at him from under her lashes. On any other woman, that look would have been coquettish, designed to convey blatant invitation, and he would have walked away without regret. On her, it was a hint of vulnerability, of uncertainty. And together, they unexpectedly whacked him in the heart.

Hadn't seen that coming. His attraction had deepened over a simple look.

"Not clumsy," he corrected smoothly. "Honest. That's refreshing."

"I'm glad someone thinks so." She scowled, but it was cute on her. "Numbers people like me are not usually sought out by party hosts. We tend to skulk about behind statues and embarrass ourselves with wardrobe problems."

"Why did you come to the party if you don't like dressing up?"

Obviously she hadn't morphed into someone who liked black-tie affairs, which was a shame. She was looking less and less like a candidate for his permanent plus one. The problem was, the more he stood here with her, the more he wanted to chuck all his marriage rules.

"You know why."

The undercurrents between them heated as their gazes locked. He couldn't have walked away from Alex if his ancestral home caught fire. He was close enough to see the brown fleck in her eye and it was oddly intimate. His attraction to her was ungodly strong and a colossal problem.

"You came for me?" he asked, but it wasn't really a question. Her smile answered affirmatively anyway. "I'm flattered you'd put on an uncomfortable dress and wear makeup just for me."

"Call it a rare burst of spontaneity. Totally unlike me. But hopefully worth it in the end."

He almost groaned. She was killing him. Why couldn't they be two normal people meeting at a party, with no agenda other than to spend time together? "I'm a fan of spontaneous women."

Especially since he didn't have nearly enough opportunity to indulge in spontaneity. It was the enemy of someone eyeing the presidency. His life consisted of carefully worded statements and planned appearances, strenuously vetted acquaintances and photo ops. The chances of, say, happening across an intriguing woman in a shadowy corner were nearly nil.

Yet here he was. They shared an inability to be spontaneous. Just this once, he wanted to indulge in spontaneity alongside her. Maybe they *could* be two people who met at a party and had fun with no expectations.

His grin widened. This was probably the most he'd smiled without being ordered to in…a long time. "Let's do something totally impulsive, then. Dance with me."

As vigorously as she shook her head, it was a wonder it didn't roll off her neck. Brown, glossy strands floated from her hairdo, drifting down around her face. "I can't dance with you in front of all these people."

"You can so. Your dress is appropriately adjusted. You're over the age of eighteen and not married."

That was the trifecta of scandal potentials and the three he always checked off the list automatically within the first half a second in a woman's company. After his uncle had lost his Senate nomination over some risqué pictures starring a woman who was not his wife, Phillip had vowed to stay on the straight and narrow.

His career wasn't just about the election but about making a difference. Changing the world. He refused to allow his star to be snuffed out early for any reason, least of all a woman. His life was privileged, no doubt, but with that privilege came great responsibility.

"This dress doesn't have magical powers, Phillip. I'm clumsy with words *and* feet."

"You don't seem to realize that you're a successful executive who cofounded a million-dollar company. You should be out on the dance floor, intimidating the hell out of all the people here because you are Alexandra Meer and you don't care what they think."

He held out his hand. There was no way he would let her spend the night in the corner. They were going to honor her spontaneous impulse to attend this party. Of course, that was just an excuse. He couldn't help but steal a few more minutes of her company.

Alex hesitated, staring at Phillip's outstretched hand.

She'd been hiding behind the statue for a reason. Other women must have some kind of special sticky skin that allowed them to wear strapless dresses without falling out of them. Alex didn't. Dancing would make everyone else aware of it, too.

"Come on," he pleaded in his deep voice that made her shiver tonight as much as it had the first time she'd heard it. "I can't leave you back here, and if you don't dance with me, I'll be an absentee host at my own party. This is my house. It would seem weird."

Alex glanced at the very large, very ugly statue she'd taken refuge behind. "You weren't supposed to see me."

No one was; that was the point. The statue was a great place to hide but still allowed her to sort of be in the midst of things. Parties always reminded her of why she didn't attend them. Social niceties were a confusing, complex set of rules that she could never seem to follow. Alex liked rules. But only when they made sense, like in finance. Numbers were the same yesterday and today as they would be tomorrow.

Normally, she followed her own number one rule to the letter—stay out of the spotlight. But she'd developed a fierce attraction to Phillip and, well…parties seemed to be his natural habitat. Thus she had to attend one to see if things might heat up between them outside of Fyra. Because there were sparks between them, but he'd yet to make a move. She wanted to find out if his glacial pace had to do with lack of interest or something else.

Cass had bullied her into a makeover and pried Alex's credit card out of her fingers to purchase this dress. It all felt very surreal and a little like trying too hard. Alex didn't have a glamorous bone in her body, but the resulting image in her mirror had turned out pretty good, if she did say so herself.

And here she and Phillip were, flirting and having fun, and he'd just asked her to dance. This dress *did* have magical powers.

Maybe she *could* dance with him. Just once. Then she'd slink back to her hiding spot before someone else tried to talk to her. Someone who wasn't as understanding as Phillip about her permanent foot-in-mouth syndrome.

Slowly, she reached out. It was almost harder to do that than it had been to walk through Phillip's palatial double front doors, knowing he was on the other side, divinely, devastatingly handsome. Actually, just about everything she'd done in the name of advancing her relationship with Phillip had taken a huge amount of bravery.

Maybe the stars had finally aligned to alleviate the loneliness Alex had been feeling lately—a by-product of both social awkwardness and a firm belief that romance was a myth perpetuated by the retail market. She dated here and there. Not often, for obvious reasons. But she liked companionship as much as the next girl, and Phillip was the first man in a long time that she couldn't stop thinking about.

Tonight was about seeing where things might go between them.

Except, this hundred-year-old house was overwhelming— with a grand foyer the size of a public library, flanked by two curved staircases reaching toward the second floor. It was a visual reminder of his elite status and that men like him lived a whole different kind of existence, one that was ill-suited for a quiet wallflower like Alex.

But when her flesh connected with Phillip's, it was a shock to her system. Need lanced through her. *Hello. Been a long time since those muscles had a workout, yes sirree.*

Their gazes collided and his hot blue eyes spoke to her, saying without words that he wanted her, too. Well, how about that?

She let it sing through her because men never noticed her. Alex had perfected the art of fading into the background, but Phillip had never overlooked her. Her reaction was powerful and visceral.

"Alex," he murmured and tightened his grip on her hand. "We have to dance now. Otherwise, something very bad might happen."

"Like what?" she asked curiously. His gaze was on her lips as if he might lean forward at any moment and take her mouth with his.

That sounded very *good* to her.

Maybe he'd even back her up farther into the corner and do it properly. His hands were smooth and strong, and she'd fantasized about them as they'd sat through long meetings together.

It wasn't a crime. Just because she didn't buy into the fantasy about love and romance didn't mean she had an aversion to sex.

She'd been dreaming of kissing him for weeks, ever since the first time he'd walked into Fyra. The sparks between them had been instant and deliciously hot. And their connection was more than just physical. He was thoughtful, well-spoken, listened to her ideas and had a wicked sense of humor. She genuinely liked him. The insane gorgeousness attached to his personality was just a big, fat bonus.

"Bad, like I might show every last person at this party to the door," he said. "And focus on no one but you."

Heat kicked up in her midsection. Oh, yes, to have all that delicious focus on her. He had this way of making her feel like the only person in the room, even when there were a hundred present.

It was an invitation. And a question. Where did she want this evening to lead?

Where did *he* want this evening to lead?

Were they on the same page about what their association might look like afterward? They were working together, after all. Not everyone could do that and become personally involved. That was where the romantics messed it all up. Relationships were black-and-white and easy to navigate as long as you didn't let yourself get bogged down in unquantifiable emotions. Her parents' divorce had been nasty enough to prove that love was one of the worst illusions ever invented.

She should probably feel him out about their future interaction before letting him do bad things to her. Also, he'd thrown this party for a reason, which would not be accomplished by allowing him to throw everyone out. It would be terrible of her to force him to end it early because she was a giant chicken about dancing in public.

More bravery needed, stat. "Let's dance."

"This way, Ms. Meer."

He led her to the dance floor and pulled her into his arms.

The crowd dynamic shifted instantly as people checked out the woman dancing with the senator. Alex's back heated with the scrutiny. The only friendly faces in the crowd were her boss, Cassandra, and Cass's fiancé, Gage, who was Phillip's cousin.

Self-consciousness turned Alex's feet into lead.

"Right here, Alex." Phillip tapped his temple and let his hand drift back to her waist. "Keep your eyes on me. Don't worry about them. They don't exist."

Ha. If only that were true. Of course, she'd had her chance to make that a reality when he'd offered to kick everyone out. She had no doubt that if she'd taken him up on his invitation, the crowd would already be in their chauffeured limousines heading for home.

Why hadn't she taken him up on it, again?

She did as instructed, locking her gaze to his molten-blue eyes. He swirled her around the hardwood floor to the tempo of the classical music piping through his expensive, invisible sound system. The crowd faded away and she became so very aware of his hands on her body, exactly as she'd envisioned them. Well, not exactly. In the majority of her fantasies, they were both naked.

Heat flushed her skin, arrowing straight to her core as he watched her closely.

"See?" he murmured. "Better."

Yes. This night, this man holding her in his arms. All better. It wasn't the dress, but *Phillip* who held the magical powers. She was someone else when she was with him, someone who didn't have to fade into the woodwork to avoid making a fool of herself. Someone who could be with a man like Phillip and it made sense, even though they were social opposites.

And she very much wanted to take advantage of the magic while it lasted. Maybe she could, just for tonight.

Two

Phillip didn't leave Alex's side all night.

It was both sweet and intoxicating. She lost all track of time and place, forgetting about the judgmental audience as Phillip had entreated her to do. He was an amazing man who made her feel special. Her starving soul ate up the attention and begged for more.

She could get used to being the center of Phillip's world. Used to how the focused glint in his blue eyes pulled on strings deep inside. Used to how her heart seemed lighter when he—

A tap on her shoulder startled her. She glanced backward. *Cass.* Alex had nearly forgotten her friend was at the party.

"Ms. Claremont." Phillip nodded to Cass without missing a beat. "My apologies for failing to tell you how stunning you look this evening. Gage is a lucky man."

"Yeah, you've been way too busy to notice me," Cass

said, tongue in cheek. "I'll be sure to let Gage make it up to me later."

Alex thought about smacking her but that would mean removing her hands from Phillip's shoulders.

"I need to borrow Alex for a minute," Cass explained, and Alex nearly sobbed as Phillip's arms dropped from around her.

Cass dragged Alex to the powder room, nodding and making nice to a couple of Hollywood types who were leaving as they walked up. The glitterati lived in a world she wasn't a part of and Alex had no idea who the glamorous women were. Cass not only knew them by name, she belonged in a roomful of beautiful people who never said the wrong thing.

Not that Alex was jealous. It was just fact. She loved the CEO of Fyra like a sister. After all, Cass had insisted on Alex taking over the financial joystick of Fyra despite full knowledge of the teenage rebellion that had landed Alex in a courtroom, staring down the barrel of jail time.

That ledger in her head would never balance. She owed Cass for taking a chance on her and she'd gladly bury herself in Fyra's numbers until the day she died, if necessary.

But that didn't mean Alex forgave the interruption.

"What was so important?" she muttered as soon as the door to the powder room closed, affording them a measure of privacy. "I was dancing."

Cass raised her perfectly penciled eyebrows. "Yes, you were. But Gage and I are ready to go."

"Already?" Alex had caught a ride with them since Gage had insisted there was plenty of room in his chauffeured town car. On the drive over, she'd been contemplating how she would get home when she sneaked out early from the party. She'd been sure attending Phillip's shindig would go down as the worst idea she'd ever had. Funny how that had turned out.

"It's midnight." Cassandra pointed at the ornate wall clock for emphasis. "We have a son who can't tell time and will be up at 6:00 a.m."

Dismayed, Alex stared at the clock, willing it to be a few hours earlier. The hands didn't change position. Why did it have to be midnight? This night should never end because in the morning, she'd go back to being invisible.

"You just hired a nanny," Alex reminded Cass with a touch of desperate logic. "Can't she get up with Robbie?"

This was a bizarre conversation. Robbie was Gage Branson's son from a previous relationship and never would Alex have taken Cass for the type to willingly enter a relationship with a single father. But she and Gage were deliriously happy. It was so optimistic of them to fall in love despite all the complications. Alex hoped they'd defy the odds and have a long, happy life together.

Cass shook her head with a laugh. "I like to get up with him when I can, since Gage and I still live in different cities for the time being. If you want to stay, just say so and catch a cab later."

That was Cassandra. A problem solver. "I can't stay."

Fyra's newest shade of lipstick appeared from the depths of Cass's sparkly bag. She slicked it over her lips and puckered before asking, "Why not?"

Because the thought of staying without the safety net of her friend induced a swirly feeling in Alex's stomach that could easily turn into full-blown panic. This was a party. The place where Alex was the least comfortable.

And while she'd danced with Phillip, she still had no idea how he intended the evening to end. What if she'd misread his signals? It wasn't like she had a lot of practice.

Then there was the soft gush inside every time he laughed

at one of her jokes or did something gallant. Those were things she could never get enough of. The fact that she liked them so much was probably the best reason of all to disentangle herself before things progressed. When a man got that far under her skin so quickly, it could only lead to trouble.

"Phillip and I have no business getting involved," Alex explained lamely.

"Honey, you and Phillip are already *involved*." Cass accompanied the word with exaggerated air quotes, an impressive feat considering she still had the tube of lipstick in her hand. "Whether you like it or not. He is the whole reason you came. You like Phillip and want to see where it goes. Right? Otherwise, why did I spend all that time coaxing you into that dress?"

Alex could hear herself being ridiculous. "I do like Phillip, but—"

"Is this about your mom again? Because, honey, she's not you. Just because your dad was a weasel doesn't mean all men are."

Alex closed her mouth. Yeah, her parents' divorce had a lot to do with her caution, but Cass never seemed to understand how deeply it had hurt Alex. How it had driven so many of her decisions, then and now. After all, Alex had a juvenile arrest record thanks to a pathetic attempt to get back at her parents for splitting up. Later, after her mom had patiently straightened Alex out, she'd realized things weren't as black-and-white as she'd assumed. That was why it never paid to get emotional over a relationship. Love was too messy and complicated.

It was much better to fade into the woodwork and focus on the numbers parading across Fyra's balance sheet.

A wave of sensation sloshed through her stomach. Definitely panic.

"Do you want to stay?" Cass asked point-blank. There was no mistaking what she was really asking.

Staying meant she was giving Phillip the green light. He'd been eyeing her all night like a gentleman, never pushing her, but it didn't take a rocket scientist to figure out that the senator wanted more than a dance. Alex was being silly even questioning that.

If it had been anyone other than Cass, she'd lie. "I do. But I'm not—"

"Yes, you are." Firmly, Cass took Alex by the shoulders. In heels, she and Cass were almost the same height. "You're making this too hard. No one is asking you to marry him. This is about right now, that man and what you want. Go after him."

Alex's insides settled a bit.

It sounded so simple. Don't worry about things she couldn't control and just enjoy the attention of a man she'd been salivating over for weeks. Don't assume he cared about anything other than sex—better yet, make it hot enough that he lost all interest in anything other than how good they could make each other feel. What would be the harm in a brief fling with a man she had a not-so-secret crush on? The magic didn't have to end at midnight.

A shiver rocked her shoulders. It had been a long time since she'd had sex that didn't require batteries, and Phillip would do just fine as reintroduction to the pleasures of a flesh-and-blood man. After all, he was a prime member of the species.

"Tell Gage I said good-night," Alex said decisively. "I have a senator to seduce."

Alex had been gone for five minutes and already a line of people had formed with Important, Pressing Matters to discuss with Phillip. One of those people was his father, whom he hadn't seen outside of Washington in over a week. Rarely did their paths cross anyway since his dad was a member of the House. They'd been discussing a secret energy project, but frankly, he couldn't concentrate on anything Congressman Robert Edgewood was saying as Phillip strained for a glimpse of the woman whose company he wasn't nearly finished enjoying.

That shimmering dress appeared in his peripheral vision. About time. A humming sense of anticipation kicked up, the same sense he'd had all evening as he immersed himself in Alexandra Meer. What had started out as a way to get to know her better had grown into something more. Something with teeth, which had clamped onto him.

He extracted himself from his dad with a very polite "Excuse me."

He drew up beside Alex, far too close. All of the other guests vanished. He tilted his head toward her ear and the scent of sweet pears made him hungry. Would it be awful if he tasted her?

He resisted. Barely. This woman had been in his arms all night, exactly what he'd needed to quit dwelling on Gina, and now he wanted Alex back against him, even if all they did was more socially approved dancing. He liked being around her, liked the way she made him feel. Of course, he'd be okay with whatever she dictated for the night's conclusion, but the sharp ache in his midsection reminded him that this woman could ease it, quite well.

"You're right," he murmured and eyed a spot he'd like to nuzzle, right along her jaw. "The mayor is a bore."

"I tried to tell you." She laughed softly, leaning into his space.

"Come with me," he said. "I have something I want to show you."

Suddenly eager to have some privacy, he led her upstairs

to a balcony that overlooked the living room. His grandfather had given him the Edgewood ancestral home in Old Preston Hollow as an engagement present with many of the original furnishings intact. An antique love seat hugged the back wall, far enough away from the wrought iron banister to hide them from prying eyes below.

Phillip had never appreciated the decor as much as he did at that moment. Hand to her back, he settled in next to her on the cushion. "You can see the whole bottom floor from here. But they can't see us."

"Handy." Then she cleared her throat. "Gage and Cass are leaving. They're my ride."

Disappointment walloped him. That sounded decidedly final. Had he misinterpreted the long heated glances? He'd just got her where he wanted her. Well, closer to where he wanted her, anyway.

"You're ditching me already?" he asked and tried to keep his voice light.

Probably for the best. What could possibly happen between them? A brief but satisfying interlude where he'd eventually have to say goodbye? A woman like Alex deserved promises he could never make. He would treat her well, of course, but if a woman got intimate with a man, she eventually wanted to fall in love and get married and have the whole heart of her mate. Phillip couldn't do that, didn't want to do that.

Gina had been enough for him. Sometimes the sadness of losing her overwhelmed him. Like it had today. Alex had distracted him and he was grateful.

But once the party ended, the cavernous house would seem even emptier. He was not looking forward to it.

Alex glanced up at him through her lashes, and her lips parted slightly. "Actually, I was wondering if you'd mind giving me a ride home. Later."

Later was a word he liked a whole lot. It held all sorts of interesting possibilities. A smile tugged at his mouth. "My car is available to you at any hour."

"Looks like the party is breaking up," she commented, and it took him a second to tear his gaze from her beautiful face to register what she meant.

He glanced down through the spindles. His living room had grown surprisingly empty. What time was it? He'd lost track of everything—the hour, his guests, the people he should have been entertaining. And now he was going to kick out the stragglers in under a minute like a bad host. Even worse, he was going to have his butler do it.

Phillip signaled to George, who'd been ushering guests out the door and coordinating with the valet. His butler had worked for the Edgewoods for over forty years, largely owing to his singular talent of being able to read minds. George nodded and began moving to the remaining groups of people, herding them toward the double front doors.

Phillip should probably care about that more. "Perfect timing, I'd say."

"I agree. I was looking forward to having you all to myself."

A current of awareness passed between them, zigzagging through his groin, waking up his body.

"Unless," she continued, "you'd rather I go?"

"Why would you think that?" It might have come out a little too forcefully.

She bit her lip, drawing it between her teeth. A habit he'd noticed she fell into when she was trying to decide what to say, not that he spent an inordinate amount of time staring at her mouth. Okay, probably more time than he should spend on it, but the meetings they'd had about the FDA approval process had been interminable and she'd been right there across the table.

"Just checking. I'm not the best at reading people."

All at once, he realized what she was fishing for.

He cupped her face. Her green eyes blazed with something warm, hopeful and slightly hungry. Even the brown dot seemed extravibrant under his scrutiny. For some reason, that sent a shaft of unadulterated desire through his gut.

"Tonight is about being spontaneous," he told her. "Neither of us is good at that. That means no expectations. Make it about what *you* want."

And he meant that seriously. If she wanted to talk all night, that was okay. Of course, he wouldn't turn down a willing woman in his bed. But he just wanted to spend time with her, realizing it was selfish. Realizing he couldn't offer her much. Realizing he should definitely aim his search for a wife of convenience in another direction.

But no expectations meant he didn't have to think about any of that, either. Not tonight.

"No expectations," she repeated and her smile grew. "I like that. I like that you get I have a hard time with being spontaneous. But I want to make it about what we *both* want. You know, assuming we both want the same thing."

His own smile widened. "I hope so."

A great, no-strings evening together. In whatever form that took.

"It won't be weird? Tomorrow? We are still working together," she reminded him. "Some people find it difficult to face each other over a boardroom table after getting naked together."

Okay, then. Now there was no question about whether they were on the same page. The burn in his loins flared hotter as he slid his hand to the back of her neck, drawing her close so he could feel for the pins.

He extracted one and let it fall. He'd been thinking

about doing that since their first moment on the dance floor. Now he could.

"Not weird," he murmured. "What happens at Phillip's house stays at Phillip's house."

With a shiver, she shook her head, loosening the pins under his questing fingers. He found them one by one, flicking them free. She tipped up her chin to pierce him with her gaze, and he fell into it as her hair rained down around her shoulders.

"Can I tell you a secret?" Her voice had gone husky.

He loved that he could affect her. "Anything."

"I sometimes lose track of the discussion in those meetings because I'm thinking about kicking everyone out and letting you kiss me. Maybe up against the table."

He groaned as that image slammed into his mind unencumbered because there was no blood left in his head to stop it. He understood her problem perfectly. "I generally lose my place because I'm thinking about what you taste like. Here."

Tracing the line of her throat starting from her ear, he slid a finger to her collarbone and replaced his finger with his mouth. Her flavor filled his senses as he fulfilled the fantasy of savoring it. Straining closer, she moaned and it was better than music.

He needed more. More contact. More music. More Alex. He drew her closer, nearly into his lap, and her dress came up over her hip as his palm gathered it. She pressed into his touch, arching into him.

And then somehow, she rolled and landed *in* his lap, straddling him. Wordlessly—because he couldn't have spoken if his life had depended on it—he cupped her rear, nestling her so their bodies aligned, and then her mouth crashed into his. The kiss ignited inside him, pounding adrenaline through his body, pumping euphoria along all his nerve endings.

More. Somehow she heard him or he communicated it telepathically because her mouth opened over his as she rolled her hips in a sensuous rhythm against the fiercest erection he'd experienced in recent memory. Maybe ever.

Heat broke over him like a blast from a detonated bomb, coalescing at the point of contact between their bodies, nearly finishing him off before they'd scarcely started. He tore his mouth from hers, panting.

"Wait," he murmured and stood with her in his arms. She clamped her legs around his waist and he stumbled to his bedroom blindly as she fastened her lips on his throat, sucking with erotic pulls that drove him insane.

"That's not the definition of *waiting*," he told her hoarsely and let her slide to the ground as he slammed the door shut with one foot.

"I'm not very patient." To prove it, she half turned and presented the zipper to her dress.

He reached out and pulled it. That glittery fabric snaked from her body and landed in a heap around her ankles as she spun back to face him. She was naked, and her high, peaked breasts called to him.

A curse worked itself loose from his mouth. "Are you trying to kill me?"

"No, I'm trying to get you into bed. Apparently I'm doing it wrong since you're still dressed."

Laughing around the raging desire clogging his throat, he stripped and scooped her up, then complied with her directive, depositing her gently on the bed. He rolled into her, and that fragrant, fruity scent encompassed him just as completely as the woman did.

"I've been fantasizing about this moment for a long time," she confessed. Her honesty tripped something inside him.

Honeyed warmth spread through his chest as they stared

at each other. This wasn't supposed to be anything other than two people connecting with no expectations. Guess that wasn't even possible with someone as unique as Alexandra Meer. She pulled things from deep inside that he'd have sworn were frozen. Things he didn't want to feel for another woman. But it was hard to shut down.

He liked her. She was smart and successful with a touch of vulnerability that set her apart from other women in his path. That had been true from the first moment he'd met her.

He might as well admit the same. "Me too."

Phillip kissed her and she slid a long, smooth leg between his, teasing, tempting and torturing all at once, and that was it. This wasn't going to happen slowly. He wanted her as badly as she seemed to want him.

He fumbled in the nightstand for some condoms he was pretty sure were still in there from the last time he'd brought a woman home maybe eight months ago. A year? He had a bad moment when he couldn't find them and then his fingers closed around one.

He tore it open and somehow got it on in one shot and then she was back in place against him, her gorgeous, sweet body aligned with his. After an eternity, he pushed inside and they joined in a clash of bodies that felt so right, Phillip could hardly stand it. She was unbelievably lush and sensuous.

They moved in a timeless rhythm that somehow became new and electrifying. She gave as much as she took and his mind drained of everything except returning the pleasure. Higher and higher they spiraled as her moans spurred him on. Their simultaneous climax was like icing on an already lip-smacking cake.

He held her quaking body tight against his as the release blasted through him. And then he couldn't let go. She smelled like pears and well-loved woman, and he craved her heat, even in the aftermath. Usually he preferred to recover on his own, but he still couldn't get enough of this amazing woman.

Sure, he'd wanted her, but sex wasn't the be-all, end-all. He'd wanted to explore the connection they'd both felt from the very first. It had been just as amazing as he'd hoped. But he'd anticipated burning off that attraction and moving on. Epic fail in that regard. He wasn't close to done and that felt like a problem.

He had to get her out of his bed before he started rehearsing a pretty speech designed to convince her to spend the night. Which was enough of a warning to scramble from the sheets. He had never *slept* with a woman other than Gina. Tonight was not the night to start.

Later, he drove Alex home in his Tesla instead of sending her with his driver, Randy, like he'd planned. He couldn't seem to let her go. The night had ended far too soon.

And though he couldn't give her everything she deserved, he didn't want to let Alex walk out of his life.

Just because they'd said no expectations didn't mean he couldn't ask to see her again. After all, he didn't really *know* what she was looking for in a relationship. How could he say what he had to offer wasn't enough if they didn't talk about it?

At the door of Alex's house just north of Dallas in University Park, he kissed her good-night and then pulled back to gorge himself on the sight of her beautiful face. Tomorrow, she'd go back to T-shirt-and-jeans Alex.

He wanted to see her again, no matter what she was wearing.

"Can I call you?" he asked hoarsely and cleared his throat. "Let me take you to dinner."

She smiled. "I'd like that."

Phillip mentally flipped through his calendar and then cursed. He'd fly to Washington tomorrow and hadn't planned to be back in Dallas for the foreseeable future. "I can't set a firm date. But please know it's not because I don't want to. I have to be in Washington. Duty calls."

"Phillip, no expectations." She cupped his face with both palms and held it. "I like spending time with you. But I'm not going to wait by the phone for you to call. I have a company to run. I'm busy, too. Call me when you're free."

A bit blindsided, he stared at her. Most women—*all* women he'd ever met—wouldn't have considered giving him a pass like that. Alex was something else. "That's very gracious."

She shrugged. "You're worth waiting for."

Something turned over in his heart. This was crazy. Instead of exploring their attraction and getting it out of their systems, he was trying to figure out how to juggle his schedule so he could see her again. He should be running back to his car and driving away very fast in pursuit of someone who was much better suited to being the wife he needed.

The wife he needed would understand he couldn't be disloyal to Gina. The wife he needed would stand by his side as he navigated the Washington social scene, wearing couture and cosmetics with ease. The wife he needed would understand that his career might require sacrifices to her own career.

Above all, the wife he needed would not generate all of these unexpected, confusing emotions. Alex was not what he needed.

His career was everything to him. It had saved him from drowning in grief two years ago, and with his eye on the White House, Alex would only complicate his life. No, she wasn't what he needed—but she was everything he wanted. And that made her very dangerous indeed.

Three

Four weeks later...

The packaging on the pregnancy test was too slick for Alex's shaking fingers to grip. Gracelessly, she stuck the end in her mouth and tore it open. The slim stick fell out and tumbled end over end into the toilet bowl with a splash. Of course.

This was surreal. The walls of the company she'd co-founded surrounded her. Fyra was a multimillion-dollar cosmetics powerhouse that she'd worked tirelessly to manage alongside her friends and partners. Every single dollar of revenue and every dime of expense had passed through her fingers from day one. She was responsible for hundreds of employees' paychecks.

And she couldn't do a simple thing like open plastic packaging.

"What happened?" Cass's voice rang out from the other side of the bathroom stall.

"I'm nauseous and clumsy," Alex shot back. "The stupid test made a break for it and landed in the water."

This was not the way Alex wanted to spend her lunch break.

She was pretty sure the test would only confirm what she already knew in her heart to be the truth. The upset stomach she'd been battling for over a week had nothing to do with the seafood she'd eaten last Friday and everything to do with the night she'd spent with Phillip.

"Can you get it out?"

"I'm working on it."

Liar. Staring at the little white stick down in the water wasn't solving the problem. Alex thought about just flushing the thing and avoiding the whole question of why no amount of prayer had started her skipped period. She and Phillip had used protection. This wasn't supposed to be happening.

"Just pee in the toilet," Cass suggested. "You don't have to be holding the stick for it to work."

Alex sighed and gave in to the inevitable. "Fine. It's done. Now, how long do I have to wait?"

"I don't know." Cass rustled the paper instructions she'd been holding when Alex had locked herself in the bathroom stall. "Three minutes."

Might as well be three hours. Alex shredded her nails in under a minute and a half, not that it mattered. No one was looking at her nails. Phillip had gone back to Washington the day after his party, as promised, and they'd conversed a few times via email. He'd called twice to say hi, but so far, they hadn't connected for dinner. She wasn't upset. He'd let her know when he was free and that obviously hadn't happened yet.

It was exactly what she'd signed up for. A night of passion with an amazing man who paid attention to her. She still dreamed about the way his mouth felt on hers and how gorgeous that man's body was. Sure, she'd have liked to see him again, but that might mean having a conversation about what dating meant for them and she didn't want to ruin the magic with real-life fears and hang-ups.

If the test came back positive, they'd be having a hell of a conversation about dates, that was for sure. Due dates, birth dates, playdates. It was mind-boggling.

She peered into the toilet. Nothing. Or maybe something. Did the results window look a little pink? Her stomach flipped over and back again. "What do the instructions say about how to read this test? What does it mean if it's pink?"

She'd read them herself but panic drove the information from her brain.

"One pink line is not pregnant. Two pink lines is pregnant. You've *never* taken a pregnancy test before?" Cass didn't bother to keep the incredulity from her tone. "Not even in college?"

"No," Alex muttered. "You'd have to have sex to need one."

She'd been just as awkward and clumsy in college as she was now. Men shied away, for the most part. Phillip was a rare exception.

Please, God, do not let that exception have irreversible consequences.

More pink bled into the window. A distinct line appeared. *One* line. That meant not pregnant. Except the pink was still wicking through the window, spreading its impersonal message about huge, life-alerting events.

"Why are you making me do this?"

"Because you clearly weren't ever going to do it yourself. It's been four weeks since Phillip's party," Cass reminded her, as if she needed reminding. "If you are pregnant, you're a third of the way through the first trimester. Denial is not a good health-care plan for you or a baby."

Baby. Oh, God. Alex had staunchly refused to even think that word. And then…a second line appeared in the window, pink and vivid and final.

"Hand me the second test," Alex demanded hoarsely. She'd wondered why they'd included two. Obviously so people in her position could make absolutely sure.

Cass did so without comment and they waited in silence for the second confirmation.

"How accurate are these things?" Alex whispered, as again, two pink lines materialized in the window.

"Pretty accurate," Cass confirmed. "Sometimes it says you're not pregnant when you really are because you've taken the test too early. But if it says you *are* pregnant, that's like 100 percent. I'm guessing it was positive. Both times."

And now it was a reality, an undeniable, unfixable reality.

Alex was pregnant with Senator Phillip Edgewood's baby.

Flipping the latch to unlock the wide door, she stumbled from the bathroom stall—how, she didn't know, when everything was numb. Except her mind, of course. That was on full speed in a Tilt-a-Whirl of thoughts, none of which were cohesive.

She was going to be a mom. A life was growing inside her through the miracle of procreation. It hardly seemed possible.

Cass took one look at Alex's face and engulfed her in a hug, holding her tight as if the sheer pressure might keep Alex together. "It'll be okay."

"How?" Alex mumbled into Cass's shoulder. "How will it be okay?"

She was going to be a *mom*. The idea terrified her. Deep inside, she knew she could do it. She had her own mom to fall back on and look to for guidance. Alex was smart—present circumstances excluded. She had her own money and house. Maybe it *would* be okay.

Phillip. She had to go see him. For one brief, bright second she envisioned him opening the door, seeing her and breaking into a wide smile that she'd feel all the way to her toes. He'd confess he'd missed her, had been thinking about her and was glad she'd come by. She'd smile back and something meaningful would pass between them. She'd admit she'd thought about him, too. That she wished he'd called even though she knew why he hadn't.

And then she'd tell him he was going to be a father. She had no idea how he'd react. Because she didn't really know him at all.

"It's a mess." Alex pulled from Cass's embrace.

"It's a wonderful, joyous event to be celebrated amongst friends," Cass corrected brightly. "You're the first of us to get pregnant. Harper and Trinity will be thrilled."

"About what?" Harper asked as the two women in question joined Alex's nightmare right on cue. Fyra's chief science officer's red hair was down today, framing Harper's lovely face, and she'd got it cut, but Alex was too shell-shocked to comment on it.

Trinity's keen gaze zigzagged between Cass and Alex as she crossed her arms over a chic suit in a vivid shade of blue that matched the stripe coloring the right side of her dark hair. "Something's going on. Did something happen on the FDA approval front? What did Phillip say?"

His name was like a knife through Alex's heart, especially since she hadn't thought about Formula-47's FDA application one time over the past week. That was what she should have been focusing on, not her stupid crush on the man helping Fyra with the approval process.

This was the absolute worst timing. Fyra was poised to hit the billion-dollars-a-year mark in revenue with Harper's revolutionary new skin-care formula, and Alex couldn't do a simple thing like working with the senator on the FDA approval process without messing it all up.

"Phillip didn't call," she told Trinity, who she knew was chomping at the bit to get started on a new marketing campaign. "I'm pregnant."

Harper and Trinity exclaimed happily and took turns hugging her. She had her friends, if nothing else. She breathed easier.

Cass smiled and rubbed her back. "See? We'll hold your hand through it and be your village. Single women raise children all the time."

Single mom. Oh, God. She hadn't even got that far in her mind. It wasn't just a pregnancy, but a child who needed nurturing and love.

The complexities nearly knocked her knees out from under her. She'd never intended to have children, never planned to expose a helpless child to pain and suffering at the hands of adults. Her own parents' divorce had changed her, hardened her, driven her into teenage experimentation with drugs and alcohol, then ultimately a brush with the law. And now she'd done the one thing she'd sworn to never do—force a child to live with his or her parents' mistakes.

This was what happened when she threw caution to the wind.

Cass had made a broad, sweeping assumption that Alex would be handling this without Phillip, but nothing could be further from what Alex had envisioned. Babies needed a family. A father. She hadn't had one and knew that pain. Her child would have one come hell or high water.

Did Phillip even want kids? What if he would be happier washing his hands of her and the baby, perfectly fine with never seeing either of them again? How would she convince him otherwise if he hated the idea of being a dad?

And what kind of relationship would she and Phillip have? How could they be parents when they weren't even a couple? Panic sloshed through her already nauseated stomach.

"When did you become an expert on motherhood?" Alex snapped, too freaked to temper her tone.

"Since Gage got full custody of Robbie," Cass said simply. "Just because I didn't give birth to him doesn't make him any less mine. I wanted to learn."

Cass had fallen in love with a single father and thus had to become a mother in short order. Looked like Alex would be doing the same.

A horrifying thought occurred to her then.

Maybe Phillip *would* want to raise the baby...without her. Oh, God. What if he tried to use his power and influence to take the baby away for some reason? Instantly, she cradled her still-flat stomach protectively. He wouldn't do that. Would he? She bemoaned the fact that she didn't know him well enough to guess.

It didn't matter. No one was taking this baby from her. The child was equally hers and Phillip's, and they were both going to have a role in its life. Period.

No child of hers was going to grow up without a loving mother *and* father. That started by talking to Phillip about how they would manage the next eighteen-plus years together and ended with honesty. She certainly didn't need his money, but what she did need from him would require courage and fortitude to secure.

"I have to see a doctor. To confirm. And then fly to Washington," she told Cass woodenly. "I know it's the worst time to be gone, but—"

"Don't be ridiculous. Go. Take the time you need to figure out the next steps. We'll be here."

Yes. Next steps. If she took this in the logical order everything would be fine.

Trinity and Harper both nodded, throwing in their own versions of support and talking a mile a minute about nursery decor, breast-feeding and maternity fashion.

"Thanks." Alex's throat closed and she couldn't say anything else. Just as well. She needed to save her voice for the long conversation with Phillip looming in her future.

Phillip typed his electronic signature and sent the email. One thing off his growing list.

Cherry trees outside his office window had burst into full bloom in the past week. Spring was Phillip's favorite time in Washington, though he enjoyed the snowy winter, too. Winter in Dallas consisted of ice storms followed by seventy-degree days. The ups and downs were maddening.

He wished his grandfather agreed. The man had spent years and years living in DC while he'd held office, but as his health declined, Max Edgewood preferred to stay in Dallas. It was the one reason Phillip commuted back and forth as much as he did; he loved his grandfather and gladly split his time between the two cities. He didn't like to think about how few days Max might have left on this earth.

In fact, they were overdue for a visit. He should go home soon. Except he was avoiding Dallas.

Linda buzzed him through the phone intercom. "Senator, Ms. Meer is here."

A myriad of emotions flushed through his body at the mention of the woman he'd fled to Washington to forget.

He'd failed spectacularly at the forgetting part, but he'd been trying to at least stay away. No matter how much he'd wanted to arrange that dinner they'd discussed, they were all wrong for each other and she'd given him the perfect out by telling him to call when he was free. If he was at the Capitol, he wasn't free.

What was Alex doing in Washington? It was almost as if she'd known he couldn't stop thinking about their night together. Or, more realistically, she was here about the FDA approval process. They *were* still working together.

This wasn't the first time she'd stopped by his office. It was, however, the first time she'd come by without an appointment. It was a testament to his admin's superior mind-reading skills that she hadn't turned Alex away.

"Send her in immediately," he told Linda.

He stood as the door opened and Alex spilled into the room. Gone were the makeup and fancy clothes, replaced by her typical ponytail and jeans.

Her bare face glowed and something seized his lungs as he stared at her. She was even more beautiful without all the trappings she'd worn to his party. Breathtaking almost, as if something inside her had suddenly become illuminated.

"Hi," he greeted her inanely after a long moment of silence.

She'd stolen his ability to think simply by walking into the room. That was not supposed to happen. He'd expressly promised things wouldn't be weird between them once he knew what she looked like under that formfitting T-shirt… and he was making it weird.

"Hi," she repeated and shifted uncomfortably. "Thanks for seeing me on short notice. I'm sorry to barge in here without calling first."

"I'm glad." He smiled, feeling a bit more on even ground. "I'm happy to see you."

"You might not feel that way in a minute."

Her eyes shone with unexpected moisture and he lost his place again. This wasn't a social visit, obviously. "Is something wrong?"

"Maybe." She hesitated, biting her lip in that way that said she didn't know what to say next. "You didn't ever issue that dinner invitation."

Not here to talk business, then. The uncertainty glinting in her eyes put a cramp in his stomach.

"I'm sorry," he said sincerely and cursed himself for being such an ass. "I could give you a bunch of excuses, but none of them would be the truth. I didn't think it was fair to you to continue our relationship. So I didn't."

But he'd dreamed of things happening differently. A lot. If only he could take her in his arms and kiss her hello, like he wanted to.

"Because you got what you were after and now you're done?" she whispered.

The simple question whacked him between the eyes. He'd hurt her feelings with his stupid rules and the loneliness that had caused him to act selfishly.

"That's not it at all." True, and yet nowhere near the whole truth. He *was* done, but not for the reasons she seemed to think. He sighed. "I like you a lot, Alex, but I'm not sure we're meant to continue our affair. It's complicated. And not your fault. I wish things could be different. And not so complicated."

She choked out a laugh that sounded a bit like a sob. "Yeah, I wish that, too. Unfortunately, things are far more complicated than you could ever dream."

"What—"

"I'm pregnant."

His expression froze into place, a practiced mechanism to keep his audience from guessing his thoughts before he was ready to share them.

Pregnant.

The simple word bled through his mind and fractured into pieces as a thousand simultaneous thoughts vied for attention. *Pregnant.* It echoed, tearing through his heart painfully. The obvious question—whether she thought he was the father—clearly didn't need to be asked. She wouldn't be here otherwise.

Now would be a good time to say something. "That's an unexpected development."

Because he needed to do something with his hands, he pushed the intercom button. "Linda, can you bring Ms. Meer a bottle of water?"

Then he rounded the three-hundred-year-old desk that had been his grandfather's, gifted to Phillip when his grandfather retired, and hustled Alex to the couch where he sometimes slept when he couldn't face his lonely condo on 2nd Street. "Please. Sit down."

She complied, sinking to the couch as if her bones couldn't hold her upright any longer. He knew the feeling. Linda hurried in with the water and handed it to Alex with a friendly nod and then disappeared, as a good admin should.

"I'm sorry to blurt it out like that," Alex said solemnly and drank the water. "I don't phrase things well under the best circumstances and I'm still kind of in shock."

"I would imagine so." Blearily, he scrubbed his face with his hands and breathed deeply. For fortitude. It didn't help. "How do you feel? Okay? Do you need a paper bag? I'll get you one as long as you share it with me."

She flashed a brief smile. "Are you having sympathy morning sickness?"

"No, I was thinking about breathing into it." Because he felt like he might pass out. "It's my baby, right?"

"Yeah." Her smile disappeared. "I'm not all that good at luring men into bed. Look how long it took for me to get you there. But we can do a paternity test while I'm here, if you want."

The sooner, the better. He trusted Alex, but he couldn't afford mistakes.

This could *not* be happening. Phillip had lived his life carefully for nearly two decades. Even as a teenager, he'd been mindful that political aspirations could die easily with the wrong decisions, and he'd never had a reason to conceal his actions. While other politicians paid off former mistresses and employed spin doctors to get them out of hot water with the media, Phillip preferred honesty—after all, if you never did anything questionable, you didn't have to cover it up.

This was all his fault. The condoms must have been older than he'd remembered. And now they'd both pay the price.

Pregnant. Alex was pregnant.

He couldn't repeat it enough times for it to stick in his brain as a fact, like the way he knew the sky was blue without looking at it. Alex was a great person, a businesswoman he was helping navigate the bureaucracy of the FDA approval process. Thinking of her like that was easy. She was also a sexy woman whose company he'd enjoyed at a party a few weeks ago.

And now she had a third designation: the mother of his child.

It changed everything.

They had to get married. His heart squeezed painfully once, and he shut it down ruthlessly. There was so much more to consider here than how he'd always thought he'd have a baby with Gina. So much more to consider than Alex's lack of credentials as the perfect wife to fit his needs.

If he planned to be honest with his constituents, there was no other solution than to surround Alex, his child and his career with the protection of marriage. No man with Phillip's political platform could ascend to the Oval Office with an illegitimate child any sooner than he could as a single man. The press would eat him alive, gleefully portraying his family values as hypocrisy.

Except all he could think about was Alex spread out on his bed, underneath him, as he made love to her. What would it be like to wake up to her in the morning? He couldn't lie to himself any more than he could to his supporters; marrying her meant they could continue that part of their relationship.

The pregnancy meant he could have Alex and keep his emotional commitment to Gina, because of course Alex wouldn't expect him to be in love with her. He could raise his baby with his child's mother. The rest of the complications were a huge compromise, but one he was willing to make for the benefits.

He had no clue whether Alex would marry him under those conditions, but he had to try to convince her.

She cleared her throat. "We need to talk about next steps."

"Agreed." His mind raced through his calendar, rearranging appointments and projects. He could carve out time for the flurry of activity that was about to become both their realities. He had to. "My mother will want to plan a huge splashy ceremony, but I can probably talk her off the ledge if you'd rather have something a bit simpler."

His parents would be thrilled he'd finally moved on. His mom had bemoaned never having grandkids twice a week for over a year, and at least this development would make her happy.

She stared at him. "Your mother will want to have a ceremony to announce the pregnancy? Don't take this the wrong way, but that's very strange."

Flubbed that up, moron.

When he'd asked Gina to marry him he'd gone the distance with a surprise trip to Venice, a hired violinist and a ten-carat diamond that had once belonged to a Vanderbilt. But he'd had considerably longer than ten minutes to plan it and a huge gaping hole in his life that only Gina could fill.

Yet he was about to start a family with Alex instead. Yes, he liked her, but the biggest decision he'd thought he had in relation to her was whether he'd break his promise to himself about not calling her. It was numbing how quickly everything had turned on its head.

This woman was going to be his wife if he had anything to say about it. He needed to start acting like it.

"I'm sorry. Let's back up." He took her hand and held it, though why he thought that small bit of contact would help, he couldn't say. "Alex, we have to get married."

And that wasn't much better as proposals went.

Her face went white and she snatched her hand away from his as if he'd scalded her. "Married? Why would we get married? That's insane. We don't know each other."

The note of desperation in her voice didn't sit well. "We don't know each other well enough to be parents either, but facts are facts. As the baby's father, I want to consider what's best for him or her. Unless the paternity-test results might offer another reason for your denial?"

Something broke open inside him as he thought about Alex with another man. Irrational, to be sure, especially since he was the one who hadn't called. He didn't own her.

But he had never stopped thinking about her, or her sweet fire as they'd connected—her skin, her eyes, all of it. He wouldn't apologize for having a strong attraction to a woman who'd just announced she was carrying his child, nor for the fact that marriage meant he was the only one allowed the privilege of sleeping with her. Fidelity was as much a part of his makeup as statesmanship. There was no denying that she still affected him, and if they were living together, it was a natural conclusion that they'd continue their physical relationship. He certainly wanted to.

"No, of course not," she said. "This is your baby."

In DC, the first thing you learned was how to tell if someone was lying. She wasn't. Regardless, he needed to make sure. The test could be done relatively quickly and would only confirm what he already knew in his gut.

"Here's what we're going to do." The plan rolled through his head. "I'll clear my schedule for the day and we'll get the test. Then will you agree to talk about what comes next?"

Hesitating, she blinked and met his gaze, vulnerability and fear in her expression. It prompted him to fix whatever was wrong so she'd smile again. He ached to take her into his arms. For comfort, not to kiss her, though he'd have sworn a minute ago that sparks were the only thing between them.

Even that was too much.

The way Alex affected him clashed with the place inside that belonged to his first wife. That unsettled him nearly as much as the idea of Alex being pregnant. But if he wanted to have a family—and he did—not only would he have to convince Alex marriage was the best option, he would have to convince himself to stay strong against the tide of emotions she elicited.

No second chances in life or love. That meant he would never have feelings for another woman. This compromise might be harder than he'd envisioned.

"Okay," she said, her voice low. "We can talk. But you'll

have to rethink the idea of marriage. I'm not a member of the cult of love and romance."

She wasn't? He stared at her as his argument for marriage shifted gears and fell into place.

Four

The results of the paternity test didn't take long. With Phillip's connections, he had paperwork in his hand before lunch proving the baby Alex carried was 100 percent his.

Like she'd told him. It stung a little to hear him question her, as if Alex might have tried to pass off another man's baby as his. Who *did* something like that?

Okay, it stung a lot. But she tried not to fume about it as Phillip's driver navigated the enormous limousine through Washington, DC, traffic. Her baby's father sat next to her on the long bench seat, still clutching the results from the private physician's office they'd visited to perform the test.

"Are you hungry?" Phillip asked, his tone polite but distant, as it had been since the moment she'd uttered the word *pregnant*.

She secretly called it his Senator Mask, and she'd noted he pulled it on when the circumstances dictated he be tolerant and friendly without inviting too much familiarity.

He'd put on the mask in meetings and at the party a couple of times but always toward others. She'd never thought he'd direct it at her.

"I don't think I could eat, no," she murmured. Her stomach wasn't in any condition to accept food and not just because of the morning sickness that should be renamed *24/7 sickness*. "But if you want to find a quiet restaurant where we can talk, you're welcome to eat. I wouldn't mind a cup of hot tea."

It was time to make some decisions. Unfortunately, she feared neither of them liked the choices all that well. And she had a feeling the subject of marriage was about to come up again.

Alex and Phillip were not getting married under any circumstances. Marriage was for other people, foolish people who believed love could last forever. Who believed in happily-ever-after. There was nothing he could say to convince her. Besides, marriage didn't make any sense.

"Maybe we should drive around. This car is about as private as it gets." Flashing her a distracted smile, Phillip hit the intercom to speak to the driver. "Randy, would you mind stopping at the next Starbucks and purchasing Ms. Meer a cup of hot tea?"

Something squished in her chest. The man never missed a trick. Alex found herself returning his smile even though his wasn't the genuine one she preferred. How was it possible that pregnancy could drive such a wedge between them? They were still the same people as the night of the party. They'd shared jokes and laughed, and he'd looked at her like she was the only person in the room he cared about.

Since that type of attention had got her in this situation, maybe it was better that he wasn't flirting with her. She missed it, though.

Phillip's driver whipped into a parking lot, and with the efficiency she'd come to expect from Phillip's staff, he handed her a white to-go cup before she'd barely registered that he'd stopped. She nodded her thanks.

Hot tea in hand, she stared out the window at the bustling city her baby's father called home for much of the year. Might as well jump right into it. "Before you start talking about marriage again, just know that I can't even consider it. Marriage doesn't work under the best of circumstances, let alone the worst."

He contemplated her as he pulled a water bottle from a hidden compartment on his left side. Did the lavishness at Phillip's disposal ever end? Alex made a healthy salary, but she rarely spent money on more than necessities. Phillip came from old oil money and his wealth far eclipsed hers. The imbalance had never seemed all that important before, but in the face of making decisions about things like custody, lifestyles, nannies and public schools versus private, the gulf between them widened.

"As long as we're sharing philosophies," Phillip said, "let me tell you something about mine."

He wasn't looking at the traffic. His focus was solely on her and it tripped her pulse.

"Sure."

"I can't remember a time when I wasn't aware that my family had something unique about it. Adults in my world discussed important issues at the dinner table. We went to rallies and talked to farmers, industrial workers, bankers and moms during cross-country trips. I was fascinated by the activity. I learned more about the daily life and burdens of the average American before the age of ten than most people are probably ever aware of."

"You were born into a political dynasty, Phillip," she interjected in the pause. "I get that."

He nodded. "You met my father, the congressman. My grandfather was a senator and so was my uncle. It's in our blood to care about making things better for our country."

Oddly enough, the more Phillip talked about his job, the more quickly his Senator Mask faded. It was a little breathtaking to watch him morph back into the man who had so charmed her from their first meeting and nearly every second since then.

She didn't dare interrupt. This was the Phillip she'd dreamed about. The one she'd gladly donned makeup and a dress to get closer to. Her pregnancy didn't erase his magnetic appeal in the slightest.

"So now I'm going to have a son or daughter," he continued. "I always envisioned my kids having a similar childhood to the one that solidified my path."

That implied he planned to have more kids. That sounded nice—for *him*—but she wasn't concerned about children that didn't exist yet. Only the one that did. "I'm sorry, but—"

"Wait." He shushed her gently. "I'm getting to the important part. I married Gina with my heart and eyes wide-open. We were going to have that life I just described and then she was gone. It was a single-car accident and no one could say for sure what had happened other than a telephone pole in the wrong place. The devastation... I can't go through that again. So I'm not a fan of marriage, either. At least not the kind of marriage I had with her."

"There's another kind?" Alex blurted out before she thought better of it.

She'd been caught up in watching his face as he talked about his first wife. The emotions were heartbreaking. What would it be like to be married to a man who loved you that much? Up until this moment, she hadn't realized it was possible to love someone so much that even the distance of two years wouldn't fully dull the pain of losing them.

Obviously Phillip was the exception to the rule that love didn't last.

"There are all kinds of marriages," Phillip said. "That's why you can't say for sure that no marriages work."

Was that where he was going with this? "Sure I can. I didn't have a fairy-tale childhood like yours. I lived through a really bad divorce and it doesn't matter what kind of marriage my parents had because the ultimate result was that it ended. Just like yours did. That's why marriages don't work, because when they end, people get hurt. That's why a marriage between *us* wouldn't work."

"Not if we do it differently," he suggested calmly, despite her rising agitation. "Hear me out."

Genuine curiosity got the better of her. If he'd spouted romantic poetry or autocratic demands, she'd order him to stop the car. But logic? The man couldn't have picked a better way to get her attention. "Okay. I'll bite. What kind of marriage could we possibly have that would work, Phillip?"

"One based on partnership. We're about to become parents. I'd like to raise our child together, without shuttling him or her between us. I want us to be on the same page about things like discipline. I want to celebrate holidays together. Share milestones. I think that's best accomplished by being a unit."

His deep voice slid along her skin as he wove a picture with words. A picture that dug into the core of her hurt and disappointment about her parents' divorce and promised that her child wouldn't have to endure what she had.

It was fool's gold, though. All the things he talked about depended on their commitment to each other never dying. It depended on no one changing their mind at some point down the road and ripping out the heart of the family that they'd built.

"But we don't have to be married to make parenting decisions together," she said. "And if we're not married, we never have to go through a divorce."

No marriage meant no one got hurt. No child of hers would ever have to be the product of a broken home.

But the line she'd just drawn might also mean her child wouldn't get to know his or her father, not like she'd envisioned. She couldn't have it both ways.

If she and Phillip didn't live in the same house, how would Christmas morning work? They'd have to split custody and explain that Santa came to two houses for some children. But she would always feel that something wasn't quite right. And the arrangements might mean that some years, she wouldn't even have her child with her on Christmas morning. Or a random Tuesday when her child took his or her first steps. The first day of school, learning to ride a bike—the list went on and on.

There were thousands of things she might miss if she and Phillip set up a custody agreement. Things he would miss. The baby was half his, no matter what, and she wanted her baby to have a father. A *present* father, not one that swooped in on weekends.

Panic fluttered her pulse. How in the world had she got here?

"Or..." He reached out then and captured her hand, threading his fingers through hers. "We have a marriage with no expectations other than divorce isn't an option."

No expectations.

It was an intentional echo of their singular night together, when passion had been the only thing that mattered.

Her gaze flew to his, caught and held. His blue eyes were mesmerizing as he tilted his head slightly and let that smile she loved spill over his face. Breath tangled in her lungs as he brushed her thumb with his.

"Tell me what a marriage with no expectations looks like," she murmured because her throat had gone completely dry.

"It means we take love out of the equation. That's what causes all the hurt. The loss of it is what drives people to end things. If we start out as friends and partners with no expectations of anything more, we can have the kind of marriage that lasts. Then divorce doesn't even come up."

The logic flowed over Alex like a balm. She'd never understood the hoopla over moonlight and candles, but Phillip had figured out how to romance her with reason. It was extremely affecting.

"I like you," Phillip continued, his smile deepening. "And I think you like me. We're obviously a match in the bedroom, which not even couples in love can always say. If we establish some ground rules from the beginning, no one gets hurt. We're just two people raising a child and living our lives together."

Rules for marriage. How…safe. And clear. She did like rules.

Never in a million years had she imagined he'd find a way to get her to consider this insane idea. But here she was…thinking about matrimony. His point made a brilliant sort of sense. Her baby would have a father. She'd never have to miss a thing.

Somehow, she'd found a man who didn't have one single emotional demand. She'd have someone by her side to help raise the baby, and they'd have a deal up front to stay together. No one was making any promises they couldn't keep.

"So no expectations." She rolled it around in her head.

"You don't care if we never fall in love? Because I don't even know if I have that capacity. Nor the desire."

Since she'd never even come close to feeling giggly and romantic about a man, she'd always assumed she didn't have the right temperament for it.

He was quiet for a moment. "It's not that I don't care. It's that I don't want to be in love with anyone other than Gina. Most women wouldn't put up with that in a marriage. Fortunately for me, you're not most women."

It should have been the final argument that won her over. She'd never have to question whether love would become a factor in their relationship because his heart wasn't available. But something wasn't adding up here.

"Just out of curiosity, why marriage, then? Why don't we just live together?"

"Simple." He shrugged. "I don't want to. It serves many purposes to marry you. I'm a senator. Marriage is something my constituents would expect. I believe in family values, which will be a central part of my platform when I run for president."

"President? Of the United States?" Her voice might have gone up a full octave but she couldn't tell for sure around the sudden rush of blood from her head. "When were you going to tell me that part?"

She couldn't be the First Lady. She didn't have the flair for it. Or the ability to talk to the press. She'd rather eat bugs than have that kind of attention dogging her for the rest of her life.

"I'm telling you now," he said calmly and squeezed her hand. "Because that's an important part of this discussion. I'm running for president within the next few years and it would greatly benefit my campaign if I was married. My child is going to be in the spotlight no matter what. My child's mother is going to be a subject of interest. If you'd like to weather that on your own, I can't decide that for you. But marriage affords you a measure of protection, especially as I'm campaigning and definitely if I win."

More logic. And it made a certain sort of sense. Enough to deepen her panic. "I can't be a politician's wife! I can barely talk to you, let alone the press."

There would be no hiding behind a statue for the rest of her life if she married Phillip. Her stomach turned over as the limo made another loop around the Washington Monument.

"I have people who can help with that, Alex. Stylists. Speech writers." He cupped her chin, and his fingers on her face soothed her as she stared at his earnest expression. "I like you the way you are, but if it would make you more comfortable to have more polish as you stand by my side at a press conference, okay. I'll help you with that."

Mute, she stared at him. No expectation for Alex to morph into the perfect politician's wife, either? Part of her was grateful and wanted to respond to such grace positively. Of course she'd try not to embarrass him. Why wouldn't she?

The other part of her was a bit suspicious. "I don't have to dress up if I don't feel like it?"

"The only thing you need to worry about is whether you want to do this with me. Whether you want our child to have the life I've been describing."

Oh, no, there was so much more to consider. Speaking of which, would she have to live in Washington if they got married? What about her career? "What about my company? I have a job. I can't walk off and leave it."

Fyra was everything to her. Surely he wasn't saying she needed to give it up. Not only did she owe Cass for giving her a chance, she loved her job.

"That could be a challenge. I won't lie. But we'll figure something out. We have to," he said.

"It's not the life either of us imagined," he continued. "It's not going to be easy. But it will be worth it for our baby and for us personally. We'll be doing it together. As partners operating under an up-front agreement but also as friends. Like we've been all along."

His smooth voice drew her in, convincing her. She might have to do some things she didn't like, but the rewards for their child would outweigh her discomfort.

And there were other potential benefits she couldn't help but wonder about.

"What about sharing a bedroom?" she murmured, and the temperature in the close confines of the limo shot up instantly as they watched each other, the question hanging between them.

"Ah, now, that's the part of this discussion I was waiting for." He tilted his head a touch closer. Almost within kissing distance. "I'm in favor of whatever you decide. But I would have a very difficult time keeping my hands off you behind closed doors. Even if we didn't share a bedroom."

"Really?" That hummed through her pleasantly. Did Phillip find her that attractive? There was something delicious about being wanted, especially by a man like Phillip. He'd rocked her with his careful attention, both in and out of bed. Imagine if that continued.

"Oh, are you confused about that?"

Without warning, he pulled her forward, almost hauling her into his lap. His mouth hit hers in a searing kiss that spoke of his desire far more clearly than words ever could.

The promise bled through his fingers, into her skin, heating her as she fell into this kiss. As her senses exploded with Phillip. He kissed her masterfully, purposefully.

When he pulled back, she nearly wept.

"I'd like an intimate marriage in every sense of the word," he rasped, clearly as affected as she was.

She'd wished for something to fill the void in her life—perhaps she'd found it. She just couldn't help but think she'd bitten off more than she could chew.

"With the exception of love," she reminded him. Just to reiterate the ground rules.

"Right. I had that once and I'm not a believer in second chances."

That was a hard line to take. Second chances were sometimes the only thing standing between a person and the rest of her life. Without a second chance, Alex wouldn't have been afforded the opportunity to start over after nearly ruining her life.

What if he didn't like the fact that she'd needed a second chance? That had to be hashed out now, not later.

Nodding once, she took a deep breath. "Then there's something you need to know before you make a final decision about marrying me. You could find this out for yourself with your connections. But I want you to hear it from me. When I was fifteen, I was arrested and convicted of theft. I got probation and my record was sealed. But the media might find a way to dig it up if my husband is running for president. I thought you should know."

Phillip's expression didn't change. "Is that the extent of your record?"

"Yes." Because it was the only crime she'd got caught doing. Not because it was the only illegal thing she'd ever done.

"I'll get my publicist on it immediately. If we talk about it up front, we can play it off as youthful indiscretion. This is exactly why marriage is important for you, too. If I can forgive it, the world can, too."

He made all of this sound too easy. She had a feeling

he'd knock down any argument she threw out because he'd decided what he wanted and planned to wear her down until she accepted the inevitable. "I never really had a choice about marrying you, did I?"

He flashed a grin. "Of course you do. Would you like some time to think about it?"

No, they could debate this to death or get started on the rest of their lives. "Where do I sign?"

That got a genuine laugh out of him. "We can let our lawyers handle that. In the meantime, we have a wedding to plan."

The idea exhausted her. Other women must love that kind of thing, but a wedding? How fancy did it have to be? Maybe they could elope. "I'd rather eat some toast and take a nap. Don't you have people who can handle a wedding?"

His eyes glowed as he smiled. "Absolutely, if that's your preference. Let me take care of everything. You pick out a dress and show up."

That sounded so nice. No picking out floral arrangements and visiting venues for the reception? Senator Edgewood had her vote. He really was making this easy on her.

She had a feeling that might not last. Especially since she had a suspicion he'd glossed over every single one of her objections for a yet-to-be-established reason. He needed her. Why remained to be seen.

Music rang out in the sanctuary, signaling the start of the ceremony. Phillip trained his eyes on the double doors at the rear of the Methodist church north of downtown Dallas where his parents had been members for thirty years. He hadn't seen Alex in over a week and for some odd reason it had put a hitch in his stride.

This wedding served a purpose. It wasn't supposed to be sentimental. Or emotional. It was a compromise. He and Alex had a deal to be partners in raising their child and they'd agreed it made sense to be legally married. She was okay with the fact that he wanted to stay loyal to his love for Gina. He was okay with her lack of social skills.

Nerves shouldn't be a factor. But as he waited for his bride to make an appearance, he couldn't call this jumpiness under his skin anything but nerves.

In the next few moments, Alexandra Meer would officially become Mrs. Edgewood. Not only was she about to become his wife, in less than seven months they'd be parents. It was mind-boggling.

The doors burst open and the first woman in lilac solemnly paraded toward him. Dr. Harper Livingston, the genius scientist behind Formula-47, the product for which Alex's company needed FDA approval, was followed by a second woman in lilac. Trinity Forrester, Fyra's chief marketing officer, cut quite a figure with her angular black hair and stilettos. CEO Cassandra Claremont glided down the aisle next, her gaze fastened firmly on the man to Phillip's right, her fiancé, Gage Branson. Gage had been the only person Phillip would have asked to be his best man, considering his cousin was the one who had introduced him to Alex.

In a marriage based on appearances, no detail was too small.

And then Alex walked into the room and his heart thumped once, then paused for the longest, strangest skipped beat.

Alex had selected white for the occasion, but the minimalist design allowed the woman to shine through. Phillip couldn't tear his gaze from her beautiful face, which had the lightest smattering of color in deference to the photographs that would be taken later. The uncharacteristic makeup only enhanced the natural beauty of the woman he had somehow convinced to marry him.

He still didn't know what had tipped the scales. Still hadn't fully taken a deep breath until this moment, because what if she changed her mind? He refused to consider any of this an emotional investment. He needed a wife, and it would be twice as difficult to find one willing to step into a marriage of convenience after the press finished crucifying him over his purported family values while his illegitimate child lived with a single mom.

Five hundred guests, ranging from the United States secretary of state, to a French hotel magnate, to Alex's mom, watched as Alex floated down the aisle toward him. She reached his side and he took her hand. She was trembling.

"You okay?" he whispered as the minister started the dearly-beloveds. Instantly, all thoughts of plans and campaigns and ground rules vanished as he focused on Alex.

"No." All the color leached out of her face, which became a remarkable match for her dress. "Will you be really mad at me if I throw up on that suit?"

Morning sickness was taking a huge toll on her, which was part of the reason they hadn't seen each other—she'd been too ill to fly and he'd had to burn the midnight oil in Washington in order to take off a few days for the wedding.

"Well, it's not what I'd envisioned for our vows," he acknowledged wryly. "But perhaps appropriate under the circumstances."

"Don't make me laugh," she muttered as a smile tugged at her mouth. "I'm trying to keep down the four bites of toast I had for breakfast. Remind me again why we couldn't elope?"

The minister launched into a series of lines that Phillip's mother had painstakingly selected after being given the job. Their immediate family and close friends knew Alex was pregnant, but they'd kept it secret otherwise. At only ten weeks, she wasn't showing yet, so there was no reason to eclipse the wedding with baby news.

"Because," Phillip said out of the side of his mouth. "Pomp and circumstance are part of the deal."

She moaned. "I don't see how it's fair that I have to both carry the baby and smile at guests."

"I'll tell you what. After the birth, I'll carry the baby. How's that for fair?"

The minister cleared his throat. Phillip glanced back at the man, having completely lost track of the ceremony. "I do."

Nodding, the minister repeated the questions to Alex, who also said, "I do," and after sliding their respective rings on each other's third fingers, it was done. They were married with none of the emotion of the first time he'd done this.

It was a relief. Alex had distracted him from thinking about Gina from the moment she'd appeared, and he was oddly grateful for her good humor in the face of not feeling well. He'd thought this day would be difficult to get through, but Alex had turned that on its head by holding a conversation during the ceremony.

No expectations. It was a strange mantra for marriage, but for an unconventional agreement like theirs, it worked. So far.

"Is it okay if I kiss you?" Phillip whispered in case she didn't want anyone else to know her stomach was upset.

She scowled. "Of course. It would seem weird if you didn't."

But then it was weird anyway because five hundred people were watching. Would they know this marriage wasn't a loving union? That was one aspect he and Alex hadn't discussed—if they were going to act like a traditional married couple in front of others.

Since there was no time to chat about it, he turned her away from the crowd so they had a measure of privacy.

When he cupped her face, she smiled and it filled him from the inside out. Suddenly, it didn't matter who was watching. He kissed her and she opened underneath his mouth. For a moment, he soaked in the perfection of how this woman he'd just married fit against him.

He hugged her deeper into his embrace and let the one part of himself that wasn't off-limits to her have free rein. His body reacted like it always did whenever Alex got within a few feet. Which wasn't necessarily appropriate for a crowded church, any more so than it had been for a crowded party. There was no giant statue here, so he reluctantly let her go to the sound of applause and swelling music.

Breathlessly, she regained her balance, her lips red and bare of lipstick. Funny, he'd got to the point where he preferred her without makeup now that he had a basis for comparison.

Phillip took his bride's hand and they walked down the aisle together as husband and wife. With the wedding out of the way, it was all downhill from here.

Five

Phillip couldn't concentrate on the guests he'd invited to the reception.

Alex had invited some friends and family but the majority of the guest list consisted of movers and shakers from around the globe: people who benefited his future campaign for the White House. People he owed favors to for previous campaigns. People he knew from Congress. Old friends of his parents, who happened to own most of Dallas. Every one of the attendees on his guest list had significant power and influence.

This wedding wasn't a joyous celebration of the union between two lovers, like the one he'd shared with Gina, but a carefully orchestrated event designed for a future presidential campaign. He had to think about it that way, or he wouldn't get through it. Or at least that had been the plan.

But instead, all Phillip could think about was his new wife, who had fled to the bathroom almost thirty minutes ago. She'd been trailed by three women in lilac, so he knew she was in good hands. But not *one* of them could be bothered to take two minutes and bring him word that Alex was okay?

He was worried about her. The baby was half his and he couldn't carry it, but he could at least be there to help ease Alex's discomfort. Get her water or *something*. Why hadn't she asked for him?

Senator Galindo breezed by with her husband, the CEO of a telecommunications company. They chatted for a moment and then Alex joined their group, a small smile in place.

Finally, he could assess her condition for himself. Make sure she didn't need to go home and lie down. She looked so uncomfortable that his heart twisted. He hated that she felt this awful at what was supposed to be their debut as a couple.

Not much point in marrying a wife to stand by his side who wasn't able to, or at least that was what he tried to tell himself. Sternly. But he didn't care about the loss of his plus one at a key networking event when his wife's face was tinted a hue best suited for frogs.

"Alex, I don't think you've met Senator Ramona Galindo." Phillip forced himself through the niceties of introductions all around, even though Alex's distress was clear. But he didn't want to be rude, and Alex wouldn't have come back from the bathroom if she wasn't okay. Would she?

Alex shook hands with the senator and her husband. "Thank you for coming."

"It was a lovely ceremony," Ramona said brightly.

"I wasn't paying attention," Alex admitted. "Also, I was up at the front, so I didn't have a great seat."

Senator Galindo chuckled nervously, clearly opting to take the comments as a joke. "I know what you mean. I remember very little about my ceremony. It went by in a blur."

That gave her husband and Phillip permission to smile through the awkwardness. Next time, maybe he should step in, smooth things over. Or not. Alex had to learn to navigate his world in her own way. He'd offered help and it was up to her to take him up on it.

Phillip bent his head toward Alex to murmur in her ear. "Feeling better?"

Her hair had been twisted into a curly fountain at her crown. With the curve of her neck exposed, the style lent her an elegance he liked. When Alex went all out, she was breathtaking. It was probably a good thing she didn't do it very often because he was having a hard time remembering all the reasons this marriage should be cold and clinical.

"Not really," she whispered back. "How soon can we leave?"

They'd talked about the importance of the reception at length and she'd agreed to the big, formal party. And he needed to treat this whole affair like a business event to keep things on an impersonal plane. But he couldn't make her stay if she wasn't feeling well. "Is it that bad? I was hoping to introduce you to some people."

"I drank ginger ale, ate some crackers and lay on the divan while Cass sponged my neck with a cold cloth. Nothing helped. But I came out anyway because I thought I'd been gone too long. I know what my job is today. It's just harder than I'd expected it to be."

The pointed comment wasn't lost on him. She was trying and it wasn't her fault the pregnancy was playing havoc with her insides. "I'm sorry. I wish I could trade places with you. The morning sickness will pass soon, right?"

The band struck up the song the wedding planner had told them would be reserved for their first dance. It was a photo-worthy, crowd-pleasing moment that Alex hadn't wanted to include. She wasn't keen on the idea of being in the spotlight as they danced solo. But he'd talked her into it, just like all the other aspects of the wedding she'd balked at.

"Not soon enough." She glanced toward the band. "Aren't we supposed to be dancing?"

Alex was being such a good sport that she deserved an out if she wanted it. "We don't have to."

"Oh, but it's our wedding." She bit her lip in that way he'd come to find adorable. "I'd like to try. If you're okay with that."

The bravery in her statement hooked Phillip in a place inside that shouldn't have been affected by simple words. How did she slide right past all his internal barriers? No other woman had ever done that. Of course, he hadn't married anyone else.

Maybe the solemnity of the occasion had got to him more than he'd realized. That was probably it. The difficulty of pushing back his emotions was messing him up. But it was only fair to Alex that he didn't spend the day dwelling on Gina. What else was he supposed to do but shut down everything inside?

"Sure. But you have to tell me if you need to stop. I'd rather not make our wedding memorable for the wrong reason."

Looked like he would get to dance with his new wife after all. It shouldn't have been a big deal. He could pretend his internal turmoil had Gina's name all over it, but this dance suddenly meant something to him.

He led Alex to the dance floor, threading through the crowd of onlookers, and honestly, he couldn't pick out one single face he recognized. They all blurred together as he took his wife into his arms and held her close, swaying slowly. She nestled into his arms, closer than appropriate for the style of music. It was supposed to be a ballroom dance that would impress and dazzle. Alex had worried she wouldn't be able to perform. He'd waved her concerns aside.

Right at this moment, he didn't care what anyone thought of either of their dancing abilities. This was their wedding. Like Alex had said. They should enjoy it regardless of the compromises that had led them here, and he planned to.

He spread his hand against the silk at her back and breathed in the scent of sugary pears. It was the same fruity flavor Alex had worn the night they'd made love, and the rub of her body against his woke up the memories in a hurry. Who was he kidding? What had led them here was a completely illogical attraction.

Pulling back a bit, he watched her as something unfolded in her expression. Her color had come back, flooding her cheeks gorgeously. Gone was the slightly glassy sheen to her eyes that had been there since the ceremony.

In its place was something wholly affecting. Wholly sensual.

Her grip on his waist tightened as awareness bled through them both. There was no mistaking the rising heat in her gaze, in her bated breath, radiating from her touch. And there was no way for her to misinterpret his body's reaction to it all, not with how closely she pressed against him.

"You look stunning," he commented hoarsely, pleased his voice had worked at all.

Her smile lanced through him. "Thanks. I wanted to. For you. It took me a long time to find a dress that wasn't too fancy but was classy enough for your crowd."

"Sweetheart, in that dress, no one here is classy enough for *you*."

She laughed softly. "Flattery will get you everywhere, Senator Edgewood."

"Really? That's the most interesting statement you've made all day, Mrs. Edgewood."

He wanted to roll that name around on his tongue some more. He didn't want it to be strange. There'd been a time when he'd been sure there would never be another Mrs. Edgewood in his life. A time when he'd cried out against the reality of having to find one.

His search had ended with the woman in his arms. He couldn't have done this with someone who had romantic expectations and stars in her eyes. Or worse, a true wife of convenience who fit his criteria to the letter and had as much personality as the paper their agreement was written on.

The real question though—whether he could do this with Alex—remained to be seen.

Her brows lifted a touch. "Oh, yeah? That was better than 'I do'?"

"They were both great," he amended as he swung Alex around with a little more gusto since she seemed to have fully recovered.

The evening was looking up. A real wedding night would make all the doubt and difficulties worth it. Solidify their partnership. Give them a chance to bond over their decisions.

The crowd applauded as the number ended and other couples streamed onto the dance floor.

"Is it time to leave yet?" he echoed and drew the laugh from her he was hoping for. "I have a sudden desire to be alone with you."

And therein lay Alex's danger. Five minutes ago, he'd been focused on the business at hand. Now he couldn't think of anything but taking her home and consummating this unconventional marriage.

She was his wife and he wanted to honor that in every sense of the word.

"That's the benefit of being the bride and groom." Her face had taken on that pregnancy glow that turned her breathtaking instead of merely beautiful. "We're expected to leave early."

Well, then. Phillip hustled Alex off the dance floor and they made a round of the room to say goodbye, but it was still a good thirty minutes before they were alone in the limousine on their way back to his house—their house now—for a brief honeymoon.

The moment they settled into the limo, Phillip turned to Alex, about to draw her into his arms. His body ached to pick up where the promises made during dancing had left off.

His wife lacked polish, connections and a comfort among his set. She hated parties and dressing up. The next few months would obviously be a difficult adjustment period for them both as they struggled to find common ground, but right this minute, he didn't care about any of that. When it was just the two of them, there was only passion. Like it had been on the night that had sealed their fate, setting them on this journey together.

At last, he'd have Alex back in his bed. The one place they made sense together. Sex worked between them. He yearned to recapture that connection.

The look at her face in the dim lighting ruined that idea.

"Sorry," she gasped. "Give me a minute. I don't—"

And then she clamped her lips together, shaking her head, looking decidedly uninterested in the type of evening activities Phillip had hoped were in store.

Based on the burn of regret in his gut, it was probably

best to stay dressed and out of bed. Intimacy had only led to complications thus far. Why would tonight be any different? He'd let his guard down, forgetting how important it was to stay detached in light of their agreement.

Phillip sighed. Maybe the Rangers were playing on TV tonight.

As weddings went, Alex's had left a lot to be desired.

Of course, she'd never sat around and daydreamed about her big day the way other women did. So the disappointment was minimal. Most of it was directed at herself. Phillip's patience was legendary, but even she could see how spectacularly she'd failed at being a politician's wife.

Thank God she hadn't actually thrown up on anyone. When he'd carried her across the threshold of his house, he'd been so sweet. But clearly didn't get the concept of how movement of any kind threatened her stomach.

Finally alone in the gargantuan bathroom attached to the bedroom she and Phillip now shared, she swiped her eyeliner and mascara off. Cass would have a heart attack if she could see Alex treating her skin so casually, but Alex wanted to lie down. Immediately.

Phillip had deposited her on the same bed where they'd given in to the heat between them after his party and wandered off to "give her some privacy."

She crawled into bed, wondering if she'd put Phillip off the idea of sleeping with her entirely. Obviously sex was out for the evening—certainly not by her choice—but surely Phillip intended to use his bed. Time ticked by. The bed swallowed her, and the masculine tone of the decorations reminded her that this had been solely a man's domain for a long time.

They'd agreed to share a bedroom and she'd thought that would start tonight. Had prepared herself for it. Had reminded herself there would be a necessary adjustment period. After all of that, where was he?

Far, far away from his wife, clearly. Because she'd ruined his opportunities for campaigning at the reception? Was he *that* mad at her?

She must have fallen asleep because something startled her awake sometime later. The dark room had a hush about it that told her she was still alone. And she was wide-awake. Her stomach was strangely settled. Of course.

No better time to feel great than the middle of the night in a new house. She hadn't officially moved in until today, though movers had brought the majority of her things yesterday. Her house was on the market, and as advised by the Realtor, she'd left the furnishings to give it more appeal to buyers. It had felt so weird to leave her house behind, almost fully intact, as if she might return to it after a long vacation. But she wouldn't be returning and it was pretty unsettling to think about new people in her house.

This was her residence now. The place where she'd raise her baby alongside Phillip. The house itself was over a hundred years old with sweeping colonial accents and artwork that should be in a museum behind glass. Certainly not a style she'd have chosen. And Phillip had three servants who lived in the converted coach house fifty yards from the flagstone side porch that flanked the west wing. Definitely not something she was used to.

She glanced at the clock. 1:00 a.m. Had Phillip fallen asleep somewhere else? Since it was her house now too, if she wanted to get up and find her husband, that was her right. If any of the servants were wandering around this late, they probably wouldn't think anything of it. Would they?

She bit her lip.

The way she felt—lost, adrift, scared—had nothing to do with what the new lady of the house should be allowed to do. She missed Phillip. Marriage was new and the house was new and being pregnant was new. She needed to not be alone right now.

Throwing on a robe as she padded to the door, Alex wandered down the hall to the ornate staircase that curved to the marble floor below. Soft, hidden lighting somewhere in the recesses of the stairs guided her path as she crept to the first floor. Otherwise, the house was dark.

Except for Phillip's study. A lamp spilled a glow into the hall through the slightly ajar door. Pushing it open, she peered over the edge of the couch, which faced away from the door and overlooked a small courtyard outside the triple bay window. Phillip indeed had fallen asleep on the couch, still dressed, still sitting up against the plush cushions.

She skirted the couch and stopped short of touching him. Her hand fell to her side as she took a moment to study this man she'd married. In sleep, his handsome face had relaxed. Normally, he had this energy about him that drew her eye…and everyone else's. Charisma was a big part of his appeal, no doubt, but in this quiet moment, she could also appreciate other subtleties, like his strength, both internal and external.

She might have leaned on that a little too hard today. But the day had been difficult. Other than her mom and bridesmaids, the crush of people at the ceremony and the reception had been Phillip's guests. And every eye had been turned on her. It had been exhausting to keep up with what little conversation she had been included in.

Then, as now, she sought the one person who was supposed to be her lifeline in this deal. Whether he was annoyed at her or not, she needed the contact. He was leaving tomorrow for Washington and they'd had precious little time together as it was, thanks to her morning sickness.

Gently, she touched his shoulder. "Come to bed."

His eyelids blinked open but he didn't immediately stand. "What are you doing here?"

She flinched and tried to catch it, but she'd never been good at hiding her thoughts. And that terse comment had not been the reception she'd anticipated. "Looking for you. I was lonely and you weren't in bed."

"For a reason," he muttered. "You should go back to sleep. You're pregnant."

Hands on her hips, she scowled down at this grumpy man she scarcely recognized. "What? *Pregnant?* When were you going to tell me about this?"

A smile tugged at his lips, though he tried to fight it. "I just meant you need your rest and I didn't want to bother you. You're sleeping for two now."

"Is that why you didn't come to bed?" The light dawned then. Maybe his absence had less to do with disappointment in her and more to do with a misguided sense of sacrifice.

"Among other reasons," he returned. "Figured it was better not to tempt fate after what happened in the limo."

The look he shot her should have been lascivious, but she sensed there was something else underneath it. Something he wasn't planning to share with her. Instead of doing as he'd practically ordered and hightailing it back upstairs, she sank onto the couch next to him. "Is it weird to think of sharing a bed?"

He shrugged without looking at her. "Not weird. Different."

How selfish was she? All this time she'd been caught up in her own fears and hang-ups, never realizing he'd stumbled into some internal roadblocks, as well.

"We don't have to," she said instantly. "There's no reason to rush things."

Perhaps it would help to give them both a bit of breathing room. She could get her bearings and figure out how to stop feeling so much like she'd stepped off the edge of a cliff with no wings. He could take some time to work through…whatever was worrying him.

Silence filled the space and she glanced at him. They'd never had trouble talking before. In fact, some of her favorite memories involved deep discussions about random subjects of which they'd always seemed to have an endless supply.

Not only was Phillip grumpy tonight, but he'd added a distance into the mix that she didn't especially like.

"Hey." Impulsively, she clasped his hand. "We're supposed to be partners. If something's bothering you, we should talk about it."

She wanted things to be like they'd been before. Was that too much to ask? Had marriage actually driven them apart? If so, that was a side effect someone should have warned her about before she'd said "I do." Regardless, she'd made a deal and she'd stick to it. She just hadn't counted on it making them both miserable.

He stared down at their joined hands for so long, she thought he wasn't going to answer. But he didn't pull away, so that was something.

"You know this is where I lived with Gina, right?" he finally asked.

His first wife. He rarely talked about her other than to say they'd been very much in love, so Alex's knowledge of the woman was limited. But she would definitely like to hear more, especially if it meant she didn't have to go back to that lonely bedroom just yet.

She nodded. "It's okay. I don't mind. We both had other lives before we met."

He flashed her a brief smile of appreciation. "That's not weird for you?"

It hadn't been until he brought it up. Should she be worried about competing with a ghost? "We talked about this last week. This is your ancestral home and I had no particular attachment to mine, so…here we are. I wouldn't say it's weird, just different."

An intentional echo of his words. Clearly they both had some adjusting to do. But for the good of the baby, they were in this together, for better or worse.

"I appreciate that. And the pass on sharing a bedroom. That is something we should probably ease into. More than anything, I want to be sure you feel like you're being treated fairly."

Fair? She wasn't being forced to raise her child alone and their marriage had the best possible basis for lasting because they'd established easy-to-follow rules up front. What wasn't fair about that? "This is still new, but I certainly don't feel like I'm being taken advantage of."

"Good. It would be hard for some women to be in a marriage of convenience with no hope of having her husband fall in love with her."

They'd had this discussion once already, but that had been before they'd actually tied the knot. Now it had a sense of finality that hadn't been there before. She was living in his house, sharing his name and pregnant with his child, but she would never have a place in his heart.

Yeah, she was okay with that. Love didn't exist. Or rather, it didn't last. Except maybe it did for some people. Phillip and his first wife obviously, and probably some other people. Cass and Gage, for example. If anyone could defy the odds and have a lasting love, her money was on those two.

She frowned. So if it lasted for some people, what if it could for her and she never had the chance to find out? That was the crux of Phillip's question. What if she woke up one day in a loveless marriage and that wasn't okay anymore?

"I signed up for no expectations, Phillip," she countered with a bravado she suddenly didn't feel. "That means I'm not expecting anything more than what we agreed to."

But that didn't mean she wasn't allowed to *hope* for something more. If Phillip had loved Gina, he obviously had the capacity for it. Maybe part of *no expectations* could be taking time to explore what could happen between Alex and her husband inside of a safe agreement. No pressure. No one scouting for the exit. No idea what it would look like. Just two people taking it slow so no one got hurt.

Maybe that was the key to getting their relationship back to the way it had been before they'd got pregnant and married. Because she wanted that easy, flirtatious camaraderie back.

If love was in the cards, that was strictly a bonus.

Six

By Sunday evening, the distance Alex sensed between her and Phillip hadn't disappeared.

He spoke. He listened. Sometimes he smiled. But he'd moved some things to a bedroom down the hall, essentially kicking himself out of his own room—which only made sense, he argued, because he was going to be in Washington most of the time. He didn't touch her, even casually, and all of their conversations skated along a very practical edge. Of course they had to talk about logistics and get used to living with each other. But did it have to be so…clinical?

It was like he'd flipped a switch.

While he packed for the trip back to Washington, Alex sat in the breakfast nook adjacent to the kitchen, a spot she'd discovered by accident, but liked very well. Franka, the stout German cook Phillip employed, had welcomed Alex into the kitchen and the two women had had a couple of friendly conversations.

Which was nice. She needed a friend in this giant house, especially now that Phillip would be gone until Friday. For the time being, he planned to commute back and forth until they could enjoy a less restrictive schedule. Alex was hoping once her morning sickness wore off, she could arrange to work remotely for three weeks a month and come home to Dallas for face-to-face meetings the fourth week. She hadn't approached Cass, Trinity and Harper about it yet, but Alex didn't anticipate much resistance to the idea. Cass did something similar since Gage lived and worked in Austin.

Cass had to drive it, though. Alex's husband owned a private jet and she intended to make full use of it. Love Field was only a few miles from their house, making plane travel a bit easier than it normally would be. Being married to a man from old oil money did have its perks.

In this day and age, nearly any business task could be managed with a cell phone, an internet connection and a laptop. Except meetings with the rest of the Senate, apparently. When Phillip had told her they'd work it out, she hadn't exactly understood that she'd be the one who had to make the most sacrifices.

It's worth it, she reminded herself. The baby would have two parents and that was what mattered.

But when Phillip hunted her down to say goodbye, he brushed her cheek with his and then headed for the airport with a cool "I'll call you." Which kind of left her wondering *why* it was worth it, especially when she spent half the night in the bathroom, hugging the floor in agony. Alone.

Alone was how she did things, she reminded herself. She *liked* solitude, or at least she used to, but something had changed.

She wanted Phillip to be *with her*. That had been the

whole point of this kind of marriage in her mind—for them to spend time together with no pressure.

When she got to work the next morning, her calendar reminded her she had a doctor's appointment on Thursday. She groaned. Somehow she'd convinced herself the appointment was today and she'd hoped to talk to the doctor about more effective remedies for morning sickness.

Because her current state was ridiculous.

Harper bounced into Alex's office, her strawberry blond curls brushing her shoulders. Normally, Fyra's chief science officer wore her hair in a no-nonsense bun to keep it away from the machines and tools in her lab.

Harper was an excellent distraction from all the angst and mood swings and general unpredictability of Alex's life. If it got her mind off Phillip, so much the better. Especially his smile as he'd danced with her at the wedding reception, which she could not erase from her brain for some reason.

"Special occasion, Dr. Livingston?" Alex asked with a nod at Harper's hairstyle.

"Dante is in town," she acknowledged with a cheeky grin. "He's taking me to lunch."

"Boring." Alex rolled her eyes, only half jesting. "When are you going on a date with someone you might actually have a chance of getting romantic with?"

Harper and Dante had been friends since freshman year in college, when they'd been paired up in chemistry. Friends with absolutely no benefits other than companionship, which put Harper in the slim minority of women who didn't notice how hot Dr. Dante Gates was underneath his hornrimmed glasses.

"I'm not the newlywed. Not all of us are looking for love." Harper waggled her brows. "Speaking of which, do kiss and tell."

Harper plopped into a chair and perched her chin on a palm, batting her eyelashes in a very clear invitation to spill everything. Instead of a quick rejoinder about how Alex wasn't looking for love either—which Harper well knew, as she was one of the few people aware of the agreement between Alex and Phillip—tears sprang up. As they rolled down Alex's face, Harper silently rounded the desk and gathered her friend up in a fierce hug. That only made the baffling anguish inside that much worse.

"Sorry," Alex choked out. "It's just hormones."

Probably. Harper didn't let go, but Alex didn't mind. Disappointment over Phillip's distance had caught up to her, increasing the flood exponentially. Which was ridiculous. Alex had entered Phillip's agreement willingly because it made sense. There was no room for emotional outbursts just because she'd hoped they'd pick up where they'd left off after the party. Last weekend should have been a honeymoon of sorts, even though they'd opted to skip any kind of trip because it seemed too traditional and sentimental.

The weekend had been nothing of the kind. Granted, she'd been nauseous pretty much the whole time.

But they could have spent time together. As friends. Oh, she understood that Phillip had to go to Washington for work during the week. But while he'd been home yesterday, she'd have been happy to watch a movie together or go to dinner. She didn't have to eat, but the conversation would have been nice. That would have tided her over until he came home.

But that hadn't even been suggested. Did he not think about their one night of passion the way she did? Because she wanted a repeat of their closeness, the tender kisses and their bodies communicating so perfectly.

More tears rushed down her face.

If you couldn't cry all over your best friends, who could you cry on? She and Harper had been friends since college. Way before they were business partners and colleagues.

When the surge had passed, Harper eased back and leaned on the desk, but she kept Alex's hand in hers. "That didn't seem like pregnancy hormones to me. Not that I'd know or anything."

What should have been a throwaway comment made by a staunch workaholic came out sounding wistful. As if Harper wished she could commiserate instead of merely being sympathetic.

Alex glanced at her friend through watery, suspicious eyes. "Trust me, you would not like to have firsthand knowledge, if that's what you're thinking."

"Oh, I'm not," Harper insisted with a forced laugh that raised Alex's concern even more. "I'm a scientist. I like to deal in facts. Since I've never been pregnant, I can't speak from personal experience, nor have I done any research. I mean, I know the basics and pregnancy can cause mood swi—"

"It's hormones," Alex interrupted before she got a full discourse on the potential side effects of pregnancy. "You were at the reception. Things did not improve and it's just not how I envisioned spending the weekend after my wedding. Phillip left to go back to DC yesterday."

"Oh. So no kiss and tell." Harper managed to look sympathetic through her disappointment, largely owing to her Irish charm, no doubt. "That would make me cry, too."

"It's hormones," Alex repeated through gritted teeth and one last tear trickled down to belie the statement. Crying on your friends wasn't cool if you were going to turn around and fib through your teeth about the genesis of the waterworks. "And okay, I'm sad that he's gone. Don't make a big deal out of it."

Saying it out loud made it real. Her marriage was forty-eight hours old and as lifeless as the paper it was written on. Maybe that was the deal she'd signed up for but, hormones or not, in the cold light of Monday morning it sounded as appealing as drinking dishwater.

Alex had a gorgeous husband, one who had been featured in magazine after magazine as one of the hottest bachelors in America. Now he was hers. Yet not hers. Was it so bad to dream of him taking her to bed and then calling the next day to say how much he hated that they were in different states?

"There's nothing wrong with missing your husband. I'm pretty sure that's allowed, even if you do have weird ideas about why to get married. Not that I'd know anything about that, either." Harper made a face, and if Alex didn't know better, she'd swear that jealousy laced the other woman's tone.

"Please. Phillip and I got married because of the baby." And a multitude of other reasons. "What better reason could there be? I'll be fine. I didn't have a husband last week either, so nothing has changed."

Everything had changed. That was the problem. And she had no idea what to do about it.

"Anything I can do?" Harper asked.

"You can distract me from my misery by telling me you found a new supplier for the pumice microbeads in your exfoliating scrub," Alex reminded Harper with raised eyebrows. The sooner they got off the subject of Phillip, the better. "Our profit margin is circling the drain."

"Are you that miserable? You should call your obstetrician." With a pat on Alex's arm, Harper leaned forward, clearly hoping to avoid the topic of suppliers and cost of goods.

"I have an appointment Thursday. I can suffer in silence until then. Now, about the pumice supp—"

"I'll go with you," Harper interjected smoothly. "To the appointment. Let me drive you."

"I can drive myself—" Alex sighed as she cut herself off. Maybe she spent so much time alone because she constantly drove people away. After all, it wasn't like she'd said anything to Phillip about spending time together. He probably didn't even know she'd hoped to. "You know what? That sounds nice."

"It's a date, then," Harper said. "Cass called a meeting this afternoon to talk about her progress on finding the leak, or lack thereof. Check your calendar. She just scheduled it."

Alex groaned. Someone in Fyra had leaked information to the media about Formula-47, which had nearly cost the company everything. Since they hadn't found the culprit yet, they'd decided to go forward with obtaining FDA approval before Harper felt ready, strictly to stave off damaging effects of the leak.

Another meeting with little progress. It was maddening. "Okay, thanks for the heads-up."

Back to business. That was a good way to get her mind off Phillip. Except she had a suspicion it wouldn't work.

Alex didn't exactly suffer in silence until Thursday. It was a little difficult when Fyra's chief science officer had taken on a personal mission to check on Alex ten times a day. Harper's pointed, yet loving, questions were hard to ignore, especially when Alex craved companionship. Alex found herself being honest about how she felt—physically at least, as the angst about Phillip was too hard for her to justify to herself, let alone to someone else. And she even let Harper run to 7-Eleven to fetch ginger ale a couple of times. On Thursday, true to her word, Harper popped into Alex's office, keys in hand, to drive her to the doctor.

"Let's go," Harper chirped and steered Alex into the two-seater Mercedes her friend had recently bought.

The smell of new car and leather engulfed Alex as she settled into the seat. "Thanks. For being there. I didn't realize how much I'd need hand-holding."

"Sure. That's what friends are for." Harper had tamed her red curls into a bun today, returning her to a more serious look.

Of her three business partners, Alex had always had the most in common with Harper, as they both approached life analytically. They'd had matching T-shirts in college that read Left-Brained Women Are Sexier. No one but the two of them had thought the saying was funny.

Thank God Alex had her friends during this challenging period. It didn't fully alleviate the loneliness of a big empty house, but Alex had solved that problem by going into the office early and staying until 10:00 p.m. Numbers were her refuge; always had been.

Phillip had called, as promised, every night at 10:30 p.m. and asked how she was feeling. It was nice that he took the time, but she was usually exhausted, so their conversations had been short. She then fell into Phillip-laced dreams, where he held her during the night and stroked her hair, then her skin. His lips would seek out the hollow of her throat and their urgency would increase until they were both naked and panting each other's names.

Hormones. They were killing her.

When the time for her appointment came, Alex's obstetrician, Dr. Dean, listened to her concerns about the severity of her morning sickness. "I'd like to do an ultrasound."

Dr. Dean had mentioned on Alex's first visit that she

didn't typically do ultrasounds until around eighteen weeks to verify the baby was growing correctly, and also to determine gender, which Alex very much wanted to know ahead of time.

"An ultrasound? But I'm only at eleven weeks," Alex said as her pulse started hammering in her throat. "Is something wrong? Is that why you want to do one?"

Dr. Dean waved at the nurse to roll the ultrasound machine over to the examination table and smiled at Alex. "I guess that depends on your definition of *wrong*. One explanation for the severity of your symptoms might be twins. An ultrasound will tell us, and if you are carrying multiples, finding out sooner is best."

"Twins?" All the blood rushed from Alex's head as Harper clapped gleefully from her spot across the room. "Oh, my God."

One baby felt like a huge enough responsibility to raise without damaging him or her. But two babies?

The sonographer pulled up Alex's gown, poured warm goop on her abdomen and then rolled the wide white wand across Alex's stomach. The black-and-gray screen near the table blurred and shifted with each movement and a blobby thing appeared.

Alex's heart stopped, and when it started beating again, it was too big and tight for her chest.

"Is that the baby?" Alex whispered, eyes wide so she didn't miss anything.

Phillip should be here. He should be holding her hand and watching this miracle unfold with her. Her throat ached with emotions she couldn't name, and she wished he'd care enough to be here to experience all of this, too.

"Yes," the sonographer confirmed, grinning. "And there's the other one. Dizygotic twins, or in layman's terms, fraternal. See how there are two distinct placentas?"

Twins. Alex's eyelids fluttered closed and then she pried them open to watch the sonographer type into the machine. Xs and dotted lines appeared.

"We're measuring their size so we can monitor growth," she explained. "Dr. Dean will want to do more ultrasounds as you progress to ensure we don't have an imbalance."

Alex nodded, too overwhelmed to speak. *Babies.* She had two babies in there sloshing around and causing so much havoc with her stomach. No wonder.

"So that explains your severe morning sickness," Dr. Dean said gently. "That's good news. Means nothing more serious is wrong. You'll probably start to feel better by about twelve or thirteen weeks, so not long now."

The doctor wrapped up the appointment with some additional tips and instructions and answered all of Alex's and Harper's questions. When Alex sank back into the seat of Harper's Mercedes, she let her head fall back against the headrest, too weary to think. Harper chatted about how great the news was all the way back to Fyra, and Alex let her talk, mostly because she couldn't get a word in edgewise. And her throat was too tight to make a sound.

Back in her office, she debated how to break the news to Phillip. There was no telling how he'd react. It was a reality they'd never even contemplated. Would they have to hire two nannies now? Have two nurseries—or did parents of twins typically put them in the same room?

In the end, it didn't matter. Phillip didn't answer his phone, even though she called him four times, fifteen minutes apart. Finally, she sent him a text message:

Went to the dr today. Guess what? It's twins.

Phillip was going to get his full-blown family much sooner than he'd anticipated.

* * *

When Phillip finally walked out of a three-hour meeting, the only thing he wanted to do was get something hot to eat and cold to drink. He grabbed his phone and briefcase from his office and waved to his admin, Linda, as he left Capitol Hill for the day.

The week had crawled by. Barely an hour had gone by that he hadn't thought about Alex, what she was doing, whether she felt better, if she was getting used to living at his house. He'd picked up his phone four or five times to send her a funny text message, like he'd done when they were still dancing around the edges of their attraction.

And then he'd remembered. They weren't flirting with the intent to eventually take it up a notch; they were married. In name only. She'd agreed to it and seemed pretty happy with the status quo as best he could tell during their nightly conversations, which he'd forced himself to cut short. Their relationship needed distance if it was going to work.

Of course, the distance wasn't working so well for him.

Every night, he would end the call and stare at the ceiling until he fell asleep, fighting the urge to call her back so he could hear her voice again. She needed to sleep, not hang out with him on the phone for no other reason than he suddenly hated the quietness of the DC condo that had always been perfectly fine before.

One more day of Washington and then he'd fly home. Somehow, he'd have to figure out how to maintain that distance while they were in the same house. It was a horrible catch-22 to want to spend time with his new wife and yet have an inner voice reminding him that the only reason he had a new wife was because Gina had died. He'd married Alex but it didn't mean he'd moved on. Not at all. Guilt weighed down his soul to the point where some mornings, he'd had a hard time getting out of bed.

Randy opened the back door of his town car and Phillip slid into the seat with a glance at his phone. Speaking of his new wife…looked like he'd missed a bunch of calls from Alex. Frowning, he noted a text message, too. Hopefully nothing was wrong.

And then the word *twins* leaped off the screen.

"Randy, change of plans," he croaked as he tapped furiously through the message app to see if she'd sent any follow-up texts. Nothing. "Drive me to the airport. I'm flying home to Dallas unexpectedly."

Twins.

The flight home took a million years, during which Phillip questioned every single decision he'd made since the first moment he walked into Fyra and saw the barefaced woman in jeans named Alex. They were having *twins*.

And Alex had found out at a doctor's visit he hadn't been asked to attend.

That was not okay.

These were his *children*. Alex was his wife. He wanted to be involved in everything, no matter how small, and he'd been robbed of that chance for some reason. He wanted to know why. Why hadn't she told him she was going to the doctor? Why hadn't she wanted him there?

The pilot announced the aircraft had entered Dallas airspace. Finally.

Phillip whipped off his seat belt the moment the wheels hit the tarmac and glared at Randy as his driver, who always traveled with him, lumbered to his feet a good thirty seconds after the plane had rolled to a stop. All Phillip had to do was raise his eyebrows for the man to clue in that time was of the essence.

"Where to, boss?" Randy asked mildly as they double-timed it to the private lot where Phillip kept his car. Normally, Randy pulled the car onto the tarmac and loaded Phillip's luggage when they returned home, but his driver had figured out that normal wasn't the theme of this trip. Plus, Phillip didn't have any luggage since he hadn't taken time to go back to his condo.

Phillip glanced at his watch. Nearly 9:00 p.m. Dallas time, a near miracle considering he'd climbed into his car at Capitol Hill just before six DC time. "To the house."

Where Alex would be at home, hopefully eating whatever Franka had made. Whatever Alex wanted, spare no expense or effort, he'd told Franka. Of course, he hadn't known his wife was eating for three then or he might have thrown Franka a side comment about watching Alex's nutrition, as well. He should have anyway.

Randy drove like a demon possessed, which Phillip appreciated, but when they got to the house, George met Phillip at the door with a puzzled frown. "Sir? We didn't expect you unt—"

"Where's Alex?" Phillip blew through the door, his gaze already searching the floor above. "She's not already in bed, is she?"

"Not hardly." George clucked, displeasure lacing his tone. "Ms. Alexandra is still at her office."

A spurt of anger ripped through Phillip's breastbone. "She's…what?"

"At work," George repeated, but Phillip had already spun to march back down the steps.

Not only pregnant, but with twins…and still at work? She should be working reduced hours, not putting her nose to the grindstone. If he had his way, she'd be sitting on the couch at home reading a book instead of working even eight hours a day, let alone fourteen. And she'd let Phillip take care of her. He wanted to.

By the time Randy pulled up at the glass-and-brick building housing Fyra Cosmetics, Phillip's temper had well passed the unreasonable stage. He and his wife had some words to exchange.

Fishing his guest security badge from his briefcase, Phillip launched from the car and stormed through the reception area, pausing long enough—just barely—to beep through the glass door leading to the executive offices.

Light spilled from the door marked Chief Financial Officer. The moment he stepped across the threshold, he opened his mouth to blast Alex.

Clearly startled, she glanced up, and as her gaze lit on him, it filled with something so warm and so tender, all his breath rushed from his lungs. Her wide smile poleaxed him in the stomach, and all of that was so definitely *not* what he'd expected that he forgot everything he'd planned to say.

His wife was so beautiful. And she was the mother of his babies. It was nearly divine how she'd suddenly filled him to the brim.

"Phillip!" She shot to her feet and rounded the desk with her arms spread as if she meant to fly into his embrace, and then, all at once, she skidded to a stop just short, her gaze hungrily taking him in. "I wasn't expecting you."

"Clearly not," he said gruffly, taken aback at how disappointed he was that she'd stopped.

What the hell.

He pulled her into his arms for what should have been a quick hug between parents...friends...spouses...whatever they were. But then she nestled in with a sigh, setting his blood on a simmer that completely changed the mood. His arms tightened and he held her, breathing in the scent of her hair.

"I guess you got my message," she murmured. "I tried to call."

"I know. I was in a meeting." It sounded as inane to his ears as it probably did to hers. He pulled back to zero in on her face. "Why didn't you tell me you had a doctor's appointment?"

"Oh." Confusion marred her beautiful bare face. "I didn't think you'd care. It was just a doctor's appointment. I have a lot of those. Goes with the territory."

"Of course I care." His voice was still gruff from the long day. Or something. "Especially if you're going to have an ultrasound. You have to tell me about these things."

"I didn't know. It was just a routine checkup, but when I mentioned how bad my morning sickness still was, Dr. Dean wanted to see if I was carrying twins." She shot him a wry smile. "I guess that's why they pay her the big bucks, because she called it in one."

"So it's true?" he whispered and his hand moved to Alex's abdomen involuntarily, as if he could validate by touching her that not one but two heartbeats lay just on the other side of her skin.

She pressed into his hand and the moment intensified as they stared at each other. He wasn't just touching the babies, but *her*. And she felt amazing under his palm. Everything in the world could vanish except for what was in his grasp and he'd be all right with that.

"It's true. I saw the pictures myself," she murmured, her gaze going soft and bright. "Oh, I have them."

She ducked out of his embrace and crossed to her desk, pulled open a drawer and rummaged around until she triumphantly held up a few pieces of paper.

She handed them to him and he glanced down at the black-and-white squares. Ultrasound pictures. And *there they were*. Two light-colored blobs in circles, surrounded by darkness. His babies. *Their* babies.

His eyes stung. *Stung*, like he might actually shed a tear. Why hadn't someone prepared him for this moment when he got to see his children for the first time? It wouldn't have mattered; he wouldn't have listened because how could he have prepared for *this*? The swell of his heart, the spike of his pulse. The sheer awe. All of it poured through him thickly and he couldn't have spoken to save his life.

"It's pretty amazing, huh?" she asked softly and he took it as a rhetorical question because of course the answer was yes. "I wish you'd been there to see them move."

"Me too." Apparently he *could* talk. "I'm going to be there next time. I want advance notice of all doctor's appointments from now on."

"Okay. I'm glad you want to be involved. I thought…" She trailed off and bit her lip. "Well, when you left on Sunday, I got the impression we weren't supposed to share things. I would have said something, but you seemed… distracted every time we talked. It almost felt like you were avoiding me."

Of course she'd thought that. His quest for distance had been a stellar success. So much so that he'd missed an important step in Alex's pregnancy because of his own bone-headedness. Paper rustled under his fingers as his hands tightened into fists. Carefully, he set down the ultrasound pictures before he crumpled them.

"I'm sorry you thought that. I wasn't trying to avoid you." Yeah, he kind of had been, but now it didn't make any sense. Either they were partners and friends or there was no reason to be married. He wanted her to feel like she could tell him things. He wanted to know about her and not just about the pregnancy.

The Distance Plan wasn't going to work. He needed a new plan in order to make this marriage succeed. Otherwise, they'd both be miserable.

"Won't it be hard to come to doctor's appointments when you're in Washington?" she asked and it was a perfectly logical question.

Yes, it would be difficult but he didn't care. He couldn't stand the thought of missing one more second of his wife's pregnancy. Of missing his wife.

Where had *that* come from? That wasn't the point here.

"Let me worry about that. Now, let's talk about what time it is and why you're still at work, shall we?" The subject change flowed out smoothly, a plus considering he'd started out this little interlude as a confrontation. And somehow, she'd got him all discombobulated with a simple smile.

She had the grace to look chagrined. "I wasn't expecting you to catch me."

"Ah, so you recognize that it's a problem for a woman in your condition to work herself too hard."

Good. Maybe this would end up being a reasonable conversation about what a woman expecting twins could and couldn't do. Back on track, he smiled gently.

"What? No." She shook her head with a scowl. "What kind of 'condition' would that be, Phillip? I'm pregnant, not incompetent. I know my limits."

Except clearly she didn't. "Then why the guilty face?"

"Because I—" She looked away, biting her lip again. A dead giveaway that she had something on her mind that she didn't want to say. "I didn't want to go home."

"You hate my house? You can't sleep? What is it? You can say it."

She was hesitating because she knew she was guilty as charged. She should be at home with her feet up, letting him cater to her every whim. She deserved to be treated like a queen and to have a husband around who could look after her well-being. Which would be hard for him to do in Washington, as well.

How had everything got so complicated?

"It's too empty," she blurted out. "I don't like being there alone."

He waved it off. "You're not alone. I have a full staff—"

"*You're* not there, Phillip! I don't like being at the house without you. I work until ten so I can go home and fall into bed, so exhausted that I don't think about how you left Sunday with barely a goodbye. I missed you. I miss the way we were before *this*—" she sliced at her midsection "—happened. Why can't the pregnancy be something that brings us together?"

A lone tear rolled down her face and the sight of it clenched his gut. The emotional distance he'd created wasn't working so well. For either of them. She'd been working late because he hadn't been engaging her as a person, as the future mother of his children.

This was his fault and he needed to fix it, before the damage to his marriage became irreparable.

Here, in the light of these revelations, it didn't seem so terrible to admit that he wanted to be with her. To hold her whenever he felt like it and let her do the same. The distance he'd created hadn't done what he'd hoped anyway. He still thought about Alex, still wanted her in his bed.

The Distance Plan sucked. New plan—make Alex glad she'd married him. Get back to where they'd been before the babies came into the picture. Be real friends and partners. Back to Basics. That was a great new plan. Hopefully along the way, he'd earn the right to be included in things like ultrasounds. The only thing he didn't have quite worked out yet was how he'd get closer to Alex and keep his commitment to Gina's memory.

But he had to. Somehow.

Seven

The first thing Phillip did when they got home was draw Alex a bath.

The second thing he did was insist she get in it while he made her a tray of tea and crackers.

After the emotional breakdown in her office, Alex had half expected Phillip to jet back to Washington. They didn't have a real marriage; theirs was based on rules. She got that, knew what she'd signed up for. The whole time she'd been admitting how much she missed him, she knew she shouldn't be, that it was a risky move, but there was no way she could have held back, not with Phillip within arm's length. Not when she was still so raw from his sudden appearance and the way he'd held her and touched her.

And yet Phillip hadn't fled. He was here, in the house, with no apparent plans to leave. Maybe that meant an opportunity to change things. But how? And to what? Alex wasn't one to jump in with both feet. Except for that one time at the party, and look where that had got her.

Bubbles up to her neck, Alex relaxed in the giant oval bathtub as best she could under the circumstances. The bathtub might be her favorite spot in the house. It was on a raised platform with windows surrounding it, and the bathtub overlooked a cheerful garden. At night, the garden's floodlights cast the bathroom in a dim, rosy glow. The day's stresses melted away.

And then Phillip bustled in, tray in hand. Gorgeous, self-assured, and oh so very sexy with his shirtsleeves rolled to midforearm and dark hair rumpled from his flight.

"I, uh…didn't know you were coming in," she squeaked.

She was naked under these bubbles. And her husband didn't seem too worried about it as he crossed over to the pale marble tub and perched on the wide lip. Carefully, he placed the tray of tea and saltines next to him on the ledge and slid it out of the way, toward the wall.

"Well, I wasn't planning on it, but that water does look tempting." His lips quirked as he let his gaze travel down the length of the tub, which consisted of nothing but bubbles. The sudden heat flashing through his expression made her wonder if he could see more than she assumed.

But then…he'd seen her naked before, so what was she freaking out about? And she'd been dreaming of the day he wanted to see her naked again. If today was that day, she didn't want to breathe too hard in case she blew away her chance to be with Phillip again.

"I meant, I didn't know you were coming into the bathroom," she corrected hastily. Did she sound as breathless to him as she did to herself? "Men don't like baths."

"As a rule, I suppose, but other men don't have you in their bathtubs." Lazily, he swirled a finger through the bubbles as he watched her. "Lucky for me I'm not other men."

It sure looked like he might be seriously contemplating

joining her. Was he going to dive right into the tub? Oh, my, she certainly hoped so.

She didn't know where to put her hands. "There's enough room for two."

Her cheeks burned as she envisioned Phillip stripping down and sliding against the marble, his skin slick against hers. Then he'd touch her and they'd fall back into the way they'd been at the party. Connected. Hot. Meaningful.

That was all she wanted—his attention on her like it had been then, so focused and delicious. No rules, just two people who wanted to be together.

His grin lit her up inside. "That's the best invitation I've had all week. But not now. This evening is about you and you only. I want to take care of you. If I got into that tub, all my good intentions would go out the window."

Now she couldn't decide if she was disappointed or intrigued. Maybe a little of both. "That sounds interesting. Tell me more about that."

Something wicked flashed through his expression. "You want to hear about how easily you could break down my good intentions? I didn't know you liked dirty talk, Mrs. Edgewood."

"I haven't heard any yet, so I honestly don't know if I'd like it," she countered primly, trying hard to be shocked at her own boldness and failing miserably.

She'd married this man to provide a family and future for her children. That didn't mean she had to live alone, be lonely or pretend she didn't want him. In fact, she didn't recall any rules against that.

"Well, see… I wanted to rub your feet." He punctuated this comment by dipping a hand in the water and fishing her ankle from the suds. Then he held it in his palm as he kneaded her instep with a thumb. "Like this. Thought you might enjoy it."

She was too busy groaning at the exquisite sensations radiating through her foot. Why hadn't she realized her feet hurt that bad? "You can do that. I don't mind."

"Oh, I had all these *good intentions* to massage your whole body." He picked up her other foot and began to rub it in kind. Her eyelids fluttered closed involuntarily. "I was about to launch into a very long description of how I'd taste your whole body if I got into that tub with you."

Every inch of her went liquid as that promise exploded in her core. Caught between the tantalizing glimpse of what could be and the amazing things currently happening to her body, her brain wasn't too quick on the draw.

"You twisted it all around," she murmured as her head sank back against the marble. "I wanted to hear about how you planned to take care of me."

"One and the same, Alex." His low voice drifted through her. "Or at least it is now. Because every second I'm seeing to your comfort, my hands will be on you. And I'll be thinking about how taking care of you might include something pleasurable for us both."

That she could get on board with in a hurry. Something had changed. She could sense it, as if he'd opened up. And now that she had his attention, she could admit, to herself at least, how much she'd craved it, how her body cried for his touch.

"I definitely want to hear more about that."

"How about I show you instead?"

Wordlessly, he found her hand and gently pulled her out of the bubbles until she was standing in the water, bared to him. Droplets of water and suds slid along the planes of her body, sensitizing it. His gaze followed the drops, lingering along the way, and that heightened the heat blooming along her skin.

Phillip grabbed a towel and dried her carefully, murmuring about how beautiful she was. He dropped flowery phrases as he worked, turning the utilitarian act of drying skin into a seduction. Her starving soul ate up the words, hiding them away. Her neglected body soaked up his touch. Everything felt bigger, better, stronger than the last time she'd been naked with Phillip.

Her left brain recognized that pregnancy hormones were heightening the experience. Her everything else couldn't wait to find out what the rest of it was going to feel like.

"Phillip," she said hoarsely. "Take me to bed."

His hand stilled on her back. "Are you sure? No morning sickness tonight?"

The questions lingered in the air. He was giving her a chance to back out if this wasn't what she wanted. A chance to analyze where this step in their relationship might lead, and he was okay if she used morning sickness as an excuse. She appreciated that more than he could possibly know. It meant he understood she didn't normally throw caution to the wind—and he wanted her to make the choice.

"None. Finish what we never got to start the night of our wedding." Actually, she hadn't even thought about her stomach since the moment he'd walked into Fyra earlier that evening.

He grinned and picked her up easily, snugging her into his arms as he nuzzled her ear. "You sure you don't want that massage?"

She nestled into his embrace. Strong. Capable. It was a good thing she wasn't standing because her knees had just gone weak. "I thought I was promised both."

"And both you shall have."

He carried her to the bed and laid her out on it, worshipping her with his gaze.

She shivered under the onslaught, though he hadn't

touched her again. His eyes on her were enough as he swept her from head to toe with that heated contemplation.

She'd forgotten how nice that felt. Phillip made her feel beautiful, even when she had nothing on her face. Her company had been built on the premise that a woman required enhancements to be attractive, to gain the attention of a lover. She'd never thought it worked, that it *should* work. If a man wanted you, he should want the woman you were, not the woman you pretended to be.

It was her shameful secret. She owed Cass so much, owed Trinity and Harper for taking her in despite her juvenile arrest record. How could Alex tell her friends that cosmetics made no sense to her?

Here under the laser-sharp, watchful eye of Phillip, she didn't have to pretend. He knew she didn't like dressing up and he didn't care. The way his gaze perused her naked body said he liked what he saw. That was so powerful.

"I hope you're planning to join me in the bed," she murmured. "The bath was one thing, but I'm pretty sure the activities I had in mind require you to get wet this time."

His brows shot up but he schooled the shock off his face. "Why, Mrs. Edgewood. Is that a sample of the dirty talk you mentioned earlier? I wasn't aware you planned to be the one doing the talking but I'm in favor of it."

"More where that came from," she promised as the sound of his voice calling her Mrs. Edgewood curled up in her belly, warming her. Strange. Who would have thought a simple title could be so affecting? Must be the way he'd said it, with a slightly naughty edge.

Whatever had shifted between them got her vote. She just wished she knew what it was. So if things shifted the other way again, she could fix it.

With a small chuckle, Phillip began shedding his clothes. She watched, shamelessly. Of course, she'd seen him naked too, but that had been months ago…and pre-whacked-out hormones, obviously, because she really didn't remember the sight of his fingers slipping buttons free of their moorings being so erotic.

But as the second one popped out, something sharp stabbed through her core, heating her from the inside out. Third one, fourth, and the heat flushed upward to encompass her torso, spreading to her breasts, peaking them.

He watched her just as shamelessly as she watched him, his eyes growing darker the more her body visibly reacted.

"You're a fan of stripteases, too?" he asked, his voice rough with appreciation. "That's incredibly hot."

His shirt was as unbuttoned as it could be, baring his chest. And then he slid it off, first one shoulder, then the other. It shouldn't have been so—*wow.*

"It's news to me, as well," she muttered as her back arched involuntarily. "Don't you dare stop."

"I wouldn't dream of it. I find myself anxious to explore all the interesting things going on with your body." His hands had moved to his pants and the zipper released with a quick tug. Then, as he shoved the fabric away, catching his briefs in the same motion, she got a good eyeful of how she'd been affecting him thus far.

Oh, my. She wanted that gorgeous length of flesh. Right now. That pleasure he'd promised her had already started in a very big way and she ached to finish it.

Silently, she held out her hands and he fell onto the bed next to her, drawing her into his arms a bit roughly, but she didn't mind. His body felt heavenly against hers, insistent, hard, hot. All of it inflamed her to the point of senselessness and a moan fell from her lips as he thrust a thigh between her legs.

He took her mouth with his in an urgent kiss that grew exponentially more heated every second. Their tongues clashed, seeking, tasting, feeling, and she nearly bucked off the bed when his hands found her breasts. He molded them to his palms, explored them as he'd told her he would, and the ache at her core morphed into something almost agonizing. She needed him more than she'd ever needed anything.

"Hurry," she mouthed against his lips and rocked her hips against his for emphasis.

"I don't think I could do it another way," he muttered as her fingers closed around his gloriously hard shaft. "And this will be over if you keep that up."

With a groan, he removed her hand and rolled her to her back. Then he kissed his way down the length of her body, spread her thighs and put his mouth in the center of the heat she couldn't contain.

The first wet touch of his tongue nearly split her apart. She might have screamed as sensation rocketed through her body. Her hips bucked against his mouth as he pleasured her and that tight coil of need spun faster and faster until it exploded in a storm of light behind her eyes.

Her whole body stiffened as she cried out his name, and then he was kissing her gently, holding her tight against him as she rode out the thick waves of release. No words. No bones. Her whole body might have disintegrated in the aftermath and she didn't care.

He let her recover—not fully, because that was frankly impossible, but enough. His hands threaded through her hair as he cupped the back of her head, drawing her face close to his so he could nibble on her lips, then her throat, and the whole tide started over again.

But this time, he murmured more flowery phrases as he kissed her, and when he poised between her thighs, ready to claim her a second time, he captured her gaze, watching her intently as he pushed inside.

The connection electrified her, sensitized her, heightened her pleasure as his blue eyes went hot. They were joined and it was magnificent, much more so than the first time. With no condom between them, it took less than a minute for her to crest that peak again.

He shuddered with his own release and they both went limp in each other's arms, torsos heaving and neither in a hurry to drift apart. His palms smoothed across her buttocks, cradling her close, and something so raw and elemental broke open inside her, she could barely breathe.

The same thing had happened when she'd shown him the ultrasound pictures… His awed, perfect reaction had touched something deep inside. The look on his face had floored her, rushing through her, awakening parts of her she didn't know existed. Kind of like now.

She'd ignored it then. But couldn't have in this moment for a million dollars. Her emotions were fully engaged in this relationship, despite her best effort to stick with what was logical, and she wanted things, so many things. Things she didn't know how to express. Things that scared her because she'd been convinced none of them were real.

Right now, all of them were oh so real.

She couldn't let go of Phillip. Didn't want to let go. But she should.

None of this internal catch-22 should have been happening just because they'd had sex. Sex had been part of the agreement. They were married; of course they were going to take care of each other's needs.

The reality? Not the nice, safe marital bed she'd imagined. Actually, nothing about her marriage had gone like she'd thought it would. The confusion and swirl of uncertainty nearly overwhelmed her, and all she wanted to do to soothe it was cling to Phillip. The author of her alarm. What was she supposed to do with that?

For his part, he seemed sated and content to lie there murmuring lovely things about round two in her ear as he stroked her hair. Maybe he was onto something. There was no cause for panic. She could stay focused on how good they made each other feel and forget about stuff she couldn't explain.

Her marriage would work because they'd both agreed to keep emotions out of it. The rules were there for a reason. Rules kept you from getting hurt and from hurting other people. Rules kept the subject of divorce at bay.

Besides, Phillip didn't believe in second chances. He'd married the great love of his life already, and there was no room for Alex in his heart. If only... No. That was the opening phrase of a path straight to madness.

But as she lay in Phillip's arms, cradled by the husband she'd never planned to have, pregnant with the babies she'd never imagined being gifted with, her heart started filling in the blank without her permission.

The Back to Basics Plan might be the best one Phillip had ever devised.

When sunlight filtered through the drawn curtains, he'd already been awake for a while, just listening to Alex breathe. Even that was a turn-on.

If only he could wake her up with a kiss and dive in again. But he resisted. Barely. She needed her sleep, especially since she'd been working until ten o'clock. The woman needed a good spanking. Among other things. His imagination got busy thinking up additional wicked items for that list.

And now he had an erection the size of the Senate chambers. Where he should currently be but wasn't because he'd flown home on a whim to have it out with his wife about her bad habits. Guess he'd skipped over that confrontation in favor of something much more necessary.

His marriage was on much better ground than it had been. Fortunately. Some things were worth the sacrifice, and Alex, the mother of his twins, definitely was. He sent Linda a text message, begging her to cover for him at Capitol Hill, and tossed his phone back on the nightstand. On Silent.

The government could do without a senator for one day.

Alex sighed and rolled over, facing him. Her eyes were still closed, her body relaxed in sleep. Even in the dim light of the rising sun, he could see the line of her hip and the length of her legs as they stretched toward the footboard.

Gina had always slept curled in a ball, one hand over her face, as if to ward off the darkness. Since she'd died, he sometimes woke up in the middle of the night and, in that half second of semiconsciousness, could feel Gina's presence in the bed. It was always so real he'd have a moment of panic when he couldn't find her.

And then reality would wash over him with biting, bitter coldness. She was gone. Irrevocably. In those moments, it felt like his heart had been clawed from his chest and buried with her.

A part of him wondered why he didn't bring home a new woman every night in an attempt to ward off such a visceral nighttime experience. But he couldn't. He hadn't let other women into his bed except very briefly, and then he always escorted them home after. Alex was the first to still be there in the morning.

He'd put off sleeping with her overnight, hoping to assuage the guilt before it affected the friendship they were developing, but he'd known marrying Alex meant she'd eventually fill the empty space.

And now that it had happened…it was so much better

than he'd imagined. Better than he'd planned to allow. His chest hurt with the conflict waging an all-out war inside. He wanted to embrace what he had with Alex, and what it might become, but how could he? It was so disloyal to Gina he could hardly breathe.

Alex blinked awake and smiled. "You owe me. I never got tea or a massage last night."

That pulled a laugh from him in spite of all the turmoil seething under his skin. "And here I thought what I did give you made up for losing out on those."

Nodding, her smile widened. "Mmm, yes. Good point. I'll give you a pass on both."

All at once, she stretched one arm over her head and the sheet slipped down. One rosy nipple popped free of the covers, drawing his eye. Her breasts had grown fuller, lusher since the party and he obviously hadn't paid enough attention to them last night because his mouth started watering as he pondered tasting them again.

He snaked an arm out and gathered her against him in one motion. Sex made sense. It was a release and then over. No disloyal emotional commitment involved.

"Oh, no," he said smoothly over her squeal. "You're far too quick to forgive. I promised you a massage. And tea. But we'll get to the tea later."

Her gaze filled with heat instantly, her eyelids dropping a touch as she tangled her legs with his, aligning their hips to bring her dampness flush with his hard-on. Yes, that would do nicely. Last night, he'd been so focused on her pleasure that he'd ignored his own needs.

This morning, he'd sate himself. As soon as he made sure the coast was clear.

He bent his head and nuzzled her ear. "You're feeling okay this morning?"

"Very okay," she purred and fused her lips to his, drawing him into a kiss that spiraled out of control in a heartbeat.

He groaned as her skin ignited his. He didn't remember her being this way before they'd got married. Hot, sure. Willing, absolutely. But this was different, an urgency he could barely keep up with. Though he'd give it the college try.

Tearing his mouth from hers, he treated himself to those gorgeous breasts, massaging them with his tongue as promised. But she arched against his mouth, moaning with little sighs that drove him crazy, and then got her hips in on the action, writhing against him.

One small shift of his hips and they joined.

It was insanely perfect. Beautiful. They fit together better than anything he could have imagined and he reveled in it for a moment, too overcome to break the spell. Alex was in his arms, hair spread over his pillow, and she was so much more than the wife he'd thought he needed, he could hardly reconcile it all.

With a sound, she rolled her hips, taking her own pleasure, apparently too impatient with his sightseeing to wait. He let her take control despite starting out this jaunt with his own pleasure in mind because in the end, they both won.

Far too quickly, she had them both gasping through a mutual, explosive orgasm. It took him by surprise, engulfing him, which made it that much more powerful.

He gathered her up and held her tight, loath to let go. After all, sex was the only normal part of their relationship. Why not spend as much time in bed as possible? Here he could pretend nothing had changed in their relationship and that the Back to Basics Plan was still about making sure he was included in doctor's appointments from now on.

He knew deep down that was a lie. But he couldn't deal with the truth.

"I have to go to work. It's Friday," she reminded him, though she didn't sound too thrilled about it. She sighed and pushed at his arms with very little strength. He didn't let go.

"Call in sick." He kissed her temple. "You're allowed to take time off, especially since you've probably already worked sixty hours this week."

She scowled. "I'm not an hourly employee. I never monitor my time like that. Fyra is my company that I built alongside my friends. I like my job."

"Okay." He held up his hands in mock surrender despite feeling anything but conciliatory. Now was not the time to push, obviously, even though part of the reason he'd come home a day early was to make sure she was taking care of herself. And not working too much.

So he'd let her think she'd won that round and help her climb from bed. As she padded across the room toward the bathroom, he called out, "I'll come by this morning and we can catch up on the FDA status."

She glanced over her shoulder. "Sure. I have an opening at eleven."

Excellent. That gave him time to devise a plan to get her out of the office for lunch. And if he played his cards right, she wouldn't be going back until Monday.

His wife needed rest and relaxation. It was his job to make sure she got that. The other stuff going on in their relationship could be ignored if he put his mind to it.

Eight

Melinda, Fyra's receptionist, smiled as Phillip strode through the glass doors of Alex's company.

"Mr. Edgewood, always a pleasure. I didn't know you were in town."

"Short notice," he allowed easily. "Alex penciled me in at eleven."

Melinda glanced at her computer screen, the corners of her mouth tilting down. "Oh, she must have gotten the time wrong. She's in a meeting with the people who run our accounting software."

"No problem." Phillip pasted on his Capitol Hill smile, the one he reserved for lobbyists and the media. "I'll wait in her office."

Cooling his heels in Alex's office gave Phillip plenty of time to think. And the FDA approval process didn't cross his mind once. There was some movement on that front, but concern for the health of his wife and babies trumped government bureaucracy. By the time said wife strolled through the door forty-five minutes later, he had his strategy laid out for how he would get her out of this place.

"Great timing," he said pleasantly as she eyed him warily. "I have reservations at the Crescent for lunch. We'll eat and talk about the status of the FDA application, and then we've been invited to the new children's hospital ribbon cutting this afternoon. We have just enough time to run by the house so you can change."

"Hello to you, too," she said with obvious sarcasm. "I have a protein bar for lunch that I brought from home and three meetings this afternoon. The ribbon cutting sounds great, but today is impossible."

Actually, he'd already convinced Melinda to rearrange Alex's schedule, and it had been far too easy to sway the receptionist to his way of thinking—namely that Alex needed the break—which told him his wife was definitely working entirely too much. But she clearly hadn't glanced at her calendar yet in order to notice her clear afternoon.

"We had an appointment that you blew off. You owe me." He raised his brows, driving the point home. He wasn't above layering on some guilt if it got her out of the office.

She sighed. "You're right. The meeting with the software people was critical since it's nearly quarter end, but I could have scheduled it another time. I didn't think you'd mind and took advantage of our relationship."

Well, that was laying it on a bit thick, but it worked in his favor, so he bit his tongue. "It's okay. I forgive you. As long as you agree to go to the ribbon cutting with me. That's one of the reasons we got married, right? So we could do things like that together."

"I'll get my purse."

Victory, Phillip. She even let Randy drive and settled into the town car without a peep about leaving her own car in the Fyra parking lot. There was a brief scuffle over Alex changing clothes, but Phillip smoothed over it with the very well-made point that the Crescent Hotel's restaurant had a strict dress code.

Once at home, Alex scowled and took the green Ralph Lauren from Phillip's outstretched hand. "I've never even seen this dress before."

"I bought it for you." Phillip twirled his finger in a get-on-with-it motion. "I'm dying to see it on you. It's the right size, isn't it?"

That must have been the correct way to play it because Alex threw it on the bed so she could slip off her jeans. A bonus Phillip hadn't expected—he was going to get to watch his wife dress.

As she slithered out of her shirt, his whole body reacted favorably to the sight of lush woman in nothing but a bra and panties. He thought seriously about blowing off his own plans for the day. What was wrong with playing hooky entirely from senator duties? When the mayor had called about the ribbon cutting, it had seemed like a perfect solution to Phillip's problem with Alex. She needed a break; the ribbon cutting was nothing more than a big party where he and his wife would be the guests of honor. It was a low-key event and he got to spend time with Alex. Win-win.

But then she pulled the dress over her head, and as it settled down around her breasts and hips, she twirled and struck a pose. "What do you think?"

His lungs felt like an elephant had just sat on them because he couldn't breathe. The brown fleck in her eye, the one that marked her so uniquely, stood out against the grass-green dress, and the hue complemented her pregnancy glow with unexpected flawlessness. She pulled the ponytail holder from her hair, letting it tumble down her back in a mass of loose waves.

"Gorgeous," he murmured. "We have to get out of here now before I undo all that."

She shot him a smug smile. "That good? You should buy me more clothes."

"I plan to," he growled. Lingerie, tiny silk robes, the works. "Later. Let's go eat before I lose my mind."

Laughing, she led the way to the car, and somehow, that had broken the mood, on her end at least. She chatted on the way to the restaurant, asking him questions about the FDA application. Since he'd been the one to bring it up— even though it had been a ploy to get himself into her office, so he could extract her—he obliged her with a status report, explaining that the FDA had scheduled a hearing a week from Monday.

It was a small measure of progress, he told her, but his mind wasn't on anything other than how quickly they could get through lunch and the party so he could be alone with his wife again.

Lunch was nearly as torturous.

If he'd have known buying Alex a dress would be so affecting, he might have picked something else. When he'd seen it in the shop window he hadn't hesitated, had just walked inside and had it shipped home. George had signed for the package and had the dress hung up in Alex's closet.

That was how things should work. Buy your wife a gift, and she wears it. Simple. It was anything but. Somehow the act of clothing her constantly reminded him of the act of unclothing her. He wanted to strip her out of the dress with his own two hands and watch as her luscious skin was revealed inch by inch. He wanted to kiss her and watch her face as he pushed into her again and again.

The dress was too distracting. His wife was too distracting.

Alex laughed at something he said, her face lighting up,

and he changed his mind. No. He needed to buy ten more dresses exactly like it. What was wrong with wanting his wife? Perfectly normal.

It just didn't feel normal or friendly or partner-y or whatever they were doing. It felt like...*more*.

And that was dangerous to his careful sense of propriety about their relationship. How could he stay true to Gina if he let himself feel all these *things* for his new wife?

He risked putting his hand against her back as they left the Crescent, guiding her toward the car as Randy sailed to the curb and stopped smoothly in the valet lane. Not because she needed help walking but because he wanted to touch her. But she ducked into the car too fast and he missed the feel of fabric stretched over her body.

The hospital parking lot was a madhouse, so Randy dropped them off in a side lot. They had to walk around to the front where the ribbon-cutting ceremony would be held, which gave Phillip exactly the opportunity he was looking for to put his arm around Alex again.

Throngs of people milled about in the clearing near the entrance. A scarlet ribbon blocked the sliding glass doors, emblazoned with Wharton Children's Hospital. Ceremonial shears the size of his desk stood on end against one of the posts, waiting for the hospital board and guest of honor.

Phillip had donated a lot of money to the hospital building fund and he was glad his schedule had allowed him to participate. Or rather, he was glad his wife's stubbornness had reared its head at the time that it had.

"There are a lot of people here," Alex muttered into his ear, leaning into his embrace a little deeper. A sure indicator that she was nervous.

"You'll be fine," he assured her with a light kiss to her temple that drew a small smile from her. Something pulled tight in his chest as she lifted her chin a touch to prolong the contact of his lips on her face. Such a small, brief moment. Why did it feel so massive?

A flash went off in his peripheral vision. Odds were good that the press had just captured that moment for all posterity. That should be a good thing. That was what they were here for. To schmooze and give photo ops, drum up support for Phillip's name and platform. All press was good press.

Except this time, it was intrusive. That moment with his wife hadn't been for public consumption and it infuriated him to have it tarnished. But his life was not his own, and neither was hers.

"Come on." He led her to the knot of suits near the entrance, most of whom comprised the hospital board.

He introduced Alex around and she shook hands demurely, opting to keep her comments minimal and largely of the noncommittal variety. Good. She was learning. Something pulled inside his chest again and he rubbed it with the flat of his hand. What the hell was going on in there?

The ceremony began and the board president took the stage to say a few words about the financial generosity of the Wharton family for whom the hospital was named and then thanked a few local businessmen who had also donated money, including Phillip.

"I didn't know you'd given money," Alex whispered and her breath warmed his ear. "This is a great cause. I'm proud to be the plus one standing next to you. Why didn't you tell me?"

"It never came up," he said, suddenly uncomfortable with the direction of the conversation. He'd inherited a vast amount of wealth. So what? "It's not a big deal. I give money to lots of stuff."

But the admiration and pride shining from her eyes said

she thought it *was* a big deal and that sharpened the strange ache in his chest. He carried it with him as the president of the hospital board called Phillip up to help him, along with four other board members, cut the ribbon. They posed for pictures and then cut as one group. Just like he'd done a dozen times before, except never with Alex watching him while she wore a dress he'd selected and a smile he'd elicited through a deed she found heroic.

The mayor's wife approached Alex and he was too far away to hear the conversation, but they shook hands, then chatted for a moment. The mayor's wife kept smiling and even laughed at one point. Not once did she get that bemused, cockeyed look on her face that so commonly appeared on people's faces after two seconds in his wife's company.

When Phillip finally sprang free of his duties, he cornered Alex. "What did the mayor's wife say to you?"

"That she had naked pictures of Channing Tatum on her phone and did I want to see them?" Alex snorted as he raised a brow. "What do you think she said? She introduced herself and apologized for missing the wedding."

Okay, he'd probably deserved that. "She seemed charmed. That's good."

"I'm trying, Phillip. Like we talked about. I want to be an asset to you or I wouldn't be here." Alex folded her hands in front of her, clearly more poised than he would have expected, and even that sat funny on his nerves.

A beep from Alex's handbag interrupted and she fished out her phone, read the message and glanced up to meet his gaze, her expression clouding. "The problem with our accounting software just got worse. The vendor is on-site trying to help and they need my guidance. Sorry. I have to cut this afternoon short."

Disappointment flooded the ache in his chest, drowning

it thoroughly. "Fyra can survive without you until Monday. I need you by my side."

Actually, he needed her for a whole lot more than that. The reality of it froze his tongue. He could do a ribbon cutting without her. He'd been solo for two years with no problem.

But that wasn't the issue. He'd wanted to go home with her after this. Lock the bedroom door and forget about the outside world. Just spend his weekend reveling in her body, her smile, the way she made him feel.

That wasn't what was supposed to be happening in their relationship. When had Alex become so critical and necessary?

Panic pounded in his breastbone and melded with disappointment he absolutely should not be feeling.

"Well, I can't stay. This is *your* job." She waved curtly at the milling ribbon-cutting attendees. "Not mine. I have to go resolve these issues or Fyra's quarter-end filing will be late."

He shrugged, hoping it had come off as nonchalant. "Your company isn't publicly traded. It's not like your stock will tank if you don't produce a financial statement."

Alex went still. "What's that supposed to mean? Because Fyra's a private company, I shouldn't worry about a little thing like quarterly numbers? I'm talking about *tax* filing. That's not optional unless you know of some IRS loophole I've been ignorant of all this time."

Arms crossed, she stared him down, and yeah, he heard himself acting like an ass but couldn't physically stop himself. Not with all the panic still racing through his veins over when and how Alex had become someone he didn't like being separated from. "You're working too hard. It's not good for the babies. Maybe you should think about taking a leave of absence. Think about that instead of your numbers."

"What are you saying?" she whispered. "That it's not okay with you if I work simply because I'm pregnant? That was never part of our deal."

"Neither were twins, Alex." His voice rose too loudly for his own comfort, so he pulled her to a more private area and tried to reel in his temper because none of this was about her working. It had everything to do with making sure she knew this marriage was about the babies. Nothing more. "No second chances. If you harm the babies through your own selfishness, how will that sit with you?"

That had been over the line. He started to apologize but she cut him off.

"Is that how you think of my career? As being selfish?"

Stricken, her eyes went wide and filled with unshed tears. The tears cooled his temper instantly. He'd hurt her with his asinine comments and inability to have a conversation simply because she'd dug too far under his skin. Which was his fault, not hers.

Nonetheless, he'd started this showdown. And his points were still valid.

"I'm not talking about giving up your career. Just take it easy until the babies are born and maybe then stay home for six months? I don't know, just thinking out loud."

It was a compromise. He'd like to say she should consider being a stay-at-home mom. Twins were a huge responsibility. Plus, he worried about her. She should be resting, not pushing herself to the point of exhaustion.

With Gina, this conversation never would have happened. His first wife had talked for hours upon hours about how she couldn't wait to be a mother, couldn't wait to raise their children. She'd had no job outside of being his wife, and he'd never realized how that had translated into making his life easier. He had no practice at resolving marital disagreements because Gina had never disagreed with him.

"Keep thinking," Alex shot back, and one tear spilled down her face. "I'm going to work. You do your thing and maybe I'll see you later. Don't worry about me. I was taking care of myself just fine before you came along. Which means I can call a taxi on my own, too."

With that, she flounced off as she angrily dashed the tear away, leaving Phillip with a burn in his chest, no plus one and no explanation for why he wanted to punch the wall. Or maybe he should just punch himself. It would probably hurt less than being responsible for making Alex cry.

Phillip slunk to his car, but instead of directing Randy to drive home, he asked to be taken to his grandfather's house. Max Edgewood was the only person on earth who would give Phillip a warm welcome no matter what. And honestly, he needed a friendly face right now.

Amelia, his grandfather's maid, answered the door the moment Phillip knocked. Randy had called ahead as he drove so Max would be expecting visitors. The older Phillip's grandfather grew, the less he got out of bed, but for some reason, he refused to receive visitors while laid up. So there was a process to get the elderly man dressed and into his wheelchair so he could be taken to the ground floor by elevator.

As expected, Max sat in the formal parlor with a wide smile on his face and an oxygen tank hooked to the back of his chair. "There's my favorite grandson."

"Last time I checked, I was your only grandson. You uncover a long-lost relative I don't know about?"

It was an old, beloved routine, but it warmed up the cold place in Phillip's gut that had formed when his wife stormed

off. Because her husband had hurt her over his own conflicted emotions.

"Never," his grandfather announced imperiously. "In
my day, we didn't lose track of our family, even without
the benefit of Facebook and thingamajigs that beep and
vibrate and who knows what all."

"Still not a fan of cell phones?" Phillip let his face fall
in mock disappointment. "Too bad. I bought you one for
your birthday."

"Well, that's a horse of a different color. A man cannot
in good conscience refuse a thoughtful gift. Give it here."
Max nodded and held out his hand.

"Ha. Your birthday isn't for two months. Don't you try to
con your way into an early present because it won't work.
But I might have something else…"

He drew it out as long as possible because he knew Max
well and the man could not stand to be left hanging. He'd
instantly become a dog fighting over a prized bone. It was
one of the qualities that had made him such a great senator.

His grandfather scowled without any real heat. "Don't
toy with me. I taught you those tricks, boy."

With a smile, Phillip handed over the ultrasound pictures
he'd tucked into his wallet yesterday. Max glanced at them,
then back up at Phillip quizzically. Then the light dawned.
His eyes went wide as he stared at the pictures. "Two?" he
whispered. "You're giving me two great-grandchildren?"

"Only because you're the best grandfather in the world,"
Phillip confirmed as Max laughed out loud, drawing the
attention of Amelia and Nancy, his full-time nurse, both
of whom rushed into the room to see what was happening.

"Look at this, ladies. I'm gonna be a great-grandpa times
two."

Amelia and Nancy oohed and aahed over the ultrasound

photos, but you could only look at blobs for so long. They congratulated Phillip and drifted back to their posts.

"You should have brought your lovely new wife by," Max suggested and waggled his bushy brows. "I haven't even met her yet."

Guilt crowded into Phillip's chest, and there hadn't been that much room in the first place with all the other stuff going on inside. His grandfather couldn't travel and hadn't been able to make the wedding, and then Phillip had been so busy commuting back and forth before and after that he hadn't made the time.

All just excuses in the end and not the real reason. If anyone would see his marriage as a sham, it would be Max, and Phillip hadn't wanted to answer any pointed questions about the nature of the agreement between him and his wife. Not in front of the one person who would instantly clue in on how it *looked* like Phillip had moved on...but really hadn't.

"Next time," he said instead.

If there was a next time. The fight he'd just had with Alex came rushing back, and it must have registered on his face because Max narrowed his gaze far too shrewdly for someone with cataracts.

"Trouble in paradise already?"

Phillip scrubbed his face. "She's working twelve, fourteen hours a day. I don't think it's good for her or the babies, and I guess trying to talk to her about it was the wrong move. She got pretty upset and stormed off."

"Take it from me. I'm an old widower but marriage hasn't changed in sixty years. You're wrong, no matter what. Apologize and make it good," Max advised and then shushed Phillip as he started to speak. "No, really. You're wrong. Trust me."

"So, I'm supposed to be okay with the fact that she's working so much?" Phillip frowned. "I can't accept that."

"Oh, I didn't say I agreed with her. I said you're wrong. You can spin that with her however you want. You handled it wrong. You were wrong to upset her. You misunderstood the question and gave the wrong answer. Whatever works to make her feel like she's understood and being heard. That's what women really want."

Phillip raised a brow. "You never gave me that advice when I was married to Gina."

"Gina was a sweet lady and you were so in love with her." Max smiled craftily. "But you were her whole world. She didn't have a life outside of Phillip Edgewood, United States senator. This new marriage is not the same. You have to give more because Alexandra is older than Gina was when you married her. More set in her ways. Less pliable. You don't want a pliable woman anyway, son. You married this one because she's totally different from Gina. Admit it."

Yes.

Shock shut Phillip's mouth so he couldn't say it out loud, but he was pretty sure he didn't have to. Of course Alex wasn't anything like Gina, but he'd been so busy following the rules to keep his new wife at arm's length that he hadn't stopped to examine *why* he'd been so attracted to someone so unlike his first wife.

He'd like to claim he'd done it deliberately, so he could guarantee he'd never fall for Alex. But that was the reason he'd married her, not the reason he was so attracted to her. That, he couldn't control. At all. Alex made him feel things he'd never felt for any woman before, and being the mother of his children had a lot to do with it. He could pretend all day long that was all it was—a fondness for the woman bearing his twins. But that wasn't all it was. No amount of guilt or pretending could change that.

"How did you get to be so smart, anyway?"

"Don't be grouchy just because I'm right." Max put a soothing gnarled hand on Phillip's shoulder and paused as his voice dissolved into a phlegmy coughing fit. When he'd recovered, he asked, "Now, what's really going on? You didn't have a fight about her working too hard because I'm pretty sure a woman who founded her own company always works a lot of hours."

That was what he got for telling his grandfather so much detail about the woman he'd married. Phillip's shoulders slumped as he recalled that Alex had said something very similar. "Yeah. It's kind of a mess."

The whole story poured out before Phillip even registered opening his mouth. How he didn't want to be in love again. Too painful. Much easier to go into a marriage without expectations. He needed a wife. Alex hadn't wanted to get married but he'd talked her into it.

Maybe *guilted* her into it was a better description.

Max nodded here and there but didn't interrupt. When Phillip finished talking, his heart felt ten pounds lighter. Who would have thought confession would be so good for his soul?

"I thought for sure that a marriage based on a mutual agreement would work." Phillip stared at his wedding ring. White gold instead of yellow because he hadn't wanted it to be the same as the first one. "But I have no idea how to handle things with Alex. Did I make a mistake, Grandpa?"

Fear seized his lungs, and he couldn't breathe. If he had made a mistake, that meant he had to make it right. That meant losing Alex. And his babies. He couldn't.

Max worked his lips, his gaze distant and thoughtful. "Here's the thing, son. Marriage isn't about how much you love someone or what *you* need. It's about how much you're willing to give. How well you're meeting *her* needs. Doesn't matter why you got married. Only whether you're willing to do the work."

His grandfather's advice ringing in his ears, Phillip flashed back to all the events since Alex had announced she was pregnant. She hadn't wanted to get married. He'd convinced her. She hadn't wanted to be a politician's wife. He'd blown that off and told her she'd be great. She hadn't wanted to be alone in the house when he wasn't there. He'd tried to take away her one refuge—numbers.

She'd done all the hard work thus far.

All this time, he'd thought he was being unfair to Alex because he'd sworn to withhold love from her, and it had blinded him to all the other imbalances going on. Instead of throwing his weight around, he should be bowing and scraping and treating her like royalty. He had to fix things or he would lose his plus one due to his own idiocy. Make that his plus three.

He'd assumed the learning curve would be steeper for Alex because she'd never been married before. But he hadn't realized that it would be a totally different ball game for him too the second time. Because he'd married a different woman. For different reasons.

"What should I do?" Phillip murmured.

"You already know the answer to that." Max nodded once for emphasis and started coughing again.

Phillip had overtaxed his grandpa with his own foolishness. It was way past time to leave. And his grandfather was right. There was no mystery here. He had to admit he was wrong and start working as hard on his marriage as Alex was. Easy. Look how brilliant she'd been at the ribbon cutting. Had he even thanked her? He couldn't remember.

He stood and rubbed Max's shoulder. "I should go. I

need to talk to my wife and let you rest. Okay if I bring her by sometime?"

"Of course. How else would I get a chance to steal her away from you?"

Phillip grinned. "Ha. You can try, old man, but you will not succeed."

"Bring it on," Max called out as Phillip left, a new plan already forming in his mind.

Back to Basics had been a great start but he needed something bigger: the Give Back Plan, which included making sure Alex got what she needed in this relationship. As long as he stuck to the rules, he could afford to be a lot more emotionally supportive.

Nine

Alex pivoted, but her stomach didn't look any less flat from that angle than it had from the left side. The mirror had to be broken. When was she going to start showing? Three months pregnant was a third of the way there.

She wanted to see some physical change, some hint of the miracle going on inside. Something that would prove she hadn't done the babies any harm by continuing to nurture her career as well as the twins.

Because at least half the reason she was still upset about the fight with Phillip a day later had to do with guilt. What if he was right? What if something terrible happened because she refused to listen to him? Morning sickness was a giant flashing warning, her body's way of saying *slow down*. And she hadn't been heeding the message.

At least all her clothes still fit. Shopping was not high on her list of pleasurable activities and she was kind of banking on Trinity and Cass picking out all her maternity clothes when the time came.

She glanced up as Phillip appeared in the mirror behind her.

"Ready to go?" he asked.

He'd come home last night with a dozen roses and a sweet apology. She'd accepted both. But hadn't forgiven or forgotten the reason they'd had a fight. Mostly because she'd got exactly what she deserved after filling in the *if only* blank. She'd let herself start to hope, just a tiny bit and *bam*...they'd got into an argument because she'd forgotten the rules. They were partners, not lovers who supported each other no matter what. No second chances, period, end of story. Hoping for something more? That had been the biggest in a long line of mistakes.

No more mistakes. If she screwed up, her kids would be fatherless, just like she'd been. That was not happening. This marriage was strictly designed to ensure her family didn't suffer because of her own selfishness.

So things between her and Phillip were...strained, for lack of a better word. Of course, they hadn't been married but a little over a week. Maybe this was normal for them.

"As ready as I'll ever be," she allowed and slicked on a coating of Harper's Crushed Blush lipstick, which she'd had for a year without using it all.

They'd been invited to a party at Phillip's parents' house, which she sorely did not want to attend but couldn't think of a good excuse for skipping. The question of her working through her pregnancy had not been broached again, but neither was it resolved, and the last thing she wanted to do was spend time faking her enthusiasm for the Edgewood clan.

But this was her role in the marriage. It was a fair trade for giving her babies a father. She just wished she didn't have to keep reminding herself that she was getting a good deal out of this.

Phillip had abracadabra-ed another dress from her closet that she'd never seen, and part of her wanted to hate it. But she didn't. It was a beautiful off-white wrap dress with a long skirt that reminded her of something Marilyn Monroe would wear.

She put it on. It fit. She looked spectacular in it. What was there to hate?

But she couldn't help feeling like a trophy wife. *Her.* Alexandra Meer...er, Edgewood. Her husband wanted to trot her out like a show pony, provided she had the right saddle. Coupled with everything else, especially the seesaw of emotions she constantly rode, it was too much.

They drove to the party in silence, though Phillip kept shooting her glances like he wanted to say something but wasn't sure how it would be received. Smart man.

The senior Edgewoods lived a short distance away in a newer part of Preston Hollow. New being relative; Phillip's house had been built in 1938. The Edgewoods' sprawling property rivaled their son's in elegance and beauty but clearly had a more modern design.

Randy opened the door and the Edgewoods' butler helped Alex from the car. Phillip put his hand on her back to escort her up the stairs. It was a simple gesture, but his touch burned through her.

Okay, that might be the sole physical response she couldn't chalk up to anything more than the pregnancy. Why did her body respond so quickly and ferociously when all Phillip had done was absently touch her? It was maddening.

The party was in full swing. People thronged the expansive grounds at the rear of the Edgewood property, all seemingly in a festive mood.

Alex pasted on a smile and greeted people she vaguely remembered from the wedding. She'd been so sick that day. She'd barely registered much of anything, let alone people's names.

Today, the swirl in her stomach had everything to do with uncertainty and a strong desire to not say anything that would raise eyebrows. Mostly that meant she had to keep her mouth shut and let Phillip do all the talking. Easy. He was a born charmer.

To her shock, he didn't park in the middle of a group and start chatting as he usually did. With barely a nod to those who called out to him, Phillip swept her past the knots of people and ushered her straight to a nearly empty gazebo overlooking the pool, pointing her to a wicker love seat. "This is your spot. Relax and I'll bring you a drink. Ginger ale?"

"Um...sure?" A bit off-kilter, she watched him thread back to the bar set up on the south end of the pool and accept a clear plastic cup from the uniformed bartender.

Phillip didn't stop to talk to one single person as he rushed her drink to her waiting hand.

"What else can I get you? Something to eat?" he asked.

"What's going on?" she blurted out. "Why are we here if you're not going to work the crowd?"

He sat on the love seat next to her, his gaze riveted to her face and not scanning the crowd for someone he needed to speak to. She was it, and oh, how she felt it deep inside.

"Because it's a party and I thought it was important that we have fun. Together. We don't do that."

"No, not as a rule." Or rather, because of the rules. They didn't have a relationship where they had *fun*. Did they? "Out of sheer curiosity, what would be the definition of *fun*?"

He smiled, and it washed over her with unexpected force. Like it had the night of another party. "A drink. Maybe I tell you a joke and you laugh. We talk about our favorite TV shows from when we were in third grade and perhaps a few interesting people happen by who join in on the conversation. Maybe we'll all weigh in on whether our parents let us watch *Blossom* or thought we were too young."

She couldn't help it. The laugh came out on its own.

"Hey," he protested. "I didn't tell you the joke yet."

"I was like seven when *Blossom* went off the air. I only cared about dolls and ponies and kitty cats, if I recall."

His grin widened and she forgot about the rest of the party. "Then you were definitely too young. Our kids won't be allowed to watch anything questionable until they turn twenty-one."

Our kids. It had such an intimate ring to it. She wanted to gather the feeling close and hold on to it. And that was enough to spring her guard back into place. "Really, you don't have to hang out with me. You should go network."

He waved off her comment. "I can do that anytime. I have to go back to Washington Sunday night and I want to spend time with you while I can."

Tenderness spread through his expression, and that was so lovely, she forgot why she wasn't supposed to let her heart squish when he looked at her.

A noise behind her alerted her to the presence of someone else, and reluctantly, she tore her gaze from her husband to see his mother clambering up the steps to the gazebo.

"Here's where you've spirited off my daughter-in-law to," Mrs. Edgewood exclaimed and swatted her son on the arm as she sank into the adjacent wicker armchair. "Whew, I was starting to think I'd never sit down. Thank you for picking such a great place to hide."

Guilt reared its ugly head, driving Alex to protest. "Oh, we're not hid—"

"You're welcome," Phillip interjected smoothly over

Alex's hasty response. "This is the best seat in the house for people watching."

Alex gave him the side-eye. Had he just admitted to his mother that he was avoiding people at his mother's own party? That was the kind of faux pas Alex usually made and had sworn to never make again.

But his mother laughed. "You used to come here all the time during parties when you were younger, Phillip. Remember? The adult ones you weren't invited to because they went on past your bedtime. You didn't think I knew, but Nana always kept me in the loop."

"Nana was my nanny," Phillip explained as an aside to Alex, still grinning fondly at his mother. "She had a real name but I couldn't pronounce it, so she was Nana until the day she left our employ. Little did I know she was a big tattletale about my nocturnal activities."

"Siobhan," Mrs. Edgewood supplied easily. "I could say it fine, but forget spelling it. Oh, she was a dear thing. We tag-teamed everything, from scraped knees to driving you to and from St. Mark's. His school," she explained to Alex.

Fascinated, Alex watched the exchange between Phillip and his mom. They had a bond that reminded her of the closeness she shared with her own mother, but different. Sure, Alex loved her mom, but their relationship had a lot of other things bound up in it: guilt and shame for the things she'd put her mother through. A sense of obligation. Her mother didn't have anyone else, had never remarried or even dated much after Alex's father left, so Alex was all she had.

And her mother had been instrumental in pulling Alex from the pit of self-destruction. She'd probably be dead or in jail right now without her mother. It made sense that Alex would remain mindful of the debt she owed.

The interaction between Phillip and his mother was totally different. They loved each other for no other reason than by virtue of being family. Not due to any rules or obligation. Just because. You could see it in their expressions, in the relaxed way they were with each other, in the tones of their voices.

Love didn't look like that in Alex's world. Never had. Her own father had left their family without a backward glance. So was it any wonder she'd never believed love existed?

Or had that belief been something she'd invented to avoid the question of *why* no one loved her like that?

"Alex, when you're ready to hire a nanny, if you want my help interviewing you just let me know." Mrs. Edgewood patted Alex's arm to punctuate that statement.

Stunned, Alex stared at Phillip's mother. Nanny? She hadn't even thought that far ahead, but of course she would need one. It wasn't like she could work sixty or seventy hours a week and raise two babies, especially not with a husband who commuted back and forth to Washington.

"That's very kind, Mrs. Edgewood."

"Oh, please don't call me Mrs. Edgewood. That just aged me twenty years. And I didn't need any help getting older." She shook her head with a laugh. "I'm Connie and we're family."

Tears pricked at Alex's eyes. Stupid pregnancy hormones. Why would Mrs. Edgewood say something like that? Alex wasn't family, not really. Not the kind she'd meant, like someone you loved for no reason other than because you wanted to. Her son certainly didn't.

But obviously he had the capacity for it. He'd loved Gina. Was there something fundamentally wrong with Alex that caused people to shy away from loving her?

A tear worked loose and slid down her face. Mortified, she swiped at it and then shrugged. It wasn't like she could hide it from the woman watching her so closely. "Thank you, Connie. I think that's the nicest thing anyone's said to me in a long time."

"Then you're hanging out with the wrong people." Glaring at her son with pointed barbs as if to include him in the category of *wrong people*, Connie smoothed a hand over Alex's shoulder. "You're the only daughter I've got. Let's make it count."

Oh, wow. That had not been anything like the reception she'd been braced for. There was an authenticity implied in the woman's statement that Alex craved all at once. Her relationship with Phillip might not be based on love but the one with Connie could be. There were no rules about that. If she wanted advice about hiring a nanny, who better to ask than a woman who'd married a politician, the same as Alex had?

They could be friends in an otherwise confusing Edgewood world. Somehow, the simple sentiment of being labeled Connie's daughter enclosed Alex in a big bubble of belonging, and now that she was inside it, she couldn't stand for it to burst.

"Okay." Alex nodded and another tear splashed to her lap. When had she started wanting so much more than rules to live by? Rules were the only thing that made sense and never changed. They kept you safe and free from consequences.

When had she started wanting to be loved?

Phillip's arm came around Alex and he pulled her close in wordless comfort. His touch warmed her, and it had nothing to do with sex. The moment swelled through her, fueled by the emotions already in play.

"You should be saying nice things to your wife all the time," his mother scolded. "Alex is the mother of your children. That automatically makes her worthy of being showered with all sorts of pretty words."

"I agree," Phillip said wryly. "But none of the stuff I'd like to say is fit for mixed company."

"Well, then, I'll leave you to your pillow talk." His mother didn't even blush, a trick Alex would like to learn because *her* cheeks had certainly prickled with heat at the blatant sexual innuendo. Connie stood and smiled at Alex. "Thank you for bringing light back into my son's life. His father and I worried he'd never get to this point after Gina passed. You're more of a blessing than you could ever know."

Connie sailed out of the gazebo, leaving Alex in a big puddle of confusion about what had just happened. Had she done that—brought some cheer into the life of a widower? Somehow she hadn't thought of him as grieving. And as revelations went, it was rather huge.

"Sorry, she didn't mean to make you uncomfortable."

Alex blinked and met Phillip's gaze. A warm breeze filtered through the gazebo, bringing with it the barest hint of honeysuckle and a clarity she hadn't realized she'd needed.

"She didn't. She's a lovely person." Her mind whirling furiously, Alex settled deeper into Phillip's embrace. "Did she make *you* uncomfortable? You don't talk about Gina much."

Bingo. Phillip shifted as if he couldn't find the right position. "Not much to talk about. She's gone."

He *was* uncomfortable talking about Gina. But if he didn't talk about her, how was he ever supposed to move past his feelings for her?

"But you loved her. That's a big, beautiful thing worth honoring."

At that, he full-out froze. Sounds of the party drifted through the sudden stillness and Alex had half a mind to quit while she was ahead. This was exactly the kind of foot in mouth she should be avoiding. But something about the way he'd talked to his mother, the relationship they had, made her ache. Physical needs she knew all about slaking. This man had a talent for it, and she had a pretty good handle on how to reciprocate. But what about emotional needs? His *and* hers? Why wasn't fulfilling those part of their deal?

Or was the real problem that neither of them knew what their emotional needs were? What if she could take this opportunity to find out and didn't?

She went for broke. "I've never been in love. What's it like?"

Phillip exhaled, and with it, some of the tension eased. "A miracle. A song that your soul can't stop singing. Energy. Light. Motivation. When you have it, things you never thought possible become achievable."

Transfixed, Alex listened to her husband express the poetry of his heart and her own twisted. The wrenching in her chest was equal parts awe and pain, like she'd glimpsed heaven only to have angry storm clouds race across the opening in the sky.

Because what he'd just described was what love meant to Phillip. Now that she'd heard it, experienced it in watching the way he interacted with his mother, she wanted it for herself. She wanted Phillip to believe he could have that again. That they could achieve it together, with each other.

And that was against the rules.

Alex bit her lip and held back additional tears. Barely. "No wonder you don't think you'll find that again. It sounds like a once-in-a-lifetime deal."

Which didn't necessarily mean that it was. There were no rules when it came to things of the heart. That was why she shied away from them so quickly. But this time, she didn't want to.

He nodded, surprise dawning in his expression. "You give me a lot of grace. I appreciate that. I keep expecting you to make demands of me that I can't fulfill and you never do. I've made some mistakes due to that and I'm sorry. I'm trying to stop operating on false assumptions."

He meant their fight about her working too hard. And the distance. All smoke screens to keep her from expecting too much. Because he didn't think he had any more to give than what he'd laid out at the beginning of their relationship.

And finally, she understood his emotional need in this relationship—to become a believer in second chances. Who better to help him learn that than someone who understood the power and mercy of being granted a do-over?

She carried the explosive secret with her for the remainder of the weekend.

When they got home from the party, where Phillip had done exactly as he said and spent the entire time with Alex having fun, he didn't disappear, mentally or physically.

They watched a movie on the giant theater screen in the media room and Phillip held her hand through the whole thing, except for the five minutes he left to get her a drink. They slept in the same bed, wrapped around each other like lovers. Because they were.

Just not yet the kind she'd started to believe—and hope—might be possible.

At breakfast Sunday morning, Phillip looked up from his English muffins, jam and scrambled eggs with a bittersweet smile. "I hate that I have to go back to Washington tonight."

"It's not ideal," she agreed. "I was hoping to get to a

point where I could come with you, but this week is impossible with quarter end. I have meetings all week."

"Speaking of which, a week from tomorrow, there's going to be a preliminary hearing about your FDA application. In Washington. I was planning to cover it for you."

"That would be great." She asked him a few questions about the process so she could report back to the other ladies in Fyra's C-suite about the next steps, which Phillip answered easily and thoroughly. Fyra had been truly blessed by his help.

He forked up a bite of eggs and chewed thoughtfully, his gaze on her. "We've known each other for a while now, and I don't think I've ever asked why cosmetics."

The question was so out of left field she had to take a minute to figure out what he was talking about. "You mean why did Cass, Trinity, Harper and I open shop to sell mascara instead of something else?"

"Yeah. I knew I wanted to be a senator by the time I was a senior in high school. And really for me, it was more of a decision on whether I wanted to go to the House or the Senate, not whether I'd go into politics at all. You had the whole world at your feet and chose mascara. I'm curious why."

She could lie. She did it all the time. But something about the way he asked, with no judgment, just a man curious about his wife's thoughts, made her want to answer honestly. If she hoped to reverse Phillip's stance on second chances, what better way to accomplish that goal than to tell the story of how she'd got hers?

"Cosmetics is their thing. I'm just along for the ride," she admitted, and the earth didn't crack open at her feet, so she went on. "I never planned to go to college. I wanted to have fun and hang out with my friends. Who were a boatload of trouble, but they were mine. You know? They listened to me and cared about me in the midst of my parents' painful divorce."

He nodded, but didn't interrupt.

"The first time we got arrested, they let us go with a warning. We thought we were invincible and did a lot of things we shouldn't have—drugs, shoplifting, graffiti. You name it, we did it."

It was a bland recitation of facts, but the anguish she still felt sometimes about her past came out in her voice. The concern painting her husband's face wasn't the revulsion she deserved.

"You needed your family and they weren't there," he said simply. "So you found a new one."

"Yeah. Then the music stopped when I was fifteen. I finally got the attention of someone who saw the train wreck about to happen and knew exactly how to fix it. Judge Miller. She was compassionate, just and really cared about her job."

Alex had realized all of this in hindsight, of course. At the time, she'd been disrespectful, mad about being caught and not about to let anyone know how scared she'd been. Judge Miller had told Alex she couldn't let her ruin her own life. The first of many second chances. Alex had quickly embraced them for the miracles they'd been.

And according to Phillip, *love* was a miracle. Maybe she'd been the recipient of more love than she'd realized over the years. The concept didn't feel so foreign all at once.

"How did she fix it?" Phillip had forgotten about his breakfast and sat with his attention squarely on Alex.

"After she sentenced me, she called me and my mother into her chambers and gave my mother the talking-to of her life. Said she was the one who could change things for me, and Judge Miller was going to hold her accountable for my probation. That was a turning point."

Her mother had taken that advice to heart, got Alex into a rehab program that actually worked and applied for every scholarship she thought her daughter had a marginal chance of receiving. With a lot of hard work, Alex had got her grades up enough to be accepted to the University of Texas.

She told Phillip about walking into freshman algebra, her first class as a college student, and sitting next to a friendly redhead who had knocked her pencil to the floor four times in fifteen minutes. Each time, Alex had picked it up with a smile of commiseration. Her own nerves had been strung tight, too.

By the end of the hour, Alex had known her classmate's name was Harper, that they shared a decided social awkwardness and that Harper had hoped to be a chemist when she grew up. Since Alex had had no clue what she'd wanted to be the following day, let alone in the future, and because she'd had a lack of friends without criminal records, Harper had seemed like someone from another planet.

A bit starstruck, Alex had expended monumental effort to match her new friend's over-the-top math skills. But it wasn't until the professor asked her to tutor another student that Alex had understood she possessed an unusual aptitude for numbers.

"The other student? It was Cass," Alex finished and had to swallow the sudden lump in her throat. "She was such a beautiful person. Still is. She believed in me from the very beginning. When she introduced me to Trinity, the first thing she said was 'I found our finance guru.' *Me*. Alex Meer, fresh from Podunk, Texas, and barely clear of my probation period. I never would have majored in finance without Cass. I never would have realized I liked numbers if I hadn't sat next to Harper that first day."

"That's a great story." Phillip squeezed her hand.

She hadn't even registered him taking it into his, but the silent comfort soothed the emotional smashup going on inside. "That's why I can't just quit. Cosmetics mean nothing to me, but friendship? That's everything. I would paint my body with mascara brushes if one of my partners asked me to."

"I see." He went quiet for a moment. "No wonder you got so angry with me when I mentioned it."

The fact that he got that squeezed her heart harder than he'd squeezed her hand. How did he affect her so much with simple words? Probably because she'd started to glimpse what could be possible between them and every moment in his presence reinforced it. She *wanted* to be affected. The emotional highs were addictive. Necessary. Wonderful.

"I didn't deserve a second chance, but I definitely believe in them." Let him do what he wanted to with that.

"I'm starting to get the point." With that cryptic comment, he kissed her fingertips and wandered down her arm to her elbow with so much serious intent that finishing breakfast became the last thing on either of their minds.

By the time he left that night, she hadn't got any closer to figuring out how to take their relationship to the next level. Or what that would even look like. Quandaries of the heart were not logical, and she was the last person who should be attempting to unravel this.

But comments like *I'm starting to get the point* gave her hope. Phillip had loved Gina so much. Maybe it was clouding his judgment about whether it could happen again. Lightning might not strike the same place twice, but who stood around in the exact same place waiting for it?

What had he said at the party? *Things you never thought possible become achievable.* She totally understood that now. Because she was pretty sure she was falling for her husband. That was so huge a revelation, it rendered her mute. And made the long week without Phillip seem that much longer.

On Monday, Melinda called her to the front desk because a dozen roses had just been delivered with Alex's name on them. Entranced, she rushed to the reception area to claim her vase. The note inside read: "One bouquet to commemorate our wedding day. —Phillip"

It was so sweet and surprising, she floated through the rest of the day.

On Tuesday, she received another delivery. Two dozen stargazer lilies with a note: "Two bouquets in honor of our twin babies. —Phillip"

She stared at the bouquets on her desk for a solid hour instead of focusing on the quarterly reports she needed to absorb before a meeting that afternoon. Phillip was obviously thinking about her. Missing her, maybe, like she was missing him. Their big house seemed so empty without him in it. Like her heart. She yearned to fill it with Phillip.

Perhaps he wanted to fill her heart and she just needed to let him.

On Wednesday, the reception area nearly burst at the seams as the entire office came to see what Phillip had sent. Three dozen larkspurs with a note: "Three bouquets. One for each month you've carried my children in your womb. —Phillip"

That one drew tears from her and at least half of the onlookers. She got it now. He was grateful for his children and wanted her to know, that was all. She'd never received flowers from anyone before and three in a row was something special. But she couldn't help wishing the flowers had been sent for more personal reasons.

Thursday, it was four dozen dendrobium orchids. The

note: "Four. That's how many orgasms I gave you last weekend. —Phillip"

No one in the reception area got to read that note and she blushed the rest of the day. Had the flower delivery people read it? Surely not. Next time, she'd be more careful what she wished for. But still. The flowers weren't just about the babies, like she'd convinced herself, strictly to avoid being disappointed. So what *were* they about?

On Friday, five dozen tulips in orange, red and yellow made the reception area look like the sun had burst open all over Fyra. The note read: "Five days I've had to wait to see you again. It's too many. —Phillip"

Something sharp and sweet spiked through her. Was all of this her husband's subtle way of saying his feelings were changing, as well? He was a rule follower, too. It was one of the many things they had in common. Maybe he was waiting for her to make the first move, in case she wasn't on board with coloring outside the lines. How could she find out?

Ask him, of course. But what if she turned out to be wrong? She was flying blind and terrified of messing up.

If she wanted something more than just being friends and partners with Phillip, she had to take that leap. They'd agreed divorce was off the table, so there was no reason to fear the consequences.

Last week, he'd come home to her. This time, she'd go to him. On the surface, she could pretend she'd elected to attend the FDA hearing on Monday in person. But in reality, for the first time since her youth, Alex was planning to break the rules.

Ten

Last week, Phillip had jetted home without even stopping by his condo. By five o'clock on Friday, he was starting to think that sounded like an even better idea this week.

Opposition to the bill he was cosponsoring with Senator Galindo had been fierce, and she and Phillip had spent the past week duking it out side by side on the Senate floor. The bill had failed to even make it to a vote.

He wanted to go home to Dallas and sink into Alex for reasons he was too tired to examine. She'd make it all go away with her smile and her pretty hair that felt like silk against his fingers. But the three-hour flight loomed, long and boring and so not what he wanted to do, and he hadn't even left Capitol Hill yet.

This commuting back and forth arrangement had serious holes in it. But he and Alex were stuck in it for the time being. He was trying to be patient with all of the complexities of their relationship, but something had to give.

A bit disgusted with the world in general, he trudged to his car and let Randy drive him back to the condo so he could dump his briefcase at least. But when he walked in the door, the light in the kitchen was on. Instantly on guard, he pulled out his phone to call 911…when Alex emerged from the bedroom.

Alex. Wearing a silk robe and a smile. And nothing else. He hoped.

The phone dropped from his nerveless fingers. "What—"

"Shh. I wanted to surprise you. Consider it an in-person thank-you for the flowers."

She advanced to the spot where he'd become rooted to the floor and he couldn't do anything other than watch the sexy sashay. He didn't want to do anything else on earth besides that.

"Yeah?" he croaked. "Found the robe I bought you, did you?"

He swallowed the question as she took hold of his tie, pulling on it sharply to bring his mouth to hers.

And then his brain dissolved as his wife devoured him, kissing him with a burst of pent-up passion. Or maybe that was his own kettle hitting full boil and whistling for all it was worth. Because holy hell, her tongue slicked along his, hot and strong and determined to unravel him in one shot.

It was working.

His wife had flown to Washington. To be with him. He'd reached out, tried to change the dynamic between them so they could get their relationship on even ground, and she'd reached back. Wow, had she reached back.

He should be the one doing the thanking. She was exactly what he'd needed, exactly what he'd wanted. All his fantasies wrapped up in an amazing package that he didn't have to wait one second to enjoy. It was like she'd read his mind.

His heart shattered and knit back together again instantly. He should probably care more about the ramifications of that.

She backed him up against one of the pillars separating the family room and the kitchen. His shoulder blades hit it a moment before her lush breasts smashed against his torso. He groaned. Even through his suit jacket he could feel her hard nipples. Lust rocketed through him, hardening everything in its path, and she purred her approval as her hands examined every inch of it.

"Too many clothes," she muttered and yanked off his suit jacket, popping a button in her haste. Enthusiastically, he helped her get the rest off and then the silk of her robe brushed across his skin, shooting sparks of sensation far and wide.

"Not you," he murmured hoarsely. "You're wearing exactly the right amount."

Provided she was naked under that robe…and lo and behold, she was. His palms cupped her bare rear and shoved, grinding her against his erection.

More. Now. Fast.

His mouth hot on hers again, he picked her up and stumbled to the kitchen…or the living room…or at least something that had a surface at waist height, and set her down. Because he wanted to use his hands and couldn't hold her up at the same time.

Falling into her, he gathered up the edges of the robe and pulled them wide, baring her breasts to his hungry gaze. Licking one nipple into his mouth, he sucked as his hands circled her stomach, thighs and then finally honed in on the sweet spot, pulling a hard gasp from her as he pushed into her slick center with two fingers, then three.

Not enough. He wanted to feel everything.

Centering her, he plunged in to the hilt and a gasp burst

from his own throat. Perfection. She rolled her hips, drawing him deeper, urging him on with little cries that inflamed his thrusts until they both came in a rush, pulsing in tandem. His knees nearly gave out from the force of his release.

And then he just held on to her, still deep inside, still caught up in the wash of pleasure. He closed his eyes and let his head rest on hers as something warm burst open in his chest.

He knew exactly what it was. Something that wasn't supposed to be there but had been for a while. Something wholly encompassing that was so much stronger in this moment after making love to his wife.

Where had that *come* from?

The black box inside had been locked up for so long. Exactly the way he'd wanted it. No emotions meant no pain.

Of course he cared about Alex. She was carrying his children. They were married. That warmth was only natural, he assured himself with something akin to panic.

She sighed against his neck, her legs clamped tight around his waist in the midst of an encounter that had only happened because she'd cut her workday short so she could fly three hours to see him. It was a huge concession, one that wasn't lost on him, and the warmth he'd been trying to deny spread to his heart, filling him.

Leftover reaction from the sex. Which had been so unbelievable. That was all this was. Of course he'd have some residual heat from that; it had been hot.

Relief settled over him. After the conversation with his grandfather, he'd known he had to do something to change his relationship with Alex or he risked losing what he'd perceived to be a tenuous hold on Alex and his babies. Looked like it had worked.

"You're welcome," he murmured when he could speak through all the *stuff* going on inside. "For the flowers."

It had been a spontaneous thought born of a long night alone last Sunday. He'd lain in bed remembering their weekend together and had wanted to do something to let her know he missed her. Part of the hard work Max had entreated him to take on, but it hadn't felt like work.

"The notes were the best part," she whispered into his ear and her legs tightened around him, increasing the contact between their bodies. "They were like a secret message."

"Oh?"

"Yeah. You picked out the most important highlights of our relationship and dedicated a note to each one. We're married. Having a family together. We can't keep our hands off each other because we've always been hot for one another." She ticked off each point against his shoulder. "And we like being with each other. Sharing a life. So much so that we miss each other. Marriage is so much better than what we thought it was going to be. That's what you meant. Right?"

Hearing it all encapsulated like that—no, that wasn't at all what he'd intended but he liked her points. What she'd said was exactly how he felt. Maybe he had subconsciously wanted to pay tribute to what was great about where they'd ended up.

"Yeah, sure. You're onto me."

Actually, it wasn't perhaps as subconscious as he'd pretended. The notes were also parameters. They carefully defined the box he'd put around their relationship. *These are the things our relationship is. The omissions are the things our relationship is not.*

It was inside of those parameters where he felt safest. Nothing bad would happen if they just stuck to the agreement. No emotional commitment meant no guilt, and it meant he'd never have to relive those hours and days after losing the most important thing in his life. And the fact that Alex got that was amazing. Wonderful. Miraculous.

The warmth in his chest started to bother him. He couldn't exactly claim to still be in the throes of post-orgasm. What was he doing still engaged with her like this? It was dangerous.

Alex cupped his face with her palms and kissed him sweetly, then drew back to bowl him over with a misty smile. Shiny moisture gathered in the corners of her eyes. "That's great. Because I'm falling for you, too."

"You're…what?" His voice cracked. "*Falling? For me? Too?*"

Parroting her words did not cause them to magically become coherent. While he'd been busy lying to himself about what was happening on his side of the fence, it had never occurred to him that *she'd* be veering from the rules.

She cocked her head, her smile slipping a touch. "Well… yeah. That's what we're talking about. Right? Our feelings toward each other are growing stronger. Deeper. The agreement didn't cover what would happen if we fell in love. So what do we do with that?"

Yes, of course their feelings were deeper than they had been. They were living together, married—but not *in love*. Okay, sometimes he couldn't sleep when she wasn't there. Sometimes his heart got a little warm when he looked at her. So what? That wasn't the same as what she was talking about.

Or was she seeing something he hadn't dared admit, even to himself?

"We're not…" His throat tightened, almost strangling him as he shut his eyes, willing back the panic clawing through his gut. "The agreement didn't cover it because it's not happening."

Crush it now. Don't let anything change.

The rules were in place for a reason; so she didn't expect something he was unwilling to give. But it was too late to backpedal. Even he could see that as she flinched.

Caution clouded her expression. "Not happening? You can't tell me how I feel, Phillip. Nor can you lie away your own feelings."

This was really, truly happening. They were having a conversation about the very thing he'd taken so many pains to avoid. The conflict inside between the guilt over his faithlessness toward Gina and the future he could have with Alex roared to life, clawing through him with metal teeth.

Wrenching away from her, he went in search of his clothes. He didn't want to have this conversation at all, let alone while naked.

She followed him into the living area, drawing her robe closed and belting the sash. She clearly didn't realize he'd been seeking distance. She perched on the edge of a wingback chair flanking the fireplace. Quickly, he threw on his shirt and pants but couldn't find the left leg hole until he sat on the couch. Dazed, he stared at the carpet, the giraffe-stone fireplace, anywhere but at his wife as he told her what she needed to hear.

"I'm not lying away my feelings," he insisted. He despised politicians who lied as a matter of course. His honesty had always been one of his trademarks; that was the reason he was in this marriage, because he hadn't wanted to mislead his constituents. "I don't mean that I'm trying to will it away. I mean it's not on the table. It's not an option."

Which was true but wasn't necessarily the same as the

whole truth, and that was something he wasn't willing to offer. Because the way he felt about Alex had veered into dangerous territory a long time ago. And he'd tried—unsuccessfully—to mitigate those circumstances.

His heart belonged to Gina and no other woman could ever breach that wall. No other woman could be allowed inside. It wasn't fair to anyone, but it was the way things were.

It rang a little less true than it had in the past. And that was the worst revelation of all. If he allowed himself to love Alex, he'd be allowing himself the possibility of being emotionally destroyed all over again. He couldn't do it.

He was hurting her. The pain etched into her face nearly undid him. This was the reason he'd avoided women who wanted a love match. What had happened to his perfect, loveless marriage? Dumb question—emotions had happened to it. His and hers, effectively killing their agreement. It was a disaster.

Everything was falling apart and he didn't have a clue how to save it.

"You say it's not an option," Alex countered far more calmly than the tango in her stomach should have allowed. "But one of your points about getting married was that you wanted our children to grow up in a home like the one you had."

This was not going like she'd envisioned. Phillip hadn't fallen into her arms and thanked her for reading between the lines of his notes. In fact, if anything, she'd say they were headed in the opposite direction. His slightly panicked expression and superquick donning of his clothes had a lot to do with that impression.

The magic she'd thought had sparked between them in

the kitchen had thoroughly fizzled. Why had she thought baring her soul would be a good idea?

"Yeah. It is one of the reasons." Even his tone of voice had flattened out.

Pandora's box had been opened, and though she'd like nothing more than to slam the lid closed, she forced out the words. Do-or-die time. If she wanted more, she had to reach out. If she wanted to be loved, she had to say so.

"Your parents are very much in love, even now. Anyone can see that. Maybe that's part of the equation. Love is what creates that environment for kids. So what if we keep fast to the agreement and that turns out to be worse for our children? Why not explore all the options?"

There it was. Her best argument for taking their relationship to places they'd never expected. The logic was sound. If there was any chance of getting her husband on board with the possibility of a love match, logic was it. She held her breath.

"It's not an option," he repeated as his expression closed in. "We talked about this. You know what I'm willing to give and what I'm not."

Because his first wife was such a paragon that Alex couldn't measure up. Being the mother of his children didn't give her any special rights to his heart. He'd been more than clear about that all along.

Bitterness rose up in her throat. "Gina is gone, Phillip. You have to get over her and live your life for you and your children."

He froze, and his entire demeanor iced over. "That's not your call."

His tone cut through her, heightening the sick wave of panic and pain that had been brewing since she first admitted she was falling for him and he didn't say it back.

She'd screwed up. She never should have said anything. That was what she got for trying to get out of her comfort zone. For daring to believe that she'd found someone who would love her madly, passionately, like Phillip had loved Gina. She'd really thought… Obviously, she'd imagined Phillip had developed any sort of feelings toward her other than gratitude. But the notes had been so sweet and the way he looked at her sometimes… Her heart lurched as she stared at his implacable expression.

No. This was not her fault. Her feelings had changed and he didn't get to dictate that.

She wanted the husband she'd convinced herself he was becoming. It wasn't what they'd talked about or what she'd thought would happen, but that didn't make it any less valid. And she'd fight for what she hoped could be the outcome of this argument. "Well, the agreement's not working for me anymore. That *is* my call."

Frowning, he eyed her. "What are you saying?"

"I want more than a partnership. I don't want to be two friends who got married because of a baby. Actually, that's not even still the same as it was when we first came up with this deal." She laughed without humor. "It's not a baby. It's a whole family that will be here in six months. Nothing is like it was when we cooked up the agreement. Especially not me."

"We agreed—"

"I know that!" Breathing in sharply, she tried to settle her stomach, which kept flipping over and back again, a little more violently each time she got more upset. "I didn't know we were having twins when I agreed. I had no idea what love looked like when I agreed. I had no idea that I'd experience such depths of feeling with you when I *agreed*. Emotions are not my forte. Don't you get that? This is hard for me and I was scared to bring it up because I don't know what I'm feeling."

Her hands shook with the effort to hold back the tears.

"Then you shouldn't have brought it up," he said flatly, refusing to look at her. "We had a line and you crossed it."

"I had to," she whispered, head bowed as something sharp tore through her chest. "I want more, Phillip. If you aren't willing to consider what I'm asking for, then I'm done here."

That got his attention. He glanced up abruptly. "What does that mean?"

"What it sounds like." An ending. What was ending, she wasn't sure. Her hopes? Her dreams? "I'm going to stay with Harper for a while until I can sort out what I want to do."

Drained, she rubbed at her temples, too shell-shocked to string together many more coherent words. Had they just broken up? Hard to say; she'd never done any of this before. She had no idea what came next, but what was happening at the moment was not something she could keep slogging through.

"I see." His eyebrows snapped together. "We agreed no love. We agreed no divorce. Apparently you're allowed to throw the entire agreement out the window if I don't bow to your wishes. Is that it? I have no say here?"

Divorce. The ugly word bit through her and something died inside. No, that wasn't what she wanted at all. But what was the alternative? They'd tried no expectations and that had been a dismal failure.

"I don't have the energy for this right now." That at least was the truth. "I have to think about the babies. I'm about to break into a million pieces and I'd prefer to do it somewhere you're not."

He nodded curtly. "Randy will take you to the airport. Fly home in my plane. Take care of yourself."

Too numb to cry, she gathered her bag and let Phillip help her into the car that would take her away from the man she suspected had just broken her heart.

Eleven

The next morning, Harper took one look at Alex's face and threw open the door of her Victory Park loft to embrace her. "Oh, honey. When you called, I had no idea it was that bad."

What was the definition of *bad*? That she didn't know whether she could be married to Phillip anymore? That he hadn't tried to stop her when she left? That in spite of everything, she'd fallen for her husband after all, and now that she knew love existed, it sucked?

Alex sniffed against Harper's shoulder. "It's bad. The worst part is that I don't even know why I'm crying."

The diminutive redhead herded Alex to the long off-white leather couch facing the Dallas skyline. A dozen floors below, traffic raced along the street, but up here, they were insulated from life's ebb and flow. If only the quiet would dull the riot of emotions seething through her stomach.

"You're crying because men are jerks and they should all be flayed alive with butter knives," Harper responded matter-of-factly. "Except Dante."

For some reason, that got a laugh from Alex. "Friends are exempt?"

Alex and Phillip had been friends once upon a time. Now they weren't even that. Were they? When she'd started this ill-advised descent into lunacy also known as admitting she cared for her husband, she should have thought it through a little better. Now she didn't have a friend, a partner *or* a father for her babies. That dull butter knife might be a kinder way to go.

Harper grinned fondly. "Dante's exempt because he's awesome and it would be a travesty for the world to lose his genius. The fact that he's one of the few people in the world who would drop everything for me is just a bonus."

That sounded so nice. She wanted Phillip to love her like that.

Stomach sloshing again, Alex groaned and leaned back against the couch. She'd flown back to Dallas last night and had been so sick by the time she got back to Phillip's house that she couldn't pack one single shirt, let alone all her belongings. She'd curled up on the bathroom floor, cheek to the marble, in hopes it would cool her tear-ravaged face or settle her stomach. It had done neither.

"I'm crying because of hormones. That's all," Alex assured Harper, though she'd stopped believing that at about three o'clock that morning. "This pregnancy is going to go down as the most difficult in history."

Harper snorted, reminding Alex she'd used the hormone excuse on her friend once already.

"I think all pregnant women say that. What's it feel like, anyway?"

"Like I drank four glasses of red wine, two shots of

Jägermeister and a gallon of Clorox in less than a minute. On an empty stomach."

Hormones weren't the reason she ached inside at the thought of never seeing Phillip again, never being held by him again. Not having that family with him that she'd envisioned where they woke up on a Saturday and went for brunch at a low-key restaurant, then swam in his parents' pool until it was time to get ready for one of Phillip's political fundraisers that evening. The kids would stay home with the nanny she'd hired with Connie's help, and in the car, Phillip would raise the privacy shield and turn to Alex with a wicked smile...

"Ha-ha." Her friend's nose wrinkled and she nodded to Alex's midsection. "I mean the being-pregnant part. You have real live babies in there. Is it weird?"

"Miraculous," she corrected and her heart thumped twice in rapid succession. Looked like that particular organ was still working after all. "They're mine. I'm the only person in the world who gets to have the experience of carrying them in my womb. When I give birth, they'll be my children forever and no one can take that away."

"Wow, your face just started glowing." Clearly fascinated, Harper zeroed in on it, her scientific brain no doubt cataloging all the nuances.

Alex didn't even have to think twice about how to describe it. "That's what love looks like."

The miracle, the energy Phillip had spoken of—that was how she felt about her babies. If nothing else, he'd given her the babies and they were a huge gift indeed.

"I'm a little jealous, honestly," Harper murmured, her smile faltering. "You and Cass are both moving to a new phase in life and I'm being left behind. Trinity is, too. I'm not sure she cares, though."

"But you care?" Alex eyed Harper but her vision was

still pretty blurry. Was she serious or just making conversation? "Since when do you think about being a mom?"

Harper shrugged, not even bothering to cover the wistfulness in her small smile. "Lately. It's not a crime."

The thought of Harper giving a man the time of day—let alone unbending enough to be intimate with one—was unfathomable. "Weren't we just talking about how men suck and should all be tortured?"

"Who needs a man? There are all sorts of ways to become a mother without introducing additional complexities like a relationship." As Alex well knew, and the point wasn't lost on her. The leather creaked under Harper's thigh as she crossed her legs. "You're going to be raising your babies alone, right? If you can do it, I could, too. We'll do it together."

Alone? As in without Phillip? *No.* That was not what was happening here. She'd needed breathing room, that was all. Her heart settled deeper in her chest as that reality clarified. She hadn't been able to pack because that wasn't the answer. She and Phillip were married. This was the part where it got hard but she'd made a commitment and she still wanted her babies to have a father. Phillip was the only one who got that title.

"Yeah, but the difference is that I don't want to be doing it alone. That's not what I'd envisioned for myself or my kids. At all."

So they'd have to find a way to make it work. Somehow. Her resolve faltered. Did that mean she'd have to go back to their original agreement and suck it up, never mentioning again the longings of her heart to have something more meaningful than a handshake?

"Well, it was just a thought, anyway." Leaning forward, she patted Alex's arm. "If you don't want to do it alone, then why are you here? Go back to Washington and work things out with Phillip. You had a great agreement going for you. Put it back together."

"It's not that simple," Alex wailed, her emotional threads bursting at the seams again. "Everything seemed so logical and reasonable and then I started wanting more, wanting things I don't even understand... He wasn't happy with me for bringing it up."

Of course he hadn't been. She'd broken the rules. Bad things happened when she did that, but she'd done it anyway. She was the poster child for letting selfishness guide her actions and then reaping what she'd sown.

Tossing her hair back, Harper narrowed her gaze. "Then I'm probably not the right person to help you sort it out. I love you like a sister but romantic love is a waste of time. When you said you and Phillip had a fight, I thought he'd brought up the issue about you working again."

"No, he got over that." Hadn't he? They'd never really talked about it again. More like it had been brushed under the carpet. Like everything else. "This is about our non-traditional marriage and whether I can keep being okay with it."

Phillip needed her and needed his marriage. That much she knew for a fact. He had his image to maintain, after all, she thought sourly.

"Then it sounds like you have some thinking to do about what you want to do. Of course, you're welcome to stay here until you figure it out." Brightly, Harper jumped up from the couch and held out her hand to help Alex to her feet. "Let's have some breakfast and you can fill me in on the status of the FDA application. As soon as we have approval, we're ready to gear up production of Formula-47, and frankly, I can't wait for two years' worth of work to come to fruition. Do I need to step in as Fyra's liaison now that things are dicey with Phillip?"

Alex groaned. The hearing on Monday. She'd forgotten all about it. The babies weren't the only reason she couldn't shed her relationship with Phillip quickly and easily, even if she wanted to. "The hearing is on Monday. I went to Washington yesterday with the sole intent to spend the weekend with Phillip and then go to the hearing, but instead, I ran away like a spoiled brat."

Some executive she was. In all her imaginings of her life with Phillip where they lived happily ever after with their family, her career hadn't entered the picture once. Because it was a given, she reminded herself fiercely. Fyra was her life.

Or at least it was right now. At some point in the future, she'd have two sweet babies added to the mix and she'd be a mother as well as a CFO. If she wanted to work things out with Phillip then she'd also be a wife, whatever that would look like.

And it was her job to deal with the FDA hearing. So she'd do it.

It was too much to contemplate and her morning sickness was back with a vengeance. So much so that she couldn't even think about breakfast. "I'll get the report from Phillip Monday night and fill you in. Don't worry about it."

Alex drifted through the rest of the weekend and somehow managed to sleep most of it. She was so tired, and Monday morning, she nearly called in sick. They'd filed the quarterly reports on Thursday last week; if there was ever a good time to take a break, this was it. But she hadn't taken one sick day since they'd opened the doors of Fyra, and now wasn't the day she'd start.

At three o'clock, an email popped into her inbox from the Office of Senator Edgewood and her heart did a slow dive, even though she knew before opening it that it was about the FDA hearing.

The committee is ready to move to the next step—touring the research facility. They'll expect to collect samples and research notes from the project. Talk to Harper and let me know when to schedule it. I'll be coming to Dallas with the committee as the liaison.

That was it. No mention of their fight or a question about how she was doing? Was that how it would be from now on? If so, she didn't like it. But she steeled her resolve and coordinated with Harper on a day and time later in the week. She responded to Phillip's email with the details, matching his businesslike tone. We'll expect you on Thursday, she wrote and hit Send.

As the week progressed, Alex's morning sickness grew to epic proportions. She barely kept down a few crackers and ginger ale, and she only ate that because Harper forced her to when Alex huddled on her friend's couch in the evenings, pretending to watch TV while the misery of her existence overwhelmed her.

She missed Phillip and couldn't stand things being so unsettled. That was the reason her stomach was so messed up. Her symptoms had improved last week or she would never have been able to go to Washington in the first place. Was this part of her punishment for daring to ask for more from her husband than a businesslike email as their sole communication in a week?

Thursday dawned as the worst day yet. Alex dragged herself from the froufrou coverlet on Harper's guest bed and forced herself into a pair of jeans that scarcely buttoned over her expanding stomach. Finally, she'd started outgrowing her clothes. Ironic that it had happened today of all days.

When the committee arrived at Fyra, Alex managed to be at the front, ready to greet them, though the dark-haired man in the center drew her gaze and kept it. Hungrily, she soaked up the sight of her husband, cataloging the fatigue around his eyes. He looked like he hadn't slept much and the thought lightened her heart at the same time it saddened her. She didn't want him to lose sleep over their situation. She wanted... Well, she wanted something that wasn't possible.

But what was possible? Could she agree to live with him again for the sake of the babies, in name only? She was sure he'd agree to go back to their original agreement. After all, becoming president one day guided all of his thoughts and actions. It was the whole reason they were married in the first place. If she wanted a father for her babies—and she did—could she forget about the fact that she'd fallen in love with him and he'd refused to reciprocate?

The answers did not arrive by way of osmosis simply by virtue of Phillip being within touching distance. The two men accompanying the senator introduced themselves and the tour started immediately thereafter. Harper met them at the door of the lab and took over to explain her setup and walk the committee through her processes. Which was a godsend, as Alex sincerely thought she might lose her breakfast of two crackers and ginger ale very shortly.

Phillip hung back, drawing near Alex, his blue eyes trained on her. "How are you doing?"

Tears pricked at her eyelids over the mere sound of his voice. "Not good. You?"

"Same." He shrugged. "I've been worried about you."

"I could tell from the way my phone never stopped ringing." A wave of dizziness cut off the rest of her sarcastic comment and she flung a hand out to steady herself, catching him square in the chest.

"Alex—" Phillip caught her in his strong arms as her

knees buckled. "What's happening? Talk to me, sweetheart."

"I...can't." Her tongue froze in panic as another wave of dizziness nearly blacked out her vision. If he hadn't been holding on to her, she would have hit the floor, no question. Something sharp tore through her abdomen. All the air rushed from her lungs as she fought to breathe, to understand, to keep her insides from falling out.

"The babies," she croaked and then blackness took her under.

Phillip had never known the true meaning of terror until the moment his wife passed out in his arms.

How he'd got her to the hospital in under twelve minutes remained a mystery he had no interest in solving. Not while everything that was precious to him hung in the balance.

Hospital personnel swarmed in and out of the triage area of the emergency room, taking vital signs and barking questions at him. He answered as best he could.

Yes, she was about fourteen weeks pregnant. No, he didn't observe anything unusual prior to the episode. Yes, she'd been complaining of an upset stomach. No, she hadn't been drinking alcohol or taking any kind of medication— that he knew of. Actually, the fact that he hadn't been right by her side every second had dug under his skin.

No matter what, he should have been there, taking care of his pregnant wife, not nursing the wounds of his black, conflicted heart.

One of the nurses escorted him from the room, very much against his will, as they began setting up a number of frightening machines and attaching them to Alex, who was lying on the hospital bed, skin as pale as the white sheets under her. What if she woke up and didn't know what was happening? Who would explain it to her? Who would hold her hand?

"Senator Edgewood, you have to clear the area and let us do our jobs," the nurse said firmly, leaving no doubt about whether his clout would have any sway here. It was a no.

He tried to take solace in the fact that the machines would help the competent doctors figure out what was wrong with his wife and assure everyone that the babies were fine.

They *were* fine. They had to be. Everyone was fine. Nothing else would be acceptable.

Time crawled to a halt as he sat in the waiting room, his head in his hands, partly because he couldn't hold it up and partly to keep anyone from recognizing him. Normally fame didn't bother him, but today he didn't want any questions about why he was in the emergency room… especially since he couldn't answer them. He had no idea what was wrong with his wife, because they weren't "together" right now.

Actually, he had no idea *what* they were. She hadn't called him, hadn't told him what she wanted to have happen next. Nothing. And he'd tried hard to honor her mandate that he give her space.

When he'd seen Alex again, it had been a punch to the throat—and then some. He'd been miserable since last Friday night. Miserable and unable to figure out what he was supposed to do to get what he wanted. And he'd had no idea how much he'd wanted her until he'd stood near Alex again, so close, yet unable to touch her like he longed to.

And then she'd been in his arms again, but not the way he'd dreamed. Oh, no. That swoon and faint was the stuff of nightmares.

Cassandra, Harper and Trinity rushed into the emergency room, heels clacking and dangly earrings sparkling with furious movement. The FDA tour must have concluded. He made a mental note to thank them all later for filling in the gaps his and Alex's absences had caused.

"What's going on?" Cassandra demanded before she'd even reached his chair.

Phillip shook his head. "I don't know yet. They haven't told me anything."

"And you're sitting there like a bump on a log?" Trinity scowled and swung around to terrorize the lady at the reception desk. They exchanged words, Trinity's rather heated, until finally, Fyra's chief marketing officer conceded defeat and returned to pace in the small waiting area off to the side where Phillip had chosen to set up camp.

After an eternity, a different nurse entered and approached Phillip. He shot to his feet, heart pounding as he braced himself for whatever news was about to be dropped. With Gina, he'd had no warning, no time to process. The authorities had come to his office personally to tell him, but she'd already been gone.

This was far worse because it was happening as he waited.

"Mrs. Edgewood is awake and asking for you," the nurse said without preamble.

Ten kinds of relief whooshed the air out of his lungs and he went a little light-headed. "What happened? Is she okay?"

The other three ladies clambered at his back, peppering the nurse with additional questions.

The nurse, who must have been used to the chaos of the waiting room, simply nodded. "She's stable. But she's dehydrated and her blood pressure was very low when she came in. We've got her on an IV."

The big, glaring omission in the status of Alex's situation iced Phillip's skin. "What about the babies? Everything's fine, right?"

The nurse's mouth firmed into a thin line. "There's a possibility of some…complications. We'll be running additional tests in the next few hours. I can't say anything else definitively at this time. You can go see her. Your wife is understandably very upset. It would be beneficial for her to relax if you can influence her."

With an apologetic backward glance at Alex's friends, he left them in the waiting room and followed the nurse through a maze of corridors to a different area than where Alex had started out.

Alex blinked up at him from the hospital bed, her skin ashen and her eyes huge and troubled. His heart went into a free fall and landed in the pit of his stomach. Mute, he stared at her as something cataclysmic shifted inside.

He could have lost her. And he knew what the pain would be like if that happened. He hadn't wanted to experience it again. But here he was, in the same exact boat despite all his efforts to the contrary. Despite all the pretending.

It would hurt to lose her.

Just like it hurt to be apart from her, and hurt to think about how his life would be meaningless if he didn't have Alex in it. He'd spent so much time shoving her away so he'd stay true to a promise he'd once made to another woman that he hadn't recognized it was already too late.

His problem wasn't that he didn't know how to get what he wanted—it was that he hadn't realized what he truly wanted until this moment.

Alex.

He was in love with Alexandra Edgewood. Letting her walk away last Friday might go down as the dumbest thing he'd ever done in his life. If he'd grabbed on to her with both hands, he could have been by her side all week as she'd grown sicker. He might have been able to fix things.

At the very least, neither of them would have spent the past week in misery.

Also his fault.

Weakly, she stretched out a few fingers, seeking his hand. "Phillip. What's happening?"

She wanted his comforting touch. The fact that she considered it such floored him. What did that mean? That it wasn't too late?

He obliged her by sliding a palm under hers, steeling his nerves so she didn't notice the shakes he'd developed in the past thirty seconds. How did you apologize for being such a moron when the woman you loved lay in a hospital bed, scared and upset? Squeezing her hand, he mustered a small smile.

"Everything's fine," he lied, which she obviously didn't believe for a second judging by the line that appeared between her eyes.

"They won't tell me what's happening with the babies." Alex bit her lip, a sure sign she had something on her mind she didn't know if she should say. "Dr. Dean is on her way. That can't be good."

"I'm sure that's standard procedure," he assured Alex with a composure he didn't feel in the slightest, but the nurse's admonition to keep Alex calm rang in his ears. "They're probably waiting on a qualified obstetrician to give her opinion."

"About what?" Alex asked tersely. "If nothing is wrong, then any doctor can look me in the eye and say that. I've felt so bad this week, but I thought it was because of…you know. What happened with us." Tears sprang up instantly in her green eyes, magnifying the brown dot that made her so unique. "I should have known something was wrong."

"Shh, you couldn't have known." Guilt settled a bit more

heavily across his shoulders. If only... "As for what happened between us, let's not worry about that now."

"I can't just not think about it," she whispered. "You were clear about the line I crossed. I've been ignoring the problems between us this week, obviously to my detriment. We have to figure out how to move forward."

Her gaze bored into him, convicting him. This was his wife to lose.

Maybe now was the perfect time to tell her how much of an idiot he'd been. "I was thinking the same thing."

"We have to consider the possibility that I might lose the babies." One tear slipped free from her eye and slid down her face. "I know we said no divorce and I agreed to that. But I have to know. If Dr. Dean gives us bad news, will you fight me on it?"

"Fight you on what?" Agape, he stared at her, his brain having an impossible time putting the horrific blocks of words together into something cohesive. And then it clicked. "You mean on granting you a *divorce*? Hell yes, I'll fight you on it. No divorce."

He couldn't lose her, especially not if the unthinkable happened and they left the hospital grief-stricken. The mourning process wasn't something you could do alone. He didn't want to do it alone and he didn't want her to grieve alone, either. They should be together. Always.

"Phillip, please." Her fingers curled around his, urgently digging into his flesh. "This is hard enough. Don't force me to stay in this marriage if there's no reason to. We only got married because of the babies. Why drag it out? I don't have the energy to indulge you in a lengthy battle, so I'm asking you point-blank if you'll agree."

"That's not the only reason we got married," he countered a bit desperately. "I—"

"I know." Her voice soured. "You have your voters to

consider. I get it. Well, I have my life to consider, too. I've had my eyes opened recently, and votes aren't my top priority. I'm sorry. I wish I could have stuck to the agreement, but things are changing. Honestly, I'm not even sure I can stay in this marriage if the babies are fine."

Misery turned her mouth down and he wanted to shut his eyes against it. "Alex, none of this has anything to do with votes. I'm trying to tell you I'm in love with you. Campaigns aside. I want to be married to you because of *you*. The babies are just an amazing bonus."

"What are you talking about?" Alex's expression grew hard. "Is this because I'm lying in a hospital bed? What happens tomorrow when I'm not in danger anymore? Once again, I'll be the convenient wife that isn't as good as your first one."

"Is that what you think?" God, he'd bungled this up but good. He squeezed his temples, wondering where all his stellar debate skills had flown off to. "I've never thought of you as second-best. You're actually better suited to me than Gina ever was."

That hadn't been what he'd planned to say. At all. But the words tumbled out, and as he heard himself say them, the truth became so clear. Gina had been wonderful but she hadn't challenged him. Alex made him better. Gina had been right for him once but Alex was right for the man he was now. A man he'd become because of Alex. A man who believed in second chances.

"You're not anything like her," he continued more strongly, determined to make up for some of the damage he'd done. "On purpose. I wanted you to be different so I could guarantee I'd never have feelings for you. But that's not how it went down. Instead, it just meant I could never compare you. I could certainly never find you lacking because you're perfect.

You don't blend into my world, which makes you unique and special. You stand out wherever you go. I love that about you."

That moment at the hospital ribbon cutting. When she'd tried so hard to speak to people, even though she'd been scared and uncomfortable and hadn't wanted to be there… that had probably been the moment when he'd fallen in love with her.

What had started as an attraction so fierce he'd dreamed about her pear scent for weeks had led him to a place he'd never imagined he'd be. In love again.

His promises to Gina had been slipping further away each day. He let them go, fully and irrevocably. His marriage to Gina was gone, but he had something wholly amazing in its place and he planned to embrace it.

Alex stared at the wall. "Too little, too late. You've had your chance to spout a bunch of pretty words. I think the only way to move forward is if we're not together."

Finally he knew what he wanted and she wasn't having any of it. "You're saying you want a divorce no matter what? I can't accept that."

"Well, guess what? I'm newly converted to the Phillip Edgewood philosophy of no second chances."

The phrase cut through him like a machete. Touché. And he totally deserved it.

A nurse bustled into the room, oblivious to how Phillip's entire world had just crashed down at the precise moment when he'd figured out exactly what he had to lose. If he hoped to keep the woman he loved, he had to go big.

Dr. Dean performed a lot of tests that took forever, but finally she declared the babies were fine. Alex breathed deeply for the first time since she'd awoken in the hospital bed.

At last it was over, and she still had two little heart-beats in her womb. The happy tears wouldn't stop cascading down her face, even though the rest of her life was in shambles.

A grim-faced Phillip had stuck by her bedside despite her telling him to go away several times. She got that he was concerned about the babies, so she didn't make a big deal out of it even though the echo of his beautiful voice saying *I love you* still pinged around inside her heart, looking for a place to latch on to.

She wasn't going to let it. No matter how much she wanted to believe it was real.

All of his declarations were an elaborate ploy to save face with his voters. He'd always cared more about appearances than she'd credited. She'd known when he brushed aside all her concerns about marriage that he'd needed her more than she'd needed him, but they'd gone far past reason and logic into something else entirely.

And to use her feelings against her—it was cruel and the height of emotional blackmail.

He could figure out how to spin the lack of a plus one whatever way he chose. She wasn't up for a repeat of the past few weeks, when she let herself believe he might be open to something more, only to be disappointed and heartbroken again. They'd have to figure out something else because she didn't want to be in this marriage any longer.

The irony of her choice to end their marriage wasn't lost on her. The one thing Alex had never wanted would come to pass because she'd dared to develop feelings for her husband.

Once she was released from the hospital, Phillip insisted on having Randy drive her home. But after a few minutes, she realized the car was traveling in the direction of Phillip's home, not Harper's, where she'd been staying.

"Randy." She tapped on the glass, only to have Phillip

snatch her hand back. She glared at her husband. "Are you kidnapping me, then?"

Figured. His dictatorial side had come out in spades.

"No." He scowled. "You just had a very serious episode. You need someone at your beck and call, twenty-four hours a day. *Me*. Harper will be busy with the FDA committee and unable to provide you with the care you need."

Yeah, Alex had heard that one before. He liked to "take care" of her all right; seduction was his favorite method to gloss over issues. Besides, as far as she knew, he'd been planning to fly back to Washington after the FDA committee tour. "That'll be a bit difficult for you to do when you'll be in another state. I can take care of myself."

Crossing her arms, she sank down in the seat. Residual wooziness hadn't worn off yet and she was so tired. Physically, mentally, spiritually.

"That's where you're wrong." He pulled his phone out and tapped a few times, then handed it to her.

She sighed, and even though she swore she wasn't going to humor him, she glanced at the screen anyway because why not? Blinking, she read over the words again. "That says you're taking an extended leave of absence. Until further notice. Phillip, you can't do that!"

"I can. And I did."

He pocketed the phone and gathered her hand in his carefully, as if handling something delicate and breakable. Since she wasn't quite sure which way was up at this point, she let him. And yeah, she still craved his touch, as much as she'd like to deny otherwise.

"But you're an elected official," she reminded him, unnecessarily, no doubt. "What's going to happen to your seat?"

"It's unpaid leave, so no taxpayers will feel defrauded. As long as I go back within the four weeks I was granted, my seat shouldn't be an issue. The biggest hit will be to goodwill. When I run for president, it will come up. I have no idea how damaging it'll be or how voters might view it." He shrugged. "But I don't care. This is more important. I want to spend time with you, pamper you. Eat meals with you."

Damaging? He'd deliberately take a leave of absence that might hurt his campaign for president? Oh, goodness. That was his brass ring. The most important thing in his life. Or at least it *used* to be. And he'd possibly thrown it all in the scrap heap for *her*.

Her greedy, traitorous heart soaked up the idea of being the center of Phillip's whole world and wouldn't let it go.

Dumbfounded, she scrabbled for something to say. And then reality set in. "Let me get this straight. You'll be here in Dallas. For four weeks. So this is a kidnapping disguised as a way to get me to take time off work?"

A double whammy. He wanted to be around to dictate her schedule so his babies were guaranteed safety.

"Alex."

She glanced at him and did a double take at his fierce expression.

"Don't make this about something other than what it is," he said. "You're pregnant with my children. I want to take care of you. When you feel better, go back to work. Or don't—I don't care. I trust that you'll make the right decisions *for you* because you're a smart person. Period, end of story."

"Really?" She eyed him. "We never established your expectations for my career. Long term. So you're okay with it if I hire a nanny and don't take off six months like you dictated?"

Madness. Why did she care? She was through with this

relationship, through with Phillip and through with trying to figure out why love was such an elusive beast.

Why did the thought of giving up make her heart hurt so badly?

"Completely. It's your choice."

He seemed so sincere, she wavered. What if her *if only* wish was actually coming true and she didn't give him a chance? One could argue she was just as bad as Phillip if she refused to give him a second chance. One could also argue that if she fell for his charm again, she was getting in line to be emotionally trounced.

She shook her head and opted to call a spade a spade. "You're just saying that so I'll change my mind about the divorce."

"When did you arrive at the conclusion that I'm someone who just tells you what you want to hear so I can get my way?" Clearly annoyed, he gripped her hand tighter. "That's the reason we're currently separated. Because I didn't do that. I've always been painfully honest with you, Alex. If I was going to lie to you in order to keep you, wouldn't a better time to do it have been that night in my Washington condo? I could have said I was falling for you then and avoided all of this. I didn't because I'm not like that."

"Uh—" Speechless, she replayed that point in her head and came up blank. "So what is all of this about, then?"

Tenderly, he smiled and cupped her face. "What I've been trying to tell you. I'm a big dummy who let some rules get in the way of what was happening between us. I didn't want to be hurt again. I lost someone I loved and I wasn't about to allow myself to go through that again. I set up the perfect scenario to make sure love was off the table, only I didn't count on you."

"What did I do?" she whispered. His warmth spilled

through her whole body, settling her nerves, her stomach, her heart.

"You kicked my rules to the curb and made me realize our agreement isn't worth the paper it's written on."

"Our agreement isn't written down," she pointed out through a throat so tight she could hardly breathe. Was he saying what she thought he was saying—that she'd broken the rules and *it was okay*?

He shrugged. "Guess there's nothing to rip up, then, in order to make way for our new agreement."

She didn't want to know. She *didn't*.

Oh, who was she kidding? "Which is?"

"Our marriage will be based on love. For better or worse. I solemnly swear that I'll spend the next fifty or sixty years giving us second, third, fourth, hell, as many chances as we need."

Maybe it really was this simple. Maybe she'd been right to open herself up to this man.

Her heart swelled. "What about divorce? Is that an option?"

"Never." Punctuating the statement by enfolding her into his arms, he smoothed her hair back as he gazed at her with something she'd swear was love in his eyes. "We're going to have the kind of marriage that lasts because I got lucky enough to find my soul mate a second time. No more talk of divorce."

It was real. This was what love looked like for her. It wasn't like in sappy movies or even what it looked like for Cass and Gage. Alex had never felt giggly and starry-eyed over a man because that wasn't who she was. The way she felt about Phillip was deep, lasting and so very real. And wonder of wonders, it seemed as if he'd fallen in love with her, as well.

"That sounds like an agreement I can get behind," she whispered through another round of happy tears.

He shook his head. "No, that was the part where you were supposed to say, 'Phillip, I love you, too. You're the best husband in the whole world. How could I ever live without you?'"

"Don't push your luck." She smiled at his mock scowl. "I do love you. Unexpectedly. Despite not even believing in it. Where did that come from?"

She knew. Phillip had demonstrated it from the first. She'd learned from him about what was possible.

"I'm very lovable. Did I forget to tell you?"

And then he kissed her as the town car turned onto the street where their house sat, silent and waiting for the laughter of the family that would live there for a very long time.

Epilogue

Harper put both hands on the conference table and leaned forward, looking very much like a redheaded pit bull in a Keith Lloyd suit. "What do you mean, the committee has questions about the formula samples?"

One hand on her expanding stomach, Alex glanced at Phillip and he took the question.

"As you know, they collected samples while they were here last month," Phillip interjected smoothly. "I'm sure it's just a formality. But they want to get additional samples because there was some question about possible tainting."

"What the hell does that mean?" Trinity piped in, finally glancing up from the ad copy that had dominated her attention thus far during the board meeting Alex and Phillip had called to discuss the progress of the FDA approval process. Or rather, the lack of progress. The committee's report had not included approval as those around this boardroom table had expected.

"It means they're suspicious about my lab," Harper threw in, steam nearly shooting from her ears as her Irish got up. "They think there's something dubious about my methods. Or something."

"No one is saying that," Alex said calmly as Phillip took her hand under the table to rub at one of her knuckles absently. He did that a lot. Random touching for no reason. And she reveled in it each time. "They just want to be sure before they approve the product. No harm in that."

"We still don't have a name attached to the leak." All heads turned toward Cass as she took control of the meeting. "That's the biggest concern when we start talking about a delay. Is the additional sample request negotiable, Phillip?"

"No. Sorry."

"Then we comply. Period." Cass held up her hand as Harper bowed up as if about to take on the entire front line of the Dallas Cowboys by herself. "Harper. Take five. Actually, let's all take a few minutes. Each one of us has an emotional stake in Formula-47."

The smile on Alex's face grew wide as she internalized the truth of that. Yes, she did. After all, it had brought her Phillip and the two babies in her womb that grew a little more each day. Who would have thought that she'd credit one of Fyra's products as the sole reason for all the wonderful things in her life?

In the hall, Phillip drew Alex into his embrace, his hand automatically smoothing across the swell of her abdomen. Instantly, one of the babies bumped against his palm.

"Oh! Did you feel that?" Alex's gaze flew to Phillip's and she was pretty sure the awe spreading across his face was mirrored in her own. "That was the first kick. And you got to feel it. How amazing is that?"

His four-week leave was nearly over and they'd already

decided that Alex would work remotely from Washington full-time once he went back to work. They couldn't stand to be apart for even a day. And when the babies were born, Alex had elected to take six months' leave from her job, during which she'd hire a nanny who would become well acquainted with the benefits of pictures and video.

"Miraculous," he murmured and pressed more firmly. "Just like you."

Fyra's Formula-47 wasn't the sole reason she had everything she'd never known she wanted. All the wonderful things in her life had to do with one simple act—breaking the rules.

* * * * *

MILLS & BOON®

Desire™

PASSIONATE AND DRAMATIC LOVE STORIES

A sneak peek at next month's titles...

In stores from 2nd June 2016:

The Baby Inheritance – Maureen Child *and*
Expecting the Rancher's Child – Sara Orwig

A Little Surprise for the Boss – Elizabeth Lane *and*
Saying Yes to the Boss – Andrea Laurence

His Stolen Bride – Barbara Dunlop *and*
The Renegade Returns – Dani Wade

Available at WHSmith, Tesco, Asda, Eason, Amazon and Apple

Just can't wait?
Buy our books online a month before they hit the shops!
visit www.millsandboon.co.uk

These books are also available in eBook format!

'Mistress,' Nikolai slotted in cool as ice.

Shock had welded Ella's tongue to the roof of her mouth because he was sexually propositioning her and nothing could have prepared her for that. She wasn't drop-dead gorgeous... *he* was! Male heads didn't swivel when Ella walked down the street because she had neither the length of leg nor the curves usually deemed necessary to attract such attention. Why on earth could he be making *her* such an offer?

'But we don't even know each other,' she framed dazedly. 'You're a stranger...'

'If you live with me I won't be a stranger for long,' Nikolai pointed out with monumental calm. And the very sound of that inhuman calm and cool forced her to flip round and settle distraught eyes n his lean darkly handsome face.

'You can't be serious about this!'

'I assure you that I am deadly serious. Move in and I'll forget ur family's debts.'

'But it's a *crazy* idea!' she gasped.

'It's not crazy to me,' Nikolai asserted. 'When I want anything, I o after it hard and fast.'

Her lashes dipped. Did he want her like that? Enough to track er down, buy up her father's debts, and try and buy rights to her nd her body along with those debts? The very idea of that made er dizzy and plunged her brain into even greater turmoil. 'It's moral… it's blackmail.'

'It's definitely *not* blackmail. I'm giving you the benefit of a choice ou didn't have before I came through that door,' Nikolai Drakos elded with a glittering cool. 'That choice is yours to make.'

'Like hell it is!' Ella fired back. 'It's a complete cheat of a supposed ffer!'

Nikolai sent her a gleaming sideways glance. 'No the real cheat as you kissing me the way you did last year and then saying no nd acting as if I had grossly insulted you,' he murmured with lethal uietness.

'You *did* insult me!' Ella flung back, her cheeks hot as fire while he wondered if her refusal that night had started off his whole chain eaction. What else could possibly be driving him?

Nikolai straightened lazily as he opened the door. 'If you take ffence that easily, maybe it's just as well that the answer is no.'

MILLS & BOON®

Mills & Boon have been at the heart of romance since 1908… and while the fashions may have changed, one thing remains the same: from pulse-pounding passion to the gentlest caress, we're always known how to bring romance alive.

Now, we're delighted to present you with these irresistible illustrations, inspired by the vintage glamour of our covers. So indulge your wildest dreams and unleash your imagination as we present the most iconic Mills & Boon moments of the last century.

Visit **www.millsandboon.co.uk/ArtofRomance** to order yours!